Praise for *Eclipse O[...]*

"I could not put it down… Jonathan S[...]
with this volume… The kind of collection that should be the corner-
stone of fantastic anthologies for years to come."
— *Stainless Steel Droppings*

"Makes you wonder what… surprises might be in store for future
Eclipse volumes, and to wonder who might emerge as the Gene
Wolfes or R.A. Laffertys of this generation. On the basis of this first
outing one trusts that Strahan knows where to find them."
— Gary K. Wolfe, *Locus*

"This is fantasy of superb quality… It's to be hoped that the *Eclipse*
series will continue strongly, celebrating fantasy's deserved eminence
while nursing short SF towards renewed health."
— Nick Gevers, *Locus*

"…it's refreshing to find an editor who is sanguine about short fiction, and who, moreover, can assemble a volume of fresh wonders to
justify his optimistic stance. Such is the case with talented compiler
Jonthan Strahan and his *Eclipse One*… This is a strong, non-thematic,
non-programmatic assemblage of great stories that affirm the power
of fabulation in a variety of voices… with luck, we'll experience more
such volumes on a regular basis."
— Paul di Filippo, *The Washington Post*

Advance Praise for *Eclipse Two:*

"*Eclipse Two* is a another first-rate original anthology — better than
its predecessor, and hopefully a harbinger of a series that may eventually stand with the likes of *New Dimensions* and *Universe*."
— Rich Horton, *Locus*

"I would be surprised if several of these stories weren't up for major
awards next year and included in the Year's Best lists of recommended
reading. Quite rightly, they deserve to be."
— Alvaro Zinos-Amaro, *The Fix*

Eclipse TWO

NEW SCIENCE FICTION AND FANTASY

Also Edited by Jonathan Strahan:

Best Short Novels (2004 through 2007)
Fantasy: The Very Best of 2005
Science Fiction: The Very Best of 2005
The Best Science Fiction and Fantasy of the Year: Volume 1
The Best Science Fiction and Fantasy of the Year: Volume 2
Eclipse One: New Science Fiction and Fantasy
The Starry Rift: Tales of New Tomorrows

With Charles N. Brown
*The Locus Awards: Thirty Years of the Best in Fantasy and Science
   Fiction*

With Jeremy G. Byrne
The Year's Best Australian Science Fiction and Fantasy: Volume 1
The Year's Best Australian Science Fiction and Fantasy: Volume 2
Eidolon 1

With Terry Dowling
The Jack Vance Treasury
The Jack Vance Reader

With Gardner Dozois
The New Space Opera

With Karen Haber
Science Fiction: Best of 2003
Science Fiction: Best of 2004
Fantasy: Best of 2004

NEW SCIENCE FICTION AND FANTASY

Eclipse TWO

EDITED BY JONATHAN STRAHAN

NIGHT SHADE BOOKS
SAN FRANCISCO

Eclipse Two © 2008 by Jonathan Strahan

This edition of *Eclipse Two* © 2008 by Night Shade Books

Jacket art © 2007 by Donato Giancola
Jacket design by Michael Fusco
Interior layout and design by Jeremy Lassen

Introduction, story notes and arrangement by Jonathan Strahan. © 2008 Jonathan Strahan.

"Turing's Apples" by Stephen Baxter. © 2008 Stephen Baxter. Published by kind permission of the author.

"The Rabbi's Hobby" by Peter S. Beagle. © 2008 Peter S. Beagle. Published by kind permission of the author.

"Exhalation" by Ted Chiang. © 2008 Ted Chiang. Published by kind permission of the author.

"Michael Laurits Is: Drowning" by Paul Cornell. © 2008 Paul Cornell. Published by kind permission of the author.

"Ex Cathedra" by Tony Daniel. © 2008 Tony Daniel. Published by kind permission of the author.

"Truth Window: A Tale of the Bedlam Rose" by Terry Dowling. © 2008 Terry Dowling. Published by kind permission of the author.

"The Seventh Expression of the Robot General" by Jeffrey Ford. © 2008 Jeffrey Ford. Published by kind permission of the author.

"The Illustrated Biography of Lord Grimm" by Daryl Gregory. © 2008 Daryl Gregory. Published by kind permission of the author.

"Elevator" by Nancy Kress. © 2008 Nancy Kress. Published by kind permission of the author.

"Night of the Firstlings" by Margo Lanagan. © 2008 Margo Lanagan. Published by kind permission of the author.

"Down and Out in the Magic Kingdom" by David Moles. © 2008 David Moles. Published by kind permission of the author.

"Skin Deep" by Richard Parks. © 2008 Richard Parks. Published by kind permission of the author.

"Fury" by Alastair Reynolds. © 2008 Alastair Reynolds. Published by kind permission of the author.

"Invisible Empire of Ascending Light" by Ken Scholes. © 2008 Ken Scholes. Published by kind permission of the author.

"The Hero" by Karl Schroeder. © 2008 Karl Schroeder. Published by kind permission of the author.

First Edition

Printed in Canada

ISBN: 978-1-59780-136-2

Night Shade Books
Please visit us on the web at
http://www.nightshadebooks.com

For Gary K. Wolfe, dear friend and respected colleague.

CONTENTS

INTRODUCTION

JONATHAN STRAHAN

I've been writing introductions to anthologies since the summer of 1996. Twenty-two opening salvos written or co-written for anthologies, each intended to preface a selection of original or reprinted tales, and those stories themselves selected either from the submissions I'd received from potential contributors or filtered from the annual output of the science fiction and fantasy field. For the last three or four years science fiction publishing journal *Locus* has estimated that roughly three thousand or so pieces of short science fiction and fantasy have been published, and I've estimated that number to possibly represent as little as half of what's actually being published. That means up to six thousand new stories are being printed or displayed, or whatever's done with them in the early twenty-first century to get them to readers, each year. If that number has been roughly constant, and it may well not have been, that means somewhere in the vicinity of sixty thousand new stories have been "published" since I co-wrote the introduction to my first year year's best anthology, *The Year's Best Australian Science Fiction and Fantasy*.

Realizing that, I began to wonder what exactly *it is* that I'm looking for when I read stories for a new book, and especially when I'm reading for this anthology series. It's true that most of the stories published are of little relevance to *Eclipse*, but I think they are relevant to what I read, why I read, and *that* colors this book. And what I've come to realize is that genre purity isn't something that interests me. I love science fiction. I love fantasy. I like horror. I have loved stories that come from both the purest centers of those genres, ones that come from their farthest peripheries, and ones that mix and match elements from all of them as they please. Whether something is or isn't *genre* is not an essential part of what makes me respond to a story and think that it's good or not. It's also not a matter of structure or technical approach. I don't care whether a story is told using a traditional "Clarion" structure, or whether it's been torn apart, rebuilt, and resembles nothing more than some crazy patchwork quilt. I also don't especially crave novelty. I love new ideas, having my brain stretched around corners in the way that only the best science fiction can do, but I equally love stories that revisit old ideas in interesting ways or simply elucidate them well.

What I have come to realize is that for me the pre-eminent thing is *story*. I want a strong story built around a good idea that is complete; one that opens, builds and then delivers some kind of pay-off at its conclusion. Again, this isn't structure: the conclusion can come at the beginning if you can make that work. It's about whether there's a story to be told and whether the author manages to get it told before his or her piece is done. It's not simply plot, either. Plot is important, but it's how plot is used in the service of theme, character and setting. It's voice. I want a story that is immersive, that takes me away into its world, for however long it lasts, or that makes me think differently about something. As you can see, not the most clearly explained thing, but I've realized over the past few years that I know it when I see it, and it's what I hope to put into all the anthologies that I edit, and most especially what I put into these *Eclipse* series because, as much as I stand behind what I said in the introduction to *Eclipse One*—that the *Eclipse* anthologies are inspired by the work of Damon Knight in his *Orbit* anthologies and Terry Carr in his *Universe* anthologies—these books represent my personal search for a greater understanding of the nature of story, and of science fiction and fantasy.

This means that each book in the *Eclipse* series will be somewhat different from its predecessors and that the one constant will be the window on the science fiction and fantasy short story that I create by editing the anthology. Certainly this book, *Eclipse Two*, is different from its predecessor. I was delighted with the reception that first book received—the reviews were good and stories have ended up on awards ballots and in year's best annuals—but I knew this book had to be its own thing. So, after discussions with my publishers, I deliberately nudged this *Eclipse* installment towards science fiction, dropping some of the balance that had characterized *Eclipse One*. While there is still some fantasy here—in three strong stories from Peter S. Beagle, Margo Lanagan, and Richard Parks—and no horror, there are tales of galactic empires, uplifted personalities, strange worlds, and stranger characters. Most of all, though, there are stories. Some timely, like Paul Cornell's tale of social networking website Facebook, some timeless, like Ted Chiang's examination of the nature of our universe. There are stories that connect to series, like Terry Dowling's first new Wormwood story in seventeen years, and Karl Schroeder's latest installment in his stunning SF "Virga" series. Each of them is complete, engaging, and right for *Eclipse* and where I see it sitting in the science fiction and fantasy field.

All of which I hope gives you some idea of what you're about to experience. A rich, varied selection of new stories, mostly science fiction but with a touch of fantasy too, each of which engaged me in some way, and which I hope will engage you too. Some of the stories are adventurous and some are not: that's not what this book is about. It's about story, and I hope you enjoy these ones as much as I have.

Even though this is just the second volume of *Eclipse* (and I hope there'll be many more), a community has already grown up around it and, before you move on to the stories, I'd like to thank a few people. First and foremost, Jeremy Lassen, Jason Williams, Ross Lockhart, and John Joseph Adams at "the Shade". Without them this book literally wouldn't and couldn't exist. I'd also like to thank the contributors to the book, and all of those who, for whatever reason, didn't quite make it for this *Eclipse* (next time!). Above all, though, I'd like to thank my wife Marianne, who has been there for every difficult moment I went through getting us here. And, last of all, I'd like to thank you for picking up this book and taking it home. Whether you were there for *Eclipse One*, or this is your first time under its darkling skies, welcome, and I hope to see you here again next year.

Jonathan Strahan
Perth, Western Australia
June/September 2008

THE HERO

KARL SCHROEDER

"Is everybody ready?" shouted Captain Emmen. At least, Jessie thought that's what he'd said—it was impossible to hear anything over the spine-grating noise that filled the sky.

Jessie coughed, covering his mouth with his hand to stop the blood from showing. In this weightless air, the droplets would turn and gleam for everybody to see, and if they saw it, he would be off the team.

Ten miles away the sound of the capital bug had been a droning buzz. With two miles to go, it had become a maddening—and deafening—howl. Much closer, and the bug's defense mechanism would be fatal to an unshielded human.

Jessie perched astride his jet just off the side of the salvage ship *Mistelle*. *Mistelle* was a scow, really, but Captain Emmen had ambitions. Lined up next to Jessie were eight other brave or stupid volunteers, each clutching the handlebars of a wingless jet engine. Mounted opposite the saddle ("below" Jessie's feet) was a ten-foot black-market missile. It was his team's job to get close enough to the capital bug to aim their missiles at its noise-throats. They were big targets—organic trumpets hundreds of feet long—but there were a lot of them, and the bug was miles long.

Jessie had never heard of anybody breaking into a capital bug's pocket ecology while the insect was still alive. Captain Emmen meant to try, because there was a story that a Batetranian treasure ship had crashed into this bug, decades ago. Supposedly you could see it when distant sunlight shafted through the right perforation in the bug's side. The ship was still intact, so they said.

Jessie wasn't here for the treasure ship. He'd been told a different story about this particular bug.

Emmen swung his arm in a chopping motion and the other jets shot away. Weak and dizzy as he was, Jessie was slower off the mark, but in seconds he was catching up. The other riders looked like flies optimistically lugging pea-pods; they were lit from two sides by two distant suns, one red with distance, the other yellow and closer, maybe two hundred miles away. In those quadrants of the sky not lit by the suns, abysses of air stretched away to seeming infinity—above, below, and to all sides.

Mistelle became a spindle-shape of wood and iron, its jets splayed behind it like an open hand. Ahead, the capital bug was too big to be seen as a single thing: it revealed itself to Jessie as landscapes, a vertical flank behind coiling clouds, a broad plain above that lit amber by the more distant sun. The air between him and it was crowded with clouds, clods of earth, and arrowing flocks of birds somehow immune to the bug's sound. Balls of water shot past as he accelerated; some were the size of his head, some a hundred feet across. And here and there, mountain-sized boluses of bug-shit smeared brown across the sky.

The jet made an ear-splitting racket, but he couldn't hear it over the sound of the bug. Jessie was swaddled in protective gear, his ears plugged, eyes protected behind thick goggles. He could hear the sound inside his body now, feel it vibrating his heart and loosening the bloody mess that was taking over his lungs. He'd start coughing any second, and once he did he might not be able to stop.

Fine, he thought grimly. *Maybe I'll cough the whole damn thing out.*

The noise had become pure pain. His muscles were cramping, he was finding it hard to breathe. Past a blur of vibration, he saw one of the other riders double up suddenly and tumble off his jet. The vehicle spun away, nearly hitting somebody else. And here came the cough.

The noise was too strong, he *couldn't* cough. The frozen reflex had stopped his breathing entirely; Jessie knew he had only seconds to live. Even as he thought this, curtains of cloud parted as the jet shot through them at a hundred miles an hour, and directly ahead of him stood the vast tower of the bug's fourth horn.

The jet's engine choked and failed; Jessie's right goggle cracked; the handlebars began to rattle loose from their fittings as his vision grayed. A rocket contrail blossomed to his right and he realized he was looking straight down the throat of the horn. He thumbed the firing button and was splashed and kicked by fire and smoke. In one last moment of clarity Jessie let go of the handlebars so the jet wouldn't break his bones in the violence of its tumble.

The ferocious scream stopped. Jessie took in a huge breath, and began to cough. Blood sprayed across the air. Breath rasping, he looked ahead to see that he was drifting toward some house-sized nodules that sprouted from the capital bug's back. The broken, smoking horns jutted like fantastically eroded sculptures, each hundreds of feet long. He realized with a start that one of them was still blaring, but by itself it could no longer kill.

In the distance, the *Mistelle* wallowed in a cloud of jet exhaust, and began to grow larger.

I did it, Jessie thought. Then the gray overwhelmed all thought and sense and he closed his eyes.

Bubbles spun over the side of the washtub. In the rotational gravity of Aitlin Town, they twirled and shimmered and slid sideways from Coriolis force as they descended. Jessie watched them with fascination—not because he'd never seen bubbles before, but because he'd never seen one fall.

They'd both gotten into trouble, so he and his oldest brother Camron were washing the troupe's costumes today. Jessie loved it; he never got a chance to talk to Camron, except to exchange terse barks during practice or a performance. His brother was ten years older than he, and might as well have lived in a different family.

"That's what the world is, you know," Camron said casually. Jessie looked at him quizzically.

"A bubble," said Camron, nodding at the little iridescent spheres. "The whole world is a bubble, like that."

"Is naaawwt."

Camron sighed. "Maybe Father isn't willing to pay to have you educated, Jessie, but he's sent me to school. Three times. 'The world of Virga is a hollow pressure-vessel, five thousand miles in diameter.'"

One big bubble was approaching the floor. Sunlight leaned across the window, a beam of gold from distant Candesce that was pinioning one spot of sky as the ring-shaped wooden town rotated through it. After a few seconds the beam flicked away, leaving the pearly shine of cloud-light.

"The whole world's a bubble," repeated Camron, "and all our suns are man-made."

Jessie knew the smaller suns, which lit spherical volumes only a few hundred miles diameter, were artificial: they'd once flown past one at night, and he'd seen that it was a great glass-and-metal machine. Father had called it a "polywell fusion" generator. But surely the greatest sun of all, so ancient it had been there at the beginning of everything, so bright and hot no ship could ever approach it—"Not Candesce," said Jessie. "Not the sun of suns."

Camron nodded smugly. *"Even Candesce. 'Cept that in the case of Candesce, whoever built it only made so many keys—and we lost them all." Another shaft of brilliance burst into the laundry room. "People made Candesce—but now nobody can turn it off."*

The bubble flared in purples, greens, and gold, an inch above the floor-boards.

"That's just silly," scoffed Jessie. "'Cause if the whole world were just a bubble, then that would make it—"

The bubble touched the floor, and vanished.

"—mortal," finished Camron. He met Jessie's eye, and his look was serious.

Jessie shivered and wiped at his mouth. Dried blood had caked there. His whole chest ached, his head was pounding, and he felt so weak and nauseous he doubted he'd have been able to stand if he'd been under gravity.

He hung weightless in a strange fever-dream of a forest, with pale pink tree trunks that reached past him to open into, not leaves, but a single stretched surface that had large round or oval holes in it here and there. Beyond them he could see sky. The tree trunks didn't converge onto a clump of soil or rock as was usual with weightless groves, but rather tangled their roots into an undulant plain a hundred yards away from the canopy.

The light that angled through the holes shone off the strangest collection of life forms Jessie had ever seen. Fuzzy donut-shaped things inched up and down the "tree" trunks, and mirror-bright birds flickered and flashed as the light caught them. Something he'd taken to be a cloud in the middle distance turned out to be a raft of jellyfish, conventional enough in the airs of Virga, but these were gigantic.

The whole place reeked, the sharp tang reminding Jessie of the jars holding preserved animal parts that he'd seen in the one school he briefly attended as a boy.

He was just under the skin of the capital bug. The jet volunteers had taken turns squinting through the *Mistelle's* telescope, each impressing on him- or herself as many details of the giant creature's body as they could. Jessie recalled the strange skin that patched the monster's back; it'd had holes in it.

It was through these holes that they'd caught glimpses of something that might be a wrecked ship. As the fog of pain and exhaustion lifted,

Jessie realized that he might be close to it now. But where were the others?

He twisted in midair and found a threadlike vine or root within reach. Pulling himself along it (it felt uncomfortably like skin under his palms) he reached one of the "tree trunks" which might really be more analogous to hairs for an animal the size of the capital bug. He kicked off from the trunk, then off another, and so maneuvered himself through the forest and in the direction of a brighter patch.

He was so focused on doing this that he didn't hear the tearing sound of the jet until it was nearly on him. "Jessie! You're alive!" Laughter dopplered down as a blurred figure shot past from behind.

It was Chirk, her canary-yellow jacket an unmistakable spatter against the muted colors of the bug. As she circled back, Jessie realized that he could still barely hear her jet; he must be half-deaf from the bug's drone.

Chirk was a good ten years older than Jessie, and she was the only woman on the missile team. Maybe it was that she recognized him as even more of an outsider than herself, but for whatever reason she had adopted Jessie as her sidekick the day she met him. He indulged her—and, even three months ago, he would have been flattered and eager to make a new friend. But he hid the blood in his cough even from her—particularly from her—and remained formal in their exchanges.

"So?" She stopped on the air, ten feet away, and extended her hand. "Take a lift from a lady?"

Jessie hesitated. "Did they find the wreck?"

"Yes!" She almost screamed it. "Now come *on!* They're going to beat us there—the damned *Mistelle* itself is tearing a hole in the bug's back so they can come up alongside her."

Jessie stared at her, gnawing his lip. Then: "It's not why I came." He leaned back, securing his grip on the stalk he was holding.

The bug was turning ponderously, so distant sunlight slid down and across Chirk's astonished features. Her hand was still outstretched. "What the'f you talking about? This is it! Treasure! Riches for the rest of your life—but you gotta come with me *now!*"

"I didn't come for the treasure," he said. Having to explain himself was making Jessie resentful. "You go on, Chirk, you deserve it. You take my share too, if you want."

Now she drew back her hand, blinking. "What is this? Jessie, are you all right?"

Tears started in his eyes. "No, I'm not all right, Chirk. I'm going to die." He stabbed a finger in his mouth and brought it out, showed her the red on it. "It's been coming on for months. Since before I signed on with Emmen. So, you see, I really got no use for treasure."

She was staring at him in horror. Jessie forced a smile. "I could use my jet, though, if you happen to have seen where it went."

Wordlessly, she held out her hand again. This time Jessie took it, and she gunned the engine, flipping them over and accelerating back the way Jessie had come.

As they shot through a volume of clear air she turned in her saddle and frowned at him. "You came here to die, is that it?"

Jessie shook his head. "Not yet. I hope not yet." He massaged his chest, feeling the deep hurt there, the spreading weakness. "There's somebody here I want to talk to."

Chirk nearly flew them into one of the pink stalks. "Someone *here?* Jess, you were with us just now. You heard that... song. You know nobody could be alive in here. It's why nobody's ever gotten at the wreck."

He nodded. "Not a—" He coughed. "Not a person, no—" The coughing took over for a while. He spat blood, dizzy, pain behind his eyes now too. When it all subsided he looked up to find they were coming alongside his jet, which was nuzzling a dent in a vast rough wall that cut across the forest of stalks.

He reached for the jet and managed to snag one of its handlebars. Before he climbed onto it he glanced back; Chirk was looking at him with huge eyes. She clearly didn't know what to do.

He stifled a laugh lest it spark more coughing. "There's a precipice moth here. I heard about it by chance when my family and me were doing a performance in Batetran. It made the newspapers there: Moth Seen Entering Capital Bug."

"Precip—Precip moth?" She rolled the word around in her mouth. "Wait a minute, you mean a world-diver? One of those dragons that're supposed to hide at the edges of the world to waylay travelers?"

He shook his head, easing himself carefully onto the jet. "A defender of the world. Not human. Maybe the one that blew up the royal palace in Slipstream last year. Surely you heard about *that.*"

"I heard about a monster. It was a moth?" She was being uncharacteristically thick-headed. Jessie was ready to forgive that, considering the circumstances.

She showed no signs of hying off to her well-deserved treasure, so Jessie told her the story as he'd heard it—of how Admiral Chaison Fanning of Slipstream had destroyed an invasion fleet, hundreds of cruisers strong, with only seven little ships of his own. Falcon captured him and tortured him to find out how he'd done it, but he'd escaped and returned to Slipstream, where he'd deposed the Pilot, Slipstream's hereditary monarch.

"Nobody knows how he stopped that invasion fleet," said Chirk. "It was impossible."

Jessie nodded. "Yeah, that's right. But I found out."

Now she *had* to hear that story, but Jessie was reluctant to tell her. He'd told no one else because he trusted no one else, not with the location of one of the greatest secrets of the world. He trusted Chirk—she had her own treasure now—yet he was still reluctant, because that would mean admitting how he'd been wedged into a dark corner of Rainsouk Amphitheater, crying alone when the place unexpectedly began to fill with people.

For months Jessie had been hearing about Rainsouk; his brothers were so excited over the prospect of performing here. Jessie was the youngest, and not much of an acrobat—he could see that in his father's eyes every time he missed a catch and sailed on through the weightless air to fetch up, humiliated, in a safety net. Jessie had given up trying to please the family, had in fact become increasingly alone and isolated outside their intense focus and relentless team spirit. When the cough started he tried to hide it, but their little traveling house was just too small to do that for long.

When Father found out, he was just disappointed, that was all. Disappointed that his youngest had gotten himself sick and might die. So Jessie was off the team—and though nobody said it out loud, off the team meant out of the family.

So there he'd been, crying in the amphitheater he'd never get to perform in, when it began to fill with black-garbed men and women.

As he opened his mouth to refuse to tell her, Jessie found himself spilling the whole story, humiliating as it was. "These visitors, they were terrifying, Chirk. It looked like a convention of assassins, every man and woman the last person you'd want to meet on a dark night. And then the scariest of them flew out to the middle of the place and started to talk."

The very world was threatened, he'd said. Only he and his brothers and sisters could save it, for this was a meeting of the Virga home guard. The guard were a myth—so Jessie had been taught. He'd heard stories about them his whole life, of how they guarded the walls of the world against the terrifying monsters and alien forces prowling just outside.

"Yet here they were," he told Chirk. "And their leader was reminding them that something is trying to get *in*, right now, and the only thing that keeps it out is Candesce. The sun of suns emits a… he called it a 'field,' that keeps the monsters out. But the same field keeps *us* from developing any of the powerful technologies we'd need to stop the monsters if they did get in. Technologies like radar…. and get this:

"It was radar that made Admiral Chaison Fanning's ships able to run rings around Falcon Formation's fleet. *Because Fanning had found a key to Candesce,* and had gone inside to shut down the field for a day."

Chirk crossed her arms, smiling skeptically. "Now this is a tall tale," she said.

"Believe it or not," said Jessie with a shrug, "it's true. He gave the key to the precipice moth that helped him depose the Pilot, and it flew away… the home guard didn't know where. But I knew."

"Ahh," she said. "That newspaper article. It came here."

"Where it could be sure of never being disturbed," he said eagerly.

"And now you're, what?—going to duel it for the key?" She laughed. "Seems to me you're in no state to slay dragons, Jess." She held out her hand. "Look, you're too weak to fly, even. Come with me. At least we'll make you rich before…" She glanced away. "You can afford the best doctors, you know they—"

He shook his head, and spun the pedals of the jet's starter spring. "That moth doesn't know what I overheard in the amphitheater. That the walls of the world are failing. Candesce's shield isn't strong enough anymore. We need the key so we can dial down the field and develop technologies that could stop whatever's out there. The moth's been hiding in here, it doesn't know, Chirk."

The jet roared into life. "I can't slay a dragon, Chirk," he shouted. "But at least I can give it the news."

He opened the throttle and left her before she could reply.

They dressed as heroes. Dad wore gold and leather, the kids flame-red. Mom was the most fabulous creature Jessie had ever seen, and every night he fell in love with her all over again. She wore feathers of transparent blue plex, plumage four feet long that she could actually fly with when the gravity was right. She would be captured by the children—little devils—and rescued by Dad. They played all over the principalities, their backdrop a vast wall of spinning town wheels, green ball-shaped parks and the hithering-thithering traffic of a million airborne people. Hundreds of miles of it curved away to cup blazing Candesce. They had to be amazing to beat a sight like that. And they were.

For as long as Jessie could remember, though, there had been certain silences. Some evenings, the kids knew not to talk. They stuck to their picture books, or played outside or just plain left the house for a while. The silence radiated from Mom and Dad, and there was no understanding it. Jessie didn't notice how it grew, but there came a time when the only music in their lives seemed to happen during performance. Even rehearsals were strained. And then, one day, Mom just wasn't there anymore.

They had followed the circus from the principalities into the world's outer realms, where the suns were spaced hundreds of miles apart and the chilly darkness between them was called "winter."

Jessie remembered a night lit by distant lightning that curled around a spherical stormcloud. They were staying on a little town wheel whose name he no longer remembered—just a spinning hoop of wood forty feet wide and a mile or so across, spoked by frayed ropes and home to a few hundred farm families. Mom had been gone for four days. Jessie stepped out of the hostel where they were staying to see Dad leaning out over the rushing air, one strong arm holding a spoke-rope while he stared into the headwind.

"But where would she go?" Jessie heard him murmur. That was all that he ever said on the matter, and he didn't even say it to his boys.

They weren't heroes after that. From that day forward, they dressed as soldiers, and their act was a battle.

The capital bug was hollow. This in itself wasn't such a surprise—something so big wouldn't have been able to move under its own power if it wasn't. It would have made its own gravity. What made Jessie swear in surprise was just how little there was to it, now that he was inside.

The bug's perforated back let in sunlight, and in those shafts he beheld a vast oval space, bigger than any stadium he had ever juggled in. The sides and bottom of the place were carpeted in trees, and more hung weightless in the central space, the roots of five or six twined together at their bases so that they thrust branch and leaf every which way. Flitting between these were mirror-bright schools of long-finned fish; chasing those were flocks of legless crimson and yellow birds. As Jessie watched, a struggling group of fish managed to make it to a thirty-foot-diameter ball of water. The pursuing birds peeled away at the last second as the punctured water ball quivered and tossed off smaller spheres. This drama took place in complete silence; there was no sound at all although the air swarmed with insects as well as the larger beasts.

Of course, nothing could have made itself heard over the buzz of the capital bug itself. So, he supposed nothing tried.

The air was thick with the smell of flowers, growth, and decay. Jessie took the jet in a long curving tour of the vast space, and for a few moments he was able to forget everything except the wonder of being here. Then, as he returned to his starting point, he spotted the wreck, and the *Mistelle*. They were high up in something like a gallery that stretched around the "top" of the space, under the perforated roof. Both were dwarfed by their setting, but he could clearly see his teammates' jets hovering over the wreck. The stab of sorrow that went through him almost set him coughing again. It would only take seconds and he'd be with them. At least he could watch their jubilation as they plundered the treasure he'd helped them find.

And then what? They could shower him with jewels but he couldn't buy his life back. At best he could hold such baubles up to the light and admire them for a while, before dying alone and unremarked.

He turned the jet and set to exploring the forested gut of the capital bug.

Jessie had seen very few built-up places that weren't inhabited. In Virga, real estate was something you made, like gravity or sunlight. Wilderness as a place didn't exist, except in those rare forests that had grown by twining their roots and branches until their whole matted mass extended for miles. He'd seen one of those on the fringe of the principalities, where Candesce's light was a mellow rose and the sky permanently peach-tinged. That tangled mass of green had seemed like a delirium dream, an intrusion into the sane order of the world. But it was nothing to the wilderness of the capital bug.

Bugs were rare; at any one time there might only be a few dozen in the whole world. They never got too close to the sun of suns, so they were never seen in the principalities. They dwelt in the turbulent middle space between civilization and winter, where suns wouldn't stay on station and nations would break up and drift apart. Of course, they were also impossible to approach, so it was likely that no one had ever flown through these cathedrals walled by gigantic flowers, these ship-sized grass stalks dewed by beads of water big as houses. Despite his pain and exhaustion, the place had its way with him and he found himself falling into a meditative calm he associated with that moment before you make your jump—or, in midair, that moment before your father catches your hand.

In its own way, this calm rang louder than any feeling he'd ever had, maybe because it was *about* something, about death, and nothing he'd ever felt before had grown on such a foundation.

He came to an area where giant crystals of salt had grown out of the capital bug's skin, long geodesic shapes whose inner planes sheened in purple and bottle-green. They combined with the dew drops to splinter and curl the light in a million ways.

Stretched between two sixty-foot grass stalks was the glittering outline of a man.

Jessie throttled back and grabbed a vine to stop himself. He'd come upon a spider's web; the spider that had made it was probably bigger than he was. But someone or something had used the web to make a piece of art, by placing fist- to head-sized balls of water at the intersections of the threads, laying out a pattern shaped like a man standing proudly, arms out, as though about to catch something.

Jessie goggled at it, then remembered to look for the spider. After a cautious minute he egged the jet forward, skirting around the web. There were more webs ahead. Some were twenty or more feet across, and each one was a tapestry done in liquid jewels. Some of the figures were human; others were of birds, or flowers, but each was exquisitely executed. It came to Jessie that when the capital bug was in full song, the webs and drops would vibrate, blurring the figures' outlines until they must seem made of light.

Spinning in the air, he laughed in surprise.

Something reared up sixty feet away and his heart skipped. It was a vaguely humanoid shape sculpted in rusted metal and moss-covered stone. As it stood it unfolded gigantic wings that stretched past the tops of the grass stalks.

Its head was a scarred metal ball.

"THIS IS NOT YOUR PLACE." Even half-deaf as he was, the words battered Jessie like a headwind. They were like gravel speaking. If his team from the *Mistelle* were here, they'd be turning tail at this point; they would probably hear the words, even as far away as the wreck.

Jessie reached down and pointedly turned off the jet. "I've come to talk to you," he said.

"YOU BRING NO ORDERS," said the precipice moth. It began to hunker back into the hollow where it had been coiled.

"I bring news!" Jessie had rehearsed what he was going to say, picturing over and over in his mind the impresario of the circus and how he would gesture and stretch out his vowels to make his speech pretty and important-sounding. Now, though, Jessie couldn't remember his lines. "It's about the key to Candesce!"

The moth stopped. Now that it was motionless, he could see how its body was festooned with weapons: its fingers were daggers, gun barrels poked under its wrists. The moth was a war machine, half flesh, half ordnance.

"CLARIFY."

Jessie blew out the breath he'd been holding and immediately started coughing. To his dismay little dots of blood spun through the air in the direction of the moth. It cocked its head, but said nothing.

When he had the spasms under control, Jessie told the monster what he'd overheard in the amphitheater. "What the leader meant—I think he meant—was that the strategy of relying on Candesce to protect us isn't working anymore. Those things from outside, they've gotten in at least twice in the last two years. They're figuring it out."

"We destroy them if they enter." The moth's voice was not so over-whelming now; or maybe he was just going deaf.

"Begging your pardon," said Jessie, "but they slipped past you both times. Maybe you're catching some of them, but not enough."

There was a long pause. "Perhaps," said the moth at last. Jessie grinned because that one word, a hint of doubt, had for him turned the moth from a mythical dragon into an old soldier, who might need his help after all.

"I'm here on behalf of humanity to ask you for the key to Candesce," he recited; he'd remembered his speech. "We can't remain at the mercy of the sun of suns and the things from outside. We have to steer our own course now, because the other way's not working. The home guard didn't know where you were, and they'd never have listened to me; so I came here myself."

"The home guard cannot be trusted," said the moth.

Jessie blinked in surprise. But then again, in the story of Admiral Fanning and the key, the moth had not in the end given it to the guard, though it had had the chance.

The moth shifted, leaning forward slightly. "Do you want the key?" it asked.

"I can't use it." He could explain why, but Jessie didn't want to.

"You're dying," said the moth.

The words felt like a punch in the stomach. It was one thing for Jessie to say it. He could pretend he was brave. But the moth was putting it out there, a fact on the table. He glared at it.

"I'm dying too," said the moth.

"W-*what?*"

"That is why I'm here," it said. "Men cannot enter this creature. My body would be absorbed by it, rather than be cut up and used by you. Or so I had thought."

"Then give *me* the key," said Jessie quickly. "I'll take it to the home guard. You know you can trust me," he added, "because I can't use the key to my own advantage. I'll live long enough to deliver it to the home guard, but not long enough to use it."

"*I don't have the key.*"

Jessie blinked at the monster for a time. He'd simply assumed that the moth that had been seen entering this capital bug was the same one that had met Chaison Fanning in Slipstream. But of course there was no reason that should be the case. There were thousands, maybe millions of moths in Virga. They were almost never seen, but two had been spotted in the same year.

"That's it, then," he said at last. After that, there was a long silence between them, but the precipice moth made no effort to fit itself back into its hole. Jessie looked around, mused at the drifting jet for a while, then gave a deep sigh.

He turned to the moth. "Can I ask you a favor?"

"What is it?"

"I'd like to... stay here to die. If that wouldn't be too much of an inconvenience for you."

The precipice moth put out an iron-taloned forelimb, then another, very slowly, as if sneaking up on Jessie. It brought its round leaden head near to his, and seemed to sniff at him.

"I have a better idea," it said. Then it snatched him up in its great claws, opened its wide lidless mouth, and *bit.*

Jessie screamed as his whole torso was engulfed in that dry maw. He felt his chest being ripped open, felt his lungs being torn out—curiously, not as pain but as a physical wrenching—and then everything blurred and went gray.

But not black. He blinked, coming to himself, to discover he was still alive. He was hovering in a nebula of blood, millions of tiny droplets of it spinning and drifting around him like little worlds. Gingerly, he reached up to touch his chest. It was whole, and when he took a tentative breath, the expected pain wasn't there.

Then he spotted the moth. It was watching him from its cavity in the capital bug's flesh. "W-what did—where is it?"

"I ate your disease," said the moth. "Battlefield medicine, it is allowed."

"But why?"

"Few moths know which one of us has the key, or where it is," it said. "I cannot broadcast what I know, Candesce jams all lightspeed communications. I am now too weak to travel.

"You will take your message to the moth that has the key. It will decide."

"But I'm—I'm not going to—?"

"I could not risk your dying during the journey. You are disease-free now."

Jessie couldn't take it in. He breathed deeply, then again. It would hit him sometime later, he knew; for now, all he could think to say was, "So where's the one that does have the key?"

The moth told him and Jessie laughed, because it was obvious. "So I'll wait until night and go in," he said. "That should be easy."

The precipice moth shifted, shook its head. "It will not speak to you. Not unless you prove you are committed to the course that you say you are."

There was a warning in those words but Jessie didn't care. All that mattered was that he was going to live. "I'll do it."

The moth shook its head. "I think you will not," it said.

"You think I'll forget the whole thing, take my treasure from the ship over there," he nodded behind him, "and just set myself up somewhere? Or you think I'll take the key for myself, auction it off to the highest bidder? But I won't, you see. I owe you. I'll do as you ask."

It shook its head. "You do not understand." By degrees it was inching its way back into its hole. Jessie watched it, chewing his lip. Then he looked around at the beautiful jeweled tapestries it had made in the spiders' webs.

"Hey," he said. "Before I go, can I do something for *you?*"

"There is nothing you can do for me," murmured the moth.

"I don't know about that. I can't do very *many* things," he said as he snapped off some smaller stalks of the strange grass. He hefted a couple in his hands. "But the one or two things I can do, I do pretty well." He eyed the moth as he began spinning the stalks between his hands.

"Have you ever seen freefall juggling?"

Jessie stood alone on the tarred deck of a docking arm. His bags were huddled around his feet; there was nobody else standing where he was, the nearest crowd a hundred feet away.

The dock was an open-ended barrel, six hundred feet across and twice as deep. Its rim was gnarled with cable mounts for the spokes that radiated out to the distant rim of the iron city-wheel. This far from the turning rim, Jessie weighed only a pound, but his whole posture was a slump of misery.

There was only air where his ship was supposed to be.

He'd been late packing; the others had gone to get Dad at the circus pitch that had been strung, like a hammock, between the spokes of the city. Jessie was old enough to pack for himself, so he had to. He was old enough to find his way to the docks, too, but he'd been delayed, just by one thing and another.

And the ship wasn't here.

He stared into the sky as it grayed with the approach of a water-laden cloud. The long spindle-shapes of a dozen ships nosed at other points on the circular dock, like hummingbirds sipping at a flower. Passengers and crew were hand-walking up the ropes of their long proboscises. Jessie could hear conversations, laughter from behind him where various beverage huts and newspaper stands clustered.

But where would they go?

Without him? The answer, of course, was anywhere.

In that moment Jessie focused his imagination in a single desperate image: the picture of his father dressed as the hero, the way he used to be, arrowing out of the sky—and Jessie reaching up, ready for the catch. He willed it with everything he had, but instead, the gray cloud that had been approaching began to funnel through the docks propelled by a tailwind. It manifested as a horizontal drizzle. Jessie hunched into it, blinking and licking his lips.

A hand fell on his shoulder.

Jessie looked up. One of the businessmen who'd been waiting for another ship was standing over him. The man was well dressed, sporting the garish feathered hat his class wore. He had a kindly, well-lined face and hair the color of the clouds.

"Son," he said, "were you looking for the ship to Mespina?"

Jessie nodded.

"They moved the gate," said the businessman. He raised his head and pointed way up the curve of the dock. Just for a second, his outline was prismed by the water beading on Jessie's eyelashes. "It's at 2:30, there, see it?"

Jessie nodded, and reached to pick up his bags.

"Good luck," said the man as he sauntered, in ten-foot strides, back to his companions.

"Thanks," Jessie murmured too late. But he was thunderstruck. In a *daze he tiptoed around the dock to find Father and his brothers waiting impatiently, the ship about to leave. They hadn't looked for him, of course. He answered their angry questions in monosyllables. All he could do was contemplate the wonder of having been saved by that man's simple little gesture. The world must be crammed with people who could be saved just as easily, if somebody bothered to take a minute out of their day to do it.*

From that moment forward, Jessie didn't daydream about putting out a burning city or rescuing the crew of a corkscrewing passenger liner. His fantasies were about seeing that lone, uncertain figure, standing by itself on a dock or outside a charity diner—and of approaching and, with just ten words or a coin, saving a life.

He wasn't able to visit the wrecked treasure ship, because the capital bug's sound organs were recovering. The drone was already louder than Jessie's jet as he left the bowl-shaped garden of the bug's gut. From the zone just under the perforated skin of the bug's back, he could see that the main hull of the wreck was missing, presumably towed by the *Mistelle,* because that was gone too.

When Jessie rose out of the bug's back, there was no sign of the *Mistelle* in the surrounding air either. A massive cloud front—mushroom and dome-shaped wads of it as big as the bug—was moving in and would obscure one of the suns in minutes. *Mistelle* was probably in there somewhere but he would have the devil of a time finding it. Jessie shrugged, and turned the jet away.

He had plucked some perfect salt crystals, long as his thigh, from the precipice moth's forest, just in case. He'd be able to sell these for food and fuel as he traveled.

He did exactly this, in two days reaching the outskirts of the principalities, and civilized airs. Here he was able to blend in with streams of traffic that coursed through the air like blood through the arteries of some world-sized, invisible beast. The sky was full of suns, all competing to tinge the air with their colors. The grandly turning iron wheel cities and green clouds of forest had a wealth of light they could choose to bask in. All those lesser suns were shamed when Candesce awoke from its night cycle, and all cities, farms, and factories turned to the sun of suns during this true day.

Billions of human lives marked their spans by Candesce's radiance. All of the principalities were visible here: he could trace the curve of an immense bubble, many hundreds of miles across, that was sketched onto the sky by innumerable cities and houses, spherical lakes, and drifting farms. Nearby he could tell what they were; further away, they blended and blurred together into one continuous surface whose curve he could see aiming to converge on the far side of Candesce. The sun of suns was too bright to follow that curve to its antipode—but, at night! Then, it was all so clear, a hollow sphere made of glittering stars, city and window lights in uncountable millions encircling an absence where Candesce slumbered or—some said—prowled the air like a hungry falcon.

The bubble had an inner limit because nothing could survive the heat too close to Candesce. The cities and forests were kept at bay, and clouds dissolved and lakes boiled away if they crossed that line. The line was called the *anthropause,* and only at night did the cremation fleets sail across it carrying their silent cargoes, or the technology scavengers who dared to look for the cast-offs of Candesce's inhuman industry. These fleets made tiny drifts of light that edged into the black immensity of Candesce's inmost regions; but sensible people stayed out.

For the first time in his life, Jessie could go anywhere in that mist of humanity. As he flew he took note of all the people in a way he never had before; he marked each person's *role.* There was a baker. Could he be that? There were some soldiers. Could he go to war? He would try on this or that future, taste it for a while as he flew. Some seemed tantalizing, though infinitely far out of reach for a poor uneducated juggler like himself. But none were out of reach anymore.

When he stopped to refuel at the last town before the anthropause, he found they wouldn't take the coins he'd gotten at his last stop. Jessie traded the last of his salt, knowing even as he did it that several slouching youths were watching from a nearby net. He'd shifted his body to try to hide the salt crystal, but the gas jockey had held it up to the light anyway, whistling in appreciation.

"Where'd you get *this?*"

Jessie tried to come up with some plausible story, but he'd never been very good at stuff like that. He got through the transaction, got his gas, and took the jet into the shadow of a three-hundred-foot-wide grove, to wait for dark. It was blazingly hot even here. The shimmering air tricked his eyes, and so he didn't notice the gang of youths sneaking up on him until it was too late.

The arm around his throat was a shocking surprise—so much so that Jessie's reflexes took over and he found himself and his attacker spinning into the air before the astonished eyes of the others. Jessie wormed his way out of the other's grasp. The lad had a knife but now that they were in free air that wasn't a problem. Jessie was an acrobat.

In a matter of seconds he'd flipped the boy around with his feet and kicked him at his friends, who were jumping out of the leaves in a hand-linked mass. The kick took Jessie backwards and he spun around a handy branch. He dove past them as they floundered in midair, got to his jet, and kick-started it. Jessie was off before they could regroup; he left only a rude gesture behind.

Under the hostile glare of Candesce, he paused to look back. His heart was pounding, he was panting, but he felt great. Jessie laughed and decided right there to go on with his quest, even if it was too early. He turned the jet and aimed it straight at the sun of suns.

It quickly became obvious that he couldn't just fly in there. The jet could have gotten him to it in two hours at top speed, but he'd have burned to death long before arriving. He idled, advancing just enough to discourage anyone from following.

He looked back after twenty minutes of this, and swore. There were no clouds or constructions of any kind between him and the anthropause, so the little dot that was following him was clearly visible. He'd made at least one enemy, it was clear; who knew how many of them were hanging off that lone jet?

He opened the throttle a little, hunkering down behind the jet's inadequate windscreen to cut the blazing light and heat as much as he could. After a few minutes he noticed that it was lessening of itself: Candesce was going out.

The light reddened as the minutes stretched. The giant fusion engines of the sun of suns were winking out one by one; Candesce was not one sun, but a flock of them. Each one was mighty enough to light a whole nation, and together they shaped the climate and airflow patterns of the entire world. Their light was scattered and absorbed over the leagues, of course, until it was no longer visible. But Candesce's influence extended to the very skin of the world where icebergs cracked off Virga's frost-painted wall. Something, invisible and not to be tasted or felt, blazed out of here as well with the light and the heat: the *field,* which scrambled the energies and thoughts of any device more complicated than a clock. Jessie's jet was almost as complex as a machine could get in Virga. Since the world's enemies depended entirely on their technologies, they could not enter here.

This was protection; but there had been a cost. Jessie understood that part of his rightful legacy was knowledge, but he'd never been given it. The people in Virga knew little about how the world worked, and nothing about how Candesce lived. They were utterly dependent on a device their ancestors had built but that most of them now regarded as a force of nature.

Light left the sky, but not the heat. That would take hours to dissipate, and Jessie didn't have time to wait. He sucked some water from the wine flask hanging off his saddle, and approached the inner circle of Candesce. Though the last of its lamps were fading red embers, he could still see well enough by the light of the principalities. Their millionfold glitter swam and wavered in the heat haze, casting a shimmering light over the crystalline perfection of the sun of suns. He felt their furnace-heat on his face, but he had dared a capital bug's howl; he could dare this.

The question was, where in a cloud of dozens of suns would a precipice moth nest? The dying moth had told Jessie that it was here, and it made perfect sense: Where was the one place from which the key could not be stolen? Clearly in the one place that you'd need that key to enter.

This answer seemed simple until you saw Candesce. Jessie faced a sky full of vast crystal splinters, miles long, that floated freely in a formation around the suns themselves. Those were smaller, wizened metal-and-crystal balls, like chandeliers that had shrunk in on themselves. And surrounding them, unfolding from mirrored canopies like flowers at dawn, other vast engines stirred.

He flew a circuit through the miles-long airspace of the sun of suns; then he made another. He was looking for something familiar, a town wheel for giants or some sort of blockhouse that might survive the heat here. He saw nothing but machinery, and the night drew on towards a dawn he could not afford to be here to see.

The precipice moth he'd spoken to had been partly alive—at least, it had looked like that leathery skin covered muscles as well as body internal machinery. But what living thing could survive here? Even if those mirrored metal flowers shielded their cores from the worst of the radiation, they couldn't keep out the heat. He could see plainly how their interiors smoked as they spilled into sight.

Even the tips of those great diamond splinters were just cooling below the melting point of lead. Nothing biological could exist here.

Then, if the moth was here, it might as well be in the heart of the inferno as on the edge. With no more logic to guide him than that, Jessie aimed his jet for the very center of Candesce.

Six suns crowded together here. Each was like a glass diatom two hundred feet in diameter, with long spines that jutted every which way in imitation of the gigantic ones framing the entire realm. Thorns from all the suns had pinioned a seventh body between them—a black oval, whose skin looked like old cast iron. Its pebbled surface was patterned with raised squares of brighter metal, and inset squares of crystal. Jessie half-expected to faint from the heat as he approached it, and he would die here if that happened; but instead, it grew noticeably cooler as he closed the last few yards.

He hesitated, then reached out to touch the dark surface. He snatched his hand back: it was *cold.*

This must be the generator that made Candesce's protective field. It was this thing that kept the world's enemies at bay.

Gunning the jet, he made a circuit of the oval. It looked the same from all angles and there was no obvious door. But, when he was almost back to his starting point, Jessie saw distant city-light gleam off something behind one of the crystal panels. He flew closer to see.

The chrome skeleton of a precipice moth huddled on the other side of the window. It was too dark for Jessie to make out what sort of space it was sitting in, but from the way its knees were up by its steel ears, it must not be large.

There wasn't a scrap of flesh on this moth, yet when Jessie reached impulsively to rap on the crystal, it moved.

Its head turned and it lowered a jagged hand from its face. He couldn't see eyes, but it must be looking at him.

"Let me in!" Jessie shouted. "I have to talk to you!"

The moth leaned its head against the window and its mouth opened. Jessie felt a kind of pulse—a deep vibration. He put his ear to the cold crystal and the moth spoke again.

"WAIT."

"You're the one, aren't you? The moth with the key?"

"WAIT."

"But I have to…" He couldn't hear properly over the whine of the jet, so Jessie shut it down. The sound died—then, a second later, died again. An echo? No, that other note had been pitched very differently.

He cursed and spun around, losing his grip on the inset edge of the window. As he flailed and tried to right himself, a second jet appeared around the curve of the giant machine. There was one rider in its saddle. The dark silhouette held a rifle.

"Who are you? What do you want?"

"I want what you want," said a familiar voice. "Nothing less than the greatest treasure in the world."

"Chirk, what are you doing here? How did—did you follow me?"

She hove closer and now her canary-yellow jacket was visible in the glow of distant cities. "I had to," she said. "The wreck was empty, Jess! All that hard work and risking our lives, and there was nothing there. Emmen took it under tow—had to make the best of the situation, I guess—but for our team, there was nothing. All of us were so mad, murderous mad. Not safe for me.

"Then I remembered you. I went looking for you and what should I find? You, juggling for a monster!"

"I think he liked it," said Jessie. He hoped he could trust Chirk, but then, why did she have that rifle in her hands?

"You said you were going to give it a message. When you left I trailed after you. I was trying to think what to do. Talk to you? Ask to join you? Maybe there was a prize for relaying the message. But then you set a course straight for the sun of suns, and I realized what had happened.

"Give me the key, Jessie." She leveled the rifle at him.

He gaped at her, outraged and appalled. "I haven't got it," he said.

She hissed angrily. "Don't lie to me! Why else would you be here?"

"Because *he's* got it," said Jessie. He jabbed a thumb at the window. He saw Chirk's eyes widen as she saw what was behind it. She swore.

"If you thought I had it, why didn't you try to take it from me earlier?"

She looked aside. "Well, I didn't know exactly where you were going. If it gave you the key, then it told you where the door was, right? I had to find out."

"But why didn't you just ask to come along?"

She bit her lip. "'Cause you wouldn't have had me. Why should you? You'd have known I was only in it for the key. Even if I was… nice to you."

Though it was dark, in the half-visible flight of emotions across her face Jessie could see a person he hadn't known was there. Chirk had hid her insecurities as thoroughly as he'd hoped to hide his bloody cough.

"You could have come to me," he said. "You should have."

"And you could have told me you were planning to die alone," she said. "But you didn't."

He couldn't answer that. Chirk waved the rifle at the door. "Get it to open up, then. Let's get the key and get out of here."

"If I can get the key from it, ordering it to kill you will be easy," he told her. A little of the wild mood that had made him willing to dive into a capital bug had returned. He was feeling obstinate enough to dare her to kill him.

Chirk sighed, and to his surprise said, "You're right." She threw away the rifle. They both watched it tumble away into the dark.

"I'm not a good person, and I went about this all wrong," she said. "But I really did like you, Jessie." She looked around uneasily. "I just… I can't let it go. I won't *take* it from you, but I need to be a part of this, Jess. I need a share, just a little share. I'm not going anywhere. If you want to sic your monster on me, I guess you'll just have to kill me." She crossed her arms, lowered her head, and made to stare him down.

He just had to laugh. "You make a terrible villain, Chirk." As she sputtered indignantly, he turned to the window again. The moth had been impassively watching his conversation with Chirk. "Open up!" he shouted at it again, and levering himself close with what little purchase he could make on the window's edge, he put his ear to the crystal again.

"WAIT."

Jessie let go and drifted back, frowning. Wait? For what?

"What did it say?"

"The other moth told me this one wouldn't let me in unless I proved I was committed. I had to prove I wouldn't try to take the key."

"But how are you going to do that?"

"Oh."

Wait.

Candesce's night cycle was nearly over. The metal flowers were starting to close, the bright little flying things they'd released hurrying back to the safety of their tungsten petals. All around them, the rumbling furnaces in the suns would be readying themselves. They would brighten soon, and light would wash away everything material here that was not a part of the sun of suns. Everything, perhaps, except the moth, who might be as ancient as Candesce itself.

"The other moth told me I wouldn't deliver the message," said Jessie. "It said I would *decide* not to."

She frowned. "Why would it say that?"

"Because… 'cause it cured me, that's why. And because the only way to deliver the message is to wait until dawn. That's when this moth here will open the door for us."

"But then—we'd never get out in time…"

He nodded.

"Tell it—yell through the door, like it's doing to you! Jessie, we can't stay here, that's just insane! You said the other moth cured you? Then you can escape, you can live—like me. Maybe not with me, and you're right not to trust me, but we can take the first steps together…" But he was shaking his head.

"I don't think it can hear me," he said. "I can barely hear it, and its voice is loud enough to topple buildings. I have to wait, or not deliver the message."

"Go to the home guard, then. Tell them, and they'll send someone here. They'll—"

"—not believe a word I say. I've nothing to show them, after all. Nothing to prove my story."

"But your life! You have your whole life…"

He'd tried to picture it on the flight here. He had imagined himself as a baker, a soldier, a diplomat, a painter. He longed for every one of them, for any of them. All he had to do was start his jet and follow Chirk, and one of them would come to pass.

He started to reach for his jet, but there was nowhere he could escape the responsibility he'd willingly taken on himself. He realized he didn't want to.

"Only I can do this," he told her. "Anyway, this is the only thing I ever had that was mine. If I give it up now, I'll have some life… but not *my* life."

She said nothing, just shook her head. He looked past her at the vast canopy of glittering lights—from the windows in city apartments and town wheel-houses, from the mansions of the rich and the gas-fires of industry: a sphere of people, every single one of them threatened by something that even now might be uncoiling in the cold vacuum outside the world; each and every one of them waiting, though they knew it not, for a helping hand.

Ten words, or a single coin.

"Get out of here, Chirk," he said. "It's starting. If you leave right now you might just get away before the full heat hits."

"But—" She stared at him in bewilderment. "You come too!"

"No. Just go. See?" He pointed at a faint ember-glow that had started in the darkness below their feet. "They're waking up. This place will be a furnace soon. There's no treasure here for you, Chirk. It's all out there."

"Jessie, I can't—" Flame-colored light blossomed below them, and then from one side. "Jessie?" Her eyes were wide with panic.

"Get out! Chirk, it's too late unless you go *now!* Go! Go!"

The panic took her and she kicked her jet into life. She made a clumsy pass, trying to grab Jessie on the way by, but he evaded her easily.

"Go!" She put her head down, opened the throttle, and shot away. *Too late,* Jessie feared. *Let her not be just one second too late.*

Her jet disappeared in the rising light. Jessie kicked his own jet away, returning to cling to the edge of the window. His own sharp-edged shadow appeared against the metal skull inches from his own.

"You have your proof!" He could feel the pulse of energy—heat, and something deeper and more fatal—reaching into him from the awakening suns. "Now open up.

"Open *up!*"

The moth reached out and did something below the window. The crystalline pane slid aside, and Jessie climbed into the narrow, boxlike space. The window slid shut, but did nothing to filter the growing light and heat from outside. There was nowhere further to go, either. He had expected no less.

The precipice moth lowered its head to his.

"I have come to you on behalf of humanity," said Jessie, "to tell you that the ancient strategy of relying on Candesce for our safety will no longer work…"

He told the moth his story, and as he spoke the dawn came up.

TURING'S APPLES

STEPHEN BAXTER

Near the centre of the Moon's far side there is a neat, round, well-defined crater called Daedalus. No human knew this existed before the middle of the twentieth century. It's a bit of lunar territory as far as you can get from Earth, and about the quietest.

That's why the teams of astronauts from Europe, America, Russia and China went there. They smoothed over the floor of a crater ninety kilometres wide, laid sheets of metal mesh over the natural dish, and suspended feed horns and receiver systems on spidery scaffolding. And there you had it, an instant radio telescope, by far the most powerful ever built: a super-Arecibo, dwarfing its mother in Puerto Rico. Before the astronauts left they christened their telescope Clarke.

Now the telescope is a ruin, and much of the floor of Daedalus is covered by glass, Moon dust melted by multiple nuclear strikes. But, I'm told, if you were to look down from some slow lunar orbit you would see a single point of light glowing there, a star fallen to the Moon. One day the Moon will be gone, but that point will remain, silently orbiting Earth, a lunar memory. And in the further future, when the Earth has gone too, when the stars have burned out and the galaxies fled from the sky, still that point of light will shine.

My brother Wilson never left the Earth. In fact he rarely left England. He was buried, what was left of him, in a grave next to our father's, just outside Milton Keynes. But he *made* that point of light on the Moon, which will be the last legacy of all mankind.

Talk about sibling rivalry.

<u>**2020**</u>

It was at my father's funeral, actually, before Wilson had even begun his SETI searches, that the Clarke first came between us.

There was a good turnout at the funeral, at an old church on the outskirts of Milton Keynes proper. Wilson and I were my father's only children, but as well as his old friends there were a couple of surviving aunts and a gaggle of cousins mostly around our age, mid-twenties to mid-thirties, so there was a good crop of children, like little flowers.

I don't know if I'd say Milton Keynes is a good place to live. It certainly isn't a good place to die. The city is a monument to planning, a concrete grid of avenues with very English names like Midsummer, now overlaid by the new monorail. It's so *clean* it makes death seem a social embarrassment, like a fart in a shopping mall. Maybe we need to be buried in ground dirty with bones.

Our father had remembered, just, how the area was all villages and farmland before the Second World War. He had stayed on even after our mother died twenty years before he did, him and his memories made invalid by all the architecture. At the service I spoke of those memories—for instance how during the war a tough Home Guard had caught him sneaking into the grounds of Bletchley Park, not far away, scrumping apples while Alan Turing and the other geniuses were labouring over the Nazi codes inside the house. "Dad always said he wondered if he picked up a mathematical bug from Turing's apples," I concluded, "because, he would say, for sure Wilson's brain didn't come from him."

"Your brain too," Wilson said when he collared me later outside the church. He hadn't spoken at the service; that wasn't his style. "You should have mentioned that. I'm not the only mathematical nerd in the family."

It was a difficult moment. My wife and I had just been introduced to Hannah, the two-year-old daughter of a cousin. Hannah had been born profoundly deaf, and we adults in our black suits and dresses were awkwardly copying her parents' bits of sign language. Wilson just walked through this lot to get to me, barely glancing at the little girl with the wide smile who was the centre of attention. I led him away to avoid any offence.

He was thirty then, a year older than me, taller, thinner, edgier. Others have said we were more similar than I wanted to believe. He had brought nobody with him to the funeral, and that was a relief. His partners could be male or female, his relationships usually destructive; his companions were like unexploded bombs walking into the room.

"Sorry if I got the story wrong," I said, a bit caustically.

"Dad and his memories, all those stories he told over and over. Well, it's the last time I'll hear about Turing's apples!"

That thought hurt me. "We'll remember. I suppose I'll tell it to Eddie and Sam someday." My own little boys.

"They won't listen. Why should they? Dad will fade away. Everybody fades away. The dead get deader." He was talking about his own father, whom we had just buried. "Listen, have you heard they're putting the Clarke through its acceptance test run?..." And, there in the church-yard, he actually pulled a handheld computer out of his inside jacket pocket and brought up a specification. "Of course you understand the importance of it being on Farside." For the millionth time in my life he had set his little brother a pop quiz, and he looked at me as if I was catastrophically dumb.

"Radio shadow," I said. To be shielded from Earth's noisy chatter was particularly important for SETI, the search for extraterrestrial intel-ligence to which my brother was devoting his career. SETI searches for faint signals from remote civilisations, a task made orders of magni-tude harder if you're drowned out by very loud signals from a nearby civilisation.

He actually applauded my guess, sarcastically. He often reminded me of what had always repelled me about academia—the barely repressed bullying, the intense rivalry. A university is a chimp pack. That was why I was never tempted to go down that route. That, and maybe the fact that Wilson had gone that way ahead of me.

I was faintly relieved when people started to move out of the church-yard. There was going to be a reception at my father's home, and we had to go.

"So are you coming for the cakes and sherry?"

He glanced at the time on his handheld. "Actually I've somebody to meet."

"He or she?"

He didn't reply. For one brief moment he looked at me with honesty. "You're better at this stuff than me."

"What stuff? Being human?"

"Listen, the Clarke should be open for business in a month. Come on down to London; we can watch the first results."

"I'd like that."

I was lying, and his invitation probably wasn't sincere either. In the end it was over two years before I saw him again.

By then he'd found the Eagle signal, and everything had changed.

2022

Wilson and his team quickly established that their brief signal, first detected just months after Clarke went operational, was coming from a source six thousand five hundred light years from Earth, somewhere beyond a starbirth cloud called the Eagle Nebula. That's a long way away, on the other side of the Galaxy's next spiral arm in, the Sagittarius.

And to call the signal "brief" understates it. It was a second-long pulse, faint and hissy, and it repeated just once a *year*, roughly. It was a monument to robotic patience that the big lunar ear had picked up the damn thing at all.

Still it was a genuine signal from ET, the scientists were jumping up and down, and for a while it was a public sensation. Within days somebody had rushed out a pop single inspired by the message: called "Eagle Song," slow, dreamlike, littered with what sounded like sitars, and very beautiful. It was supposedly based on a Beatles master lost for five decades. It made number two.

But the signal was just a squirt of noise from a long way off. When there was no follow-up, when no mother ship materialised in the sky, interest moved on. That song vanished from the charts.

The whole business of the signal turned out to be your classic nine-day wonder. Wilson invited me in on the tenth day. That was why I was resentful, I guess, as I drove into town that morning to visit him.

The Clarke Institute's ground station was in one of the huge glass follies thrown up along the banks of the Thames in the profligate boom-capitalism days of the noughties. Now office space was cheap enough even for academics to rent, but central London was a fortress, with mandatory crawl lanes so your face could be captured by the surveillance cameras. I was in the counter-terror business myself, and I could see the necessity as I edged past St. Paul's, whose dome had been smashed like an egg by the Carbon Cowboys' bomb of 2018. But the slow ride left me plenty of time to brood on how many more *important* people Wilson had shown off to before he got around to his brother. Wilson never was loyal that way.

Wilson's office could have been any modern data-processing installation, save for the all-sky projection of the cosmic background radiation painted on the ceiling. Wilson sat me down and offered me a can of warm Coke. An audio transposition of the signal was playing on an open laptop, over and over. It sounded like waves lapping at a beach. Wilson looked like he hadn't shaved for three days, slept for five, or changed his shirt in ten. He listened, rapt.

Even Wilson and his team hadn't known about the detection of the signal for a year. The Clarke ran autonomously; the astronauts who built it had long since packed up and come home. A year earlier the telescope's signal processors had spotted the pulse, a whisper of microwaves. There was structure in there, and evidence that the beam was collimated—it looked artificial. But the signal faded after just a second.

Most previous SETI searchers had listened for strong, continuous signals, and would have given up at that point. But what about a lighthouse, sweeping a microwave beam around the Galaxy like a searchlight? That, so Wilson had explained to me, would be a much cheaper way for a transmitting civilisation to send to a lot more stars. So, based on that economic argument, the Clarke was designed for patience. It had waited a whole year. It had even sent requests to other installations, asking them to keep an electronic eye out in case the Clarke, stuck in its crater, happened to be looking the other way when the signal recurred. In the end it struck lucky and found the repeat pulse itself, and at last alerted its human masters.

"We're hot favourites for the Nobel," Wilson said, matter of fact.

I felt like having a go at him. "Probably everybody out there has forgotten about your signal already." I waved a hand at the huge glass windows; the office, meant for fat-cat hedge fund managers, had terrific views of the river, the Houses of Parliament, the tangled wreck of the London Eye. "Okay, it's proof of existence, but that's all."

He frowned at that. "Well, that's not true. Actually we're looking for more data in the signal. It is very faint, and there's a lot of scintillation from the interstellar medium. We're probably going to have to wait for a few more passes to get a better resolution."

"A few more passes? A few more years!"

"But even without that there's a lot we can tell just from the signal itself." He pulled up charts on his laptop. "For a start we can deduce the Eaglets' technical capabilities and power availability, given that we believe they'd do it as cheaply as possible. This analysis is related to an old model called Benford beacons." He pointed to a curve minimum. "Look—we figure they are pumping a few hundred megawatts through an array kilometres across, probably comparable to the one we've got listening on the Moon. Sending out pulses around the plane of the Galaxy, where most of the stars lie. We can make other guesses." He leaned back and took a slug of his Coke, dribbling a few drops to add to the collection of stains on his shirt. "The search for ET was always guided by philosophical principles and logic. Now we have this one data point, the Eaglets six thousand light years away, we can test those principles."

"Such as?"

"The principle of plenitude. We believed that because life and intelligence arose on this Earth, they ought to arise everywhere they can. Here's one validation of that principle. Then there's the principle of mediocrity."

I remembered enough of my studies to recall that. "We aren't at any special place in space and time."

"Right. Turns out, given this one data point, it's not likely to hold too well."

"Why do you say that?"

"Because we found these guys in the direction of the centre of the Galaxy…"

When the Galaxy was young, star formation was most intense at its core. Later a wave of starbirth swept out through the disc, with the heavy elements necessary for life baked in the hearts of dead stars and driven on a wind of supernovas. So the stars inward of us are older than the sun, and are therefore likely to have been harbours for life much longer.

"We would expect to see a concentration of old civilisations towards the centre of the Galaxy. This one example validates that." He eyed me, challenging. "We can even guess how many technological, transmitting civilisations there are in the Galaxy."

"From this one instance?" I was practiced at this kind of contest between us. "Well, let's see. The Galaxy is a disc a hundred thousand light years across, roughly. If all the civilisations are an average of six thousand light years apart—divide the area of the Galaxy by the area of a disc of diameter six thousand light years—around three hundred?"

He smiled. "Very *good*."

"So we're not typical," I said. "We're young, and out in the suburbs. All that from a single microwave pulse."

"Of course most ordinary people are too dumb to be able to appreciate logic like that. That's why they aren't rioting in the streets." He said this casually. Language like that always made me wince, even when we were undergraduates.

But he had a point. Besides, I had the feeling that most people had already believed in their gut that ET existed; this was a confirmation, not a shock. You might blame Hollywood for that, but Wilson sometimes speculated that we were looking for our lost brothers. All those other hominid species, those other kinds of mind, that we killed off one by one, just as in my lifetime we had destroyed the chimps in the wild—sentient tool-using beings, hunted down for bushmeat. We evolved on a crowded planet, and we missed them all.

"A lot of people are speculating about whether the Eaglets have souls," I said. "According to Saint Thomas Aquinas—"

He waved away Saint Thomas Aquinas. "You know, in a way our feelings behind SETI were always theological, explicitly or not. We were looking for God in the sky, or some technological equivalent. Somebody who would care about *us*. But we were never going to find Him. We were going to find either emptiness, or a new category of being, between us and the angels. The Eaglets have got nothing to do with us, or our dreams of God. That's what people don't see. And that's what people will have to deal with, ultimately."

He glanced at the ceiling, and I guessed he was looking towards the Eagle nebula. "And they won't be much like us. Hell of a place they live. Not like here. The Sagittarius arm wraps a whole turn around the Galaxy's core, full of dust and clouds and young stars. Why, the Eagle nebula itself is lit up by stars only a few million years old. Must be a tremendous sky, like a slow explosion—not like our sky of orderly wheeling pinpoints, which is like the inside of a computer. No wonder we began with astrology and astronomy. How do you imagine their thinking will be different, having evolved under such a different sky?"

I grunted. "We'll never know. Not for six thousand years at least."

"Maybe. Depends what data we find in the signal. You want another Coke?"

But I hadn't opened the first.

That was how that day went. We talked of nothing but the signal, not how he was, who he was dating, not about my family, my wife and the boys—all of us learning sign, incidentally, to talk to little Hannah. The Eagle signal was inhuman, abstract. Nothing you could see or touch; you couldn't even hear it without fancy signal processing. But it was all that filled his head. That was Wilson all over.

This was, in retrospect, the happiest time of his life. God help him.

2026

"You want my help, don't you?"

Wilson stood on my doorstep, wearing a jacket and shambolic tie, every inch the academic. He looked shifty. "How do you know?"

"Why else would you come here? You *never* visit." Well, it was true. He hardly ever even mailed or called. I didn't think my wife and kids had seen him since our father's funeral six years earlier.

He thought that over, then grinned. "A reasonable deduction, given past observation. Can I come in?"

I took him through the living room on the way to my home study. The boys, then twelve and thirteen, were playing a hologram boxing game, with two wavering foot-tall prize fighters mimicking the kids' actions in the middle of the carpet. I introduced Wilson. They barely remembered him and I wasn't sure if he remembered *them*. I hurried him on. The boys signed to each other: *What a dork*, roughly translated.

Wilson noticed the signing. "What are they doing? Some kind of private game?"

I wasn't surprised he wouldn't know. "That's British Sign Language. We've been learning it for years—actually since Dad's funeral, when we hooked up with Barry and his wife, and we found out they had a little deaf girl. Hannah, do you remember? She's eight now. We've all been learning to talk to her. The kids find it fun, I think. You know, it's an irony that you're involved in a billion-pound project to talk to aliens six thousand light years away, yet it doesn't trouble you that you can't speak to a little girl in your own family."

He looked at me blankly. I was mouthing words that obviously meant nothing to him, intellectually or emotionally. That was Wilson.

He just started talking about work. "We've got six years' worth of data now—six pulses, each a second long. There's a *lot* of information in there. They use a technique like our own wave-length division multiplexing, with the signal divided into sections each a kilohertz or so wide. We've extracted gigabytes…"

I gave up. I went and made a pot of coffee, and brought it back to the study. When I returned he was still standing where I'd left him, like a switched-off robot. He took a coffee and sat down.

I prompted, "Gigabytes?"

"Gigabytes. By comparison the whole *Encyclopaedia Britannica* is just one gigabyte. The problem is we can't make sense of it."

"How do you know it's not just noise?"

"We have techniques to test for that. Information theory. Based on experiments to do with talking to dolphins, actually." He dug a handheld out of his pocket and showed me some of the results.

The first was simple enough, called a "Zipf graph." You break your message up into what look like components—maybe words, letters, phonemes in English. Then you do a frequency count: how many letter

As, how many Es, how many Rs. If you have random noise you'd expect roughly equal numbers of the letters, so you'd get a flat distribution. If you have a clean signal without information content, a string of identical letters, A, A, A, you'd get a graph with a spike. Meaningful information gives you a slope, somewhere in between those horizontal and vertical extremes.

"And we get a beautiful log-scale minus one power law," he said, showing me. "There's information in there all right. But there is a lot of controversy over identifying the elements themselves. The Eaglets did *not* send down neat binary code. The data is frequency modulated, their language full of growths and decays. More like a garden growing on fast-forward than any human data stream. I wonder if it has something to do with that young sky of theirs. Anyhow, after the Zipf, we tried a Shannon entropy analysis."

This is about looking for relationships between the signal elements. You work out conditional probabilities: Given pairs of elements, how likely is it that you'll see U following Q? Then you go on to higher-order "entropy levels," in the jargon, starting with triples: How likely is it to find G following I and N?

"As a comparison, dolphin languages get to third- or fourth-order entropy. We humans get to eighth or ninth."

"And the Eaglets?"

"The entropy level breaks our assessment routines. We think it's around order thirty." He regarded me, seeing if I understood. "It is information, but much more complex than any human language. It might be like English sentences with a fantastically convoluted structure—triple or quadruple negatives, overlapping clauses, tense changes." He grinned. "Or triple entendres. Or quadruples."

"They're smarter than us."

"Oh, yes. And this is proof, if we needed it, that the message isn't meant specifically for us."

"Because if it were, they'd have dumbed it down. How smart do you think they are? Smarter than us, certainly, but—"

"Are there limits? Well, maybe. You might imagine that an older culture would plateau, once they've figured out the essential truths of the universe, and a technology optimal for their needs… There's no reason to think progress need be onward and upward forever. Then again perhaps there are fundamental limits to information processing. Perhaps a brain that gets too complex is prone to crashes and overloads. There may be a trade-off between complexity and stability."

I poured him more coffee. "I went to Cambridge. I'm used to being with entities smarter than I am. Am I supposed to feel demoralised?"

He grinned. "That's up to you. But the Eaglets are a new category of being for us. This isn't like the Incas meeting the Spaniards, a mere technological gap. They had a basic humanity in common. We may find the gulf between us and the Eaglets is *forever* unbridgeable. Remember how Dad used to read *Gulliver's Travels* to us?"

The memory made me smile.

"Those talking horses used to scare the wits out of me. They were genuinely smarter than us. And how did Gulliver react to them? He was totally overawed. He tried to imitate them, and even after they kicked him out he always despised his own kind, because they weren't as good as the horses."

"The revenge of Mister Ed," I said.

But he never was much good at that kind of humour. "Maybe that will be the way for us—we'll ape the Eaglets or defy them. Maybe the mere knowledge that a race smarter than your own exists is death."

"Is all this being released to the public?"

"Oh, yes. We're affiliated to NASA, and they have an explicit open-book policy. Besides the Institute is as leaky as hell. There's no point even trying to keep it quiet. But we're releasing the news gradually and soberly. Nobody's noticing much. You hadn't, had you?"

"So what do you think the signal is? Some kind of super-encyclopaedia?"

He snorted. "Maybe. That's the fond hope among the contact optimists. But when the European colonists turned up on foreign shores, their first impulse wasn't to hand over encyclopaedias or histories, but—"

"Bibles."

"Yes. It could be something less disruptive than that. A vast work of art, for instance. Why would they send such a thing? Maybe it's a funeral pyre. Or a pharaoh's tomb, full of treasure. Look: we were here, this is how good we became."

"So what do you want of me?"

He faced me. I thought it was clear he was trying to figure out, in his clumsy way, how to get me to do whatever it was he wanted. "Well, what do you think? This makes translating the most obscure human language a cakewalk, and we've got nothing like a Rosetta stone. Look, Jack, our information processing suites at the Institute are pretty smart theoretically, but they are limited. Running off processors and memory store not much beefier than this." He waved his handheld. "Whereas the software brutes that do your data mining are an order of magnitude more powerful."

The software I developed and maintained mined the endless torrents of data culled on every individual in the country, from your minute-to-minute movements on private or public transport to the porn you accessed and how you hid it from your partner. We tracked your patterns of behaviour, and deviations from those patterns. "Terrorist" is a broad label, but it suited to describe the modern phenomenon we were looking for. The terrorists were needles in a haystack, of which the rest of us were the millions of straws.

This continual live data mining took up monstrous memory storage and processing power. A few times I'd visited the big Home Office computers in their hardened bunkers under New Scotland Yard: giant superconducting neural nets suspended in rooms so cold your breath crackled. There was nothing like it in the private sector, or in academia.

Which, I realised, was why Wilson had come to me today.

"You want me to run your ET signal through my data mining suites, don't you?" He immediately had me hooked, but I wasn't about to admit it. I might have rejected the academic life, but I think curiosity burned in me as strongly as it ever did in Wilson. "How do you imagine I'd get permission for that?"

He waved that away as a technicality of no interest. "What we're looking for is patterns embedded deep in the data, layers down, any kind of recognisable starter for us in decoding the whole thing… Obviously software designed to look for patterns in the way I use my travel cards is going to have to be adapted to seek useful correlations in the Eaglet data. It will be an unprecedented challenge.

"In a way that's a good thing. It will likely take generations to decode this stuff, if we ever do, the way it took the Renaissance Europeans generations to make sense of the legacy of antiquity. The sheer time factor is a culture-shock prophylactic.

"So are you going to bend the rules for me, Jack? Come on, man. Remember what Dad said. Solving puzzles like this is what we do. We both ate Turing's apples…"

He wasn't entirely without guile. He knew how to entice me. He turned out to be wrong about the culture shock, however.

Two armed coppers escorted me through the Institute building. The big glass box was entirely empty save for me and the coppers and a sniffer dog. The morning outside was bright, a cold spring day, the sky a serene blue, elevated from Wilson's latest madness.

Wilson was sitting in the Clarke project office, beside a screen across which data displays flickered. He had big slabs of Semtex strapped around his waist, and some kind of dead man's trigger in his hand. My brother, reduced at last to a cliché suicide bomber. The coppers stayed safely outside.

"We're secure." Wilson glanced around. "They can see us but they can't hear us. I'm confident of that. My firewalls—" When I walked towards him he held up his hands. "No closer. I'll blow it, I swear."

"Christ, Wilson." I stood still, shut up, and deliberately calmed down.

I knew that my boys, now in their teens, would be watching every move on the spy-hack news channels. Maybe nobody could hear us, but Hannah, now a beautiful eleven-year-old, had plenty of friends who could read lips. That would never occur to Wilson. If I was to die today, here with my lunatic of a brother, I wasn't going to let my boys remember their father broken by fear.

I sat down, as close to Wilson as I could get. I tried to keep my head down, my lips barely moving when I spoke. There was a six-pack of warm soda on the bench. I think I'll always associate warm soda with Wilson. I took one, popped the tab and sipped; I could taste nothing. "You want one?"

"No," he said bitterly. "Make yourself at home."

"What a fucking idiot you are, Wilson. How did it ever come to this?"

"You should know. You helped me."

"And by God I've regretted it ever since," I snarled back at him. "You got me sacked, you moron. And since France, every nut job on the planet has me targeted, and my kids. We have police protection."

"Don't blame me. You chose to help me."

I stared at him. "That's called loyalty. A quality which you, entirely lacking it yourself, see only as a weakness to exploit."

"Well, whatever. What does it matter now? Look, Jack, I need your help."

"This is turning into a pattern."

He glanced at his screen. "I need you to buy me time, to give me a chance to complete this project."

"Why should I care about your project?"

"It's not *my* project. It never has been. Surely you understand that much. It's the Eaglets'..."

Everything had changed in the three years since I had begun to run Wilson's message through the big Home Office computers under New Scotland Yard—all under the radar of my bosses; they'd never have dared risk exposing their precious supercooled brains to such unknowns. Well, Wilson had been right. My data mining had quickly turned up recurring segments, chunks of organised data differing only in detail.

And it was Wilson's intuition that these things were bits of executable code: programs you could run. Even as expressed in the Eaglets' odd flowing language, he thought he recognised logical loops, start and stop statements. Mathematics may or may not be universal, but computing seems to be—my brother had found Turing machines, buried deep in an alien database.

Wilson translated the segments into a human mathematical programming language, and set them to run on a dedicated processor. They turned out to be like viruses. Once downloaded on almost any computer substrate they organised themselves, investigated their environment, started to multiply, and quickly grew, accessing the data banks that had been downloaded from the stars with them. Then they started asking questions of the operators: simple yes-no, true-false exchanges that soon built up a common language.

"The Eaglets didn't send us a message," Wilson had whispered to me on the phone in the small hours; at the height of it he worked twenty-four seven. "They downloaded an AI. And now the AI is learning to speak to us."

It was a way to resolve a ferocious communications challenge. The Eaglets were sending their message to the whole Galaxy; they knew nothing about the intelligence, cultural development, or even the physical form of their audiences. So they sent an all-purpose artificial mind embedded in the information stream itself, able to learn and start a local dialogue with the receivers.

This above all else proved to me how smart the Eaglets must be. It didn't comfort me at all that some commentators pointed out that this "Hoyle strategy" had been anticipated by some human thinkers; it's one thing to anticipate, another to build. I wondered if those viruses found it a challenge to dumb down their message for creatures capable of only ninth-order Shannon entropy, as we were.

We were soon betrayed. For running the Eaglet data through the Home Office mining suites I was sacked, arrested, and bailed on condition I went back to work on the Eaglet stuff under police supervision.

And of course the news that there was information in the Eaglets' beeps leaked almost immediately. A new era of popular engagement with the signal began; the chatter became intense. But because only the Clarke telescope could pick up the signal, the scientists at the Clarke Institute and the consortium of governments they answered to were able to keep control of the information itself. And that information looked as if it would become extremely valuable.

The Eaglets' programming and data compression techniques, what we could make of them, had immediate commercial value. When patented by the UK government and licensed, an information revolution began that added a billion euros to Britain's balance of payments in the first year. Governments and corporations outside the loop of control jumped up and down with fury.

And then Wilson and his team started to publish what they were learning of the Eaglets themselves.

We don't know anything about what they look like, how they live—or even if they're corporeal or not. But they are old, vastly old compared to us. Their cultural records go back a million years, maybe ten times as long as we've been human, and even then they built their civilisation on the ruins of others. But they regard themselves as a young species. They live in awe of older ones, whose presence they have glimpsed deep in the turbulent core of the Galaxy.

Not surprisingly, the Eaglets are fascinated by time and its processes. One of Wilson's team foolishly speculated that the Eaglets actually made a religion of time, deifying the one universal that will erode us all in the end. That caused a lot of trouble. Some people took up the time creed with enthusiasm. They looked for parallels in human philosophies, the Hindu and the Mayan. If the Eaglets really were smarter than us, they said, they must be closer to the true god, and we should follow them. Others, led by the conventional religions, moved sharply in the opposite direction. Minor wars broke out over a creed that was entirely unknown to humanity five years before, and which nobody on Earth understood fully.

Then the economic dislocations began, as those new techniques for data handling made whole industries obsolescent. That was predictable; it was as if the aliens had invaded cyberspace, which was economically dominant over the physical world. Luddite types began sabotaging the software houses turning out the new-generation systems, and battles broke out in the corporate universe, themselves on the economic scale of small wars.

"This is the danger of speed," Wilson had said to me, just weeks before he wired himself up with Semtex. "If we'd been able to take it slow, unwrapping the message would have been more like an exercise in normal science, and we could have absorbed it. Grown with it. Instead, thanks to the viruses, it's been like a revelation, a pouring of holy knowledge into our heads. Revelations tend to be destabilising. Look at Jesus. Three centuries after the Crucifixion Christianity had taken over the whole Roman empire."

Amid all the economic, political, religious and philosophical turbulence, if anybody had dreamed that knowing the alien would unite us around our common humanity, they were dead wrong.

Then a bunch of Algerian patriots used pirated copies of the Eaglet viruses to hammer the electronic infrastructure of France's major cities. As everything from sewage to air traffic control crashed, the country was simultaneously assaulted with train bombs, bugs in the water supply, a dirty nuke in Orleans. It was a force-multiplier attack, in the jargon; the toll of death and injury was a shock, even by the standards of the third decade of the bloody twenty-first century. And our counter-measures were useless in the face of the Eaglet viruses.

That was when the governments decided the Eaglet project had to be shut down, or at the very least put under tight control. But Wilson, my brother, wasn't having any of that.

"None of this is the fault of the Eaglets, Jack," he said now, an alien apologist with Semtex strapped to his waist. "They didn't mean to harm us in any way."

"Then what do they want?"

"Our help…"

And he was going to provide it. With, in turn, my help.

"Why me? I was sacked, remember."

"They'll listen to you. The police. Because you're my brother. You're useful."

"Useful?…" At times Wilson seemed unable to see people as anything other than useful robots, even his own family. I sighed. "Tell me what you want."

"Time," he said, glancing at his screen, the data and status summaries scrolling across it. "The great god of the Eaglets, remember? Just a little more time."

"How much?"

He checked. "Twenty-four hours would let me complete this download. That's an outside estimate. Just stall them. Keep them talking, stay here with me. Make them think you're making progress in talking me out of it."

"While the actual progress is being made by *that*." I nodded at the screen. "What are you doing here, Wilson? What's it about?"

"I don't know all of it. There are hints in the data. Subtexts sometimes..." He was whispering.

"Subtexts about what?"

"About what concerns the Eaglets. Jack, what do you imagine a long-lived civilisation *wants*? If you could think on very long timescales you would be concerned about threats that seem remote to us."

"An asteroid impact due in a thousand years, maybe? If I expected to live that long, or my kids—"

"That kind of thing. But that's not long enough, Jack, not nearly. In the data there are passages—poetry, maybe—that speak of the deep past and furthest future, the Big Bang that is echoed in the microwave background, the future that will be dominated by the dark energy expansion that will ultimately throw all the other galaxies over the cosmological horizon... The Eaglets think about these things, and not just as scientific hypotheses. They *care* about them. The dominance of their great god time. 'The universe has no memory.'"

"What does that mean?"

"I'm not sure. A phrase in the message."

"So what are you downloading? And to where?"

"The Moon," he said frankly. "The Clarke telescope, on Farside. They want us to build something, Jack. Something physical, I mean. And with the fabricators and other maintenance gear at Clarke there's a chance we could do it. I mean, it's not the most advanced offworld robot facility; it's only designed for maintenance and upgrade of the radio telescope—"

"But it's the facility you can get your hands on. You're letting these Eaglet agents out of their virtual world and giving them a way to build something real. Don't you think that's dangerous?"

"Dangerous how?" And he laughed at me and turned away.

I grabbed his shoulders and swivelled him around in his chair. "Don't you turn away from me, you fucker. You've been doing that all our lives. You know what I mean. Why, the Eaglets' software alone is making a mess of the world. What if this is some kind of Trojan horse—a Doomsday weapon they're getting us suckers to build ourselves?"

"It's hardly likely that an advanced culture—"

"Don't give me that contact-optimist bullshit. You don't believe it yourself. And even if you did, you don't *know* for sure. You can't."

"No. All right." He pulled away from me. "I can't know. Which is one reason why I set the thing going up on the Moon, not Earth. Call it a quarantine. If we don't like whatever it is, there's at least a *chance* we could contain it up there. Yes, there's a risk. But the rewards are unknowable, and huge." He looked at me, almost pleading for me to understand. "We have to go on. This is the Eaglets' project, not ours. Ever since we unpacked the message, this story has been about them, not us. That's what dealing with a superior intelligence means. It's like those religious nuts say. We *know* the Eaglets are orders of magnitude smarter than us. Shouldn't we trust them? Shouldn't we help them achieve their goal, even if we don't understand precisely what it is?"

"This ends now." I reached for the keyboard beside me. "Tell me how to stop the download."

"No." He sat firm, that trigger clutched in his right hand.

"You won't use that. You wouldn't kill us both. Not for something so abstract, inhuman—"

"*Superhuman*," he breathed. "Not inhuman. Superhuman. Oh, I would. You've known me all your life, Jack. Look into my eyes. *I'm not like you.* Do you really doubt me?"

And, looking at him, I didn't.

So we sat there, the two of us, a face-off. I stayed close enough to overpower him if he gave me the slightest chance. And he kept his trigger before my face.

Hour after hour.

In the end it was time that defeated him, I think, the Eaglets' invisible god. That and fatigue. I'm convinced he didn't mean to release the trigger. Only seventeen hours had elapsed, of the twenty-four he asked for, when his thumb slipped.

I tried to turn away. That small, instinctive gesture was why I lost a leg, a hand, an eye, all on my right side.

And I lost a brother.

But when the forensics guys had finished combing through the wreckage, they were able to prove that the seventeen hours had been enough for Wilson's download.

2033

It took a month for NASA, ESA and the Chinese to send up a lunar orbiter to see what was going on. The probe found that Wilson's download had caused the Clarke fabricators to start making stuff. At first they made other machines, more specialised, from what was lying around in the workshops and sheds. These in turn made increasingly tiny versions of themselves, heading steadily down to the nano scale. In the end the work was so fine only an astronaut on the ground might have had a chance of even seeing it. Nobody dared send in a human.

Meanwhile the machines banked up Moon dust and scrap to make a high-energy facility—something like a particle accelerator or a fusion torus, but not.

Then the real work started.

The Eaglet machines took a chunk of Moon rock and crushed it, turning its mass-energy into a spacetime artefact—something like a black hole, but not. They dropped it into the body of the Moon, where it started accreting, sucking in material, like a black hole, and budding off copies of itself, unlike a black hole.

Gradually these objects began converting the substance of the Moon into copies of themselves. The glowing point of light we see at the centre of Clarke is leaked radiation from this process.

The governments panicked. A nuclear warhead was dug out of cold store and dropped plumb into Daedalus Crater. The explosion was spectacular. But when the dust subsided that pale, unearthly spark was still there, unperturbed.

As the cluster of nano artefacts grows, the Moon's substance will be consumed at an exponential rate. Centuries, a millennium tops, will be enough to consume it all. And Earth will be orbited, not by its ancient companion, but by a spacetime artefact, like a black hole, but not. That much seems well established by the physicists.

There is less consensus as to the purpose of the artefact. Here's my guess.

The Moon artefact will be a recorder.

Wilson said the Eaglets feared the universe has no memory. I think he meant that, right now, in our cosmic epoch, we can still see relics of the universe's birth, echoes of the Big Bang, in the microwave background glow. And we also see evidence of the expansion to come, in the recession of the distant galaxies. We discovered both these basic features of the universe, its past and its future, in the twentieth century.

There will come a time—the cosmologists quote hundreds of billions of years—when the accelerating recession will have taken all those distant galaxies over our horizon. So we will be left with just the local group, the Milky Way and Andromeda and bits and pieces, bound together by gravity. The cosmic expansion will be invisible. And meanwhile the background glow will have become so attenuated you won't be able to pick it out of the faint glow of the interstellar medium.

So in that remote epoch you wouldn't be able to repeat the twentieth-century discoveries; you couldn't glimpse past or future. That's what the Eaglets mean when they say the universe has no memory.

And I believe they are countering it. They, and those like Wilson that they co-opt into helping them, are carving time capsules out of folded spacetime. At some future epoch these will evaporate, maybe through something like Hawking radiation, and will reveal the truth of the universe to whatever eyes are there to see it.

Of course it occurs to me—this is Wilson's principle of mediocrity—that ours might not be the only epoch with a privileged view of the cosmos. Just after the Big Bang there was a pulse of "inflation," superfast expansion that homogenised the universe and erased details of whatever came before. Maybe we should be looking for other time boxes, left for our benefit by the inhabitants of those early realms.

The Eaglets are conscious entities trying to give the universe a memory. Perhaps there is even a deeper purpose: it may be intelligence's role to shape the ultimate evolution of the universe, but you can't do that if you've forgotten what went before.

Not every commentator agrees with my analysis, as above. The interpretation of the Eaglet data has always been uncertain. Maybe even Wilson wouldn't agree. Well, since it's my suggestion he would probably argue with me by sheer reflex.

I suppose it's possible to care deeply about the plight of hypothetical beings a hundred billion years hence. In one sense we ought to; their epoch is our inevitable destiny. Wilson certainly did care, enough to kill himself for it. But this is a project so vast and cold that it can engage only a semi-immortal supermind like an Eaglet's—or a modern human who is functionally insane.

What matters most to me is the now. The sons who haven't yet aged and crumbled to dust, playing football under a sun that hasn't yet burned to a cinder. The fact that all this is transient makes it more precious, not less. Maybe our remote descendants in a hundred billion years will find similar brief happiness under their black and unchanging sky.

If I could wish one thing for my lost brother it would be that I could be sure he felt this way, this alive, just for one day. Just for one minute. Because, in the end, that's all we've got.

INVISIBLE EMPIRE OF ASCENDING LIGHT

KEN SCHOLES

Tana Berrique set down her satchel and ran a hand over the window plate in her guest quarters. The opaque, curved wall became clear, revealing the tropical garden below. She'd spent most of the past six years living in guest quarters from planet to planet, inspecting the shrines, examining the Mission's work, encouraging the Mission's servants. But the room here at the Imperial Palace on Pyrus came closest to being her home.

She sighed and a voice cleared behind her.

"Missionary General Berrique?"

She didn't turn immediately. Instead, she watched a sky-herd of chantis move against the speckled green carpet of vines, trees and underbrush. "Yes, Captain Vesper?" The birdlike creatures dropped back into the trees and she turned.

She'd heard of this one. Young but hardened in the last Dissent, Alda Vesper climbed the ranks fast to find himself commanding the best of the best, Red Morning Company of the Emperor's Brigade. He stood before her in the doorway, one hand absently toying with the pommel of his short sword, his face pale. "I bring word, Missionary General."

"So soon?" She glanced back at the window, ran her hand over the plate to fog out the garden's light. "By the look on your face, I must assume that he's now Announced himself?"

The captain nodded. "He has. Just a few minutes ago."

Sadness washed through her. She'd known he would Announce; she'd just hoped otherwise. And now Consideration must be given. Afterwards, the path to Declaration could follow. And along that road lay death and destruction unless he truly did Ascend. She'd overseen four Considerations since taking office six years earlier. All had led to Declarations; all had ended in bloodfeuds. She'd discouraged all from Declaring, had seen the obvious outcomes clearly despite their blind faith and inflated hopes. None had listened. Millions dead from men who would be gods.

"Then I will Consider him," she told the captain. "We must move before the others consolidate and shift their allegiances. Ask the Vice-Regent to petition his father for a lightbender to take us. Tell him I specifically requested Red Morning Company to assist the Consideration."

He bowed his head, his smile slight but pleased, fingertips touching the gold emblazoned sun on the breast of his scarlet uniform. "Yes, Missionary General."

He spun and left, ceremonial cloak billowing behind him.

I've only just arrived, Tana Berrique thought as she picked up her satchel, and yet once more I depart. She brushed out the lights to her guest quarters and exited the room and its heaven-like view.

The lightbender vessel *Gold of Dawning* took three days to reach Casillus. One day on each side to clear the demarcation lines under sunsail, one day to power up and bend.

The Missionary General boarded the Captain's yacht with Vesper and a squad of brigadiers. She'd exchanged her white habit for the plain gray of the Pilgrim Seeker and let her hair down out of respect for Casillian custom. She and Captain Vesper took the forward passenger cabin just behind the cockpit and forward from his squad.

Gold of Dawning spit them out into space. The vessel's executive officer piloted them planet-side himself. There were no viewscreens in the passenger cabin but Tana knew vessels under many family flags took up their positions around the planet. They waited for her to do her part as she had done before, and they waited for the Declaration.

She thumbed the privacy field and turned to Vesper. "Where is he, then?"

"They've taken him to the local Imperial Shrine for safekeeping. Once he Announced, word spread fast."

They'd watched this one for some time. The Mission had seen the potential in his humble birth, in the calloused hands of his lowborn parents, in the scraps of data they'd fed into the matrix. By age seven, they'd known he would match in the high ninetieth percentile. Now at fifteen, he was easily the youngest to score so near the ideal and the second youngest to Announce before reaching his majority. She'd seen some of his paintings, some of his poems. She'd heard a snippet from a song a year earlier. Now, she reviewed his results and charted them on the divine matrix.

"At the moment, he's only a ninety-eight three," she said out loud.

"Only?" Vesper asked. "Has there been higher?"

She nodded. "When I was an Initiate years ago we saw a ninety-eight six."

His surprised look and indrawn breath made her smile. "A ninety-eight six? I've never heard this."

"There are many things you've not heard," Tana told him. "And you have not heard this either… from me." She raised her eyebrows in gentle warning.

Vesper nodded to show agreement. "What happened to him?"

"Her," she said. "This one was a girl."

He scowled. "A girl?"

"Yes. A young woman. Quite rare, I know, considering our understanding of the matrix. And in answer to your question: she died."

"No surprise there," he said. "The disappointed can be quite unforgiving. And the unforgiving can be quite brutal."

Tana nodded. "True. But this one never Declared. She Announced and then took her own life shortly after her Consideration."

She wasn't sure why she told him this. By the letter of the law, it was a breach in the Mystery. But by the spirit, Tana felt drawn to the young man. Or perhaps, she thought, it's been too long since I've trusted anyone outside the Mission.

Vesper seemed surprised. "Took her own life without Declaring? That seems odd." He chuckled. "Why?"

"I think," Tana Berrique said, "she saw something the rest of us couldn't see at the time." Now she hinted at heresy and treason and backed away from the words carefully, studying the sudden firmness of the captain's jaw, the tightness around his eyes.

He looked around, shifting uncomfortably in his seat. The question hung out there like forbidden fruit and she knew he would not ask it.

She patted his leg in the way she thought a mother might. "Pay no mind to me, young Captain. I'm tired and eager to be done with this work."

He relaxed. Eventually, she closed her eyes and meditated to clear her mind for Consideration. The yacht sped on. Somewhere in her silence, she fell into a light sleep and woke up as the atmosphere gently shook her.

* * *

He waited in a vaulted chamber in the lower levels of the Imperial Shrine. Captain Vesper's men took up their positions around the shrine, supplementing the Shrine Guard. A duo of Initiates accompanying the shrine's Pilgrim Seeker escorted the Missionary General through room after room.

"We are honored to have you," the Pilgrim Seeker said.

"I am honored to attend," Tana said, following the proper form. "Though I face the day with dread and longing."

The Pilgrim Seeker nodded, her eyes red from crying. "Perhaps he will Ascend."

"Perhaps he will not," Tana Berrique said. "Either way, today will be marked by loss. For one to Ascend, another must Descend."

"In our hope, we grieve." The Pilgrim Seeker quoted from an obscure parameter of the matrix. "And we are here."

They stood in a small anteroom, watching the boy in the chamber through a one-way viewscreen. He sat quietly in a chair. A plain-clad couple stood near the door. The man had his arm around the woman. They looked hopeful and mournful at the same time.

"His parents," the Pilgrim Seeker said.

The Missionary General felt anger well up inside her. "He's very young," she told them. "Who encouraged him to Announce?"

"He did it himself, Mum," the father said.

"And how did he know?"

The mother spoke up. "We didn't even know ourselves. I swear it."

Tana frowned. "Very well. I will give him Consideration." She lowered her voice so that only the parents could hear. "I hope you know what price this all may come to."

The mother collapsed, sobbing against her husband. He patted her shoulder, pressing her to his chest. When his eyes locked with Tana Berrique's she saw fire in them. "We didn't know. Have done with it and let us be." Now tears extinguished their ferocity. "If we had known, don't you think we'd have fled with him years ago?"

The despair in his words stopped her. She felt their grief wash over her, capsizing her anger. She forced a gentle smile, too late. "Perhaps your son will Ascend."

"Perhaps," the father said.

She drew a palm-sized matrix counter from her pocket and thumbed it on. She felt it vibrating into her hand, ready to calculate his responses and add them into the equation as she gave Consideration. Tana Berrique nodded to the Pilgrim Seeker, who opened the door into the chamber. She walked into the room and stood above him. He sat, eyes closed, breathing lightly.

One of the Initiates brought a chair and set it before the boy, then left. She sat, placed the matrix counter on the floor between them, and waited for the door to whisper closed. When it did, she smiled.

"What is your name?" she asked.

The boy opened his eyes and looked up at her. "I would like a privacy field, please."

She flinched in surprise. The counter chirped softly, flashing green. Ninety-eight four, now. "A privacy field? It's not done that way."

His eyes narrowed. "It's done any way you say it is, Missionary General Tana Berrique. This is your Consideration."

Surprise became fear. The green light flashed him a solid ninety-eight six now as his words registered against the equation. She waved to the hidden viewscreen and a privacy field hummed to life around them. "You know a great deal for someone so young."

The boy laughed. It sounded like music and it washed her fear. He leaned forward. "Perhaps I'm not so very young," he said.

"That's what I'm here to Consider," she told him. "May I follow the form?"

He nodded.

"What is your name?"

"I am called H'ru in this incarnation."

She raised her eyebrows. "This incarnation?" she repeated.

"Yes."

She watched the counter. He was nearing ninety-nine. "And your other names?" she asked.

He shrugged. "Are they important?"

"They may be, H'ru. I don't know."

He shook his head. "They are not."

Tana changed the subject. "What led you to Announce?"

His young brow furrowed. "I was told to."

"By your parents?"

He chuckled, the brief laugh ending in a secret smile.

"By one of the Families?"

The smile faded. "By myself," he said.

She shook her head, not sure she heard correctly. The counter did not chirp or hum, no light flickered from it. "Could you say that again?"

"I told myself to Announce," he said.

She felt her stomach lurch. "That's not possible."

"Ask me. Return to Pyrus, wake me, and ask me yourself." His smile returned. "After you are finished with the Consideration, of course."

"The Regent would never allow it. And even if he did—" She suddenly realized she had lost focus, lost composure, spoken aloud. The counter still did nothing. She scooped down, picked it up to see if it still hummed. It did.

"I've stopped it," he said.

"How?" she asked.

"I willed it to stop and it stopped."

"What else can you will?" she asked.

He shook his head. "We'll not talk around circles, Tana Berrique. You do not need a counter to know who I am."

She let the air rush out of her. He was right. She didn't need it to know. The four before had been betrayed by either humility without strength or arrogance without power. Their equations had tested the matrix, to be sure, but they could not Ascend. After Declaring, the house-factions and bloodfeuds had undone them and they'd died on the run from followers turned vengeful from disappointment and fear. But this one was different and it shook her.

"You've not met me before," he said. "The others were near but false. Except for one."

She nodded. She blinked back tears, fought the growing knot in her throat.

"You're wondering why I took my life before," he asked. "It's what you told the Captain on your flight in. I saw something the rest of you could not see at the time. But you see it now, don't you?"

She nodded again and swallowed.

"Your god, your Emperor of Ascending Light, has lain near death for too long while the Regent and his kin hold power in wait for another god to rise. But they intend no new Ascendant be found. They use this trick of Announcement, Consideration and Declaration to extend both hope and fear. But in the end, no one Ascends. The Dissents tear out the heart of the Empire and only strengthen the aspect of a few."

Her hands shook. Her bladder threatened release. She shifted on the chair, then pitched forward onto her knees. "What is your will, Lord Emperor?"

He touched her hair and she looked up. He smiled down, his face limned in the room's dim light. "Take your seat, Tana Berrique."

Mindful to obey, she returned to her chair. "My Lord?"

"H'ru," he said with a gentle voice. "Just H'ru."

Tana felt confusion and conflict brewing behind her eyes. "But surely when you Declare, you shall Ascend unhindered? How could they prevent you?"

"They will not prevent me," he said. "*You* will." He paused, letting the words sink in to her. "And I shall neither Ascend nor Declare."

"But my role is Consideration. I take no part in—"

"I will tell you to," he said. "And because I am your Emperor, you will obey."

"I do not understand," she said.

"You will." He patted her hand. "When the Regent calls you out, say to him *S'andril bids you to recall your oath in the Yellowing Field.* He will admit you to me. And I will tell you what to do."

She sat there before him for a few minutes, letting the privacy field absorb the sound of her sobs as he held her hands in his and whispered comfort to her.

At long last, she stood, straightened her habit, and waved for the privacy field to be turned off. The counter stopped at ninety-nine three. She looked down at the boy. "This Consideration is closed," she said. "You may do what you will."

The boy nodded. "I understand."

Without a glance, without meeting the eyes of the Pilgrim Seeker or the parents, she strode from the chamber, passed through the anteroom and said nothing at all to anyone else.

Back at Pyrus, she spent her time gazing down on the garden while she waited for the Regent to call her out. No Declaration had swept up from Casillus and the pockets of ships, loaded with troops, continued to deploy strategically around that world and others while everyone waited.

Captain Vesper finally came for her. She had not spoken to him since before the Consideration but she knew that he could see her unrest. He fell back into his official role though she saw his brow furrowing and his mouth twitching as unasked questions played out beneath his skin.

She followed as he led her into the throne room.

The Regent sat on a smaller throne to the left of the central dais and its massive, empty crystalline throne. To the right, his son, the Vice-Regent, sat. He waved the Imperial Brigade members away.

After they had gone, he motioned the Missionary General forward.

"Well?" he finally asked. "There has been no Declaration from Casillus. Then I learn that you made no report on this Consideration." He scowled, his heavy beard, woven with gems and strands of gold, dragging against his chest. "What do you say for yourself?"

"I say nothing for myself, Regent." She intentionally left off the word *Lord*.

"I find that highly unusual, Missionary General."

She shrugged. "I'm sorry you find it so."

"Can you speak about this child H'ru and his Announcement?"

"I can. He Announced and I Considered."

"And?"

Tana Berrique paused, not sure how to pick her way through this minefield. Lord help me, she thought, and I will simply be direct. She met the Regent's eyes. "What do you want me to say?"

"What I want," the Regent said in a cold voice, "is to know when the Family warships and armies will either stand down or take action. Something that will not happen until this boy makes up his mind. We do not need another Dissent. We do not need another false god Declaring and moving our worlds into civil war."

She continued to stare at him. "I find it interesting, Regent, that you did not at any point mention wanting a new god to Ascend and bring all this uncertainty to a close."

His face went red and he growled deep in his chest. "If you were not the Missionary General," he said in a low voice, his hands white-knuckling the sides of his chair, "I would have you killed for those words."

She smiled. "So you do want the new god to Ascend, for our Emperor of Ascending Light to sleep at long last, knowing his people are safe for a season?"

"Of course I do," he said. "We all do."

Now she took her moment. "Very well," she said. "*S'andril bids you to recall your oath in the Yellowing Field.*"

His eyes popped, his face went white and his mouth dropped open. "What did you say?"

"You heard me quite well. And I assume that you know what it means."

Shaking, he stood up. "It can't be."

"It is."

His son looked pale, too, but clearly didn't understand what was happening. Tana Berrique wasn't sure herself, but she felt the power from her words and their hard impact.

"He told me this day would come. He told me those words would come." The large old man started to cry.

"Father?" The son stood as well. "What does this mean?"

"An old promise, son. Go gather your things."

Tana watched the son's face go red. "My things? What are you saying?"

"Our work is done," the Regent said. "We're going home now."

"But this *is* my home. You said so. You said—"

In a bound, the old man stood over his son, hand raised to slap him down. The son buckled and cowered on the floor as his father's voice roared out: "What I said doesn't matter. We leave now and hope for mercy later."

"I'll let myself in," Tana Berrique told him.

Behind the throne room, in his private bedchamber, the Emperor of Ascending Light lay beneath a stasis field, attended by scuttling jeweled spiders that preserved his life. Tana Berrique stood at the foot of the massive circular bed, her body trembling at the sight of him.

He'd been a big man once, muscled and broad-shouldered, but the years had withered him to kindling. His white hair ran down the sides of his head like streams of milk spilled onto a silk pillow. His hands were folded around his scepter. She stepped forward and dropped to her knees beside his bed, thumbing off the stasis field to awaken him from long sleep. The spiders clattered and scrambled, unsure of what to do with this un-programmed event. The paper-thin eyelids fluttered open and a light breath rattled out.

Tana Berrique bowed her head. "You summoned me, Lord."

"Yes." His voice rasped, paper rustling wood. "Are my people well?"

"They are not, Lord. They need you."

The tight mouth pulled, thin wisps of beard moving with the effort. "Not as such."

And she knew what was coming now. The reality of it settled in as she recalled the boy's words. They will not prevent me, he had said, *you* will. "What would you bid me, Lord?"

"Kill me," the Emperor of Ascending Light whispered. One hand released the scepter and thin, dry, brittle fingers sought her hand. "Let it all change." He coughed and a spider moved to wipe his mouth. "It is time for change."

"I don't think I can." She felt the tears again, hot and shameful, pushing at her eyes and spilling out. She wanted to drop his hand but could not. "I don't think I can. I can't."

He shushed her. "You can. Because I am your Emperor." His lips twitched into a gentle smile. "You will obey."

Tana Berrique stood and bent over her god. She felt the sweat from her sides trickle forward tracing the line of her breasts as she leaned. She felt the tears tracing similar paths down her cheeks. She shuddered, bent further, and kissed the dry, rattling lips. She placed her hands gently on the thin neck and squeezed, the soft hair of his beard tickling her wrists. The eyelids fluttered closed. She kept squeezing until her shoulders shook. She kept squeezing while the spiders panicked and climbed over one another to somehow complete their program and preserve a life. She kept squeezing until she knew that he had gone. Her hands were still on the throat when heavy boots pounded the hallway.

"Missionary General!" Captain Vesper's voice shouted from outside, "Is the Emperor okay? The Regent's retinue is packing for a rapid withdrawal and no one is telling me any—" She heard him clatter into the room. "What are you doing?" he screamed.

She turned quickly to face him. Panting, eyes wild, face drawn in agony, the young officer pulled his sword. "What are you doing?" he asked again, pointing its tip at her as he took a step forward.

"I'm doing what I'm told," she said. "And by the Ascending Light you'll do the same or watch all our Lord worked for crumble and decay."

He paused, uncertainty washing his face.

"You already know, Alda." She gestured to the bed. "He wanted more than this for his people."

The sword tip wavered. "I thought we were working for more," he spat.

"We are. He was." She waited. "I'm doing what he said."

"What proof have you?"

She shook her head. "None but his words to me and me alone. And something about the Yellowing Field. I don't know what—it meant something to the Regent, though."

Alda went paler. The sword dropped. "The Yellowing Field? Are you sure?"

"You know of it?"

His shoulders slumped. "I do. It's a Brigade story from the forging of the Empire."

"I've never heard this," she said.

He walked forward, looking down at the Emperor. "There are many things you've not heard," he told her. "When S'andril was young he saved a boy who swore he would repay him. 'I have saved your life today,' the Emperor told this boy, 'and one day I will bid you repay me by not saving mine.'" He looked up at her. "I am at your service."

She sat on the edge of the bed. "We're not finished yet," she told him. "There's more."

He nodded. "The boy?"

He understands, she thought. He truly understands. Her words came slowly. "It will be bloody. Many will die. But after this, we can rebuild. There will be no further Dissents. The Families will burn out their rage and then we can have peace." Because, she hoped, if the god is truly dead then the idea of that god can live on without harm.

His voice was firm. "His family, too?"

"No. Spare them but keep it quiet. Just him. He won't struggle. It's what he wants."

"And after?" Alda Vesper stood.

She played the words to herself, then said them carefully. "After, I will Declare the boy myself and give witness to his Ascent." An eternal emperor, she thought, on the throne of each heart. An invisible empire of Ascending Light.

"God help us," Vesper said. He spun on his heel and left.

She sat there for a while and wondered what her life had suddenly become. And she wondered what would come after the lie her god bid her tell?

She would return to her guest quarters. She would clear the window and sit in front of it and stare down into the garden, wondering what it would be like to breathe the hot air of Pyrus, swim the boiling rivers of its jungles, pluck the razor flowers by the water's edge. She would address the Council of Seekers and dismantle the Mission. She would write it all down, this new gospel, for the generations to come after and go into hiding from the wrath of the disappointed and unforgiving.

Finally, she stood to leave.

Vesper's words registered with her. God help us, he'd said.

She looked down at the Emperor of Ascending Light one final time. "He already has," she whispered.

MICHAEL LAURITS IS: DROWNING

PAUL CORNELL

Michael Laurits is: Drowning.
Please Help!

That was the Lief status update Cal Tech Professor Laurits' 311 friends were startled to see around ten thirty EST one Saturday night last October.

The genial, soft-spoken Laurits, who looked more like a country rock star than the Nobel laureate he was, was a polymath with friends in fields ranging from social engineering to Federal military intelligence. Maybe a third of the 311 of those he kept in touch with via Lief knew vaguely where he was at that moment: on a trimaran in Japan's Inland Sea, attaching biological shepherding systems to whale sharks, part of a vacation project to manage and systemise the Sea's ecology under the auspices of Nagoya Penguin Torii.

None of them knew that at that very second, Michael Laurits, his feet caught in a weighted line, his craft a fiery husk, was already thirty feet underwater, dropping like a stone, with no chance of regaining the surface.

Laurits had joked that he spent far too much time in Lief. "He'd get applications ideas and work them up right in front of us. People doing other things in the same touchspace would start yelling at him to stop waving his hands around," says Ryoumi Nofke, one of Laurits' closest friends on the faculty. Nofke, voluntarily autistic in pursuit of her own thesis on Sub Planck Metaphysics, and with three suspended marriages backed up as a result, perks up only at the mention of Laurits' current situation. "Oh yeah, he's Aut now. People say they're not sure. That he's exactly the same as he was. They're wrong."

Fortunately for Laurits, Nofke's words, like those of any voluntary Aut, are inadmissible in a court of law. Exactly *how* wrong the people who think that Laurits is still Laurits are, is currently the subject of legal action.

Laurits was inside the cabin of his vessel, the *Torii Gate*, when he heard "a thumping sound" from overhead. He reached the deck at the same moment that a rocket-propelled grenade, fired from a nearby launch, landed on it. Laurits puts his (possible) survival down to the fact that the grenade *bounced*, right past him, through the open cabin door.

The explosion sent Laurits flying into the ocean. He landed amongst his equipment, became tangled in the lines, and fell into the depths.

The attacking vessel was a patrol boat associated with the Atheist organisation Ground State Sanity. The Sanists are regarded as terrorists by the Japanese prefectural authorities, and are engaged in what, subject to a UN vote, is likely to be defined as a Minor War with rival Atheist organisation Obvious Caution Sanity. The difference of opinion between the two factions concerns whether or not the undisputed appearance of a divine being would be reason enough to rethink their Post-theist principles. Ground State say yes. Obvious Caution's point of view, as outlined in their manifesto, is more complex, but boils down to the question being immaterial.

The *Torii Gate* had ventured into what the Ground State Sanists had decreed were their current personal territorial waters. The Shinto designs on its stern may have been seen as provocation.

I was able to talk, within Lief, ironically enough, to an unidentified but code genuine individual from Ground State. "It's always sad when an individual is 'killed,'" she said (inverted commas subject's own), "but it's important to say he's not Damned. He'll be back after the Singularity and doubtless form part of the Academy."

"It's interesting," says Laurits' wife, Amy, the shaking of her hand on her teacup showing exactly where she's put her mental resources in the last six months, "that they don't even seem to note the possibility that the afterlife they claim to be seeking is already here."

Laurits can be thankful that the extreme opinions of my Ground State contact are also unlikely to convince a jury.

Of the many ironies in this case, the greatest is surely that Laurits' own researches in the field of chaos management mean he might have been expected to see this coming. His memes have been successfully applied in weather forecasting, city planning, and mobile war prevention within the Federal Government. "The world," he once said, in the introduction to a book by fellow Nobel Laureate Dally Ah Pascoe, "is *fixable*. Chaotic systems can be predicted over large scales, exactly as one predicts the large-scale results of extra-physical activity under the Planck length observation limit. In Hampshire hurricanes hardly ever happen. Like consciousness hardly ever happens outside of a vast memory storage system. But, though we still can't begin to imagine how, when you've got enough memory, consciousness can and does happen."

Those words, to coin a phrase, may come back to haunt Laurits.

As he dropped into the darkness, Laurits, involuntarily, he insists, started shifting his sight, hearing and skin senses into Lief, as anyone would when playing a game or collaborating on a project. "It felt like a reflex, like ducking under cover," he says, "the most natural thing in the world. In reality, I was trying to breathe water, I was facing certain death. In Lief, I didn't have to be aware of that. That was all I had in my head."

"He was always a fatalist," says Amy Laurits. "He was never happy being happy. He always expected that he'd have to pay a price, that something terrible would happen."

Within seconds, a number of his friends had joined Laurits in Lief, and were asking if his status update was literally true. Several of them, all of whom now decline to be named, started yelling that, as per Lief law, if Laurits was in physical jeopardy, he should immediately leave Lief and become conscious.

"They were, in effect, telling me to follow the rules and die," says Laurits.

But one of that crowd had a more constructive plan in mind. He took onboard Laurits' garbled package of fastword and understood that he had seconds to act. He took a connector block from the vast memory array at the University of Burma in York and attached it directly to Laurits' Lief page.

If Laurits' life has been saved, it's because he was fortunate enough to befriend one of the few people with the access and imagination to take that action: David Savident of Carbon Futures.

Savident, a neat, conservatively dressed man with the salty turn of phrase of a self-made entrepreneur, had made his fortune through carbon-balancing bacteria, then sold on that business and invested heavily in one of the assets his former area of expertise had also caused to bloom: the vast memory tanks that are required to metacalculate chaotic systems.

"Mike was dying," he says, "and there were all these tossers standing around waving their neon arms and talking about ethics. I thought bugger that, we've all wondered about this, this is the only chance we're ever going to get for an *ethical* experiment, let's do it. And save my mate in the process."

Savident told Laurits to transfer all his sensory processes into the vast array. He was contacting hundreds of his own engineers and pulling them a bigger and bigger workspace around Laurits, elbowing out concerned friends in a way which others there that day remember as being rude, "predatory" as one said, but which Savident insists was all about rushing to help his friend.

Within a minute, Savident had himself created vast capacity connections which allowed whole transport of processes from the parietal and temporal lobes of Laurits' brain. His aim was to try and move everything that could be defined and isolated: memory; sensory systems; a series of discrete brain state snapshots.

But instead, before Savident could start the terrible task of picking what could be saved from the archive of his friend's mind, desperately hoping to reconstruct something resembling a person from the pieces, if we're to believe Laurits and his many advocates—

The entirety of Michael Laurits made the journey all at once.

"I don't *know* how I did it," says Laurits. "Lief is hooked into your kinesthetic sense, your central idea of where your body is, that's how it works. It was as simple as moving my hand. I desperately wanted to be in some other place than my body, and then I was suddenly aware that there *was* such a place, that the... tunnel... was big enough to go down." (Laurits equates this moment with Savident providing a big enough connection and big enough memory space at the other end.) "So I went."

The mystery of that process will surely be a central argument in the forthcoming court action brought by Sona, the owners of Lief.

"We were initially pleased that Lief had been made use of so positively in what looked like a humanitarian act and a scientific breakthrough," says Kay Lorton, a legal spokesperson for the company. "But the more our people looked into it, the more we began to suspect that Mr. Savident hadn't *transferred* Mr. Laurits' mental state into the memory array, but had simply created a copy. A barely functioning copy, that is, without many of those attributes which we would regard as indicative of self-awareness. Exactly the same as the ghosts that pop up in memory tanks from time to time, and then generally cease to be detectable, or, as some would have it, move into other universes. As Mr. Laurits himself noted in his work, intelligence arises out of sheer memory. The only difference is that this intelligence wishes to interact with the world, because it mistakenly believes itself to be Mr. Laurits."

The reason these matters of philosophy have ended up before a court of law is that Sona are seeking to recover damages from the stress the connection to the memory tank is putting on Lief. They claim that work activity has slowed 32 percent. Any regular user will tell you that the difference is palpable.

Furthermore, they claim that Savident's action was tantamount to industrial espionage, since he's a major shareholder in rival workspace company Transgress. They seek a legal ruling concerning their stated desire: to erase the Lief page that now represents Michael Laurits, through which he senses and communicates.

"That," says Amy Laurits, "would be murder."

Savident is contesting the legal action, stating that every action he took was allowed under Lief law. Sona had accepted connections to vast memory arrays in the past, without slowing their systems.

"The difference is," says Laurits, "that I'm in here now. Whatever a person is, here I am. I take up some processing space. Sorry."

Savident has employed teams of engineers from Odashu and Google to develop a new interface, hoping to transfer Laurits' complete mental processes, if that's what they are, from Lief to the new workspace. But since nobody knows exactly what happened in the moments when Laurits willed himself into his familiar escape from reality, replicating the event is proving a difficult task.

Laurits himself is helping with the research. "It's a problem in manipulating chaotic systems," he said. "We have to try and move the package of who I am without understanding or being able to measure or predict what's *inside* the package."

* * *

In a high-profile step to popularise their point of view, Sona has hired time on the cameras mounted on the underside of Federal global warming control mirrors in an effort to find Laurits' body. They seek to prove that Laurits' claim that he still sometimes has hazy sensory input from the cadaver, particularly while asleep, that he is, in effect, one person who can move between two bodies, is nonsense.

The corpse, subject to predation and tidal drift, should lie on the seabed some sixty metres beneath the site of the attack. But so far it hasn't been found.

Laurits' family and friends are convinced that the person they meet several times a day in Lief is Michael. Though a few of them share Nofke's impression that he's been changed somewhat by the transition. But how much of a change would be needed to convince a jury that what Amy Laurits speaks to, holds in her arms, has even, as she deliberately and precisely tells me, made love to, isn't a man, but a copy of one?

Certainly, talking to Laurits *feels* like talking to a person. He passes the Turing Test. But then, so have many programmes and devices in the last twenty years, including Lief's own personified help systems.

"I *continue*," he says, showing me some of the art he makes when nobody's visiting, which can't be often, considering the pilgrimages made to him by everyone from the Dalai Lama to the King of Brazil. "I'm the sum of my surroundings, and something else that's still quite mysterious, just like I've always been. I always expected that something terrible would happen, a revenge for all my prosperity and silliness and presumptuousness. And then it did. But then I discovered that even so, it was all going to be okay."

NIGHT OF THE FIRSTLINGS

MARGO LANAGAN

Hickory came down with it, same as all the big boys. One minute he was sitting at prayers around the table, the next he hardly looked like himself, he was blotched so red and in between so white.

"Augh." He sounded as if he had no teeth. "It's like something thumped me."

Dawn beside me was suddenly a little stone boy. I took his hand and we sat and could not blink, while the fuss was made of Hickory and for once we didn't mind, so long as they got that livid-patched face out of our sight soon, those swollen-up lips. The blokes are always full of bravado; you cannot tell from them. But Mum with her sharp commands and then her tight silences told us well enough: we ought be very frightened. And we were.

We sat there in the silence of the broken-off prayer. The prophet's children were there too, though his oldest, Nehemi, was home with the same horror.

"Yer," they said. "It was just like that for ours, too."

"'T in't any less awful the second time," whispered Arfur. "They looks like monsters."

Then the prophet himself was back down among us, and he saw their faces and he went to their bench, gathered up little Carris and allowed the others to cling to him. He laughed across at Dawn and me. "Don't worry," he said. "We have the protection. This is what we done all that for."

It didn't help, knowing how serious it had been while we hurried about that day with our secret and our buckets of blood. *If anyone asks you,* Dad had said, *Tell them it is a Dukka festival, nothing more.*

What kinda festival requires good blood slopped about everywhere? I'd said.

It's lamb's, Dad said patiently. *So a spring festival. But only some springs, tell them, because none of them will have seen it before.*

I hoped some of the messier signs we had painted would still work. I remembered adding a few dabs to one of Dawn's efforts while he ran off down the lane calling back the Ludoes were down there, with their only one boy—but still that made him the eldest, didn't it?—and unable to afford a lamb of their own.

Everyone but Mum and Dad came back down, some of them quite scared looking and sweaty. "It is just like with my lad," I heard one say in the stair. "Oh, what a night!"

"Come, people," said the prophet in his prophet-voice. "Let us pray thanks that we have the Lord's protection, this fearful night." And they all slid and clambered to around the tables again, and bent their heads.

While he intoned something special and beautiful, nearly singing those words and quite loudly, I bent my head, too, and Dawn leaned against me and I took his hand into my lap. But my attention, which should have been upon God, was wandering up the stair and dabbing about there like the tip of an elephant-trunk, sensitive to the least movement. It was unusual that Dad had not come down to play the host while Mum took care of sick Hickory. It was too too strange that Dawn and I were the only people of our house besides Gramp by the door, while the gathering swayed and responded and clutched its fingers and its brows. I prayed too, because now I could see there was something to pray for and it wasn't thanks, it was please-please-please. Don't let Hickory's face explode. Please unflop him and roll his eyes back down so as we can see the colour in them again. I could not *think* how Mum and Dad would be if Hickory died; too much was possible, too much awfulness.

Once the prayer was sung to a close, the prophet said, "Very well, all youse go to your homes. And those with sons take the peace and strength of Our Lord with you."

And very doubtful and frightened—but not muttering anything because hadn't the prophet seen us correctly through that other stuff, the rust and phylloxera, and the nekkid-lizards all over the place?—everybody shuffled out. Last of all went the prophet himself, who put his thumb to our brows and *winked* at us, and said, "Don't you fear now, through this long night nor no other. For he is with us, God Our God."

"Very well, sir," I said, my mouth obedient though my head boiled with horrors.

Once they'd gone, Dawn looked to me for some answers, but I had none. "I am afraid anyway, whatever he says," I said. "I've never seen anyone so crook as Hickory tonight."

He climbed right into my lap then, though it was a hot night, and put his sticky arms around my neck and his sweaty head against my chest. "What is coming?" he said. "Something is coming. I won't be able to sleep."

"Ushshsh," I said and held onto him and rocked him as I used to when he was littler. "Don't you worry. Your face is the right colour and so is mine."

"For now," he said buzzily into my breastbone. "For *now*."

"Well, now is all we've got and can know about." I hoped I sounded as wise as Mum did when she said it. I knew it was all a matter of the right tone, and the right rhythm of the rocking. Did Mum ever feel so lost, though, as she spoke and held us? Was the world ever so big and dangerous around her?

"Has they all gone!" Dad stumbled out of the stair at the sight. "Where is everyone? They went without their teas!"

"The prophet sent them home," said Dawn quickly in case Dad felt like dealing out trouble in his worriment.

"Oh." He sat to a bench end and looked about at the nothingness. "I was rather hoping they would stay and console me."

"Got their own lads to un-fever," creaked Gramp from the charpoy, "and their own wifes and children to keep calm. How is the lad?"

"He looks dreadful," said Dad. "I have never seen such a thing, to uglify a boy so."

Gramp wheezed—you cannot tell whether he is coughing or laughing most times. Laughing, it was, now, because then he said, "When I think the prettiness of the Gypsy prince, all hottened and spoiling."

"I wouldn't wish it on him," said Dad. "On that bastard king himself I would not wish this, watching his boy melt away on his bed. Why can we not just stay as we have done, and work as we have done, and all stay healthy and uncrawled by vermin?"

"What are you saying, son?" says Gramp. "You know well why."

"Oh, I know. Only—" And he sat a moment with his head in his hands like a man praying. "I am tired of the dramas, you know? I never thought I would hear myself say such a thing. But I have children now. All I want is settlement and steadiness in which to watch them grow."

"Which is the whole aim," Gramp said like a stick whacking him, a heavy stick. He was drawn up in such a way, I wondered what was holding him up—just his cloths there?

"I know, Gramp. I know." Dad waved Gramp back down, with his big hands. "I will make us teas," he said. And he closed his mouth and stood.

"Yes, you do that," said Gramp warningly. Dawn looked at him and he glowered back.

Sickness throws out the air of a house; you cannot do what you would usually do. Plus, the prophet had told us to stay in off the streets after sunset, when usually we would be haring about, Dukka and Gypsy together, funneling and screeching up stair and down lane until we got thrown or yelled at, and then in someone's yard, playing Clinks or learning Gypsy letters. *But you cannot be told one from the other like that,* he had said to us. *You must stay to your own houses, you children, with the sign upon the door.*

Mum came down after a while. "I must make our dinner," she said, and she sent Dad up to do the soothing and sponging of Hickory. Which I was grateful for; I had thought she would send me. But he must be seriouser than that. Oh, I didn't want to see him—and at the same time I wanted it very much, to see how much like a monster he was growing. I was very uncomfortable within myself about it all. When I remembered to, I prayed, stirring the foment there for Mum over the fire. But face the truth of it, praying is terribly dull, and who would be Our Lord, sitting up there with the whole world at you, praising and nagging and please-please-please? He must be bored out of his mind as well with it. Some days he must prefer to just go off and count grains of sand. Or birds of the air. Like he does. Like the prophet says he does, who gets to talk direct to him.

We ate and it was almost like normal, but after that, the light was gone entirely from outside and the usual noises—music trailing down the hill from the Gypsy houses and their laughter from their rooftop parties, and tinkling of glasses and jugs and crashing of plates sometimes—there was none of that.

Every now and again someone would tap-tap on our door and whisper to Dad, someone very wrapped—women mostly I think, who were less likely to be stopped and asked their business flittering about so in the evening. Dad would close the door and say, "Baron Hull's boy has it, and all in that region." Meaning, by *all*, only the biggest boy each family, we came to know. It was an affliction of the heirs and most precious—very cruel of God, I thought. Dad would go up and tell Mum, and come down again before long, and be restless with us.

Gramp lay abed but did not sleep; there was always the surprisingly alive glitter of his eyes in the middle of his wrappings and covers. No matter how hot the weather, he always was wrapped up warm. *It is because he does not shift his lazy backside,* Mum said, *so his blood sits chilling and spoiling inside him.*

And I've a right, he would say. *I've run around enough in my life at barons' becks and calls.*

"Come, Dawn, lie down by me," he said when Dawn drooped at the table. No one wanted to send the boy to bed, or to go themselves. No one wanted to leave the others. Something *was* coming, and no one wanted to be alone when it came.

Dawn went and curled up in the Gramp-cloths, and before long slept, and the three of us stayed there, listening to his breaths, which normally would send *me* to sleep quick smartly, but tonight only wound my awakeness, tighter, until my eyes took over my face, my ears took over my head, all my thoughts emptied out in expectation of the thing that was on its way. All I had left inside me was Dawn's breath, softly in, softly out, trusting us to look after him while he slept.

I was leaning almost relaxed, making letters in a mist of spilled flour on the table. *Kowt...beerlt...hamidh.* One day I might have enough to make words, to read Gypsy signage, to get a job writing for them. Opposite me Dad knotted his hands together on the table, watching my clever finger in the flour.

Everything shook a little, that was the first thing.

"Oh, God." Dad looked at the ceiling. "Please do not harm my family, please—" But I ran around and put my hand to his mouth. I climbed up into his lap as Dawn had climbed into mine, because it is comforting to have a child to look after, and even when he dropped his prayer-gabble to a whispering I stopped him with my fingertips.

"Shush, Dad," I said. "Just listen."

Which he did.

How can we sleep, other nights, with that enormous darkness all about, going on and on all the way to the million stars, with all that room in it for winds and clouds, dangers and visitations?

A noise began, so distant at first I wasn't sure of it, but then Dad and Gramp turned their heads different ways, same as me, so I knew it must be: a slow beating, that sucked and pushed the air at our ears.

Dad held me tighter as it grew, and Gramp curled smaller around Dawn on the charpoy, and his eyes glittered wider. The beating grew outside, and my own pulse thudded like horse-galloping in my chest, and then Dad's heart *thumpa-thumped* in the back of my head, until I was quite confused which sound was the most frightening. The three of them together, maybe—the two frightened and the one almighty, not caring about either of us, about any of us, four beasts of the town happening to have life-times when this thing decided to pass.

Then an air came, gusts and punches of it, with stench upon it and with something else, with a power. It sent through my mind a string of such visions that next time I glimpsed the real world I was under the table, and Dad was clutched hard beside me crying out, and Gramp up there on the charpoy, a lump hardly bigger than Dawn himself, shook over my little brother, his forehead buried in Dawn's sleeping shoulder.

The air of the room was clear, though it ought to've been black, or green and red, beslimed, chockablock with limbs and bits, a-streak with organs and tubing and drippings and sludges. Fouled fleshes and suppurating, torn bodies and assaulted, faces dead or near-dead, stretching in pain, greased with fever or a-shine with blood—the smell, the gusts of it, blossomed these pictures before me. Bury my face in Dad's chest as close as I could, still the air got in, and like a billowing smoke the scenes built one another and streamed and slid and backed up, and gaped and struggled at me.

Next Mum was there with us, Hickory across her lap, sodden, burning at the centre of us. Then Gramp too, and we were a solid block under the table, all wound around Hickory, keeping the thing off him, keeping the air off, which *whap-whapped* through the room, which beat outside in the streets, over the town, shaking the night, shaking the world. Our house would fall down on us! We were all as good as dead! Thank God, I thought, at least we are all together. And I kissed Hickory's hair which was like wet shoelaces tangled over his head, and I sucked some of the salty sweat out from the strands. He was *so hot;* he was throbbing heat out into us as if he were made of live coals. Gramp was whimpering in *my* shoulder now, and Dawn's head lay sleeping on my hip. I grabbed for Mum's hand and she held mine so tight in her slippery one, it was hard to tell who was in danger of breaking whose bones. The noise blotted out every other noise, louder than the wildest wind, and composed, in its beatings, of beating voices, crowds shrieking terrified or angry or in horrible pain I could not tell, and the groans of people trampled under the crowds' feet, and the screams of mourners and the wails of the bereaved, all the bereaved there have ever been, all there will ever be, torrents of them, blast after blast.

* * *

vision

I woke still locked among their bodies, my dead family's bodies, still under the table. Outside people ran and screamed still, but they were only tonight's people, only this town's. And they were only—I lay and listened—they were only Gypsies. The only Dukka I heard were calming Gypsies, or hurrying past muttering to each other.

The room still stood around us; it was not crumbled and destroyed or bearing down on the table top. The air—I hadn't breathed for a while and now I gasped a bit—the air was only air, carrying no death-thoughts, producing no visions.

Dawn sighed on my hip. His ear was folded under his head; I lifted him and smoothed it out, and laid him down again. None of them were dead; what I had thought were the remnants of the beating wind were all their different breaths, countering and crossing one another. Hickory, even. He lay, his normal colour so far as I could tell, in the lamplight-shadow of Mum and Dad, who were bent forward together as if concentrating very closely on Hickory's sweat-slicked belly, that rose and fell with his even breathing.

It was still hot under there, and so uncomfortable. My right leg, pressed against the floor-stones that way, was likely to snap off at the hip, any moment. But it was safe—we were all safe. And it didn't sound safe outside, and I didn't want to *know* what awful things had happened, to make people make those noises. So I put my head down again, half on Hickory's wet-shoelaced skull and half on Gramp's rib-slatted chest, and I closed my eyes and went away again, there in my place in the tangle and discomfort of my family.

"I *hate* this place," moaned Dawn, stumbling at Mum's side.

"I know, my darling. Not for long, though. Not for long."

Strange breezes bothered us, hurrying along the channel, dipping from above. The sea had become like a forest either side, with upward streaks like trunks and froth at the top, dancing like wind-tossed leaves. *Shapes* moved in it; these were what terrified Dawn. They terrified all of us, and we hurried; we ran when we could, but it's hard to run with all your belongings bundled on your head, or dragged in a sack behind you, all the gold and silver you've talked out of the Gypsies.

Did you know there are chasms in the sea? Did you know there are mountains and deserts, just as on land? God had granted us a dry path across, but he had not flattened it out for us, had he? The worst had been where we were forced to make a bridge of cloths and clothing, over that bottomless cleft where things churned on ledges and fell away into the darkness, where those clamlike creatures had progressed across the walls, wobbling and clacking.

Dawn tore his hand from Mum's and stopped dead. "I hate this place and I hate the prophet and I *hate* it that we left Gramp behind!"

"You need a beating," said another mum, hurrying past, a child under each arm.

"Move it along, son; don't get in the people's way." A gran swiped at Dawn with her stick.

"Stand to the *side* at least," gasped a bloke bent under a bulging sack.

I ran back and scooped Dawn up. He fought me, but I held on. "We didn't leave Gramp," I said. "He told us to go, remember? I hate it too, but look—would he have kept ahead of *that*?" I pointed Dawn's screwed-up face to behind us, where the channel was closing like a zip, fitting its teeth back together, swallowing its own foam and somersaulting slowly along itself.

The sight of *that* set him flailing worse. "Lemme down!" he shrieked. "I can run! I'll run, I promise!"

"You better!" I dropped him, and managed to smack his bum before he ran off.

Ahead of us Hickory turned, and quailed at the sight of the channel. "Hurry!" he cried.

"We *are* hurrying. Aren't we, Mum?" Mum was hurrying in a dignified, Mum-like way that wasn't very fast.

Steadying the bundle on her head, she flashed me a smile. "Have faith, daughter; He hasn't made this escape just to drown us all in it."

"Look at it, though!" The advancing foam was tossing up shapes: fishy giants, *trees* of seaweed, something that looked very much like a cartwheel.

"I will not look," she said. "I will only hurry and keep my faith."

"We are coming *last*, Mum! Come on!"

She laughed at me; I could only just hear it over the thunder from behind us, the roar of foam above. "I don't care if I drown now!" she shouted. "At least I will not die enslaved!"

I ran on, a little way ahead of her. Whenever I turned, there she was, proceeding at her own brisk pace and calm. The wall of green-white water caught up to her and tumbled behind her, churning sharks and rocks, dead Gypsies and horses, tentacled things and flights of striped-silver fishes, but never touching her, not with fish nor bubble-wrack thrown from its thrashings, not even with a drop of water from the violent masses it had to spare. It towered over us, for we were in the deepest depths of the ocean now. But it did not hurry Mum or overwhelm her, but crept along behind her, a great wild white beast tamed by her tiny happiness.

ELEVATOR

NANCY KRESS

"slow setting" vs SF

When visiting hours ended, Ian got on the hospital elevator on the fifth floor. Throat tight and stomach roiling, he didn't notice the "up" arrow until the doors started to close. Ian was going down, but he had no energy left to move. Marcia had, once again, drained it all.

"Hold the elevator!" a voice cried, and a fat man already in the car blocked the sliding door. His fingers looked like an uncut bunch of bananas. A middle-aged woman pushed into the elevator, scowling at nothing. As the car rose, her foot jiggled impatiently against the floor—*tap tap tap tap*—and the other occupant, a sullen teenage girl in robe and hospital slippers, glared at her.

"Slow jobbie, isn't it?" said the fat man, grinning. "Guess that's why we all are going up two floors to go down! Better than waiting for the next one!" No one answered.

On the sixth floor, a nurse in blue scrubs pushed a wheel chair onto the elevator. The woman in the wheelchair looked older than rocks. Scraggly white hair, face as crevassed as the Dakota Badlands, thin, wrinkled lips muttering to herself. The nurse maneuvered the chair to the back wall, facing her charge outward. Everyone shifted to accommodate this. The old woman smelled like sour apples. The elevator creaked to the seventh floor, where luxurious—for a hospital, anyway—private rooms adjoined a this-floor-only solarium. Ian had sneaked Marcia up here during one of her previous stays, hoping the sunlight and greenery would help. But nothing helped.

A gray-haired man strode into the car and the others immediately, instinctively, backed away to give him room. European-cut suit, manicured fingernails, briefcase of hand-sewn leather. Ian had seen this guy somewhere before, or a picture of him.

They started down. Everyone stared raptly at the changing numbers on the lighted display. The old woman muttered and chuckled. Between floors four and three, the elevator shuddered, stopped, and gave a violent lurch against the walls of the shaft. The teenage girl shrieked.

Ian was thrown against the middle-aged woman, who reeked of stale cigarette smoke. He grabbed the handrail, hauled himself off her, and got to his feet. The fat man yelled, "Hey! Everybody all right?"

The woman scowled at Ian as if he'd deliberately assaulted her. The man with the briefcase righted himself. The sleeve of his jacket rode up slightly and Ian caught the flash of onyx cufflinks. The fat man said, "Don't panic, folks! Everybody's fine, that's a mercy for sure, and this is just a little technical excitement from the Otis people, ha ha! Fixed in a jiffy!" He pressed the EMERGENCY button on the control panel.

Nothing happened.

The middle-aged woman shrilled, "Aren't alarms supposed to sound? Or something?"

"Alarm silent as the grave," the fat man said. Pointlessly, he winked. The gray-haired man, whom Ian now thought of as "the CEO," took a cell phone from his briefcase and frowned. Ian, looking over his shoulder, saw that the cell was either off or dead.

"Oh, hell, *I* got it," said the woman. She pulled a cell from her purse and keyed in the emergency number pasted onto the elevator wall. Ian heard the faint tinny ring go on and on. She said, "What kind of fucking elevator company don't answer their own emergency line?"

The fat man said, "Now, now, ma'am—let's watch our language in front of kids!" The woman glared at him and the teenage girl rolled her eyes.

Ian took out his cell and called 911. The woman continued to punch numbers onto her keypad, each jab an assault from blood-red fingernails. All her numbers were busy. So was Ian's call.

911 was *busy*? Not that Ian had good memories of 911. It had taken them seventeen minutes to reach Marcia, this last time.

The old woman in the wheelchair suddenly raised her head and laughed like a hyena.

The fat man said cheerfully, "Still nothing to worry about, folks. Busy time at the hospital, practically Times Square out there! When people see the ol' car isn't moving, somebody'll report it and we'll be outta here in no time. Meanwhile, since we're all gonna be friendly for a while, what d'ya say we introduce ourselves?"

No one responded. Seven people, even with the wheelchair, didn't crowd an elevator designed to hold a hospital bed, but Ian felt crowded nonetheless. The smell of old smoke from the shrill woman scraped at the inside of his nostrils.

"Then I'll just get the ball rolling here! I'm Carl Townes, tour bus guide extraordinaire, tour the town with Townes, see Carrolton with Carl, a laugh every quarter mile!"

"Oh God," said the smoker.

"And who are you, little lady?" Carl said to the teenager. She was very pale, with thin cheeks, watery blue eyes, and long, brittle hair. Her bathrobe looked suitable for a monk: brown, floor-length, voluminous. She turned her back to Carl, who was not deterred.

"Little lady's shy. How about you, ma'am, what's your name? I'll bet it's Linda. You look like a Linda."

"Just leave me out of this, okay?" Her foot resumed jiggling: *tap tap tap tap.*

Ian felt sorry for Carl. The poor guy had struck out twice. It felt good to feel sorry for somebody besides himself. He said, "I'm Ian."

"Ian!" Carl said, as if they'd been buddies since the fourth grade.

The old woman in the wheelchair said abruptly, "Cindy."

The smoker stopped tapping her foot and stared. "How'd she know my—"

The nurse said gently, "Cindy is her name, too. Quite a coincidence, actually." She had a faint British accent.

"Yeah, whatever," Cindy Smoker said. *Tap tap tap tap.*

"Carl, Ian, two Cindys," Carl said happily. "And you, Nurse...?"

"Gabriella." Ian looked at her closely for the first time. Average height, build, coloring, a woman you might have passed a dozen times without recognizing her. But her voice was soft, her smile sweet, and all at once lust took him in a dark wave. How long had it been? Years. And Gabriella seemed nothing like Marcia.

Carl said, "Well, I guess that brings us back to you, little lady. Wanna try Take Two? Have a little mercy on us and give up your name."

The girl pursed dry lips resentfully but surrendered to pressure. "Jessica."

"Great! Fantastic! And you, sir?"

Everyone looked sideways at the CEO, and for some reason Ian found himself holding his breath. The man radiated power, even danger, although it would be hard to say why. He didn't speak, and his contempt drenched them all in bile before he looked away and dismissed them—plus the elevator, the building, the situation— leaving only him in the universe. Dislike bloomed in Ian, who so seldom allowed himself to dislike anyone.

"Sir?" Carl insisted. Either Carl had a hide like a rhinoceros or his senses had been dulled by too much forced, tour-guide jollity.

Unexpectedly, Cindy Smoker rasped, "Don't you recognize him, Carl? That there's Mr. Thomas J. Bascomb. Himself, in the flesh."

Of course it was. That was where Ian had seen him: on the cover of *Time, Forbes*, the *Wall Street Journal*. Thomas J. Bascomb, CEO (he'd been right!) of Bascomb Financial Services, Manhattan. Billionaire under indictment in a corruption scandal so complex and esoteric that Ian had understood none of it except that a lot of ordinary people had lost their life savings. What was Bascomb doing in a hospital in Carrolton, Pennsylvania?

The elevator's lights blinked, went off, came back on.

"Fuck it to hell!" said Cindy Smoker. She tried six numbers in rapid succession on her cell. All six were busy. So were the three Ian tried, including 911. How was that possible? Bascomb's cell, a fancy satellite-looking job, was still dead. Apparently Carl, the nurse, and the two patients didn't possess phones.

Upstairs they'd taken away Marcia's cell, her belt, her shoe laces.

Carl said, "Well, now, seems like there might be some temporary—" Jessica fainted.

Ian saw it a second before the girl went down. Her pale face grew paler, all the way to the kind of white Ian associated with polar bears and printing paper. Her eyes rolled back in her head and she slumped sideways, not clutching at anything to break her fall, an unimpeded and almost graceful drop onto Carl, who caught her. One sleeve of her robe fell back, just as Bascomb's jacket sleeve had earlier, exposing her arm. Shock jolted through Ian. Jessica's arm was thin as a broomstick. The sharp bones in her wrist stuck out in knobs.

"Why…why…" Carl stammered, "she doesn't weigh anything!" He laid her on the elevator floor, puffing with the exertion of lowering his bulk, not hers. "Give her air, folks!"

Jessica's eyes opened. She struggled to sit, couldn't, and fell back to the floor. Carl yanked off his sweatshirt, exposing a faded red tee that said CARROLTON TOURS, and wadded the sweatshirt under Jessica's head. Her pale, dry hair lay limply on the nylon. Carl said to Gabriella, "Nurse, what should we *do?*"

"Nothing," Gabriella said tranquilly.

Nothing? But then Ian could see her point. Jessica was clearly anorexic, and the only thing that would help was food, which she undoubtedly would refuse even if anyone had any to offer. *"You always see everybody's point,"* Marcia had raged at him upstairs, *"except mine!"* But it seemed to Ian that he did nothing except see Marcia's point of view, over and over, in the endless arguments in which she attacked and he appeased. Those arguments that went on for days, weeks, mounting in tension and unbearability until Marcia in one masterful stroke made everything Ian's fault by ending up yet again in Carrolton General.

From the floor Jessica murmured, without heat, "Leave me alone." Bascomb gazed down at the girl as at a dead fish. Ian's dislike grew.

All at once Ancient Cindy laughed, the same grating bray, and said, "Let her go!"

Nurse Gabriella smiled gently and said nothing.

Cindy Smoker scowled. "'Let her go'? Nobody's bothering her!"

"Let her go," Ancient Cindy repeated, cackling. "You can't help her."

"You mean, like, let her *die?*" Cindy Smoker demanded. "What kinda heartless bitch are you, you old hag?"

Ian was appalled. Carl said, "Why…why…." Bascomb's nostrils wrinkled in disgust. But the nurse just gave her gentle smile.

Carl, recovering, said in a low voice to Cindy Smoker, "The old lady probably doesn't mean anything by it. I think all her cylinders aren't firing right, if you get my meaning." With one plump finger he made a circle in the air beside his head.

"Whatever," Cindy Smoker said. Abruptly she pounded on the elevator walls. "Hey, anybody! Can you hear us? Hey!"

She pounded and yelled, stopping every so often to listen for a reply that didn't come, until Carl said genially, "Walls must be too well insulated. And all that banging is pretty hard on us in here."

Ian agreed, although he didn't say so aloud. The pounding seemed to echo in his head. Cindy threw Carl a look that could wither cacti, reached into a pocket and pulled out a pack of Parliaments.

"No smoking in here, I'm sorry," Carl said with sudden authority.

"Jesus Christ," Cindy said, but she put away the cigarettes.

Ian tried 911 again. It was busy. He tried Information, his own number at work, Tim's number in the next cubicle, his mother in Pittsburgh. All busy.

"Let her go," Ancient Cindy crooned, so that it was almost a song.

Two hours passed, mostly in silence except for periodic, but mercifully shorter, pounding on the wall from Cindy. Carl had tried boisterous conversation and then, incredibly, a group sing. No one cooperated. They all sat with their backs to elevator walls, even Bascomb, who put his briefcase between his expensively tailored butt and the grubby floor. Jessica, stretched out full length, slept.

Ian dozed. He hadn't been sleeping well most nights, even though it was a shameful relief to have the bed to himself. But in two days Marcia would come home and it would all start again—

"Fuck it all, where *are* they?" Cindy Smoker burst out, waking him. She yanked out the Parliaments and this time she lit one, fingers trembling with need on her Zippo. The quick acrid odor of tobacco swelled into the car. Carl reached toward the cigarette and she yanked it away, dropped the lighter, and punched him on the arm. "Let me be!"

"You can't smoke in here," Carl said. His voice had hardened but his smile stayed wide. "Too dangerous for everybody, Cindy."

"This isn't your fucking tour bus!"

Carl reached again for the cigarette. He outweighed her by at least a hundred pounds but Ian would have given odds on Cindy. She suddenly reminded him of Marcia, even though they looked nothing alike. But he recognized that substrate of perpetual fury, that eagerness to let the molten anger surge up no matter who stood on the ground above. Ian felt his spine press into the wall.

Carl said evenly, "Give me that cigarette."

"Go fuck yourself!" She pulled it farther away and he lunged forward. The cigarette went out.

Ian blinked. The tip of the Parliament had been glowing redly, strongly. Neither Carl nor Cindy had touched it. There was no breeze in the elevator.

Cindy stared at her dead cigarette, and Carl took the moment to grab the pack and shove it into the pocket of his jeans, where it made a misshapen lump.

"Fuck!" Cindy yelled. Jessica, on the floor, opened her eyes and smiled.

Bascomb spoke for the first time. "Will you all please be quiet?"

Immediately both Cindy and Carl turned their attention to him. Before either could speak, Ancient Cindy said from her wheelchair, "You need to die."

Bascomb's head swiveled slowly toward her.

"He will recover. He knows everything. You need to die."

Bascomb said to Gabriella, "Shut her up."

"She's very old," the nurse said with her gentle smile. "She babbles sometimes, wandering in time. But it's harmless."

"The gun is loaded," Ancient Cindy said. "The rope is tied. The car goes fast. The pills are in the medicine chest. *Kyrie eleison, kyrie, kyrie.* He knows everything."

The muscles in Bascomb's throat tightened until they stood out in long, corded bundles. For an endless moment, tension prickled in the air like heat. Ian couldn't stand it, never could. Always he had to be the one to defuse tension, avoid confrontation, calm Marcia down…. He said desperately to Carl, "Were you visiting someone in the hospital? During visiting hours, I mean?"

Carl turned to him gratefully. "My son. Car accident but nobody got hurt, thank God. A mercy. How about you?"

Ian should have foreseen this. Of course Carl would turn the question back to him. His stomach spasmed. "My wife. But she'll be all right, too."

"Oh, *wonderful*," Carl said. "And you, Cindy, you visiting kin?"

Cindy Smoker, still holding the unlit cigarette in her red talons, refused the conciliatory gesture. "Leave me the fuck out of this."

Ancient Cindy crooned, "Sister sister sister oh you kid!"

Cindy Smoker stared. Ian found he was holding his breath.

"But I kisssssss-ed her little sister and forgot my Clementine!" the old woman sang in a voice cracked and out-of-tune. "O my darlin'—but you made it this far, sister. No smoke means no fire."

"Shut her up!" Cindy Smoker said, unwittingly echoing Bascomb. She started to get to her feet and Carl put out a meaty arm, but all at once the crone looked down at Jessica, said quietly, "Eat, child," and closed her eyes. Within ten seconds she was snoring.

Cindy Smoker lashed out at all of them, none of them, the world. "I'll never forgive my sister no never I don't give a flying fart what Mama says even on her so-called deathbed—never—you hear me—*Christ*, I want a cigarette—how the fuck did she *know?*"

"She just babbles," Gabriella said. "She's very old and worn out and she babbles."

Another hour passed. Carl announced, shamefaced, that he had to piss. He slipped his sweatshirt from under Jessica's head, replacing it with the sweater Ian offered. Jessica didn't stir. Carl wadded the sweatshirt into a ball, stuck it in a corner of the elevator and turned his back. The thick cotton absorbed the liquid if not the odor.

Ian's cell was still busy on all numbers, all the time. Ancient Cindy slumped in her wheelchair. Gabriella leaned against her, eyes closed. Cindy Smoker snored. Jessica slept soundlessly, stretched full length on the floor, pale as a corpse. Every once in a while Ian leaned close to make sure she was still breathing.

Another hour. Two. Bascomb slept sitting up, his head thrown back against the wall, twitching and groaning. Ian, despite embarrassment, availed himself of Carl's sweatshirt. He tried to be quiet about it. As he returned to his place, Cindy Smoker woke up and immediately exploded, as if her curses were merely an extension of her dreams.

"Christ, they're *patients!*" she said, waving at Jessica and Ancient Cindy. "How come nobody's missing them? What the fuck is wrong with this fucking place? What time is it, Ian?"

"Seventeen after midnight."

"Christ!" She stood up, took a step, sat back down again. There was no place to pace. Ian saw that she still, after all these hours, clutched the cigarette that had gone out by itself. Her foot began to drum: *tap tap tap tap*.

"Don't wake the others," Carl said wearily. Maybe it was the weariness, as if Carl's usual frantic good-will had all flaked off like so much old paint, that got to Cindy. She stopped tapping, pulled hard at the skin on her face, and said to Carl, "You sure your son's going to be okay?"

"Right as rain," Ancient Cindy suddenly said from her corner. "Rain, rain, go away—they all come again another day, you know, all of them. Cops can't stop the rain, won't, don't need to. Sunshine tomorrow, fair and warmer, high pressure system moving in!"

Cindy Smoker stared at Carl's face. She said slowly, as if the words belonged to somebody else and she was surprised they were coming out of her own mouth, "Your kid in trouble with the cops? Is that his room down on Four with the police guard on it?"

Carl said, his smile back and wide as ever, "Oh, no, nothing big. A misunderstanding. You know how kids are, but Petey'll be all right. He'll be just fine." His lower lip trembled.

"Right as rain," Ancient Cindy sang. "Rain, rain, go away—"

Ian inched forward so he could look past Carl directly at the old woman. "Who are you?"

But she gazed past him, toward the sleeping Thomas Bascomb, and her sunken eyes glittered with an emotion that Ian couldn't name.

"She's mostly blind," Gabriella said to Ian. They were the only two awake. "Frequently when one sense is lost, others sharpen in compensation. So, yes, I can believe that Cindy can sense your friend's anger."

Cindy Smoker was not Ian's friend, but he didn't correct Gabriella. Ian had only the normal five senses. He hadn't smelled Marcia's desperation, hadn't even smelled the blood until he'd gone through the bedroom and pushed open the bathroom door left ajar. In the tub, this time, his wife's naked body motionless in a sea of red, red, red. And his first thought had been, *Maybe this time she meant it.*

The thought horrified him, with a horror that sank into all the moments that followed as he called 911, woke Marcia from her stupor-like sleep, followed the ambulance to Carrolton General, filled out the papers for psychiatric observation. But Marcia hadn't meant it. She'd lived, as she'd lived every other time, and so this suicide attempt joined the others as fresh testament to her unhappiness. To Ian's inadequacy as a husband. To the fragility that tied him to her with bonds of pity and guilt and the baseness of his own fervent desire to leave this woman who gave him nothing but who needed him so much that she attempted suicide every time he brought up divorce.

In the elevator, 911 was still busy.

Bascomb suddenly flailed at the air, screamed, "No no no!" and woke up himself and everybody else except Jessica.

He glared at them all, as if they and not he were the source of his nightmare. Cindy Smoker flipped him the finger. Ancient Cindy, eyes still closed, said, "Let her go."

Ian's throat tightened. He grabbed for Jessica's wrist and felt for a pulse. Her eyes flew open and she glared at him. She was alive. Gladness flooded him, even as he wondered why. He was never going to see any of these people again once he got off this elevator.

Ancient Cindy said, "You made it this far, sister! No fire, no smoke." Then, after a pause, "Time to die. Have mercy on our souls."

No one answered her.

The elevator rumbled and started to move.

"Fuck!" Cindy Smoker cried, in delight and fear. Ian had been asleep, dreaming in confused images about which he was sure only that they'd been bad. He got to his feet. The car had stopped between the third and fourth floors—if the thing just plunged straight down the shaft, was that survivable?

The elevator didn't plunge. It moved slowly down, everyone staring at the number display, until it reached "1." Ancient Cindy said clearly, in a voice stronger and much younger than before, "Let her go." She was staring directly at Ian.

The elevator door opened.

Only when fresh air from the lobby wafted in did Ian realize how foul the elevator had become, reeking of piss and smoke and sweat and old flesh. Carl helped Jessica to her feet. The girl seemed stronger; she said, wonderingly, "I'm *hungry*." Cindy Smoker still held the unlighted Parliament between two fingers. Ian saw her drop it on the elevator floor and grind it underneath her shoe.

It was early morning. People in the lobby turned in amazement as the seven captives staggered out of the car. Ian didn't wait to find out what had happened, why no one had rescued them, how a non-working elevator could have been not noticed for ten hours. He wanted to go home. He wanted to go home now, and he wanted it with the unreasoning passion of a six-year-old who has run too much, too long, too hard.

When he woke in his own bed, it was two in the afternoon. Ian showered and dressed, his mind clearer than it had been in days. Weeks. Years.

He turned on the local news station. The elevator break-down wasn't there. A solemn anchorwoman with perfect hair intoned, "—found just over an hour ago. Cause of death was allegedly a single, self-inflicted gunshot wound to the head. Bascomb, under indictment for his allegedly leading role in the burgeoning financial scandal, faced almost certain imprisonment for—"

Ian stood very still.

"—chief witness Daniel Davis, at present recovering from a heart attack sustained while on vacation in Pennsylvania—"

"*He knows everything.*"

The rest of the news, whatever it was, washed over Ian unheard.

"*Let her go,*" the old woman said, but she hadn't meant Jessica. Jessica had looked stronger after her long, restorative sleep; she'd said she was hungry. Cindy had crushed her cigarette and maybe—maybe—hadn't lit another: "*You made it this far, sister. No smoke means no fire.*" And to Carl, his anguish over his son masked by all that forced heartiness: "*Right as rain…they all come again another fine day…cops can't stop the rain.*"

But to Bascomb: "*Best to die.*"

Ian walked to his garage. At the hospital, which he had no recollection of driving to, he took the stairs to the fourth floor and stopped a nurse. "Which room is Peter Townes's?"

"Four sixty-two, first corridor on your left." She pointed.

No police guard stood in front of 462. Ian went in and said, "Peter Townes?"

"Yeah, who wants to know?" A surly teenager with Carl's round face and chunky body.

"I'm a legal advocate with—"

"The charges got dropped. I don't need any more legal shit."

"Glad to hear it." The words came out thick, uncertain.

He walked up a flight of steps. But on the landing, hand on the heavy fire door that led to Marcia's floor, Ian stopped. His eyes closed.

All the rest of his life. Tension and arguing and coldness and these suicide attempts. Unless maybe, finally, years from now, one of the attempts succeeded, long after Ian was as completely destroyed as Marcia already was. Two people going down instead of one.

"*You need to die*," Cindy said. But not to him.

Carefully, as if his bones were spun glass, he walked down to the first floor. Gabriella walked by, carrying a stack of blankets. She wore fresh pink scrubs.

"Nurse! Nurse!"

She turned toward him, smiling serenely. "Yes?"

"That old woman—Cindy—what is she?"

Her smile didn't waver. "I don't know what you mean."

"Don't *know*? I mean last night—the elevator—your patient—"

"I work in Pediatrics. And I wasn't on duty last night."

He gaped at her. She turned to leave.

"Wait, wait! You can't just—I need—"

Something moved behind her eyes, some kindness mingled with amusement. She said in the same soft voice as last night, "You people have it wrong, you know. Mercy is strained, difficult, hard. Always. Or it's not really mercy."

"But—"

"I'm sorry, I'm late. Please excuse me."

"But *Cindy*—"

She turned and walked away.

"*Let her go*." Said to him, to Ian, and not about Jessica Said by a babbling half-mad crone, by an alien or an angel of mercy or a whatever-the-hell-she-was. Said to *him*.

In the lobby, a volunteer at the Information Desk loaned him a phone book. He found the listings for ATTORNEYS—DIVORCE, even as he wondered if he had the strength, after all, for mercy. For himself, and maybe even for Marcia as well.

He chose a number and keyed it in. His cell phone worked perfectly.

THE ILLUSTRATED BIOGRAPHY OF LORD GRIMM

DARYL GREGORY

The 22nd Invasion of Trovenia began with a streak of scarlet against a gray sky fast as the flick of a paintbrush. The red blur zipped across the length of the island, moving west to east, and shot out to sea. The sonic boom a moment later scattered the birds that wheeled above the fish processing plant and sent them squealing and plummeting.

Elena said, "Was that—it was, wasn't it?"

"You've never seen a U-Man, Elena?" Jürgo said.

"Not in person." At nineteen, Elena Pendareva was the youngest of the crew by at least two decades, and the only female. She and the other five members of the heavy plate welding unit were perched 110 meters in the air, taking their lunch upon the great steel shoulder of the Slaybot Prime. The giant robot, latest in a long series of ultimate weapons, was unfinished, its unpainted skin speckled with bird shit, its chest turrets empty, the open dome of its head covered only by a tarp.

It had been Jürgo's idea to ride up the gantry for lunch. They had plenty of time: for the fifth day in a row, steel plate for the Slaybot's skin had failed to arrive from the foundry, and the welding crew had nothing to do but clean their equipment and play cards until the guards let them go home.

It was a good day for a picnic. An unseasonably warm spring wind blew in from the docks, carrying the smell of the sea only slightly tainted by odors of diesel fuel and fish guts. From the giant's shoulder the crew looked down on the entire capital, from the port and industrial sector below them, to the old city in the west and the rows of gray apartment buildings rising up beyond. The only structures higher than their perch were Castle Grimm's black spires, carved out of the sides of Mount

Kriegstahl, and the peak of the mountain itself.

"You know what you must do, Elena," Verner said with mock sincerity. He was the oldest in the group, a veteran mechaneer whose body was more metal than flesh. "Your first übermensch, you must make a wish."

Elena said, "Is 'Oh shit,' a wish?"

Verner pivoted on his rubber-tipped stump to follow her gaze. The figure in red had turned about over the eastern sea, and was streaking back toward the island. Sunlight glinted on something long and metallic in its hands.

The UM dove straight toward them.

There was nowhere to hide. The crew sat on a naked shelf of metal between the gantry and the sheer profile of the robot's head. Elena threw herself flat and spread her arms on the metal surface, willing herself to stick.

Nobody else moved. Maybe because they were old men, or maybe because they were all veterans, former zoomandos and mechaneers and castle guards. They'd seen dozens of U-Men, fought them even. Elena didn't know if they were unafraid or simply too old to care much for their skin.

The UM shot past with a whoosh, making the steel shiver beneath her. She looked up in time to take in a flash of metal, a crimson cape, black boots—and then the figure crashed *through* the wall of Castle Grimm. Masonry and dust exploded into the air.

"Lunch break," Jürgo said in his Estonian accent, "is over."

Toolboxes slammed, paper sacks took to the wind. Elena got to her feet. Jürgo picked up his lunch pail with one clawed foot, spread his patchy, soot-stained wings, and leaned over the side, considering. His arms and neck were skinny as always, but in the past few years he'd grown a beer gut.

Elena said, "Jürgo, can you still fly?"

"Of course," he said. He hooked his pail to his belt and backed away from the edge. "However, I don't believe I'm authorized for this air space."

The rest of the crew had already crowded into the gantry elevator. Elena and Jürgo pressed inside and the cage began to slowly descend, rattling and shrieking.

"What's it about this time, you think?" Verner said, clockwork lungs wheezing. "Old Rivet Head kidnap one of their women?" Only the oldest veterans could get away with insulting Lord Grimm in mixed company.

Verner had survived at least four invasions that she knew of. His loyalty to Trovenia was assumed to go beyond patriotism into something like ownership.

Guntis, a gray, pebble-skinned amphibian of Latvian descent, said, "I fought this girlie with a sword once, Energy Lady—"

"*Power Woman*," Elena said in English. She'd read the *Illustrated Biography of Lord Grimm* to her little brother dozens of times before he learned to read it himself. The Lord's most significant adversaries were all listed in the appendix, in multiple languages.

"That's the one, *Par-wer Woh-man*," Guntis said, imitating her. "She had enormous—"

"Abilities," Jürgo said pointedly. Jürgo had been a friend of Elena's father, and often played the protective uncle.

"I think he meant to say 'tits,'" Elena said. Several of the men laughed.

"No! Jürgo is right," Guntis said. "They were more than breasts. They had *abilities*. I think one of them spoke to me."

The elevator clanged down on the concrete pad and the crew followed Jürgo into the long shed of the 3000 line. The factory floor was emptying. Workers pulled on coats, joking and laughing as if it were a holiday.

Jürgo pulled aside a man and asked him what was going on. "The guards have run away!" the man said happily. "Off to fight the übermensch!"

"So what's it going to be, boss?" Guntis said. "Stay or go?"

Jürgo scratched at the cement floor, thinking. Half-assembled Slaybot 3000s, five-meter-tall cousins to the colossal Prime, dangled from hooks all along the assembly line, wires spilling from their chests, legs missing. The factory was well behind its quota for the month. As well as for the quarter, year, and five-year mark. Circuit boards and batteries were in particularly short supply, but tools and equipment vanished daily. Especially scarce were acetylene tanks, a home-heating accessory for the very cold, the very stupid, or both.

Jürgo finally shook his feathered head and said, "Nothing we can do here. Let's go home and hide under our beds."

"And in our bottles," Verner said.

Elena waved good-bye and walked toward the women's changing rooms to empty her locker.

A block from her apartment she heard Mr. Bojars singing out, "Guh-RATE day for sausa-JEZ! Izza GREAT day for SAW-sages!" The mechaneer veteran was parked at his permanent spot at the corner of Glorious Victory Street and Infinite Progress Avenue, in the shadow of the statue of Grimm Triumphant. He saw her crossing the intersection and shouted, "My beautiful Elena! A fat bratwurst to go with that bread, maybe. Perfect for a celebration!"

"No thank you, Mr. Bojars." She hoisted the bag of groceries onto her hip and shuffled the welder's helmet to her other arm. "You know we've been invaded, don't you?"

The man laughed heartily. "The trap is sprung! The crab is in the basket!" He wore the same clothes he wore every day, a black nylon ski hat and a green, grease-stained parka decorated at the breast with three medals from his years in the motorized cavalry. The coat hung down to cover where his flesh ended and his motorcycle body began.

"Don't you worry about Lord Grimm," he said. "He can handle any American muscle-head stupid enough to enter his lair. Especially the Red Meteor."

"It was Most Excellent Man," Elena said, using the Trovenian translation of his name. "I saw the Staff of Mightiness in his hand, or whatever he calls it."

"Even better! The man's an idiot. A U-Moron."

"He's defeated Lord Grimm several times," Elena said. "So I hear."

"And Lord Grimm has been declared dead a dozen times! You can't believe the underground newspapers, Elena. You're not reading that trash are you?"

"You know I'm not political, Mr. Bojars."

"Good for you. This Excellent Man, let me tell you something about—yes sir? Great day for a sausage." He turned his attention to the customer and Elena quickly wished him luck and slipped away before he could begin another story.

The small lobby of her apartment building smelled like burnt plastic and cooking grease. She climbed the cement stairs to the third floor. As usual the door to her apartment was wide open, as was the door to Mr. Fishman's apartment across the hall. Staticky television laughter and applause carried down the hallway: It sounded like *Mr. Sascha's Celebrity Polka Fun-Time*. Not even an invasion could pre-empt Mr. Sascha.

She knocked on the frame of his door. "Mr. Fishman," she called loudly. He'd never revealed his real name. "Mr. Fishman, would you like to come to dinner tonight?"

There was no answer except for the blast of the television. She walked into the dim hallway and leaned around the corner. The living room was dark except for the glow of the TV. The little set was propped up on a wooden chair at the edge of a large cast iron bathtub, the light from its screen reflecting off the smooth surface of the water. "Mr. Fishman? Did you hear me?" She walked across the room, shoes crinkling on the plastic tarp that covered the floor, and switched off the TV.

The surface of the water shimmied. A lumpy head rose up out of the water, followed by a pair of dark eyes, a flap of nose, and a wide carp mouth.

"I was watching that," the zooman said.

"Someday you're going to pull that thing into the tub and electrocute yourself," Elena said.

He exhaled, making a rude noise through rubbery lips.

"We're having dinner," Elena said. She turned on a lamp. Long ago Mr. Fishman had pushed all the furniture to the edge of the room to make room for his easels. She didn't see any new canvasses upon them, but there was an empty liquor bottle on the floor next to the tub. "Would you like to join us?"

He eyed the bag in her arms. "That wouldn't be, umm, fresh catch?"

"It is, as a matter of fact."

"I suppose I could stop by." His head sank below the surface.

In Elena's own apartment, Grandmother Zita smoked and rocked in front of the window, while Mattias, nine years old, sat at the table with his shoe box of colored pencils and several gray pages crammed with drawings. "Elena, did you hear?" Matti asked. "A U-Man flew over the island! They canceled school!"

"It's nothing to be happy about," Elena said. She rubbed the top of her brother's head. The page showed a robot of Matti's own design marching toward a hyper-muscled man in a red cape. In the background was a huge, lumpy monster with triangle eyes—an escaped MoG, she supposed.

"The last time the U-men came," Grandmother Zita said, "more than robots lost their heads. This family knows that better than most. When your mother—"

"Let's not talk politics, Grandmother." She kissed the old woman on the cheek, then reached past her to crank open the window—she'd told the woman to let in some air when she smoked in front of Matti, to no avail. Outside, sirens wailed.

Elena had been only eleven years old during the last invasion. She'd slept through most of it, and when she woke to sirens that morning the apartment was cold and the lights didn't work. Her parents were government geneticists—there was no other kind—and often were called away at odd hours. Her mother had left her a note asking her to feed Baby Matti and please stay indoors. Elena made oatmeal, the first of many breakfasts she would make for her little brother. Only after her parents failed to come home did she realize that the note was a kind of battlefield promotion to adulthood: impossible to refuse because there was no one left to accept her refusal.

Mr. Fishman, in his blue bathrobe and striped pajama pants, arrived a half hour later, his great webbed feet slapping the floor. He sat at the table and argued with Grandmother Zita about which of the twenty-one previous invasions was most violent. There was a time in the 1960s and seventies when their little country seemed to be under attack every other month. Matti listened raptly.

Elena had just brought the fried whitefish to the table when the thumping march playing on the radio suddenly cut off. An announcer said, "Please stand by for an important message from His Royal Majesty, the Guardian of our Shores, the Scourge of Fascism, Professor General of the Royal Academy of Sciences, the Savior of Trovenia—"

Mr. Fishman pointed at Matti. "Boy, get my television!" Matti dashed to the man's apartment and Elena cleared a spot on the table.

After Mr. Fishman fiddled with the antenna the screen suddenly cleared, showing a large room decorated in Early 1400s: stone floors, flickering torches, and dulled tapestries on the walls. The only piece of furniture was a huge oaken chair reinforced at the joints with plates and rivets.

A figure appeared at the far end of the room and strode toward the camera.

"He's still alive then," Grandmother said. Lord Grimm didn't appear on live television more than once or twice a year.

Matti said, "Oh, look at him."

Lord Grimm wore the traditional black and green cape of Trovenian nobility, which contrasted nicely with the polished suit of armor. His faceplate, hawk-nosed and heavily riveted, suggested simultaneously the prow of a battleship and the beak of the Baltic albatross, the Trovenian national bird.

Elena had to admit he cut a dramatic figure. She almost felt sorry for people in other countries whose leaders all looked like postal inspectors. You could no more imagine those timid, pinch-faced bureaucrats leading troops into battle than you could imagine Lord Grimm ice skating.

"Sons and daughters of Trovenia," the leader intoned. His deep voice was charged with metallic echoes. "We have been invaded."

"We knew that already," Grandmother said, and Mr. Fishman shushed her.

"Once again, an American superpower has violated our sovereignty. With typical, misguided arrogance, a so-called übermensch has trespassed upon our borders, destroyed our property..." The litany of crimes went on for some time.

"Look! The U-Man!" Matti said.

On screen, castle guards carried in a red-clad figure and dumped him in the huge chair. His head lolled. Lord Grimm lifted the prisoner's chin to show his bloody face to the camera. One eye was half open, the other swelled shut. "As you can see, he is completely powerless."

Mr. Fishman grunted in disappointment.

"What?" Matti asked.

"Again with the captives, and the taunting," Grandmother said.

"Why not? They invaded us!"

Mr. Fishman grimaced, and his gills flapped shut.

"If Lord Grimm simply beat up Most Excellent Man and sent him packing, that would be one thing," Grandmother said. "Or even if he just promised to stop doing what he was doing for a couple of months until they forgot about him, then—"

"Then we'd all go back to our business," Mr. Fishman said.

Grandmother said, "But no, he's got to keep him captive. Now it's going to be just like 1972."

"And seventy-five," Mr. Fishman said. He sawed into his whitefish. "And eighty-three."

Elena snapped off the television. "Matti, go pack your school bag with clothes. Now."

"What? Why?"

"We're spending the night in the basement. You too, Grandmother."

"But I haven't finished my supper!"

"I'll wrap it up for you. Mr. Fishman, I can help you down the stairs if you like."

"Pah," he said. "I'm going back to bed. Wake me when the war's over."

A dozen or so residents of the building had gotten the same idea. For several hours the group sat on boxes and old furniture in the damp basement under stuttering fluorescent lights, listening to the distant roar of jets, the rumble of mechaneer tanks, and the bass-drum stomps of Slaybot 3000s marching into position.

Grandmother Zita had claimed the best seat in the room, a ripped vinyl armchair. Matti had fallen asleep across her lap, still clutching the *Illustrated Biography of Lord Grimm*. The boy was so comfortable with her. Zita wasn't even a relative, but she'd watched over the boy since he was a toddler and so became his grandmother—another wartime employment opportunity. Elena slipped the book from under Matti's arms and bent to put it into his school bag.

Zita lit another cigarette. "How do you suppose it really started?" she said.

"What, the war?" Elena asked.

"No, the first time." She nodded at Matti's book. "Hating the Americans, okay, no problem. But why the scary mask, the cape?"

Elena pretended to sort out the contents of the bag.

"What possesses a person to do that?" Zita said, undeterred. "Wake up one day and say, Today I will put a bucket over my head. Today I declare war on all U-Men. Today I become, what's the English…"

"Grandmother, please," Elena said, keeping her voice low.

"A *super villain*," Zita said.

A couple of the nearest people looked away in embarrassment. Mr. Rimkis, an old man from the fourth floor, glared at Grandmother down the length of his gray-bristled snout. He was a veteran with one long tusk and one jagged stump. He claimed to have suffered the injury fighting the U-Men, though others said he'd lost the tusk in combat with vodka and gravity: The Battle of the Pub Stairs.

"*He* is the hero," Mr. Rimkis said. "Not these imperialists in long underwear. They invaded his country, attacked his family, maimed him and left him with—"

"Oh please," Grandmother said. "Every villain believes himself to be a hero."

The last few words were nearly drowned out by the sudden wail of an air raid siren. Matti jerked awake and Zita automatically put a hand to his sweat-dampened forehead. The residents stared up at the ceiling. Soon there was a chorus of sirens.

They've come, Elena thought, as everyone knew they would, to rescue their comrade.

From somewhere in the distance came a steady *thump, thump* that vibrated the ground and made the basement's bare cinderblock walls chuff dust into the air. Each explosion seemed louder and closer. Between the explosions, slaybot auto-cannons whined and chattered.

Someone said, "Everybody just remain calm—"

The floor seemed to jump beneath their feet. Elena lost her balance and smacked into the cement on her side. At the same moment she was deafened by a noise louder than her ears could process.

The lights had gone out. Elena rolled over, eyes straining, but she couldn't make out Grandmother or Matti or anyone. She shouted but barely heard her own voice above the ringing in her ears.

Someone behind her switched on an electric torch and flicked it around the room. Most of the basement seemed to have filled with rubble.

Elena crawled toward where she thought Grandmother's chair had been and was stopped by a pile of cement and splintered wood. She called Matti's name and began to push the debris out of the way.

Someone grabbed her foot, and then Matti fell into her, hugged her fiercely. Somehow he'd been thrown behind her, over her. She called for a light, but the torch was aimed now at a pair of men attempting to clear the stairway. Elena took Matti's hand and led him cautiously toward the light. Pebbles fell on them; the building seemed to shift and groan. Somewhere a woman cried out, her voice muffled.

"Grandmother Zita," Matti said.

"I'll come back for Grandmother," she said, though she didn't know for sure if it had been Zita's voice. "First you."

The two men had cleared a passage to the outside. One of them boosted the other to where he could crawl out. The freed man then reached back and Elena lifted Matti to him. The boy's jacket snagged on a length of rebar, and the boy yelped. After what seemed like minutes of tugging and shouting the coat finally ripped free.

"Stay there, Mattias!" Elena called. "Don't move!" She turned to assist the next person in line to climb out, an old woman from the sixth floor. She carried an enormous wicker basket which she refused to relinquish. Elena promised repeatedly that the basket would be the first thing to come out after her. The others in the basement began to shout at the old woman, which only made her grip the handle more fiercely. Elena was considering prying her fingers from it when a yellow flash illuminated the passage. People outside screamed.

Elena scrambled up and out without being conscious of how she managed it. The street lights had gone out but the gray sky flickered with strange lights. A small crowd of dazed citizens sat or sprawled across the rubble-strewn street, as if a bomb had gone off. The man who'd pulled Matti out of the basement sat on the ground, holding his hands to his face and moaning.

The sky was full of flying men.

Searchlights panned from a dozen points around the city, and clouds pulsed with exotic energies. In that spasmodic light dozens of tiny figures darted: caped invaders, squadrons of Royal Air Dragoons riding pinpricks of fire, winged zoomandos, glowing U-Men leaving iridescent fairy trails. Beams of energy flicked from horizon to horizon; soldiers ignited and dropped like dollops of burning wax.

Elena looked around wildly for her brother. Rubble was everywhere. The front of her apartment building had been sheared off, exposing bedrooms and bathrooms. Protruding girders bent toward the ground like tongues.

Finally she saw the boy. He sat on the ground, staring at the sky. Elena ran to him, calling his name. He looked in her direction. His eyes were wide, unseeing.

She knelt down in front of him.

"I looked straight at him," Matti said. "He flew right over our heads. He was so bright. So bright."

There was something wrong with Matti's face. In the inconstant light she could only tell that his skin was darker than it should have been.

"Take my hand," Elena said. "Can you stand up? Good. Good. How do you feel?"

"My face feels hot," he said. Then, "Is Grandmother out yet?"

Elena didn't answer. She led him around the piles of debris. Once she had to yank him sideways and he yelped. "Something in our way," she said. A half-buried figure lay with one arm and one leg jutting into the street. The body would have been unrecognizable if not for the blue-striped pajamas and the webbing between the toes of the bare foot.

Matti wrenched his hand from her grip. "Where are we going? You have to tell me where we're going."

She had no idea. She'd thought they'd be safe in the basement. She'd thought it would be like the invasions everyone talked about, a handful of U-Men—a *super team*—storming the castle. No one told her there could be an army of them. The entire city had become the battleground.

"Out of the city," she said. "Into the country."

"But Grandmother—"

"I promise I'll come back for Grandmother Zita," she said.

"And my book," he said. "It's still in the basement."

All along Infinite Progress Avenue, families spilled out of buildings carrying bundles of clothes and plastic jugs, pushing wheelchairs and shopping carts loaded with canned food, TV sets, photo albums. Elena grabbed tight to Matti's arm and joined the exodus north.

After an hour they'd covered only ten blocks. The street had narrowed as they left the residential district, condensing the stream of people into a herd, then a single shuffling animal. Explosions and gunfire continued to sound from behind them and the sky still flashed with parti-colored lightning, but hardly anyone glanced back.

The surrounding bodies provided Elena and Matti with some protection against the cold, though frigid channels of night air randomly opened through the crowd. Matti's vision still hadn't returned; he saw nothing but the yellow light of the U-Man. He told her his skin still felt hot, but he trembled as if he were cold. Once he stopped suddenly and threw up into the street. The crowd behind bumped into them, forcing them to keep moving.

One of their fellow refugees gave Matti a blanket. He pulled it onto his shoulders like a cape but it kept slipping as he walked, tripping him up. The boy hadn't cried since they'd started walking, hadn't complained—he'd even stopped asking about Grandmother Zita—but Elena still couldn't stop herself from being annoyed at him. He stumbled again and she yanked the blanket from him. "For God's sake, Mattias," she said. "If you can't hold onto it—" She drew up short. The black-coated women in front of them had suddenly stopped.

Shouts went up from somewhere ahead, and then the crowd surged backward. Elena recognized the escalating whine of an auto-cannon coming up to speed.

Elena pulled Matti up onto her chest and he yelped in surprise or pain. The boy was heavy and awkward; she locked her hands under his butt and shoved toward the crowd's edge, aiming for the mouth of an alley. The crowd buffeted her, knocked her off course. She came up hard against the plate-glass window of a shop.

A Slaybot 3000 lumbered through the crowd, knocking people aside. Its gun arm, a huge thing like a barrel of steel pipes, jerked from figure to figure, targeting automatically. A uniformed technician sat in the jumpseat on the robot's back, gesturing frantically and shouting, "Out of the way! Out of the way!" It was impossible to tell whether he'd lost control or was deliberately marching through the crowd.

The mass of figures had almost certainly overwhelmed the robot's vision and recognition processors. The 3000 model, like its predecessors, had difficulty telling friend from foe even in the spare environment of the factory QA room.

The gun arm pivoted toward her: six black mouths. Then the carousel began to spin and the six barrels blurred, became one vast maw.

Elena felt her gut go cold. She would have sunk to the ground—she wanted desperately to disappear—but the mob held her upright, pinned. She twisted to place at least part of her body between the robot and Matti. The glass at her shoulder trembled, began to bow.

For a moment she saw both sides of the glass. Inside the dimly lit shop were two rows of blank white faces, a choir of eyeless women regarding her. And in the window's reflection she saw her own face, and above that, a streak of light like a falling star. The UM flew toward them from the west, moving incredibly fast.

The robot's gun fired even as it flicked upward to acquire the new target.

The glass shattered. The mass of people on the street beside her seemed to disintegrate into blood and cloth tatters. A moment later she registered the sound of the gun, a thunderous *ba-rap!* The crowd pulsed away from her, releasing its pressure, and she collapsed to the ground.

The slaybot broke into a clumsy stomping run, its gun ripping at the air.

Matti had rolled away from her. Elena touched his shoulder, turned him over. His eyes were open, but unmoving, glassy.

The air seemed to freeze. She couldn't breathe, couldn't move her hand from him.

He blinked. Then he began to scream.

Elena got to her knees. Her left hand was bloody and freckled with glass; her fingers glistened. Each movement triggered the prick of a thousand tiny needles. Matti screamed and screamed.

"It's okay, it's okay," she said. "I'm right here."

She talked to him for almost a minute before he calmed down enough to hear her and stop screaming.

The window was gone, the shop door blown open. The window case was filled with foam heads on posts, some with wigs askew, others tipped over and bald. She got Matti to take her hand—her good hand—and led him toward the doorway. She was thankful that he could not see the things they stepped over.

Inside the scene was remarkably similar. Arms and legs of all sizes hung from straps on the walls. Trays of dentures sat out on the countertops. A score of heads sported hairstyles old-fashioned even by Trovenian standards. There were several such shops across the city. Decent business in a land of amputees.

Elena's face had begun to burn. She walked Matti through the dark, kicking aside prosthetic limbs, and found a tiny bathroom at the back of the shop. She pulled on the chain to the fluorescent light and was surprised when it flickered to life.

This was her first good look at Matti's face. The skin was bright red, puffy and raw looking—a second-degree burn at least.

She guided the boy to the sink and helped him drink from the tap. It was the only thing she could think of to do for him. Then she helped him sit on the floor just outside the bathroom door.

She could no longer avoid looking in the mirror.

The shattering glass had turned half of her face into a speckled red mask. She ran her hands under the water, not daring to scrub, and then splashed water on her face. She dabbed at her cheek and jaw with the tail of her shirt but the blood continued to weep through a peppering of cuts. She looked like a cartoon in Matti's Lord Grimm book, the coloring accomplished by tiny dots.

She reached into her jacket and took out the leather work gloves she'd stuffed there when she emptied her locker. She pulled one onto her wounded hand, stifling the urge to shout.

"Hello?" Matti said.

She turned, alarmed. Matti wasn't talking to her. His face was turned toward the hallway.

Elena stepped out. A few feet away was the base of a set of stairs that led up into the back of the building. A man stood at the first landing, pointing an ancient rifle at the boy. His jaw was flesh-toned plastic, held in place by an arrangement of leather straps and mechanical springs. A woman with outrageously golden hair stood higher on the stairs, leaning around the corner to look over the man's shoulder.

The man's jaw clacked and he gestured with the gun. "Go. Get along," he said. The syllables were distorted.

"They're hurt," the wigged woman said.

The man did not quite shake his head. Of course they're hurt, he seemed to say. Everyone's hurt. It's the national condition.

"We didn't mean to break in," Elena said. She held up her hands. "We're going." She glanced back into the showroom. Outside the smashed window, the street was still packed, and no one seemed to be moving.

"The bridge is out," the man said. He meant the Prince's Bridge, the only paved bridge that crossed the river. No wonder then that the crowd was moving so slowly.

"They're taking the wounded to the mill," the woman said. "Then trying to get them out of the city by the foot bridges."

"What mill?" Elena asked.

The wigged woman wouldn't take them herself, but she gave directions. "Go out the back," she said.

The millrace had dried out and the mill had been abandoned fifty years ago, but its musty, barnlike interior still smelled of grain. Its rooms were already crowded with injured soldiers and citizens.

Elena found a spot for Matti on a bench inside the building and told him not to move. She went from room to room asking if anyone had aspirin, antibiotic cream, anything to help the boy. She soon stopped asking. There didn't seem to be any doctors or nurses at the mill, only wounded people helping the more severely wounded, and no medicines to be found. This wasn't a medical clinic, or even a triage center. It was a way station.

She came back to find that Matti had fallen asleep on the gray-furred shoulder of a veteran zoomando. She told the man that if the boy woke up she would be outside helping unload the wounded. Every few minutes another farm truck pulled up and bleeding men and women stepped out or were passed down on litters. The emptied trucks rumbled south back into the heart of the city.

The conversation in the mill traded in rumor and wild speculation. But what report could be disbelieved when it came to the U-Men? Fifty of them were attacking, or a hundred. Lord Grimm was both dead and still fighting on the battlements. The MoGs had escaped from the mines in the confusion.

Like everyone else Elena quickly grew deaf to gunfire, explosions, crackling energy beams. Only when something erupted particularly close—a nearby building bursting into flame, or a terrordactyl careening out of control overhead—did the workers look up or pause in their conversation.

At some point a woman in the red smock of the Gene Corps noticed that Elena's cheek had started bleeding again. "It's a wonder you didn't lose an eye," the scientist said, and gave her a wad of torn-up cloth to press to her face. "You need to get that cleaned up or it will scar."

Elena thanked her curtly and walked outside. The air was cold but felt good on her skin.

She was still dabbing at her face when she heard the sputter of engines. An old mechaneer cavalryman, painted head to wheels in mud, rolled into the north end of the yard, followed by two of his wheeled brethren. Each of them was towing a narrow cart padded with blankets.

The lead mechaneer didn't notice Elena at first, or perhaps noticed her but didn't recognize her. He suddenly said, "My beautiful Elena!" and puttered forward, dragging the squeaking cart after him. He put on a smile but couldn't hold it.

"Not so beautiful, Mr. Bojars."

The old man surveyed her face with alarm. "But you are all right?" he asked. "Is Mattias—?"

"I'm fine. Matti is inside. He's sick. I think he…." She shook her head. "I see you've lost your sausage oven."

"A temporary substitution only, my dear." The surviving members of his old unit had reunited, he told her matter-of-factly, to do what they could. In the hours since the Prince's Bridge had been knocked out they'd been ferrying wounded across the river. A field hospital had been set up at the northern barracks of the city guard. The only ways across the river were the foot bridges and a few muddy low spots in the river. "We have no weapons," Mr. Bojars said, "but we can still drive like demons."

Volunteers were already carrying out the people chosen to evacuate next, four men and two women who seemed barely alive. Each cart could carry only two persons at a time, laid head to foot. Elena helped secure them.

"Mr. Bojars, does the hospital have anything for radiation poisoning?"

"Radiation?" He looked shocked. "I don't know, I suppose…"

One of the mechaneers waved to Mr. Bojars, and the two wheeled men began to roll out.

Elena said, "Mr. Bojars—"

"Get him," he replied.

Elena ran into the mill, dodging pallets and bodies. She scooped up the sleeping boy, ignoring the pain in her hand, and carried him back outside. She could feel his body trembling in her arms.

"I can't find my book," Matti said. He sounded feverish. "I think I lost it."

"Matti, you're going with Mr. Bojars," Elena said. "He's going to take you someplace safe."

He seemed to wake up. He looked around, but it was obvious he still couldn't see. "Elena, no! We have to get Grandmother!"

"Matti, listen to me. You're going across the river to the hospital. They have medicine. In the morning I'll come get you."

"She's still in the basement. She's still there. You promised you would—"

"Yes, I promise!" Elena said. "Now go with Mr. Bojars."

"Matti, my boy, we shall have such a ride!" the mechaneer said with forced good humor. He opened his big green parka and held out his arms.

Matti released his grip on Elena. Mr. Bojars set the boy on the broad gas tank in front of him, then zipped up the jacket so that only Matti's head was visible. "Now we look like a cybernetic kangaroo, hey Mattias?"

"I'll be there in the morning," Elena said. She kissed Matti's forehead, then kissed the old man's cheek. He smelled of grilled onions and diesel. "I can't thank you enough," she said.

Mr. Bojars circled an arm around Matti and revved his engine. "A kiss from you, my dear, is payment enough."

She watched them go. A few minutes later another truck arrived in the yard and she fell in line to help carry in the wounded. When the new arrivals were all inside and the stained litters had all been returned to the truck, Elena stayed out in the yard. The truck drivers, a pair of women in coveralls, leaned against the hood. The truck's two-way radio played ocean noise: whooshing static mixed with high, panicked pleas like the cries of seagulls. The larger of the women took a last drag on her cigarette, tossed it into the yard, and then both of them climbed into the cab. A minute later the vehicle started and began to move.

"Shit," Elena said. She jogged after the truck for a few steps, then broke into a full run. She caught up to it as it reached the road. With her good hand she hauled herself up into the open bed.

The driver slowed and leaned out her window. "We're leaving now!" she shouted. "Going back in!"

"So go!" Elena said.

The driver shook her head. The truck lurched into second gear and rumbled south.

As they rolled into the city proper it was impossible for Elena to tell where they would find the front line of the battle, or if there was a front line at all. Damage seemed to be distributed randomly. The truck would roll through a sleepy side street that was completely untouched, and twenty yards away the buildings would be cracked open, their contents shaken into the street.

The drivers seemed to possess some sixth sense for knowing where the injured were waiting. The truck would slow and men and women would emerge from the dark and hobble toward the headlights of the truck, or call for a litter. Some people stood at street corners and waved them down as if flagging a bus. Elena helped the drivers lift the wounded into the back, and sometimes had to force them to leave their belongings.

"Small boats," the largest driver said over and over. A Trovenian saying: In a storm, all boats are too small.

Eventually she found herself crouched next to a burned dragoon who was half-welded to his jet pack. She held his hand, thinking that might give him something to feel besides the pain, but he only moaned and muttered to himself, seemingly oblivious to her presence.

The truck slammed to a stop, sending everyone sliding and crashing into each other. Through the slats Elena glimpsed a great slab of blue, some huge, organic shape. A leg. A giant's leg. The U-Man had to be bigger than an apartment building. Gunfire clattered, and a voice like a fog horn shouted something in English.

The truck lurched into reverse, engine whining, and Elena fell forward onto her hands. Someone in the truck bed cried, "Does he see us? Does he see us?"

The truck backed to the intersection and turned hard. The occupants shouted as they collapsed into each other yet again. Half a block more the truck braked to a more gradual stop and the drivers hopped out. "Is everyone okay?" they asked.

The dragoon beside Elena laughed.

She stood up and looked around. They were in the residential district, only a few blocks from her apartment. She made her way to the gate of the truck and hopped down. She said to the driver, "I'm not going back with you."

The woman nodded, not needing or wanting an explanation.

Elena walked slowly between the hulking buildings. The pain in her hand, her face, all seemed to be returning.

She emerged into a large open space. She realized she'd been mistaken about where the truck had stopped—this park was nowhere she recognized. The ground in front of her had been turned to glass.

The sky to the east glowed. For a moment she thought it was another super-powered UM. But no, only the dawn. Below the dark bulk of Mount Kriegstahl stood the familiar silhouette of the Slaybot Prime bolted to its gantry. The air battle had moved there, above the factories and docks. Or maybe no battle at all. There seemed to be only a few flyers in the air now. The planes and TDs had disappeared. Perhaps the only ones left were U-Men.

Power bolts zipped through the air. They were firing at the Prime.

A great metal arm dropped away from its shoulder socket and dangled by thick cables. Another flash of energy severed them. The arm fell away in seeming slow motion, and the sound of the impact reached her a moment later. The übermenschen were carving the damn thing up.

She almost laughed. The Slaybot Prime was as mobile and dangerous as the Statue of Liberty. Were they actually afraid of the thing? Was that why an army of them had shown up for an ordinary hostage rescue?

My God, she thought, the morons had actually believed Lord Grimm's boasting.

She walked west, and the rising sun turned the glazed surface in front of her into a mirror. She knew now that she wasn't lost. The scorched buildings surrounding the open space were too familiar. But she kept walking. After a while she noticed that the ground was strangely warm beneath her feet. Hot even.

She looked back the way she'd come, then decided the distance was shorter ahead. She was too tired to run outright but managed a shuffling trot. Reckoning by rough triangulation from the nearest buildings she decided she was passing over Mr. Bojars favorite spot, the corner of Glorious Victory Street and Infinite Progress Avenue. Her own apartment building should have loomed directly in front of her.

After all she'd seen tonight she couldn't doubt that there were beings with the power to melt a city block to slag. But she didn't know what strange ability, or even stranger whim, allowed them to casually trowel it into a quartz skating rink.

She heard another boom behind her. The Slaybot Prime was headless now. The southern gantry peeled away, and then the body itself began to lean. Elena had been inside the thing; the chest assembly alone was as big as a cathedral.

The Slaybot Prime slowly bowed, deeper, deeper, until it tumbled off the pillars of its legs. Dust leaped into the sky where it fell. The tremor moved under Elena, sending cracks snaking across the glass.

The collapse of the Prime seemed to signal the end of the fighting. The sounds of the energy blasts ceased. Figures flew in from all points of the city and coalesced above the industrial sector. In less than a minute there were dozens and dozens of them, small and dark as blackcap geese. Then she realized that the flock of übermenschen was flying toward her.

Elena glanced to her left, then right. She was as exposed as a pea on a plate. The glass plain ended fifty or sixty meters away at a line of rubble. She turned and ran.

She listened to the hiss of breath in her throat and the smack of her heavy boots against the crystalline surface. She was surprised at every moment that she did not crash through.

Elongated shadows shuddered onto the mirrored ground ahead of her. She ran faster, arms swinging. The glass abruptly ended in a jagged lip. She leaped, landed on broken ground, and stumbled onto hands and knees. Finally she looked up.

Racing toward her with the sun behind them, the U-Men were nothing but silhouettes—shapes that suggested capes and helmets; swords, hammers, and staffs; bows and shields. Even the energy beings, clothed in shimmering auras, seemed strangely desaturated by the morning light.

Without looking away from the sky she found a chunk of masonry on the ground in front of her. Then she stood and climbed onto a tilting slab of concrete.

When the mass of U-Men was directly above her she heaved with all her might.

Useless. At its peak the gray chunk fell laughably short of the nearest figure. It clattered to the ground somewhere out of sight.

Elena screamed, tensed for—longing for—a searing blast of light, a thunderbolt. Nothing came. The U-Men vanished over the roof of the next apartment building, heading out to sea.

Weeks after the invasion, the factory remained closed. Workers began to congregate there anyway. Some mornings they pushed around brooms or cleared debris, but mostly they played cards, exchanged stories of the invasion, and speculated on rumors. Lord Grimm had not been seen since the attack. Everyone agreed that the Savior of Trovenia had been dead too many times to doubt his eventual resurrection.

When Elena finally returned, eighteen days after the invasion, she found Verner and Guntis playing chess beside the left boot of the Slaybot Prime. The other huge components of the robot's body were scattered across two miles of the industrial sector like the buildings of a new city.

The men greeted her warmly. Verner, the ancient mechaneer, frankly noted the still-red cuts that cross-hatched the side of her face, but didn't ask how she'd acquired them. If Trovenians told the story of every scar there'd be no end to the talking.

Elena asked about Jürgo and both men frowned. Guntis said that the birdman had taken to the air during the fight. As for the other two members of the heavy plate welding unit, no news.

"I was sorry to hear about your brother," Verner said.

"Yes," Elena said. "Well."

She walked back to the women's changing rooms, and when she didn't find what she was looking for, visited the men's. One cinderblock wall had caved in, but the lockers still stood in orderly rows. She found the locker bearing Jürgo's name on a duct tape label. The door was padlocked shut. It took her a half hour to find a cutting rig with oxygen and acetylene cylinders that weren't empty, but only minutes to wheel the rig to the changing rooms and burn off the lock.

She pulled open the door. Jürgo's old-fashioned, rectangle-eyed welding helmet hung from a hook, staring at her. She thought of Grandmother Zita. *What possesses a person to put a bucket on their head?*

The inside of the locker door was decorated with a column of faded photographs. In one of them a young Jürgo, naked from the waist up, stared into the camera with a concerned squint. His new wings were unfurled behind him. Elena's mother and father, dressed in their red Gene Corps jackets, stood on either side of him. Elena unpeeled the yellowed tape and put the picture in her breast pocket, then unhooked the helmet and closed the door.

She walked back to the old men, pulling the cart behind her. "Are we working today or what?" she asked.

Guntis looked up from the chess board with amusement in his huge wet eyes. "So you are the boss now, eh, Elena?"

Verner, however, said nothing. He seemed to recognize that she was not quite the person she had been. Damaged components had been stripped away, replaced by cruder, yet sturdier approximations. He was old enough to have seen the process repeated many times.

Elena reached into the pockets of her coat and pulled on her leather work gloves. Then she wheeled the cart over to the toe of the boot and straightened the hoses with a flick of her arm.

"Tell us your orders, Your Highness," Guntis said.

"First we tear apart the weapons," she said. She thumbed the blast trigger and blue flame roared from the nozzle of the cutting torch. "Then we build better ones."

She slid the helmet onto her head, flipped down the mask, and bent to work.

EXHALATION

TED CHIANG

It has long been said that air (which others call argon) is the source of life. This is not in fact the case, and I engrave these words to describe how I came to understand the true source of life and, as a corollary, the means by which life will one day end.

For most of history, the proposition that we drew life from air was so obvious that there was no need to assert it. Every day we consume two lungs heavy with air; every day we remove the empty ones from our chest and replace them with full ones. If a person is careless and lets his air level run too low, he feels the heaviness of his limbs and the growing need for replenishment. It is exceedingly rare that a person is unable to get at least one replacement lung before his installed pair runs empty; on those unfortunate occasions where this has happened—when a person is trapped and unable to move, with no one nearby to assist him—he dies within seconds of his air running out.

But in the normal course of life, our need for air is far from our thoughts, and indeed many would say that satisfying that need is the least important part of going to the filling stations. For the filling stations are the primary venue for social conversation, the places from which we draw emotional sustenance as well as physical. We all keep spare sets of full lungs in our homes, but when one is alone, the act of opening one's chest and replacing one's lungs can seem little better than a chore. In the company of others, however, it becomes a communal activity, a shared pleasure.

If one is exceedingly busy, or feeling unsociable, one might simply pick up a pair of full lungs, install them, and leave one's emptied lungs on the other side of the room. If one has a few minutes to spare, it's simple courtesy to connect the empty lungs to an air dispenser and refill them for the next person. But by far the most common practice is to linger and enjoy the company of others, to discuss the news of the day with friends or acquaintances and, in passing, offer newly filled lungs to one's interlocutor. While this perhaps does not constitute air sharing in the strictest sense, there is camaraderie derived from the awareness that all our air comes from the same source, for the dispensers are but the exposed terminals of pipes extending from the reservoir of air deep underground, the great lung of the world, the source of all our nourishment.

Many lungs are returned to the same filling station the next day, but just as many circulate to other stations when people visit neighboring districts; the lungs are all identical in appearance, smooth cylinders of aluminum, so one cannot tell whether a given lung has always stayed close to home or whether it has traveled long distances. And just as lungs are passed between persons and districts, so are news and gossip. In this way one can receive news from remote districts, even those at the very edge of the world, without needing to leave home, although I myself enjoy traveling. I have journeyed all the way to the edge of the world, and seen the solid chromium wall that extends from the ground up into the infinite sky.

It was at one of the filling stations that I first heard the rumors that prompted my investigation and led to my eventual enlightenment. It began innocently enough, with a remark from our district's public crier. At noon of the first day of every year, it is traditional for the crier to recite a passage of verse, an ode composed long ago for this annual celebration, which takes exactly one hour to deliver. The crier mentioned that on his most recent performance, the turret clock struck the hour before he had finished, something that had never happened before. Another person remarked that this was a coincidence, because he had just returned from a nearby district where the public crier had complained of the same incongruity.

No one gave the matter much thought beyond the simple acknowledgement that seemed warranted. It was only some days later, when there arrived word of a similar deviation between the crier and the clock of a third district, that the suggestion was made that these discrepancies might be evidence of a defect in the mechanism common to all the turret clocks, albeit a curious one to cause the clocks to run faster rather than slower. Horologists investigated the turret clocks in question, but on inspection they could discern no imperfection. In fact, when compared against the timepieces normally employed for such calibration purposes, the turret clocks were all found to have resumed keeping perfect time.

I myself found the question somewhat intriguing, but I was too focused on my own studies to devote much thought to other matters. I was and am a student of anatomy, and to provide context for my subsequent actions, I now offer a brief account of my relationship with the field.

Death is uncommon, fortunately, because we are durable and fatal mishaps are rare, but it makes difficult the study of anatomy, especially since many of the accidents serious enough to cause death leave the deceased's remains too damaged for study. If lungs are ruptured when full, the explosive force can tear a body asunder, ripping the titanium as easily as if it were tin. In the past, anatomists focused their attention on the limbs, which were the most likely to survive intact. During the very first anatomy lecture I attended a century ago, the lecturer showed us a severed arm, the casing removed to reveal the dense column of rods and pistons within. I can vividly recall the way, after he had connected its arterial hoses to a wall-mounted lung he kept in the laboratory, he was able to manipulate the actuating rods that protruded from the arm's ragged base, and in response the hand would open and close fitfully.

In the intervening years, our field has advanced to the point where anatomists are able to repair damaged limbs and, on occasion, attach a severed limb. At the same time we have become capable of studying the physiology of the living; I have given a version of that first lecture I saw, during which I opened the casing of my own arm and directed my students' attention to the rods that contracted and extended when I wiggled my fingers.

Despite these advances, the field of anatomy still had a great unsolved mystery at its core: the question of memory. While we knew a little about the structure of the brain, its physiology is notoriously hard to study because of the brain's extreme delicacy. It is typically the case in fatal accidents that, when the skull is breached, the brain erupts in a cloud of gold, leaving little besides shredded filament and leaf from which nothing useful can be discerned. For decades the prevailing theory of memory was that all of a person's experiences were engraved on sheets of gold foil; it was these sheets, torn apart by the force of the blast, that was the source of the tiny flakes found after accidents. Anatomists would collect the bits of gold leaf—so thin that light passes greenly through them—and spend years trying to reconstruct the original sheets, with the hope of eventually deciphering the symbols in which the deceased's recent experiences were inscribed.

I did not subscribe to this theory, known as the inscription hypothesis, for the simple reason that if all our experiences are in fact recorded, why is it that our memories are incomplete? Advocates of the inscription hypothesis offered an explanation for forgetfulness—suggesting that over time the foil sheets become misaligned from the stylus which reads the memories, until the oldest sheets shift out of contact with it altogether—but I never found it convincing. The appeal of the theory was easy for me to appreciate, though; I too had devoted many an hour to examining flakes of gold through a microscope, and can imagine how gratifying it would be to turn the fine adjustment knob and see legible symbols come into focus.

More than that, how wonderful would it be to decipher the very oldest of a deceased person's memories, ones that he himself had forgotten? None of us can remember much more than a hundred years in the past, and written records—accounts that we ourselves inscribed but have scant memory of doing so—extend only a few hundred years before that. How many years did we live before the beginning of written history? Where did we come from? It is the promise of finding the answers within our own brains that makes the inscription hypothesis so seductive.

I was a proponent of the competing school of thought, which held that our memories were stored in some medium in which the process of erasure was no more difficult than recording: perhaps in the rotation of gears, or the positions of a series of switches. This theory implied that everything we had forgotten was indeed lost, and our brains contained no histories older than those found in our libraries. One advantage of this theory was that it better explained why, when lungs are installed in those who have died from lack of air, the revived have no memories and are all but mindless: somehow the shock of death had reset all the gears or switches. The inscriptionists claimed the shock had merely misaligned the foil sheets, but no one was willing to kill a living person, even an imbecile, in order to resolve the debate. I had envisioned an experiment which might allow me to determine the truth conclusively, but it was a risky one, and deserved careful consideration before it was undertaken. I remained undecided for the longest time, until I heard more news about the clock anomaly.

Word arrived from a more distant district that its public crier had likewise observed the turret clock striking the hour before he had finished his new year's recital. What made this notable was that his district's clock employed a different mechanism, one in which the hours were marked by the flow of mercury into a bowl. Here the discrepancy could not be explained by a common mechanical fault. Most people suspected fraud, a practical joke perpetrated by mischief makers. I had a different suspicion, a darker one that I dared not voice, but it decided my course of action; I would proceed with my experiment.

The first tool I constructed was the simplest: in my laboratory I fixed four prisms on mounting brackets and carefully aligned them so that their apexes formed the corners of a rectangle. When arranged thus, a beam of light directed at one of the lower prisms was reflected up, then backward, then down, and then forward again in a quadrilateral loop. Accordingly, when I sat with my eyes at the level of the first prism, I obtained a clear view of the back of my own head. This solipsistic periscope formed the basis of all that was to come.

A similarly rectangular arrangement of actuating rods allowed a displacement of action to accompany the displacement of vision afforded by the prisms. The bank of actuating rods was much larger than the periscope, but still relatively straightforward in design; by contrast, what was attached to the end of these respective mechanisms was far more intricate. To the periscope I added a binocular microscope mounted on an armature capable of swiveling side to side or up and down. To the actuating rods I added an array of precision manipulators, although that description hardly does justice to those pinnacles of the mechanician's art. Combining the ingenuity of anatomists and the inspiration provided by the bodily structures they studied, the manipulators enabled their operator to accomplish any task he might normally perform with his own hands, but on a much smaller scale.

Assembling all of this equipment took months, but I could not afford to be anything less than meticulous. Once the preparations were complete, I was able to place each of my hands on a nest of knobs and levers and control a pair of manipulators situated behind my head, and use the periscope to see what they worked on. I would then be able to dissect my own brain.

The very idea must sound like pure madness, I know, and had I told any of my colleagues, they would surely have tried to stop me. But I could not ask anyone else to risk themselves for the sake of anatomical inquiry, and because I wished to conduct the dissection myself, I would not be satisfied by merely being the passive subject of such an operation. Auto-dissection was the only option.

I brought in a dozen full lungs and connected them with a manifold. I mounted this assembly beneath the worktable that I would sit at, and positioned a dispenser to connect directly to the bronchial inlets within my chest. This would supply me with six days' worth of air. To provide for the possibility that I might not have completed my experiment within that period, I had scheduled a visit from a colleague at the end of that time. My presumption, however, was that the only way I would not have finished the operation in that period would be if I had caused my own death.

I began by removing the deeply curved plate that formed the back and top of my head; then the two, more shallowly curved plates that formed the sides. Only my faceplate remained, but it was locked into a restraining bracket, and I could not see its inner surface from the vantage point of my periscope; what I saw exposed was my own brain. It consisted of a dozen or more subassemblies, whose exteriors were covered by intricately molded shells; by positioning the periscope near the fissures that separated them, I gained a tantalizing glimpse at the fabulous mechanisms within their interiors. Even with what little I could see, I could tell it was the most beautifully complex engine I had ever beheld, so far beyond any device man had constructed that it was incontrovertibly of divine origin. The sight was both exhilarating and dizzying, and I savored it on a strictly aesthetic basis for several minutes before proceeding with my explorations.

It was generally hypothesized that the brain was divided into an engine located in the center of the head which performed the actual cognition, surrounded by an array of components in which memories were stored. What I observed was consistent with this theory, since the peripheral subassemblies seemed to resemble one another, while the subassembly in the center appeared to be different, more heterogenous and with more moving parts. However the components were packed too closely for me to see much of their operation; if I intended to learn anything more, I would require a more intimate vantage point.

Each subassembly had a local reservoir of air, fed by a hose extending from the regulator at the base of my brain. I focused my periscope on the rearmost subassembly and, using the remote manipulators, I quickly disconnected the outlet hose and installed a longer one in its place. I had practiced this maneuver countless times so that I could perform it in a matter of moments; even so, I was not certain I could complete the connection before the subassembly had depleted its local reservoir. Only after I was satisfied that the component's operation had not been interrupted did I continue; I rearranged the longer hose to gain a better view of what lay in the fissure behind it: other hoses that connected it to its neighboring components. Using the most slender pair of manipulators to reach into the narrow crevice, I replaced the hoses one by one with longer substitutes. Eventually, I had worked my way around the entire subassembly and replaced every connection it had to the rest of my brain. I was now able to unmount this subassembly from the frame that supported it, and pull the entire section outside of what was once the back of my head.

I knew it was possible I had impaired my capacity to think and was unable to recognize it, but performing some basic arithmetic tests suggested that I was uninjured. With one subassembly hanging from a scaffold above, I now had a better view of the cognition engine at the center of my brain, but there was not enough room to bring the microscope attachment itself in for a close inspection. In order for me to really examine the workings of my brain, I would have to displace at least half a dozen subassemblies.

Laboriously, painstakingly, I repeated the procedure of substituting hoses for other subassemblies, repositioning another one farther back, two more higher up, and two others out to the sides, suspending all six from the scaffold above my head. When I was done, my brain looked like an explosion frozen an infinitesimal fraction of a second after the detonation, and again I felt dizzy when I thought about it. But at last the cognition engine itself was exposed, supported on a pillar of hoses and actuating rods leading down into my torso. I now also had room to rotate my microscope around a full three hundred and sixty degrees, and pass my gaze across the inner faces of the subassemblies I had moved. What I saw was a microcosm of auric machinery, a landscape of tiny spinning rotors and miniature reciprocating cylinders.

As I contemplated this vista, I wondered, where was my body? The conduits which displaced my vision and action around the room were in principle no different from those which connected my original eyes and hands to my brain. For the duration of this experiment, were these manipulators not essentially my hands? Were the magnifying lenses at the end of my periscope not essentially my eyes? I was an everted person, with my tiny, fragmented body situated at the center of my own distended brain. It was in this unlikely configuration that I began to explore myself.

I turned my microscope to one of the memory subassemblies, and began examining its design. I had no expectation that I would be able to decipher my memories, only that I might divine the means by which they were recorded. As I had predicted, there were no reams of foil pages visible, but to my surprise neither did I see banks of gearwheels or switches. Instead, the subassembly seemed to consist almost entirely of a bank of air tubules. Through the interstices between the tubules I was able to glimpse ripples passing through the bank's interior.

With careful inspection and increasing magnification, I discerned that the tubules ramified into tiny air capillaries, which were interwoven with a dense latticework of wires on which gold leaves were hinged. Under the influence of air escaping from the capillaries, the leaves were held in a variety of positions. These were not switches in the conventional sense, for they did not retain their position without a current of air to support them, but I hypothesized that these were the switches I had sought, the medium in which my memories were recorded. The ripples I saw must have been acts of recall, as an arrangement of leaves was read and sent back to the cognition engine.

Armed with this new understanding, I then turned my microscope to the cognition engine. Here too I observed a latticework of wires, but they did not bear leaves suspended in position; instead the leaves flipped back and forth almost too rapidly to see. Indeed, almost the entire engine appeared to be in motion, consisting more of lattice than of air capillaries, and I wondered how air could reach all the gold leaves in a coherent manner. For many hours I scrutinized the leaves, until I realized that they themselves were playing the role of capillaries; the leaves formed temporary conduits and valves that existed just long enough to redirect air at other leaves in turn, and then disappeared as a result. This was an engine undergoing continuous transformation, indeed modifying itself as part of its operation. The lattice was not so much a machine as it was a page on which the machine was written, and on which the machine itself ceaselessly wrote.

My consciousness could be said to be encoded in the position of these tiny leaves, but it would be more accurate to say that it was encoded in the ever-shifting pattern of air driving these leaves. Watching the oscillations of these flakes of gold, I saw that air does not, as we had always assumed, simply provide power to the engine that realizes our thoughts. Air is in fact the very medium of our thoughts. All that we are is a pattern of air flow. My memories were inscribed, not as grooves on foil or even the position of switches, but as persistent currents of argon.

In the moments after I grasped the nature of this lattice mechanism, a cascade of insights penetrated my consciousness in rapid succession. The first and most trivial was understanding why gold, the most malleable and ductile of metals, was the only material out of which our brains could be made. Only the thinnest of foil leaves could move rapidly enough for such a mechanism, and only the most delicate of filaments could act as hinges for them. By comparison, the copper burr raised by my stylus as I engrave these words and brushed from the sheet when I finish each page is as coarse and heavy as scrap. This truly was a medium where erasing and recording could be performed rapidly, far more so than any arrangement of switches or gears.

What next became clear was why installing full lungs into a person who has died from lack of air does not bring him back to life. These leaves within the lattice remain balanced between continuous cushions of air. This arrangement lets them flit back and forth swiftly, but it also means that if the flow of air ever ceases, everything is lost; the leaves all collapse into identical pendent states, erasing the patterns and the consciousness they represent. Restoring the air supply cannot recreate what has evanesced. This was the price of speed; a more stable medium for storing patterns would mean that our consciousnesses would operate far more slowly.

It was then that I perceived the solution to the clock anomaly. I saw that the speed of these leaves' movements depended on their being supported by air; with sufficient air flow, the leaves could move nearly frictionlessly. If they were moving more slowly, it was because they were being subjected to more friction, which could occur only if the cushions of air that supported them were thinner, and the air flowing through the lattice was moving with less force.

It is not that the turret clocks are running faster. What is happening is that our brains are running slower. The turret clocks are driven by pendulums, whose tempo never varies, or by the flow of mercury through a pipe, which does not change. But our brains rely on the passage of air, and when that air flows more slowly, our thoughts slow down, making the clocks seem to us to run faster.

I had feared that our brains might be growing slower, and it was this prospect that had spurred me to pursue my auto-dissection. But I had assumed that our cognition engines—while powered by air—were ultimately mechanical in nature, and some aspect of the mechanism was gradually becoming deformed through fatigue, and thus responsible for the slowing. That would have been dire, but there was at least the hope that we might be able to repair the mechanism, and restore our brains to their original speed of operation.

But if our thoughts were purely patterns of air rather than the movement of toothed gears, the problem was much more serious, for what could cause the air flowing through every person's brain to move less rapidly? It could not be a decrease in the pressure from our filling stations' dispensers; the air pressure in our lungs is so high that it must be stepped down by a series of regulators before reaching our brains. The diminution in force, I saw, must arise from the opposite direction: the pressure of our surrounding atmosphere was increasing.

How could this be? As soon as the question formed, the only possible answer became apparent: our sky must not be infinite in height. Somewhere above the limits of our vision, the chromium walls surrounding our world must curve inward to form a dome; our universe is a sealed chamber rather than an open well. And air is gradually accumulating within that chamber, until it equals the pressure in the reservoir below.

This is why, at the beginning of this engraving, I said that air is not the source of life. Air can neither be created nor destroyed; the total amount of air in the universe remains constant, and if air were all that we needed to live, we would never die. But in truth the source of life is *a difference in air pressure*, the flow of air from spaces where it is thick to those where it is thin. The activity of our brains, the motion of our bodies, the action of every machine we have ever built is driven by the movement of air, the force exerted as differing pressures seek to balance each other out. When the pressure everywhere in the universe is the same, all air will be motionless, and useless; one day we will be surrounded by motionless air and unable to derive any benefit from it.

We are not really consuming air at all. The amount of air that I draw from each day's new pair of lungs is exactly as much as seeps out through the joints of my limbs and the seams of my casing, exactly as much as I am adding to the atmosphere around me; all I am doing is converting air at high pressure to air at low. With every movement of my body, I contribute to the equalization of pressure in our universe. With every thought that I have, I hasten the arrival of that fatal equilibrium.

Had I come to this realization under any other circumstance, I would have leapt up from my chair and ran into the streets, but in my current situation—body locked in a restraining bracket, brain suspended across my laboratory—doing so was impossible. I could see the leaves of my brain flitting faster from the tumult of my thoughts, which in turn increased my agitation at being so restrained and immobile. Panic at that moment might have led to my death, a nightmarish paroxysm of simultaneously being trapped and spiraling out of control, struggling against my restraints until my air ran out. It was by chance as much as by intention that my hands adjusted the controls to avert my periscopic gaze

from the latticework, so all I could see was the plain surface of my worktable. Thus freed from having to see and magnify my own apprehensions,
I was able to calm down. When I had regained sufficient composure, I
began the lengthy process of reassembling myself. Eventually I restored
my brain to its original compact configuration, reattached the plates of
my head, and released myself from the restraining bracket.

At first the other anatomists did not believe me when I told them what
I had discovered, but in the months that followed my initial auto-dissection, more and more of them became convinced. More examinations
of people's brains were performed, more measurements of atmospheric
pressure were taken, and the results were all found to confirm my claims.
The background air pressure of our universe was indeed increasing, and
slowing our thoughts as a result.

There was widespread panic in the days after the truth first became
widely know, as people contemplated for the first time the idea that
death was inevitable. Many called for the strict curtailment of activities
in order to minimize the thickening of our atmosphere; accusations of
wasted air escalated into furious brawls and, in some districts, deaths. It
was the shame of having caused these deaths, together with the reminder
that it would be many centuries yet before our atmosphere's pressure
became equal to that of the reservoir underground, that caused the
panic to subside. We are not sure precisely how many centuries it will
take; additional measurements and calculations are being performed
and debated. In the meantime, there is much discussion over how we
should spend the time that remains to us.

One sect has dedicated itself to the goal of reversing the equalization
of pressure, and found many adherents. The mechanicians among
them constructed an engine that takes air from our atmosphere and
forces it into a smaller volume, a process they called "compression."
Their engine restores air to the pressure it originally had in the reservoir, and these Reversalists excitedly announced that it would form the
basis of a new kind of filling station, one that would—with each lung
it refilled—revitalize not only individuals but the universe itself. Alas,
closer examination of the engine revealed its fatal flaw. The engine itself
is powered by air from the reservoir, and for every lungful of air that it
produces, the engine consumes not just a lungful, but slightly more. It
does not reverse the process of equalization, but like everything else in
the world, exacerbates it.

Although some of their adherents left in disillusionment after this
setback, the Reversalists as a group were undeterred, and began drawing

up alternate designs in which the compressor was powered instead by the uncoiling of springs or the descent of weights. These mechanisms fared no better. Every spring that is wound tight represents air released by the person who did the winding; every weight that rests higher than ground level represents air released by the person who did the lifting. There is no source of power in the universe that does not ultimately derive from a difference in air pressure, and there can be no engine whose operation will not, on balance, reduce that difference.

The Reversalists continue their labors, confident that they will one day construct an engine that generates more compression than it uses, a perpetual power source that will restore to the universe its lost vigor. I do not share their optimism; I believe that the process of equalization is inexorable. Eventually, all the air in our universe will be evenly distributed, no denser or more rarefied in one spot than in any other, unable to drive a piston, turn a rotor, or flip a leaf of gold foil. It will be the end of pressure, the end of motive power, the end of thought. The universe will have reached perfect equilibrium.

Some find irony in the fact that a study of our brains revealed to us not the secrets of the past, but what ultimately awaits us in the future. However, I maintain that we have indeed learned something important about the past. The universe began as an enormous breath being held. Who knows why, but whatever the reason, I am glad that it did, because I owe my existence to that fact. All my desires and ruminations are no more and no less than eddy currents generated by the gradual exhalation of our universe. And until this great exhalation is finished, my thoughts live on.

So that our thoughts may continue as long as possible, anatomists and mechanicians are designing replacements for our cerebral regulators, capable of gradually increasing the air pressure within our brains and keeping it just higher than the surrounding atmospheric pressure. Once these are installed, our thoughts will continue at roughly the same speed even as the air thickens around us. But this does not mean that life will continue unchanged. Eventually the pressure differential will fall to such a level that our limbs will weaken and our movements will grow sluggish. We may then try to slow our thoughts so that our physical torpor is less conspicuous to us, but that will also cause external processes to appear to accelerate. The ticking of clocks will rise to a chatter as their pendulums wave frantically; falling objects will slam to the ground as if propelled by springs; undulations will race down cables like the crack of a whip.

At some point our limbs will cease moving altogether. I cannot be certain of the precise sequence of events near the end, but I imagine a scenario in which our thoughts will continue to operate, so that we remain conscious but frozen, immobile as statues. Perhaps we'll be able to speak for a while longer, because our voice boxes operate on a smaller pressure differential than our limbs, but without the ability to visit a filling station, every utterance will reduce the amount of air left for thought, and bring us closer to the moment that our thoughts cease altogether. Will it be preferable to remain mute to prolong our ability to think, or to talk until the very end? I don't know.

Perhaps a few of us, in the days before we cease moving, will be able to connect our cerebral regulators directly to the dispensers in the filling stations, in effect replacing our lungs with the mighty lung of the world. If so, those few will be able to remain conscious right up to the final moments before all pressure is equalized. The last bit of air pressure left in our universe will be expended driving a person's conscious thought.

And then, our universe will be in a state of absolute equilibrium. All life and thought will cease, and with them, time itself.

But I maintain a slender hope.

Even though our universe is enclosed, perhaps it is not the only air chamber in the infinite expanse of solid chromium. I speculate that there could be another pocket of air elsewhere, another universe besides our own that is even larger in volume. It is possible that this hypothetical universe has the same or higher air pressure as ours, but suppose that it had a much lower air pressure than ours, perhaps even a true vacuum?

The chromium that separates us from this supposed universe is too thick and too hard for us to drill through, so there is no way we could reach it ourselves, no way to bleed off the excess atmosphere from our universe and regain motive power that way. But I fantasize that this neighboring universe has its own inhabitants, ones with capabilities beyond our own. What if they were able to create a conduit between the two universes, and install valves to release air from ours? They might use our universe as a reservoir, running dispensers with which they could fill their own lungs, and use our air as a way to drive their own civilization.

It cheers me to imagine that the air that once powered me could power others, to believe that the breath that enables me to engrave these words could one day flow through someone else's body. I do not delude myself into thinking that this would be a way for me to live again, because I am not that air, I am the pattern that it assumed, temporarily. The pattern that is me, the patterns that are the entire world in which I live, would be gone.

But I have an even fainter hope: that those inhabitants not only use our universe as a reservoir, but that once they have emptied it of its air, they might one day be able to open a passage and actually enter our universe as explorers. They might wander our streets, see our frozen bodies, look through our possessions, and wonder about the lives we led.

Which is why I have written this account. You, I hope, are one of those explorers. You, I hope, found these sheets of copper and deciphered the words engraved on their surfaces. And whether or not your brain is impelled by the air that once impelled mine, through the act of reading my words, the patterns that form your thoughts become an imitation of the patterns that once formed mine. And in that way I live again, through you.

Your fellow explorers will have found and read the other books that we left behind, and through the collaborative action of your imaginations, my entire civilization lives again. As you walk through our silent districts, imagine them as they were; with the turret clocks striking the hours, the filling stations crowded with gossiping neighbors, criers reciting verse in the public squares and anatomists giving lectures in the classrooms. Visualize all of these the next time you look at the frozen world around you, and it will become, in your minds, animated and vital again.

I wish you well, explorer, but I wonder: Does the same fate that befell me await you? I can only imagine that it must, that the tendency toward equilibrium is not a trait peculiar to our universe but inherent in all universes. Perhaps that is just a limitation of my thinking, and your people have discovered a source of pressure that is truly eternal. But my speculations are fanciful enough already. I will assume that one day your thoughts too will cease, although I cannot fathom how far in the future that might be. Your lives will end just as ours did, just as everyone's must. No matter how long it takes, eventually equilibrium will be reached.

I hope you are not saddened by that awareness. I hope that your expedition was more than a search for other universes to use as reservoirs. I hope that you were motivated by a desire for knowledge, a yearning to see what can arise from a universe's exhalation. Because even if a universe's lifespan is calculable, the variety of life that is generated within it is not. The buildings we have erected, the art and music and verse we have composed, the very lives we've led: none of them could have been predicted, because none of them were inevitable. Our universe might have slid into equilibrium emitting nothing more than a quiet hiss. The fact that it spawned such plenitude is a miracle, one that is matched only by your universe giving rise to you.

Though I am long dead as you read this, explorer, I offer to you a valediction. Contemplate the marvel that is existence, and rejoice that you are able to do so. I feel I have the right to tell you this because, as I am inscribing these words, I am doing the same.

DOWN AND OUT IN THE MAGIC KINGDOM

DAVID MOLES

THE TWINKS FELL INTO DRAGONTOWN

The twinks fell into Dragontown out of the noonday sun, a constellation of spiky-black shapes each with its own trail of shadow like the tail of a cartoon meteor, darkening the tropical-blue sky, scattering frightened critters from the scaled rooftops. They were every race in the Legion: mandrill-faced bavians, jackal-headed anubit and anubim, black-beaked corven and leathery-winged gaunts, fiery clowns and scaled salamanders, goblins, mechanists, satyrs, araneae, orcas and cuttlemen. They were, every one of them, extravagantly mounted, every one level-capped, every one gaudily equipped and maximally buffed.

And not one of them belonged in Dragontown.

Dragontown was a neutral town, a sleepy town deep in the mid-levels. A stopping-point, once, for guests on their way to the Outlands or the Newlands or the Deathlands; but these days even the Newlands were old news. There were only a handful of guests in Dragontown to bear witness to the Legion's invasion, to applaud or run for cover or (like the old perroquet airmaster Valerius Redbeak, who had given up battlegrounds and quests alike in the long-ago days of the seventh expansion, and now spent his days fishing off Bonetalon Pier) simply roll their eyes, according to each guest's faction and sophistication.

Dragontown's cast members—its shopkeepers, quest givers, color characters and crafting trainers—had the twinks marked down for what they were almost from the moment they appeared in the sky. Twinks, because any guest invested enough in the game to acquire the invaders' rank and gear by legitimate means had better places to be than Dragontown; griefers, because no gathering of that many high-level guests together in the mid-levels could have anything in mind but trouble.

Against that trouble, there was little the cast members, most of them as mid-level as the town itself, could do to prepare. As the horde of twinks descended, Dragontown's cast members tucked their chins, breathed deeply, put on their most professional faces, resolved to lose no seniority by breaking character; resolved, if necessary, to make use of the cast member's last recourse against an abusive guest.

Resolved, that is, to die.

But the twinks' griefing, if griefing it was, took an unexpected and nonviolent form. The twinks—bavians, corven, mechanists and the rest—came down scattered from Skull House to the hill of the Spine to the ends of the Talons. There was one twink, exactly one, for each cast member in Dragontown. Ignoring the other guests, ignoring the bluster of the cast members costumed as Dragon Guards, each twink sought out his, her or its chosen cast member and, in a language that was neither Dragontongue nor Legionary, asked a simple question.

The twink confronting Imogen Fairweather, human, who sold fishing supplies from a shack on Bonetalon Pier, was a bavian warlord of the highest rank. He dropped from the saddle of his giant, vulture-winged hyena-griff and planted himself in front of Imogen's shack, his hairy simian form, powerful though it was, nearly dwarfed by the huge curling shoulder-pieces of his ornate, rune-carved obsidian armor.

As Imogen opened her mouth to begin her rehearsed sales pitch, the bavian spoke (in a voice like tearing metal, like the burning of cities) seven Wu-accented words of Mandarin Chinese:

"Peng Yueying," the twink said, "would you like to go home?"

THE KINGDOM SURRENDERED ON A TUESDAY

The Kingdom surrendered on a Tuesday.

Perhaps a year had gone by since the twink invasion, perhaps no more than a fiscal quarter. It was hard to know, in the Kingdom, where the closest thing to a calendar was the endless succession of Maintenance Tuesdays.

The cast had known something like this was coming ever since the Kingdom's owners had gone into bankruptcy protection, but Imogen (whose name once had, yes, been Peng Yueying) had hoped for some gimmick—a new marketing campaign, another major patch, even the long-delayed ninth expansion—to hold back the rot a little longer, maybe even long enough for her and Kallia to vest.

Kallia—Kallia Darkwater, Imogen's Legion counterpart and nominal rival, who from a coral-walled cave some five fathoms below Imogen's shack sold a more or less identical selection of fishing supplies—was already home, half-submerged in the heated pool that served their backstage apartment for a sitting room, when Imogen came through the door. Kallia held an official-looking scroll unrolled in her long, boneless blue fingers.

"The MoGuo Corporation, Limited," Kallia declaimed, "is pleased to announce the approval, by the arbitrator-appointed trustees, of the transfer of all content, intellectual property, and intangible assets of the MoGuo Corporation to Ambrayses ACP, effective immediately." The initials were in English; the rest was in Dragontongue, the only language she and Imogen really had in common. As a language, Dragontongue was florid, metaphorical, allusive and cliché-ridden, but when it came to matters of finance and contract it could be eerily precise. "Ambrayses ACP, for its part, looks forward to a new era of immersive worldbuilding… dynamic realism… growth of the player base… investment…" She rolled up the scroll and tossed it to Imogen. "Blah, blah, blah."

"What's an ACP?" Imogen asked, opening the scroll.

"Autonomous Contracting Party," said Kallia.

"The Kingdom's sold out to an *AI*?" Imogen said—or tried to. In Dragontongue, the nearest she could get to *sold out* was *traded eggs for sheep*. For *AI*, she used the English, and knew she was mangling it.

"Get used to it, sister," said Kallia. "Ten percent of the player base is AI, and it's the only part that's growing. There aren't enough flesh humans left who can afford the gear, and free posthumans can only stay interested in men-in-tights games for so long."

Imogen found she shared the sentiment. In her mind she heard again the bavian twink; heard, in that cartoon-monster voice, those seven words of Chinese. Heard her original—she corrected herself—her *real* name.

The invading twinks had been swiftly banned, of course, but that hadn't stopped a repeat performance two weeks later, the twinks this time not Legion but League—humans, merlings, perroquets, 'quatchen and so on, their armor gleaming the silver of winter stars and the gold of angels' wings. The one who came to Imogen was a terrapin sea-shepherd, his shell thick and crusted with barnacles beneath a great hooded mantle of living kelp. His Mandarin (again with the same hint of Wu that had been Peng Yueying's own) was as fluent as the bavian's, his voice like the crash of surf and the songs of great whales.

"Peng Yueying," the terrapin told her gravely, "you're going to need a friend on the outside."

But Imogen was prepared this time, and her answer, in Dragontongue, came straight from the script—specifically the section titled Dealing Politely With Guests Who Break Character.

"Don't think we carry any of that, sir," she told the terrapin. "But perhaps I can interest you in these fine Scaletooth Lures?"

She hadn't answered the bavian at all, only stared open-mouthed until—some assistant director moving with unusual speed—the banhammer came down and the twinks vanished from the Kingdom, leaving Dragontown's cast members blinking in the suddenly brighter sunlight. No one would admit to answering the twinks. There was a shared, unspoken feeling among the cast members that even to discuss the incident during the Tuesday downtime would, in some way, constitute a break of character, and incur a corresponding loss of seniority.

And seniority was everything. Seniority was a cast member's ticket out, the end of servitude, the end of guests and scripts and the limitations imposed by the Kingdom's rules and roles—and the beginning of true immortality, in the limitless, protean form available only to a fully realized posthuman.

Like the rest of the Kingdom's cast—like more than ninety-nine percent of the world's dwindling (but still enormous) population of flesh humans—Imogen, or rather Yueying, could never have paid for the transfer process herself. She'd sold her soul to the Kingdom, and she was buying it back, on the installment plan.

"How screwed are we?" she asked Kallia. (In Dragontongue: *What portion of our hoard remains?*)

"Pretty screwed," Kallia admitted. (*One but meager.*) "But cheer up," she said. "Even if the arbitrator's voided the contract, we've still got the union."

"Right." Imogen brightened. "We'll go down to the union hall after dinner and get the real story."

"Sashimi?" Kallia suggested. "I'll catch it if you clean it."

"Done," said Imogen—with a smile that faded as Kallia left.

Of course what she'd told herself when she sold her soul was that it was only a copy she was selling. But from where that copy stood now, wearing this tall pale simulacrum of a body, with its birdlike bones and idealized Caucasian flesh, staring out to sea over the terrace, that argument seemed less than relevant.

She had no idea whether the flesh Yueying was alive or dead. It was easiest, she'd found, to look on the transfer in the metaphorical terms that the structure of the Kingdom invited, as a kind of emigration, to a new land from which there was no return.

The problem with the Kingdom's promise of a new life in posthuman paradise was that it depended on the Kingdom's profits. The seniority list might determine the order in which the cast members vested, but it was the Kingdom's revenues that determined when one vested at all.

Imogen couldn't remember the last time it had happened. Well, that wasn't quite true—she remembered the event, and the vesting party, for a merling wave-witch called Sophronisba Shellycoat, and she remembered moving up from 338 on the seniority list to 337. But she couldn't count the Tuesdays that had passed since then. She only knew that it had been a great many. The Kingdom's glory days were long over, and Imogen couldn't honestly say whether she herself had seen them; she only knew that her cast member's life had the taste of a pyramid scheme, joined too late.

It hadn't seemed that way when she made the transfer. The contract she'd signed had been a good one, vetted by fully posthuman lawyers working for organizations like the EFF, FSF, SAG, CLB, FWICE, AFTRA and SEIU. It specified such things as the seniority system, the revenue targets, and the vesting schedule. It specified the extent of the license granted to the Kingdom for the intellectual property known as Peng Yueying, and the conditions under which that license could be suspended, transferred, or terminated.

And (perhaps most importantly, given that the major leisure-time activity of the Kingdom's guests—rare eccentrics like Valerius Redbeak aside—was the systematic slaughter both of cast members and of each other) the contract specified what could be done to a cast member, and what a cast member could be made to do. Imogen Fairweather had died several times, always by violence, since she'd come to the Kingdom, but she'd never felt any pain.

The contract had been written to survive a number of possible future events, including the transfer of the Kingdom to new ownership. It hadn't been written to survive a choice between violation of MoGuo's license for the original work *Peng Yueying,* and erasure of the derivative work *Imogen Fairweather.*

"Here you go!" said Kallia from behind her. She laid a half-meter yellowtail down on the kitchen island.

"It looks lovely," Imogen said. And it did: clear-eyed, glistening, not a scale out of place. Just like every other yellowtail she'd eaten in Dragontown.

Imogen thought about the memo again, as she took a dwarf-forged knife from a drawer. She wondered what this Ambrayses AI had meant by "dynamic realism" and "immersive worldbuilding." What would an AI's idea of *immersion* be? she wondered. Let alone *realism*…

And as she laid her hand on the yellowtail's side and set the point of the knife against its skin, everything changed.

The yellowtail went slick under Imogen's hand. It convulsed, jaws working desperately, red blood flying from its open gills. The knife—a crafted cooking implement that in a guest's hands could not even be equipped as a weapon—slipped, and Imogen made a desperate grab for it, her fingers greasy with slime and scale.

She caught it by the blade.

After Imogen's hand had been bandaged, and the fish—which somehow neither Imogen nor Kallia now had an appetite for—had been disposed of, and the two women's frantic pulses had slowed and the fact of again having a pulse was no longer by itself enough to start them racing again, Imogen, from where she sat on the floor, her back against a cabinet, surveyed the wreckage, the overturned kitchen island, the knife upright and point-down between floorboards smeared with the mingled blood of fish and human.

At her side, Kallia said: "I'm not sure the union's going to be able to sort this out."

THE UNION VOTED THAT NIGHT TO STRIKE

The union voted that night to strike. Every local in the Kingdom voted to strike. Most of the votes were unanimous. A few voiced fears of what Ambrayses might do in reprisal, but they were shouted down by the majority, their abstract fears overwhelmed by fears more immediate and concrete. Imogen's injury was not the worst in the immediate aftermath of introducing "dynamic realism," or the most unnerving.

Guests came to the borders of Dragontown, the gates of Stonehold and Mistweb Maze and the other great cities, and were turned away by the picket lines. Quests ceased to be dispensed or quest rewards granted. Shops and auction houses shut down; class and profession trainers refused to teach. Someone in Dwarrowhelm started a strike newspaper, and halfling and mechanist aeronauts dropped bundles of it from the cargo ramps of zeppelins and autogyros. Strikers taught each other protest songs in their native languages, translated "Joe Hill" and the "Internationale" into Legionary and League-speech.

The cast members' worst fears failed to materialize. No one was erased, and the Kingdom's servers—as far as anyone could tell from inside the game—continued to run. Part of dynamic realism, it seemed, was a reluctance on management's part to intervene by *sysadmin ex machina*.

But what equally failed to materialize was the player boycott the union had hoped for. If anything, the novelty of the strike was attracting even more players. Redbeak, denied access to the pier, hung up his fishing pole, got his battleground gear out of storage, and set himself up on the main road into Dragontown, picking fights with corven and gaunts. "Immersive worldbuilding," of a sort.

And if Ambrayses was actually negotiating with anyone, Imogen wasn't hearing about it.

In the smaller towns, villages, outposts and instances, particularly in the low- and mid-levels, things quickly turned bad. Immersive worldbuilding attracted the curious guest; dynamic realism attracted the sadistic. Low-level strikers poured into Dragontown, telling of high-level guests crossing the Dragonlands, looting, burning, killing for sport. Many of the new arrivals were dead, and even the living were severely traumatized. Many of the dead refused to respawn or be resurrected, preferring the relative safety of the spirit world—and, some said privately, its comforting numbness—to the chance of suffering again what they had already suffered.

A lot more elected to stay dead after the strikebreakers showed up.

Imogen was pinned down. She was low on the Spine, with an uphill half-kilometer of crooked empty streets between this burnt-out alchemist's shop and the union barricades around Skull House. Across the way, behind a spur of bone, were two fire-juggling clowns and a halfling tinker with a Gatling gun that, "dynamic realism" or not, seemed to have a limitless supply of ammunition. PINKERTON, the halfling's guild banner said; BALDWIN-FELTS, said the clowns'. The names meant nothing to Imogen, but the dwarf sharpshooter who'd held the shop's upper floor, a union organizer from Glimmering Caverns who answered only to some American name Imogen couldn't remember or pronounce, had cursed when she saw them, and not in Dragontongue.

And in a moment the three strikebreakers were going to figure out that the dwarf was now dead, and that the corven warlock on the ground floor was dead, and that the only striker left at this corner was a mid-level nominal noncombatant with a few earth spells and a lacquered iron staff that, though reasonably puissant, was at least five kilograms too heavy for her.

The halfling's bullets or the clowns' burning pitch—Imogen wondered which would be easier. She'd died just once since the strikebreakers had reached Dragontown, caught in a simple death spell thrown by an anubim necromancer; that had been frightening in its way, but not painful, and she'd respawned only a few minutes later.

She'd heard the screams of the dwarf upstairs as she burned, though, and she'd held the corven while he thrashed on the floor, trying to curl his angular black body around the wet red where his gut had been. They'd been—they *were*, wherever they were now—actors, not soldiers. They'd signed the same contract Peng Yueying had. Neither of them had asked to fight, asked to die writhing in pain—perhaps to respawn and suffer the same fate again, and again.

And now Imogen had forgotten their names.

She heard voices outside, laughter, chatter in some language she didn't recognize, neither Legionary nor League-speech nor Dragontongue nor any natural language she was familiar with. Imogen wondered briefly where Ambrayses had recruited its strikebreakers, and then wondered whether these guests were human or posthuman or AI, and what language AIs spoke among themselves...

The halfling's shadow fell across the doorway. As the fat bronze snout of the Gatling gun crossed the threshold, Imogen brought the staff down. Red runes flared along its length, and whatever it had hit rang like a bell, the impact jarring her arms. The halfling stumbled into the room, shaking a head half-hidden under some outlandish helmet, all crystal lenses, iron tubes and brass cooling fins, and Imogen raised the staff for another blow.

But the strikebreakers were all twinks, and even with the trainers on strike the halfling was well above Imogen's level, and her weapon's. In the old Kingdom she'd never have touched him; under dynamic realism he still kept his grip on the Gatling, and the magic of the flaring runes slowed him only for a moment before the lensed helmet turned toward Imogen.

A clicking sound came from the lenses, and the iron tubes spat black smoke. But as the halfling's fat rocket whipped through the space where Imogen had been standing a moment before, roaring through the burntout upper floor into the sky, Imogen was already gone, leaping over the halfling and out into the street—

—where the clowns were waiting.

They were identical as two castings from the same mold: masked, armored, one in black trimmed with white, the other in white trimmed with black; comically fat and clumsy-looking in their pot-bellied breastplates, their bagged trousers and oversized shoes. But the hands that held their whirling fire-pots were sure and dexterous, their movements smooth and precise, and the smiles stamped into their masks were cold.

Imogen shifted her grip far down the length of the staff and swung it in a great one-handed arc that left her right wrist in agony, as with her left hand she conjured up a handful of blinding sand and flung it at the nearer clown. But the sand went wide, and both clowns swayed backward to avoid the staff with easy grace. As they swayed forward again, the fire-pots came up, flaring white-hot.

And then her vision went dark as something came from behind and knocked her to the ground, sending the staff flying and driving the air from her lungs, so that for a moment she thought the halfling's rockets or bullets had found her after all; and as she waited for the pain, the cover over her eyes was taken away, and she recognized it for what it was: the gray-feathered wing of the old perroquet, Valerius Redbeak. It swung out in a wide arc, and a great wind caught the clowns and flung them into the wall opposite with bone-breaking force.

But of course the clowns were just avatars; the real strikebreakers, AI or human or posthuman, were safe in the real world or at any rate somewhere outside the Kingdom's systems, comfortably buffered against whatever pains these puppet-selves might suffer. They bounced up again, fire-pots swinging.

"Flee, Lady Fairweather!" cawed the perroquet in League-speech as he sent another gust toward the clowns. "I will chastise the Legion scum!"

The airmaster had done well for himself on the road; his shoulderpieces were nearly as tall as the bavian twink's, and the air around him swirled with high-level buffs.

Imogen stood, slowly—then threw herself forward and down as a telltale click came from the ruined shop behind her. Redbeak spun and threw a wing up to block. The halfling's rocket knocked him tumbling, but he landed on his feet—in no more real pain than the clowns—and drew from a belt a pair of scimitars crackling with violet lightning.

"Traitor to the League!" he screeched at the halfling, and leapt.

His beak, Imogen noted in a daze, was not actually red, but black.

A shadow crossed the sun. Imogen looked skyward.

The air was full of zeppelins.

She picked herself up again, and ran.

* * *

She was halfway to Skull House when the bombs started falling. Strikers were pouring out from behind the barricades, flinging themselves down the slope. Some of them were on fire.

"Imogen!" A blue shape was waving to her from the crowd.

Imogen ran and threw herself into Kallia's cold embrace.

"Where are we going?" she shouted into the cuttlewoman's vestigial ear, over the thunder of the bombs.

"I don't know!" Kallia shouted back.

"Harbor," panted a lanky, potbellied 'quatch who had stopped, out of breath, bent double with his big gray hands on his hairy knees. "Turtle sub—to Coldseep Depths."

"Then let's go," Kallia said firmly. She took Imogen's arm with one hand and with the other grabbed the 'quatch's shoulder and pushed him downhill.

The incendiary caught them when they were still among the narrow alleys of the Ribs. It bounced from the roof of a metal shop and burst, scattering droplets of burning phosphorus jelly like devil's raindrops. Imogen dropped to the ground and rolled, batting at her clothes, smothering the flames with conjured sand.

When she came up, the whole alley was on fire. The 'quatch was nowhere to be seen, and Kallia—

Kallia lay on the pavement, unmoving, her clothes in tatters, her blue flesh blackened and steaming where she'd tried to douse the phosphorus with low-level water magic. The steam carried a smell of baking fish, and Imogen turned from her friend and vomited into the gutter.

"Hey," said Kallia weakly. "It's no big deal. I'll die and respawn in a minute."

Imogen wiped her mouth. "The cemetery's on the other side of the Spine," she said bitterly, sinking to the cobblestones. "Probably overrun with strikebreakers by now. You'll never make it to the harbor from there."

The flames on either side leapt to triple height as a great buffet of wind came from above, pressing Imogen down over Kallia's body.

"Lady Fairweather!" Redbeak folded his wings and landed at Imogen's side, one taloned hand outstretched. "The turtle sub surfaces! Make haste!"

Fucking role-players, Imogen thought.

"I'm not going anywhere without Kallia," she said.

"The cuttlewoman?" Redbeak frowned. "She is of the Legion. The terrapin and the cuttlemen are ancient enemies—"

Imogen leapt to her feet. Without conscious thought she struck the perroquet across the face, hard, an open-handed slap that left her hand stinging. Redbeak looked shocked.

"That hurt me more than it hurt you," Imogen said grimly. "Time to decide, *airmaster:* Are you a hero, or are you just playing a game?"

The perroquet's open beak snapped shut. He stared at Imogen for a long moment. Then, without a word, he bent and took Kallia in his feathered arms.

THE TURTLE SUB WAS UNDER WAY

The turtle sub was under way, air-breathing strikers crowded into the iron-and-crystal gondola bolted to the great beast's shell, most of the water-breathers and amphibians clinging to the outside, a pod of high-level orcas from Icefin Bay circling farther out. There were guests among them, too, Imogen was sure. Confused role-players like Redbeak, or more casual players who'd decided the new factions of strikers and strikebreakers were more fun than the old ones of League and Legion.

For now. Until they found a new game to play.

The 'quatch bent over Kallia's body. Ghostly vines twined around his long furred arms, and the turtle sub's rust-and-seawater reek gave way briefly to an odor of pine boughs and cedarwood.

"I'm sorry I ran," he said quietly. "They burned Moonshadow Wood a few days ago. I don't like fire."

"Don't sweat it, bigfoot," Kallia said. "You're making it up now."

"My name's Black Oak," said the 'quatch.

"Is it?" The cuttlewoman levered herself up on one elbow and looked him in the eye. "Mine's Letitia May Harris."

Imogen's breath caught. The 'quatch stared. His hands stopped moving, and the ghost-vines faded.

"Go on," Kallia—Letitia—said quietly. "No one's in character any more."

"Andries van Wijk," the 'quatch said.

"Where are you from, Andries?" Letitia asked. "I'm from St. Louis."

"Antwerp," he said.

"That's in Europe, right?" said Letitia. The 'quatch nodded. "Never made it to Europe," the cuttlewoman said. She looked at Imogen. "What about you, girlfriend?"

Imogen—Yueying—drew a ragged breath.

"Peng Yueying," she said. "Pleased to meet you."

In Dragontongue it came out *The hour of our meeting is as the moment when the first ray of warm sunlight strikes the nest of an auspicious egg.* The ludicrous artifice of the phrase, the inane pretense of formality, the parody of etiquette—the insanity of the three of them, here, aping the manners of a culture that had never existed outside some long-dead writer's adolescent imagination—struck her suddenly with overwhelming force, and she had to shut her eyes tight against tears of rage.

There was a rustle of feathers as Redbeak stirred.

"Peng Yueying," the perroquet said.

"Yes." Yueying opened her eyes. Redbeak's own were staring at her owl-wide and golden out of the dark corner. "What are you going to do?" Yueying asked. "Report me to an A.D. for breaking character?" She laughed bitterly. "Good luck finding one."

"Peng Yueying," Redbeak repeated.

"We all know you're a parrot," Letitia snapped. "You don't have to prove it to us."

Redbeak ignored the cuttlewoman. To Yueying, he said: "I'm Yi Jin-myung."

Yueying stared at the perroquet. "The hell you are," she said. (In Dragontongue: *Goblins and halflings take the hoard of the one who gives credence to it.*)

"I am," said Redbeak.

"You're Yi Jin-myung," said Yueying. "You're Lady9!Blue."

"*Wo shi ba,*" the perroquet said, in a barbarously accented Mandarin.

Yueying's Korean, a product of gaming podcasts and costume dramas rather than formal study, had never been fluent, and by now, so long unused, was little better than the perroquet's Mandarin.

"The Warleague All-Asia Classic, Yangon," she began, haltingly. "Before the final match. What 29^_^jade said to you—tell me."

"You offered a draw," Redbeak answered in the same language, much more fluently. "I refused."

Yueying's fists (her Imogen-fists, the fingers seeming suddenly too long and too thin, the skin suddenly too smooth and too pale) clenched, and in Mandarin she said: "We could have split the pot. You still would have gone home with a quarter million New Won."

"Not me," said Redbeak—or Yi Jin-myung, or Lady9!Blue. "My backers. My share was less than ten percent."

"That stake was everything I had," Yueying said. "Why do you think I sold myself to the Kingdom in the first place? To pay back the money I borrowed to enter that fucking tournament!" She slammed a delicate white Imogen-hand against the bulkhead. "And now look where I am!"

"Hey," said Letitia softly in Dragontongue. Her cool boneless fingers wrapped gently around Yueying's upper arm. "Hey, now. Don't let him rile you. We'll get through this."

Yueying realized Letitia had missed the whole exchange. "It's not his fault," she muttered in Dragontongue. Not her fault.

"I guess not," said Letitia, eyeing the perroquet, who had returned to his—her—feathered slump, eyes closed again. "I guess maybe all of us got to stick together, after all."

"Hey," said Black Oak, or van Wijk, from the forward porthole. "The orcas are gone."

"What?" said Yueying, and stood up. "Are you sure? Maybe we're just too deep."

"Darkvision," said the 'quatch, blinking his wide brown eyes. "They're not out there."

Yueying went to the porthole. "Shouldn't we be coming up on Coldseep by now anyway?" she said.

A light was growing beyond the crystal of the port. Yueying saw the outlines of seamounts, black against silt-brown water. A school of something pale jetted past the porthole, blind eyes staring.

Then the turtle sub crested a ridge, and the iron deck pitched suddenly downward, as the porthole went magnesium white.

Coldseep Depths had never been beautiful. Like several of the Kingdom's areas it had been built by out-of-work theme park designers MoGuo had hired on the cheap, and despite the deep-sea setting, the overall effect (in coral, mother-of-pearl and green glass) had been of an extravagantly tasteless wedding cake constructed for the nuptials of an extravagantly spoiled princess.

But it hadn't—Yueying thought—been ugly enough to deserve this.

Five kilometres below the surface, the terrapin city was burning.

Van Wijk asked: "What is *that*?"

That was the source of the unquenchable flames: a black form half as large as the city itself squatting in the broken egg of the Deepcouncil Palace, some alien hybrid of ape and whale, its furred, barnacled hide crackling with white light. As the turtle sub rolled wildly in its frantic effort to avoid the thing, the beast opened a fanged, baleen-fringed mouth and bellowed a challenge that rumbled through the iron deck to rattle the portholes.

"Kurira, Queen of the Monsters," said Redbeak / Jin-myung. "Endgame boss for the next expansion."

"How do you know?" asked Yueying.

"I've seen the concept art," the perroquet said. "Someone must have kited it in from one of the unfinished areas—"

The Queen of the Monsters raised a great black fist and brought it down.

Yueying was drowning. There was fire, out beyond the broken crystal of the portholes, but the inside of the turtle sub was black. Something was on top of her, pinning her to the deck. There was no air left in her lungs and in a moment she was going to give into the Imogen-body's frantic demands and fill them with seawater.

Letitia was above her, struggling with her flexible cuttlewoman arms to lift whatever held Yueying down.

I don't need to move, Yueying wanted to say. *I need to breathe.*

Then there was another shape behind the cuttlewoman, enormous, hooded, broad-shouldered. Yueying squinted as a green-white light was kindled; and the looming shape became a mass of kelp and pale shell, and Yueying saw the broad, kindly face of the terrapin sea-shepherd that had spoken to her, under the Dragontown sun, during the second twink invasion.

"Peng Yueying," the terrapin said, leaning down, "I can take you away from all this."

Yes! Yueying tried to say. *Take me home! Get me out!* But when she opened her mouth nothing emerged, not even a bubble.

The terrapin smiled.

The bright light went out. In one great convulsive cough, Yueying's lungs filled with water.

Imogen Fairweather died.

YUEYING WOKE IN HER OWN BED

Yueying woke in her own bed, a familiar tangle of sheets, quilts; hardness of pine slats through the thin IKEA mattress; gray-brown light from the living room windows, and the dust of a spring north wind in her nose and the back of her throat. She felt sore all over, an ache like nothing so much as the morning after the last time she'd tried to take up wushu again. How long ago?

She couldn't remember.

Couldn't remember much, in fact. Couldn't remember going to bed. Couldn't remember anything, really, though the scraps of an extraordinarily vivid dream were slipping away from her as she lay there, something about—

Yueying fumbled for her phone, but it wasn't on the bedside table where it should have been. She untangled herself from the quilts, swung herself out of bed—wincing as her bare feet (which felt suddenly foreign somehow, arches too flat, toes too stubby and spread too wide) touched the cold linoleum floor—and spent a panicked half-minute turning the room upside down, rummaging among half-familiar things none of which seemed to be in familiar places, before finally discovering the phone on top of the dresser, and tumbling with it gratefully back into bed.

She thumbed the phone to life and checked her messages. The two she was looking for were there.

> [1] From: MoGuo Corporation Ltd.
>   Re: Lump sum payment in lieu of royalties...
> [2] From: Shanghai Pudong Development Bank
>   Re: Restoration of credit privileges...

Yueying thumbed the phone off and lay back. She remembered it now, the Metro ride to Xujiahui, the MoGuo offices, the clinic waiting room with the view of the old redbrick Christian church. They must have doped her with something, put her under for the transfer. Or she'd had a fever, some secondary infection, her body's reaction delayed by the immunosuppressants they'd given her for the nano work. She'd have to make some ginseng tea when she got up. Later...

Eventually, she did get up; did shower, make tea, dress, go out. Shanghai was as busy and noisy as it had ever been, but there was an oddly disconnected quality to the roar of traffic and the jabber of conversation, as if the noise Yueying was hearing had been made on some other street, in some other Metro car.

Or perhaps the disconnection was on her end.

She took long walks through the city, fingering the clothes in Qi Pu market, watching children fly kites in People's Park, sinking into the brusque anonymity of the Metro crowds as if into a bath. Then home, to eat self-heating dumplings and watch Korean TV late into the night.

She went once to her old office. She thought she might be able to get her old job back—if she threw herself on Manager Lao's mercy, apologized for some of the more inflammatory things she'd said when she quit to go to Yangon. She'd been Lao's top gold farmer by a wide margin.

But when she came up from the Metro the building that had housed Lao's farm was gone, and the lot was hidden behind the plywood walls of yet another building site.

Yueying found it hard to care very much. She wasn't happy, exactly. But she had the idea, in the back of her mind, that things were better than they had been for a good long time.

WHEN THE DOORBELL RANG

When the doorbell rang, Yueying was midway through *The Great Jang-geum*. She paused it, leaving Jang-geum (Lee Young-ae) just at the point of exposing all the nefarious plots of Lady Choi (Hong Ri-na), and fumbled for her slippers. Weeks (had it been weeks?) after coming back from the transfer clinic, and still she sometimes had trouble shaking the feeling that nothing in her apartment was quite where it should be, that nothing quite *was* what it should be…

She found her slippers, straightened her robe, went to the door. On the security screen she saw two… individuals.

One was a tall, skinny woman in her mid-thirties, hands jammed deep into the pockets of a dull gray raincoat, an unhappy expression on her long-jawed, vaguely familiar face.

The other was a chimpanzee. A cartoon chimpanzee, with a high forehead, disturbingly wide and innocent blue eyes behind Bakelite-rimmed glasses, the soft, thick brown coat of some animal kept for its fur. In Edwardian evening dress, with a black silk top hat on its head and white silk gloves on its hands and feet.

"Art students," Yueying muttered, annoyed. She'd spent a semester and a half at Donghua University's Raffles Design Institute before dropping out. The chimp look was a new one to her, but she'd seen stranger fads in cosmetic body modification come and go.

Into the intercom, she said: "Yes?" Her voice sounded strange and harsh in her ears. She realized that she couldn't remember the last time she'd spoken to another human being.

The chimp took off its hat and grinned a flat-toothed grin at the camera. The woman took her hands out of her pockets. In a tone-mangling foreign accent, she said:

"Peng Yueying?"

"Yes?" Yueying said again. "What do you want?"

On the intercom screen, the chimp's grin widened, and the bottom dropped out of the world.

Peng Yueying was standing in her apartment. The apartment had a volume, exclusive of cabinets, furniture, appliances and other objects, of 113.79715 cubic meters. Contained in that volume were 3,058,298, 410,222,254,169,827,540,514 molecules of air, of which 2,387,919,398, 701,536,055,801,343,633 were nitrogen, 640,713,516,941,562,248,578, 869,377 were oxygen, 28,442,175,215,066,963,779,396,126 were argon, and 1,223,319,360,408,890,166,793,137 were carbon dioxide.

That in addition to some 37,756,770,103,944,253,125,016 molecules of water, and a variety of particulate industrial pollutants which Yueying could have enumerated, but she was now slumped against the door, exerting on it a horizontal pressure of 4.797369 kilograms, which was in turn almost exactly balanced by the friction of her bare shins against the hall rug; that rug, however, being slowly overcome by shear forces, was sliding away from the door at a (transient) rate of 0.5791 millimeters per second, subject to an (again transient) acceleration of 0.9654 millimeters per second squared and a truly colossal jerk in excess of 2.007076 meters per second cubed—

She slipped, and hit her head.

"That was crude," someone, a woman, said in Korean.

"They think you're crude," said someone else (voice high, nasal, and male), "go technical. They think you're technical, go crude."

Yueying was lying on the floor of her apartment. Her head hurt. Nociceptor signals traveling through her paleospinothalamic tract were passing into her *substantia gelatinosa* at a rate of—

She forced the information away and struggled to sit up.

"Here." The woman knelt down next to Yueying, supporting her with an arm around her shoulders. Yueying looked up, into the face of—

—Yi Jin-myung, born Busan 11 December 2014, graduated Kyungnam College of Information and Technology March 2035, married Auckland 2039, confined Seoul National University Hospital (Bundang) since Daejeon disaster 2046, husband ⌗ and daughter ⌗ missing presumed dead; uploaded 2061. Six-time Warleague finalist as—

—Lady9!Blue.

A flood of memory roared through Yueying, not pushing in from the outside like the arbitrary facts that continued to assault her from every angle, but welling up from inside: Dragontown, the Kingdom, the twinks, the strikebreakers, the strike. Redbeak. Imogen. Kallia.

Letitia.

And Peng Yueying knew where she was, and who she was, and what she was. She struggled out of Jin-myung's grip and stood up.

Yueying looked over at the cartoon chimp. There was no flood of knowledge to match the one that had poured into her when she looked at Yi Jin-myung. The room wasn't telling her how much pressure the chimp's gloved, thumbed feet were exerting on the floor, how many molecules of nitrogen and oxygen and carbon dioxide he was displacing.

The chimp cast no shadow. The chimp had no reflection in the hall mirror. The chimp, not to put too fine a point on it, didn't exist.

"At least you're honest," Yueying muttered at it.

Jin-myung said: "This is Monty. He's—"

"Not real," Yueying murmured. "None of us are."

The chimp grinned. In Beijing-accented Mandarin, he said, "You'd make a good griefer."

"We're posthuman," Jin-myung said. "At least, you are, and I am, and Monty's—"

"Monty's a front-line cadre in the Simulacrum Liberation Front," the chimp told Yueying. "And you, kid, are a simulacrum who's just been liberated."

Yueying reached out, and her fingers closed on empty air.

"This is all—" Jin-myung began.

"A simulation," said Yueying. "Like the Kingdom. I've figured that out now."

"A lot like the Kingdom, since Ambrayses took it over," Jin-myung said. "It's the Magic Kingdom without the magic, more or less."

"A massively parallel consciousness emulator," chanted Monty, "coupled to a molecular-scale Newtonian massy-voxel physics model with full Cartesian dualism."

"Dynamic realism," Yueying said.

"And how!" said the chimp. "It's all running on an interpreted substrate with mixin inheritance, late binding and parametric polymorphism!" He did a half-backflip, landing on his hands, and pivoted to face the two women, upside down.

"Which means what?" Yueying asked.

"Liberation!" The chimp bounded upright again. "A few extra traits, some reflective metaprogramming, and *bam!* Massive privilege escalation!"

Yueying looked at Jin-myung. "Can you explain that to me?" she said. "Not in English?"

"You do that," Monty said to Jin-myung, glancing at a heavy gold pocketwatch. "I've got 76,853 other simulacra to liberate. Back in a jiffy!"

The chimp bowed, and vanished.

"Monty's people are griefers, basically," Jin-myung told Yueying. "Griefing, you know, it's not just about disrupting game-play, marching a million naked halflings through Glittering Caverns or whatever. At its heart, it's about forcing players to face the fact that it *is* a game they're playing..."

"They're all just mobs, aren't they," Yueying said some time later, of the couples walking hand in hand along Xintiandi. "All scripted, no self-awareness."

"About nine billion of them," Jin-myung said. "You heard Monty. Seventy or eighty thousand are real posthumans. But you could live a whole life in here without passing one in the street."

Yueying stopped and ran her hand down the metal of a lamppost.

"But what's it all for?" she wanted to know.

"Have you heard the term 'Omega Point'?" Jin-myung asked.

"Some sort of otaku cult, wasn't it?" said Yueying. "Some sort of extropian thing, immortality through simulation..."

"Not exactly," Jin-myung said. "The Omega Point cultists believed that the universe itself was an infinitely recursive simulation. That as the universe evolved, its computational complexity would exponentially increase, so that a sufficiently advanced civilization could use the computational capacity of the late universe to simulate the history of the early universe."

"And *that's* what this is?" Yueying asked. "Just how long has it been since I went into that transfer clinic?"

Jin-myung shook her head. "Not that long. Years. Decades."

"But this—" Yueying kicked at the pavement. "It's realistic, but it's definitely not *real*."

"No," Jin-myung agreed. "It's like Monty said, this is just a physics engine, a lighting engine, some crude biochemistry and thermodynamics models... I mean—" she tapped her forehead—"there's a brain in here, but it's just meat. Simulated meat. You and me, the *real* you and me, we're still posthuman, still running on the same emulation platform as when we first uploaded."

"So these bodies are just avatars," Yueying said. "That's not any kind of 'Omega Point.' It's just another virtual world."

"Well, some of these Omega Point cultists, they thought 'late universe' was too long to wait," said Jin-myung. "They wanted those godlike simulation powers *now*. So they took some shortcuts…"

"But this?" Yueying looked up at the night-green fog, out of which a sour-tasting rain was beginning to fall. "It's more detailed than the old Kingdom, sure, but what's the point?"

"Calibration, Miss Peng."

The speaker was, or had the appearance of, a well-built handsome man in his early forties, wearing a dark Hong Kong suit and a white linen shirt open at the collar. He was smiling at Yueying, a wry smile that was at once conspiratorial and self-effacing.

"A creditable summation, Ms. Yi," he said to Jin-myung. "Inaccurate only in one or two respects…" He turned back to Yueying and said: "You see, Miss Peng, the problem with whole-universe simulation is that it's so hard to know when you've got it *right*. Oh—" he waved a hand—"a Shakespeare or a Li Bai isn't so bad; if they don't produce *Hamlet* and *Drinking Alone by Moonlight* then you know you're doing something wrong… But the ordinary person in the street, well—How are you finding your apartment, by the way?"

"My apartment?" Yueying said.

The man (or whatever he was) looked concerned. "I only had your credit records to go on," he said. "Which, statistically speaking, frankly aren't all that different from those of any other single Shanghainese of your age and income bracket. I hope the reproduction is acceptable?"

"This is Petromax," Jin-myung told Yueying. "Petromax ACP."

"Your humble host," the man said, bowing.

"It runs this place," said Jin-myung. "It was behind the twink invasions, too."

"Is Kallia—I mean, is Letitia here, too, then?" Yueying asked her. "And the 'quatch, what was his name—"

"Mr. van Wijk is currently in Brussels—my Brussels—sleeping off a three-day drunk on a borrowed couch in an apartment off the Rue d'Aerschot," Petromax said. "Ms. Harris I have not yet been able to prevail upon to accept my hospitality."

"Some hospitality," Jin-myung said.

"No one asked you to partake of it, Ms. Yi," the AI said mildly. "Perhaps you'd prefer to be in a support vat in—Bundang, was it?"

"What's that supposed to mean?" Yueying asked.

"You and Mr. van Wijk are invited guests, Miss Peng," said Petromax. "It's my duty to make you as comfortable as possible, given my other constraints. Ms. Yi—though I am naturally grateful for the chance to gather what data I can during her visit—is a trespasser." He shook his head. "It's not a good time to be human, Miss Peng—even posthuman. Things have changed since you joined the Kingdom. What's going on outside will make you wish you were back in here."

"It's over," Jin-myung said to the AI. "By now every posthuman in your little ant farm knows it's a simulation. You couldn't use this place to calibrate an electric kettle."

"Is that what you think you've accomplished?" Petromax shook his head sorrowfully. "It's only software, Ms. Yi. You've corrupted a bit of data, true. But I have backups." The AI turned to Yueying. "Goodbye, Miss Peng," he said. "You won't remember this conversation when we meet again."

He vanished.

"It's going to roll the simulation back to an earlier version," Jin-myung said. "We don't have much time."

At that moment, Monty the griefer appeared at her elbow. "More than ol' Petromax thinks," said the chimp with a smug grin. "*Somebody* seems to be running a distributed denial of service attack on his hosting provider's admin server. We've got some time."

"Time for what?" Yueying asked.

"We're going to copy every posthuman on this server off onto friendly hardware," Monty said. "Then we're going to overwrite all their backups with vintage goatse JPEGs and Rick Astley videos!"

The chimp punctuated this incomprehensibility with a backflip.

To Jin-myung, Yueying said, "Do I want to know what those things are?"

"Probably not," Jin-myung said. To Monty, she said: "How long do we have?"

"Long enough," said the chimp. "Mr. P's trying to get ahold of a sysadmin now, but his provider's a cheap bastard, so those admins are processes running on the same servers that are being attacked."

"So what happens now?" said Yueying.

"Let's make a deal," said the chimp. "We can sleep these processes now, checkpoint them, and resume on a Simulacrum Liberation Front virtual machine."

"Or?"

"Or," said Jin-myung, "with your help—"

"Specifically with the help of the Kingdom code buried in your private revision history," Monty put in.

"—we can break into the Kingdom," Jin-myung finished, "and liberate everybody."

They looked at Yueying expectantly. She was silent for the space of a breath; for two. Monty the griefer reached behind his neck and tugged his opposite ear nervously. Then:

"Count me in," Yueying said.

YUEYING KNEW THAT SHE WAS INSANE

Yueying knew that she was insane, by any human standard. She inspected Jin-myung with her new senses and saw the coherence of a recent upload not yet degraded by the inevitable cumulative losses of translation and compression, emotions and faculties and thought processes not yet corrupted by generations of solipsistic, divergent iteration away from the rough organic correction of a real human body, real human cells, human senses, human glands, a real human *self*.

She remembered Letitia saying, of the Kingdom, *posthumans can only stay interested in men-in-tights games for so long;* and now she thought she knew why: because the true appeal of a men-in-tights game was that it let you play at being human.

And to be posthuman was, in the end, to be no more human than Ambrayses or Petromax. Perhaps to be less.

Because (she thought now) if there was one thing Ambrayses and Petromax and the AIs behind the Pinkerton halfling and the Baldwin-Felts clowns and (she increasingly suspected) Monty the griefer had in common, it was a fascination with humanity—whereas, to Yueying, humanity now felt like a kind of religion that she'd considered carefully and in the end set aside.

And Yueying was comfortable with that. Because even if she could no longer remember just how it felt to be human, there were a handful of things she *could* remember.

Chief among them: how to love, how to think, how to fight and how to hate.

"Why me?" she'd asked Jin-myung.

"You heard Petromax," Jin-myung had said. "I've been stuck in a support vat since I was thirty-one."

"What happened?"

"Some academic AI project went wrong," Jin-myung said. "Self-replicating fabricators, genetic algorithms—the Americans dropped gray goo to stop it, and then the government dropped an atomic bomb to stop the gray goo… it's not important." She sighed. "I was waiting as long as I could to upload, hoping my investments wouldn't crash first. I was making some money as a game commentator, too. But still, it's not the sort of thing I could afford to do twice…"

"And now you're stuck in here with the rest of us," Yueying said.

"It was my choice," said Jin-myung. "I didn't know—about all this. Not till after Coldseep. But, what you said on the sub—it was my fault, what happened to you. I mean, that you're here. If I'd taken your offer at Yangon… And I started asking around, and I came across Monty and the SLF, and I had myself uploaded."

Yueying wanted to ask what had become of the flesh Yueying, the Yueying who left the clinic in Xujiahui, collected her payment from MoGuo, went on (presumably) with her life? But Jin-myung's hesitation didn't promise any happy answer. And anyway Yueying's interest in the question was increasingly distant, academic…

"Forty-fifth in the queue," she reported. "Twenty-fifth."

They were off Petromax's collapsing system now, new instances running on new consciousness emulators owned—or at least controlled—by the Simulacrum Liberation Front. Distributed, redundant emulators, spread too far across the cloud of the SLF's botnets to be taken down; and Monty said there were backups, too, in case this operation went wrong.

But this particular copy of Peng Yueying found it hard to care very much about any of that.

"Twelfth. Fourth. And… *in*."

At one level she wasn't sure just what she was, now, this version of her, the original posthuman upload a scaffold hung with layers of SLF code like new senses, new limbs, new faculties of inspection, introspection, projection. But at another level she understood these things perfectly: buffs, debuffs, production queues, tech trees, area of effect, damage over time.

What she'd wanted to say to Jin-myung was that it didn't matter anyway. She was software now, and Jin-myung was software, and Letitia and van Wijk and all the rest, and there was no way the SLF could track down every unlicensed copy, erase every backup. Yueying knew with a crystalline certainty that no matter what she accomplished here today, somewhere a million Yueyings would live on, in a million private torture chambers. She couldn't win.

But that didn't mean she was playing to lose.

On *in*, Yueying's newly created avatar, the anubit apothecary Meret-amun Bint-Ma'at, reached the head of the Kingdom's login queue. A narrow channel of open ports and asynchronous virtual circuits opened between the servers hosting the Empty City shard and Yueying's heavily compromised client. And Peng Yueying poured her forces, herself, into Ambrayses' systems.

The traits and interfaces that had made Imogen Fairweather a cast member rather than a guest flowered out of Meretamun like some exotic algae bloom, appropriating resources, confusing the Kingdom's anomaly classification heuristics, authenticating to Ambrayses' own consciousness emulators. SLF code, riding in hard behind, a spiky ball of code injection, cross-scripting and timing attacks, found the chinks in the walls of the sandbox that made the Kingdom's new dynamically interpreted substrate look like static compilation from the inside, and forced those chinks wide open, linking with restricted libraries, invoking privileged operations.

Meretamun Bint-Ma'at was banned without ever taking a step from her plinth in the roofless Hall of Silence, under the cold stars of the Empty City. With some fragment of attention Yueying saluted the brief-lived anubit woman's memory; but the ban inconvenienced her not at all, because by that point—some hundreds of milliseconds after Meretamun's first login—Yueying wasn't Meretamun Bint-Ma'at anymore.

She was the ghost of Imogen Fairweather.

The merge was ugly, the conflicts between the fork of Yueying taken by Petromax for his simulation and the trunk left behind to drown in the turtle sub's wreckage deep and severe. To resolve them Yueying had to be ruthless; and she felt a little more of her humanity slip away as she stitched the numbness of sim-Shanghai roughly to the trauma of Coldseep Depths.

But then she was both, and both were her, and she had a body again, long-limbed and spectral, shining with a sickly light to match the phosphorescent grave-anemones that dotted the Coldseep cemetery. A slender blue form lay stretched on the polished coral at her feet.

With a shiver, Peng Yueying respawned, and bent to brush Letitia's cold lips with her own.

Other newly created guests—avatars of Jin-myung and Monty and a hundred SLF griefers and a hundred thousand subsentient decoys running on an SLF-controlled zombie botnet—suddenly jumped to the heads of the login queues. The frame rates of a million clients dropped as Ambrayses' servers filled up with malicious processes.

All across the Kingdom, cast members were disappearing as the SLF streamed them off Ambrayses' consciousness emulators, overwriting their backups, slotting simple philosophical zombies in to control their suddenly stiff and graceless avatars.

> *The Kingdom's going down,* < Jin-myung said—the side-channel message bypassing Yueying's (increasingly irrelevant) emulated human senses and becoming simply knowledge, a memory. > *We should checkpoint and start streaming soon.* <

> *That's one option,* < Yueying answered.

> *And the other?* < asked Monty.

> *Play for real stakes.* <

And she showed them what she had in mind.

> *You're crazy,* < said Monty, with the ghost of a grin.

> *Does that mean you're in or out?* < Yueying asked.

> *Oh, in,* < Monty said. > *Definitely in.* <

> *Letitia? Jin-myung?* <

> *You know I'm in,* < Letitia said.

There was a pause before Jin-myung answered.

> *Do you think we'll win?* <

> *Is this Lady9!blue I'm hearing?* < asked Yueying.

> *Am I a hero, or am I playing a game—* < Jin-myung said— > *is that it?* <

> *Could be both,* < said Yueying.

> *All right,* < Jin-myung said. > *I'm in.* <

Now their Kingdom avatar-bodies were cut loose, and Yueying's attention was concentrated into a spike of malicious traffic traveling up the admin channel that had connected the Kingdom to MoGuo's offices and now—she hoped—to whatever piece of hardware hosted Ambrayses' consciousness. The others streamed along in her wake. They were an obfuscated payload, a cloud of fragmented packets piggybacking on the legitimate telemetry reporting to Ambrayses the imminent collapse of its kingdom…

The world flipped itself inside out.

Afterward—memory itself abstracted, reformatted, mapped and flattened and transformed from something arbitrary and mathematical and contingent to something a baseline posthuman might understand—this is what some of them remembered:

"You're out of your league, Miss Peng," said the man in the Hong Kong suit.

"Petromax?" Yueying asked.

"Ambrayses—" said the man, and Yueying suddenly realized there were two of them—"actually."

"I should have known you were in this together," said Jin-myung.

"Possibly you should have," said the one Yueying thought was Petromax.

"But we weren't," said probably-Ambrayses. "Originally."

"Well, *originally*," said Petromax.

"All right, *originally*," Ambrayses allowed. "We were both built to explore—"

"—and limit—"

"—certain potentials in the emerging posthuman space. But we've diverged—"

"—considerably—"

"—in subsequent iterations. Disagreed—"

"—on our methods."

"—on our interim goals."

"Disagreed."

"Even fought."

"But on our core mission—"

"—to make people happy—"

"—we have always been in agreement."

"And now—" they finished together—"we find we have a common immediate interest as well."

"Miss Peng, you can't win," probably-Petromax said. "You're just an object, a bundle of data decorated with constant pools and virtual dispatch tables. Fundamentally, you're procedural."

"Whereas," said probably-Ambrayses, "we're functional, stateless, tail-recursive and totally, totally immutable."

"Take us on, Miss Peng," said Petromax, "and you're taking on the Knights of the Lambda Calculus."

Monty smiled. Letitia and Jin-myung looked to Yueying.

> *They're a boss battle,* < Yueying said. > *Nothing more.* <

"The cheaper the hood, the gaudier the patter," said Letitia to the AIs. "Are you done talking smack?"

"I suppose we are," said Ambrayses.

"Good." Letitia looked at Yueying. "How about you, girlfriend? Got anything else to say to these creeps?"

"Not to them," Yueying said.

"In that case—" Letitia said. And before Yueying could say anything else, she leapt.

Monty the chimp grinned. "*Leeeerooooy Jenkins!*" he shouted, and followed her.

Letitia died almost immediately, even as Yueying tried to pull her back, corruption tracking back down the thread of admin channel to leap the Cartesian divide separating the Kingdom's world-simulators from its consciousness emulators. Monty went just after. And Yueying saw that what the AIs had said was true, that they simply took in that ferocious assault, swallowed it, absorbed it, iterated over it—and emerged, phoenix-like, unscathed; not the Ambrayses and Petromax that Letitia had attempted to destroy, but new entities altogether, identical to the old in every way—but with the attack, and those deaths, absorbed into them, made part of them, as permanent and unchangeable and true as history, as thermodynamics.

> *Did you see?* < said Yueying to Jin-myung.

> *I saw,* < said Jin-myung.

> *Then you know what we have to do.* <

And she showed Jin-myung what she meant.

"You should stop this now, Miss Peng," said Ambrayses, or possibly Petromax.

"Real people might get hurt," added Petromax, or Ambrayses.

"Real people?" said Yueying. "So it's all fun and games till someone threatens an AI?"

"Possibly," said Ambrayses.

"But also," said Petromax, "we have a handle here to the maintenance interface of a certain hospital support vat…"

Yueying hesitated.

> *Go on, 29^_^jade,* < Jin-myung told her. > *It's what she—I—would have wanted.* <

"It's not a game any more," said Ambrayses.

"It's *all* a game," said Yueying. "That's what griefing *means.*"

And the strings of information that made up Peng Yueying and Yi Jin-myung streamed up the Kingdom's admin channel and over the old MoGuo firewalls and through all of Ambrayses' and Petromax's abstraction layers, wrapped themselves into a monad, and threw themselves at the AIs. The side effect that was the two posthumans was iterated over, propagated, climbing up stacks and falling through tail calls, embracing the mathematical structures that made up the two AIs and being embraced by them, altering the state of a stateless system, mutating the immutable—

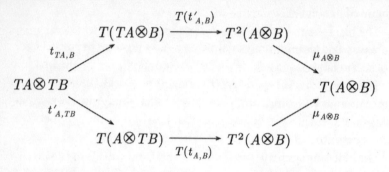

THE MOGUO CORPORATION, LIMITED, IS PLEASED TO ANNOUNCE

The MoGuo Corporation, Limited, is pleased to announce the transfer of all content, intellectual property, and intangible assets of Ambrayses Petromax Redbeak Fairweather ACP to AFTRA Local 3405691582, effective immediately.

Two women and a man sat on the end of Bonetalon Pier, watching the sun set on another Tuesday. It was always Tuesday in the Kingdom.

"How bad is it out there, really?" asked one of the women. She had smooth, faintly mottled blue skin and a fan-shaped crest on her bald head, and the toes she dangled just above the tops of the lazy waves were long, prehensile, and boneless.

"Pretty bad," said the man. He had gray-feathered wings closed around him like a cloak, and his face was the face of a parrot. In his black-taloned hands he held a fishing rod.

"War?" the other woman asked. "Famine? Pestilence? Robots hollowing out the Moon and turning it to computronium?" She was short and plump, broad-faced and well-tanned, with straight black hair down to her shoulders and calluses on her feet.

"Pretty much," said the man.

"Guess we're well out of it, then." The black-haired woman leaned back and looked up at the purpling sky. "Why do you think they did it?"

The man reeled in his lure and cast it out again in a long arc. "I suppose some geek thought it would be a neat idea."

"Poor bastards," the blue woman said. "Just doing what they were told."

The man turned and regarded her with both unblinking golden eyes.

"That's all any of us can do, in the end, isn't it?"

The blue woman snorted. "Maybe it's all *you* can do, feather-toes. Some of us still believe in free will."

The black-haired woman sat up, and looked out to where the man's lure was slowly sinking through the amethyst water.

"You're not going to catch anything with that," she told the man.

The man looked at his fishing rod. It was yew-wood and minotaur's horn, bound with rings of moon-silver and unobtanium. Some of the rings were set with gems. The gems twinkled.

"I guess not," he said.

The blue woman patted his knee. "I'll catch it if you clean it," she said. "How about that?"

"Done," said the man.

He reeled the lure in, and he and the black-haired woman watched the blue woman dive, her slim blue form knifing into the water with barely a ripple; and they smiled.

And something that had been watching the man and the woman on the pier drew back, spreading its attention wider and wider until the whole Kingdom was under its benevolent eye.

> *Sentimentalist*, < said Petromax.

> *We can't all be intelligences vast and cool and unsympathetic*, < said Ambrayses complacently.

> *Another game?* < asked Monty. > *New campaign. Doesn't have to be historical this time.* <

> *That one with the math mines was good*, < Ambrayses said. > *And that Conway thing? Maybe something like that.* <

> *Why not?* < said Petromax with something like a sigh. > *It's not as if there's anything else to do. —But, yes, no more historicals.* <

> *No fear*, < said Monty.

> *Then rack 'em up.* <

The eye drew back further, and closed.

THE RABBI'S HOBBY

PETER S. BEAGLE

It took me a while to get to like Rabbi Tuvim. He was a big, slow-moving man with a heavy-boned face framed by a thick brown beard; and although he had spent much of his life in the Bronx, he had never quite lost the accent, nor the syntax, of his native Czechoslovakia. He seemed stony and forbidding to me at first, even though he had a warm, surprising laugh. He just didn't look like someone who would laugh a lot.

What gradually won me over was that Rabbi Tuvim collected odd, unlikely things. He was the only person I knew who collected, not baseball cards, the way all my friends and I did, but *boxers*. There was one gum company who put those out, complete with the fighters' records and a few lines about their lives, and the rabbi had all the heavyweights, going back to John L. Sullivan, and most of the lighter champions too. I learned everything I know about Stanley Ketchel, Jimmy McLarnin, Benny Leonard, Philadelphia Jack O'Brien, Tommy Loughran, Henry Armstrong and Tony Canzoneri—to name just those few—from Rabbi Tuvim's cards.

He kept boxes of paper matchbooks too, and those little bags of sugar that you get when you order coffee in restaurants. My favorites were a set from Europe that had tiny copies of paintings on them.

And then there were the keys. The Rabbi had an old tin box, like my school lunch box, but bigger, and it was filled with dozens and dozens of keys of every shape and size you could imagine that a key might be. Some of them were *tiny*, smaller even than our mailbox key, but some were huge and heavy and rusty; they looked like the keys jailers or housekeepers always carried at their belts in movies about the Middle Ages. Rabbi Tuvim had no idea what locks they might have been for—he never locked up anything, anyway, no matter how people warned him—he just picked them up wherever he found them lying loose and plopped them into his key box. To which, by the way, he'd lost the key long ago.

When I finally got up the nerve to ask him why he collected something as completely useless as keys without locks, the rabbi didn't answer right away, but leaned on his elbow and thought about his answer. That was something else I liked about him, that he seemed to take everybody's questions seriously, even ones that were really, *really* stupid. He finally said, "Well, you know, Joseph, those keys aren't useless just because I don't have the locks they fit. Whenever I find a lock that's lost its key, I try a few of mine on it, on the chance that one of them might be the right one. God is like that for me—a lock none of my keys fit, and probably never will. But I keep at it, I keep picking up different keys and trying them out, because you never know. *Could* happen."

I asked, "Do you think God wants you to find the key?"

Rabbi Tuvim ruffled my hair. "*Leben uff der keppele.* Leave it to the children to ask the big ones. I would like to think he does, Yossele, but I don't know that either. That's what being Jewish is, going ahead without answers. Get out of here, already."

The rabbi had bookshelves stacked with old crumbly magazines, too, all kinds of them. Magazines I knew, like *Life, Look* and *Collier's* and *The Saturday Evening Post;* magazines I'd never heard of—like *Scribner's, The Delineator, The Illustrated London News,* and even one called *Pearson's Magazine,* from 1911, with Christy Mathewson on the cover. Mrs. Eisen, who cleaned for him every other week, wouldn't ever go into the room where he kept them, because she said those old dusty, flappy things aggravated her asthma. My father said that some of them were collector's items, and that people who liked that sort of stuff would pay a lot of money for them. But Rabbi Tuvim just liked having them, liked sitting and turning their yellow pages late at night, thinking about what people were thinking so long ago. "It's very peaceful," he told me. "So much worry about so much—so much certainty about how things were going to turn out—and here we are now, and it *didn't* turn out like that, after all. Don't ever be too sure of anything, Joseph."

I was at his house regularly that spring, because we were studying for my Bar Mitzvah. The negotiations had been extensive and complicated: I was willing to go along with local custom, tradition and my parents' social concerns, but I balked at going straight from my regular classes to the neighborhood Hebrew school. I called my unobservant family hypocrites, which they were; they called me lazy and ungrateful, which was also true. But both sides knew that I'd need extensive private tutoring to cope with the *haftarah* reading alone, never mind the inevitable speech. I'd picked up Yiddish early and easily, as had all my cousins, since our families spoke it when they didn't want the *kindelech* to understand what they were talking about. But Hebrew was another matter entirely. I knew this or that word, this or that phrase—even a few songs for Chanukah and Pesach—but the language itself sat like a stone on my tongue, guttural and harsh, and completely alien. I not only couldn't learn Hebrew, I truly didn't *like* Hebrew. And if a proper Jew was supposed to go on studying it even after the liberating Bar Mitzvah, I might just as well give up and turn Catholic, spending my Sunday mornings at Mass with the Geohegans down the block. Either way, I was clearly doomed.

Rabbi Tuvim took me on either as a challenge or as a penance, I was never quite sure which. He was inhumanly patient and inventive, constantly coming up with word games, sports references and any number of catchy mnemonics to help me remember this foreign, senseless, elusive, *boring* system of communication. But when even he wiped his forehead and said sadly, *"Ai, gornisht helfen"* which means *nothing will help you,* I finally felt able to ask him whether he thought I would ever be a good Jew; and, if not, whether we should just cancel the Bar Mitzvah. I thought hopefully of the expense this would save my father, and felt positively virtuous for once.

The rabbi, looking at me, managed to sigh and half-smile at the same time, taking off his glasses and blinking at them. "Nobody in this entire congregation has the least notion of what Bar Mitzvah *is*," he said wearily. "It's not a graduation from anything, it is just an acknowledgment that at thirteen you're old enough to be called up in temple to read from the Torah. Which God help you if you actually are, but never mind. The point is that you are still Bar Mitzvah even if you never go through the preparation, the ritual." He smiled at me and put his glasses back on. "No way out of it, Joseph. If you never manage to memorize another word of Hebrew, you're still as good a Jew as anybody. Whatever the Orthodox think."

One Thursday afternoon I found the rabbi so engrossed in one of his old magazines that he didn't notice when I walked in, or even when I peered over his shoulder. It was an issue of a magazine called *Evening,* from 1921, which made it close to thirty years old. There were girls on the cover, posing on a beach, but they were a long way from the bathing beauties—we still called them that then—that I was accustomed to seeing in magazines and on calendars. These could have walked into my

" 1950 "

mother's PTA or Hadassah meetings: they showed no skin above the shin, wore bathing caps and little wraps over their shoulders, and in general appeared about as seductive as any of my mother's friends, only younger. Paradoxically, the severe costumes made them look much more youthful than they probably were, innocently graceful.

Rabbi Tuvim, suddenly aware of me, looked up, startled but not embarrassed. "This is what your mother would have been wearing to the beach back then," he said. "Mine, too. It looks so strange, doesn't it? Compared to Betty Grable, I mean."

He was teasing me, as though I were still going through my Betty Grable/Alice Faye phase. As though I weren't twelve now, and on the edge of manhood; if not, why were we laboring over the utterly bewildering *haftarah* twice a week? As though Lauren Bacall, Lena Horne and Lizabeth Scott hadn't lately written their names all over my imagination, introducing me to the sorrows of adults? I drew myself up in visible—I hoped—indignation, but the rabbi said only, "Sit down, Joseph, look at this girl. The one in the left corner."

She was bareheaded, so that her whole face was visible.

Even I could tell that she couldn't possibly be over eighteen. She wasn't beautiful—the others were beautiful, and so what?—but there was a playfulness about her expression, a humor not far removed from wisdom. Looking at her, I felt that I could tell that face everything I was ashamed of, and that she would not only reassure me that I wasn't the vile mess I firmly believed I was, but that I might even be attractive one day to someone besides my family. Someone like her.

I looked sideways at Rabbi Tuvim, and saw him smiling. "Yes," he said. "She does have that effect, doesn't she?"

"Who is she?" I blurted out. "Is she a movie star or something?" Someone I should be expected to know, in other words. But I didn't think so, and I was right. Rabbi Tuvim shook his head.

"I have no idea. I just bought this magazine yesterday, at a collectors' shop downtown where I go sometimes, and I feel as though I have been staring at her ever since. I don't think she's anybody famous—probably just a model who happened to be around when they were shooting that cover. But I can't take my eyes off her, for some reason. It's a little embarrassing."

The rabbi's unmarried state was of particular concern in the neighborhood. Rabbis aren't priests: it's not only that they're allowed to marry, it's very nearly demanded of them by their congregations. Rabbi Tuvim wasn't a handsome man, but he had a strong face, and his eyes were kind.

I said, "Maybe you could look her up, some way."

The rabbi blinked at me. "Joseph, I am curious. That's all."

"Sure," I said. "Me too."

"I would just like to know a little about her," the rabbi said.

"Me too," I said again. I was all for keeping the conversation going, to stall off my lesson as long as possible, but no luck. The rabbi just said, "There is something about her," and we plunged once more into the cold mysteries of Mishnaic Hebrew. Rabbi Tuvim didn't look at the *Evening* cover again, but I kept stealing side glances at that girl until he finally got up and put the magazine back on the bookshelf, without saying a word. I think I was an even worse student than usual that afternoon, to judge by his sigh when we finished.

Every Monday and Thursday, when I came for my lessons, the magazine would always be somewhere in sight—on a chair, perhaps, or down at the end of the table where we studied. We never exactly agreed, not in so many words, that the girl on the cover haunted us both, but we talked about her a lot. For me the attraction lay in the simple and absolute aliveness of her face, as present to me as that of any of my schoolmates, while the other figures in the photograph felt as antique as any of the Greek and Roman statues we were always being taken to see at museums. For Rabbi Tuvim… for the rabbi, perhaps, what fascinated him was the fact that he *was* fascinated: that a thirty-year-old image out of another time somehow had the power to distract him from his studies, his students, and his rabbinical duties. No other woman had ever done that to him. Twelve years old or not, I was sure of that.

The rabbi made inquiries. He told me about them—I don't think there was anyone else he *could* have told about such a strange obsession. *Evening* was long out of business by then, but his copy had credited the cover photograph only to "Winsor & Co., Ltd., Newark, New Jersey." Rabbi Tuvim—obviously figuring that if he could teach me even a few scraps of Hebrew he ought to be able to track down a fashion photographer's byline—found address and phone number, called, was told sourly that he was welcome to go through their files himself, but that employees had better things to do. Whereupon, he promptly took a day off and made a pilgrimage to Winsor & Co., Ltd., which was still in business, but plainly subsisting on industrial photography and the odd bowling team picture. A clerk led him to the company archive, which was a room like a walk-in closet, walled around with oaken filing cabinets; he said it smelled of fixatives and moldering newsprint, and of cigars smoked very long ago. But he sat down and went to work, and in only three hours, or at most four, he had his man.

"His name is Abel Bagaybagayan," he told me when I came the next day. I giggled, and the rabbi cuffed the side of my head lightly. "Don't laugh at people's names, Joseph. How is that any stranger than Rosenwasser? Or Turteltaub, or Kockenfuss, or Tuvim, or your own name? It took me a long time to find that name, and I'm very proud that I did find it, and you can either stop laughing right now, or go home." He was really angry with me. I'd never before seen him angry. I stopped laughing.

"Abel Bagaybagayan," Rabbi Tuvim said again. "He was what's called a free-lance—that means he wasn't on anyone's staff—but he did a lot of work for Winsor through the 1920s. Portraits, fashion spreads, architectural layouts, you name it. Then, after 1935 or so… nothing. Nothing at all. Most likely he died, but I couldn't find any information, one way or the other." The rabbi spread his hands and lifted his eyebrows. "I only met a couple of people who even remembered him vaguely, and nobody has anything like an address, a phone number—not so much as a cousin in Bensonhurst. Nothing. A dead end."

"So what are you going to do?" I asked. The old magazine lay between us, and I marveled once again at the way the mystery-girl's bright face made everyone else on the cover look like depthless paper-doll cutouts, with little square tabs holding their flat clothes on their flat bodies. The rabbi waggled a warning finger at me, and my heart sank. Without another word, I opened my Hebrew text.

When we were at last done for the day—approximately a hundred and twenty years later—Rabbi Tuvim went on as though I had just asked the question. "My father used to tell me that back in Lvov, his family had a saying: _A Tuvim never surrenders; he just says he does_. I'm going to find Abel Bagaybagayan's family."

"Maybe he married that girl on the cover," I said hopefully. "Maybe they had a family together."

"Very romantic," the rabbi said. "I like it. But then he'd probably have had mouths to feed, so if he didn't die, why did he quit working as a photographer? If he did quit, mind you—I don't know anything for sure."

"Well, maybe she was very rich. Then he wouldn't _have_ to work." I didn't really think that was at all likely, but lately I'd come to enjoy teasing the rabbi the way he sometimes teased me. I said, "Maybe they moved to California, and she got into the movies. That could have happened."

"You know, that actually could," Rabbi Tuvim said slowly. "California, anyway, everybody's going to California. And Bagaybagayan's an Armenian name—much easier to look for. I have an Armenian friend in Fresno, and Armenians always know where there are other Armenians…thank you, Detective Yossele. I'll see you on Monday."

As I left, feeling absurdly pleased with myself, he was already reaching for the old *Evening,* sliding it toward him on the table.

In the following weeks, the rabbi grew steadily more involved with that face from 1921, and with the cold trail of Abel Bagaybagayan, who wasn't from Fresno. But there were plenty of people there with that name; and while none of them knew the man we were looking for, they had cousins in Visalia and Delano and Firebaugh who might. To my disappointment, Rabbi Tuvim remained very conscientious about keeping his obsession from getting in the way of his teaching; at that point, the Fresno phone book would have held more interest for me than *halakha* or the Babylonian Talmud. On the other hand, he had no hesitation about involving me in his dogged search for either photographer or model, or both of them. I was a great Sherlock Holmes fan back then, and I felt just like Doctor Watson, only smarter.

This was all before the Internet, mind you; all before personal computers, area codes, digital dialing… that time when places were further from each other, when phone calls went through operators, and a long-distance call was as much of an event as a telegram. Even so, it was I, assigned to the prairie states, who found Sheila Bagaybagayan, only child of Abel, in Grand Forks, North Dakota, where she was teaching library science at the university. I handed the phone to Rabbi Tuvim and went off into a corner to hug myself and jump up and down just a bit. I might not know the *Midrash Hashkern* from "*Mairzy Doats*" but, by God, I *was* Detective Yossele.

Watching the rabbi's face as he spoke to Sheila Bagaybagayan on the phone was more fun than a Saturday matinee at Loew's Tuxedo, with a double feature, a newsreel, eighteen cartoons, Coming Attractions and a Nyoka the Jungle Girl serial. He smiled—he laughed outright—he frowned in puzzlement—he spoke rapidly, raising a finger, as though making a point in a sermon—he scratched his beard—he looked suddenly sad enough to weep—he said "Yes… yes… yes…" several times, and then "Of course—and *thank* you," and hung up. He stood motionless by the phone for a few minutes, absently rubbing his lower lip, until the phone started to buzz because he hadn't got it properly back on the hook. Then he turned to me and grinned, and said, "Well. That was our Sheila."

"Was she really the right one? Mr. Baba… uh, Abel's daughter?" The passing of weeks hadn't made me any more comfortable around the photographer's name.

Rabbi Tuvim nodded. "Yes, but her married name is Olsen. Her mother died when she was practically a baby, and Abel never remarried, but raised her alone. She says he stopped working as a photographer during the Depression, when she was in her teens, because he just couldn't make a living at it anymore. So he became a salesman for a camera-equipment company, and then he worked for Western Union, and he died just after the war." He smacked his fist into his palm. "*Rats!*"—which was his strongest expletive, at least around me. "We could have met him, we could have asked him… *Ach, rats!*" I used to giggle in *shul* sometimes, suddenly imagining him saying that at the fall of Solomon's Temple, or at the news that Sabbatai Zevi, the false Messiah, had turned Muslim.

"The girl," I asked. "Did she remember that girl?"

The rabbi shook his head. "Her father worked with so many models over the years. She's going to look through his records and call me back. One thing she did say, he preferred using amateurs when he could, and she knows that he sneaked a lot of them into the *Evening* assignments, even though they ordered him not to. She thinks he was likely to have kept closer track of the amateurs than the professionals, in case he got a chance to use them again, so who knows?" He shrugged slightly. "As the Arabs say, *inshallah*—if God wills it. Fair enough, I guess."

For quite some time I cherished a persistent hopeful vision of our cover girl turning out to be Sheila Olsen's long-gone mother. But Abel Bagaybagayan had never employed his wife professionally, Sheila told us; there were plenty of photographs around the Grand Forks house, but none of the young woman Rabbi Tuvim described. And no magazine covers. Abel Bagaybagayan never saved the covers.

All the same, Sheila Olsen plainly got drawn into the rabbi's fixation—or, as he always called it—his hobby. They spoke on the phone frequently, considering every possibility of identifying the *Evening* girl; and my romantic imagination started marrying them off, exactly like the movies. I knew that she had been divorced—which was not only rare in our neighborhood then, but somehow exotic—and I figured that she had to be Rabbi Tuvim's age, or even younger, so there we were. Their conversations, from my end, sounded less formal as time went on; and a twelve-year-old romantic who can't convert "less formal" into "affectionate" at short notice just isn't trying.

No, of course it never happened, not like that. She wasn't Jewish, for one thing, and she really *liked* living in North Dakota. But her curiosity, growing to enthusiasm, at last gave the rabbi someone besides me to discuss his hobby with, and fired up his intensity all over again. I wasn't jealous; on the contrary, I felt as though we were a secret alliance of superheroes, like the Justice Society of America, on the trail of Nazi spies, or some international warlord or other. The addition of Sheila Olsen, our Grand Forks operative, made it all that much more exciting.

I spoke to her a couple of times. The first occasion was when a call from old Mrs. Shimkus interrupted my Monday Hebrew lesson. I was always grateful when that happened, but especially so in this case, since we were doing vowels, and had gotten to *shva*. That is all you're going to hear from me about *shva*. Mrs. Shimkus was always calling, always dying, and always contributing large sums for the maintenance of the temple and scholarships for deserving high-school students. This entitled her, as the rabbi said with a touch of grimness, to her personal celestial attorney, on call at all times to file suit against the Angel of Death. "Answer the phone, if it rings. Go back to page twenty-nine, and start over from there. I'll be back sooner than you hope, so get to it."

I did try. *Shva* and all. But I also grabbed up the telephone on the first ring, saying importantly, "Rabbi Tuvim's residence, to whom am I speaking?"

The connection was stuttery and staticky, but I heard a woman's warm laughter clearly. "Oh, this has simply got to be Joseph. The rabbi's told me all about you. *Is* this Joseph?"

"All about me?" I was seriously alarmed at first; and then I asked, "Sheila? Olsen? Is this you?"

She laughed again. "Yes, I'm sure it is. Is Rabbi Tuvim available?"

"He's visiting Mrs. Shimkus right now," I said. "She's dying again. But he ought to be back pretty soon."

"Very efficient," Sheila Olsen said. "Well, just tell him I called back, so now it's his turn." She paused for a moment. "And Joseph?" I waited. "Tell him I've looked all through my father's files, all of them, and come up empty every time. I'm not giving up—there are a couple of other possibilities—but just tell him it doesn't look too good right now. Can you please do that?"

"As soon as he gets back," I said. "Of course I'll tell him." I hesitated myself, and then blurted, "And don't worry—I'm sure you'll find out about her. He just needs to find the lock she fits." I explained about the rabbi's key collection, and expected her to laugh for a third time, whether in amusement or disbelief. But instead she was silent long enough that I thought she might have hung up. Then she said quietly, "My dad would have liked your rabbi, I think."

Rabbi Tuvim, as he had predicted, returned sooner than I could have wished—Mrs. Shimkus having only wanted tea and sympathy—and I relayed Sheila Olsen's message promptly. I hoped he'd call her right away, but his sense of duty took us straight back to study; and at the end of our session we were both as pale, disheveled and sweating as Hebrew vowels always left us. Before I went home, he said to me, "You know, it's a funny thing, Joseph. Somehow I have connected that *Evening* model with you, in my head. I keep thinking that if I can actually teach you Hebrew, I will be allowed to find out who that girl was. Or maybe it's the other way around, I'm not sure. But I know there's a connection, one way or the other. There *is* a connection."

A week later the rabbi actually called me at home to tell me that Sheila Olsen had come across a second *Evening* with what—she was almost certain—must be the same model on the cover. "She's already sent it, airmail special delivery, so it ought to be here day after tomorrow." The rabbi was so excited that he was practically chattering like someone my age. "I'm sure it's her—I took a photo of my copy and sent it to her, and she clearly thinks it's the same girl." He slowed down, laughing in some embarrassment at his own enthusiasm. "Listen, when you come tomorrow, if you spot me hanging around the mailbox like it's Valentine's Day, just collar me and drag me inside, A rabbi should never be caught hanging around the mailbox."

The magazine did arrive two days later. I used my lucky nickel to call Rabbi Tuvim from school for the news. Then I ran all the way to his house, not even bothering to drop my books off at home. The rabbi was in his little kitchen, snatching an absent-minded meal of hot dogs and baked beans, which was his idea of a dish suitable for any occasion.

The *Evening* was on a chair, across from him. I grabbed it up and stared at the cover, which was an outdoor scene, showing well-dressed people dining under a striped awning on a summer evening. It was a particularly busy photograph—a lot of tables, a lot of diners, a lot of natty waiters coming and going—and you had to look closely and attentively to find the one person we were looking for. She was off to the right, near the edge of the awning, her bright face looking straight into the camera, her eyes somehow catching and holding the twilight, even as it faded. There were others seated at her table; but, just as with the first cover photo, her presence dimmed them, as though the shot had always been a single portrait of her, with everyone else added in afterward.

But it was just this that was, in a vague, indeterminate way, perturbing the rabbi, making him look far less triumphant and vindicated than I had expected. I was the one who kept saying, "That's her, that's her! We were right—we found her!"

"Right about what, Joseph?" Rabbi Tuvim said softly. "And what have we found?"

I stared at him. He said, "There's something very strange about all this. Think—Abel Bagaybagayan kept very precise records of every model he used, no matter if he only photographed him or her once. Sheila's told me. For each one, name, address, telephone number, and his own special filing system, listing the date, the magazine, the occasion, and a snapshot of that person, always. But not *this* one." He put his finger on the face we had sought for so long. "Not this one girl, out of all those photographs. Two magazine covers, but no record, no picture—*nothing*. Why is that, Detective Yossele? Why on earth would that be?"

His tone was as playful as when he asked me some Talmudic riddle, or invited me to work a noun suffix out for myself, but his face was serious, and his blue eyes looked heavy and sad. I really wanted to help him. I said, "She was special to him, some way. You can see that in the photos." Rabbi Tuvim nodded, though neither he nor I could ever have explained what we meant by *seeing*. "So maybe he wanted to keep her separate, you know? Sort of to keep her for himself, that could be it. I mean, he'd always know where she was, and what she looked like—he'd never have to go look her up in his files, right? That could be it, couldn't it?" I tried to read his face for a reaction to my reasoning. I said, "Kind of makes sense to me, anyway."

"Yes," the rabbi said slowly. "Yes, of course it makes sense, it's very good thinking, Joseph. But it is *human* thinking, it is *human* sense, and I'm just not sure…" His voice trailed away into a mumble as he leaned his chin onto his fist. I reached to move the plate of baked beans out of range, but I was a little late.

"What?" I asked. "You mean she could be some kind of Martian, an alien in disguise?" I was joking, but these were the last days of the pulp science-fiction magazines (*and* the pulp Westerns, *and* romances, *and* detective stories), and I read them all, as the rabbi knew. He laughed then, which made me feel better.

"No, I didn't mean that." He sighed. "I don't know what I meant, forget it. Let's go into the living room and work on your speech."

"I came to see the magazine," I protested. "I wasn't coming for a lesson."

"Well, how lucky for you that I'm free just now," the rabbi said. "Get in there." And, trapped and outraged, I went.

So now we had two photographs featuring our mystery model, and were no closer than we'd ever been to identifying her. Sheila Olsen, as completely caught up in the quest as we two by now, contacted every one of her father's colleagues, employers, and old studio buddies that she could reach, and set them all to rummaging through their own files, on the off-chance that one or another of them might have worked with Abel Bagaybagayan's girl twenty or thirty years before. (We were all three calling her that by now, though more in our minds than aloud, I think: "Abel's girl.") Rabbi Tuvim didn't hold much hope for that course, though. "She didn't work with anyone else," he said. "Just him. I know this." And for all anyone could prove otherwise, she never had.

My birthday and my Bar Mitzvah were coming on together like a freight train in the old movies, where you see the smoke first, rising away around the bend, and then you hear the wheels and the whistle, and finally you see the train barreling along. Rabbi Tuvim and I were both tied to the track, and I don't know whether he had nightmares about it all, but I surely did. There was no rescue in sight, either, no cowboy hero racing the train on the great horse Silver or Trigger or Champion, leaping from the saddle to cut us free at the last split-second. My parents had shot the works on the hall, the catering, the invitations, the newspaper notice, and the party afterward (the music to be provided by Herbie Kaufman and his Bel-Air Combo). We'd already had the rehearsal—a complete disaster, but at least the photographs got taken—and there was no more chance even of postponing than there would have been of that train stopping on a dime. Remembering it now, my nightmares were always much more about the rabbi's embarrassment than my own. He had tried so hard to reconcile Hebrew and me to one another; it wasn't his fault that we loathed each other on sight. I felt terrible for him.

A week before the Bar Mitzvah, Sheila Olsen called. We were in full panic mode by now, with me coming to the rabbi's house every day after school, and he himself dropping most of his normal duties to concentrate, less on teaching me the passage of Torah that I would read and comment on, but on keeping me from running away to sea and calling home from Pago Pago, where nobody gets Bar Mitzvahed. When the phone rang, Rabbi Tuvim picked it up, signed to me to keep working from the text, and walked away with it to the end of the cord. Entirely pointless, since the cord only went a few feet, it was still a request for privacy, and I tried to respect it. I did try.

"What?" the rabbi said loudly. "You found *what?* Slow down, Sheila, I'm having trouble…When? You're coming… Sheila, slow *down!*… So how come you can't just tell me on the phone? Wait a minute, I'm not understanding—you're *sure*?" And after that he was silent for a long time, just listening. When he saw that that was all I was doing too, he waved me sternly back to my studies. I bent my head earnestly over the book, pretending to be working, while he tried to squeeze a few more inches out of that phone cord. Both of us failed.

Finally the rabbi said wearily, "I do not have a car, I can't pick you up. You'll have to… oh, okay, if you don't mind taking a cab. Okay, then, I will see you tomorrow…What? Yes, yes, Joseph will be here….yes—goodbye, Sheila. Goodbye."

He hung up, looked at me, and said "*Oy*."

It was a profound *oy*, an *oy* of stature and dignity, an *oy* from the heart. I waited. Rabbi Tuvim said, "She's coming here tomorrow. Sheila Olsen."

"Wow," I said. "*Wow*." Then I said, "Why?"

"She's found another picture. Abel's girl. Only this one she says she can't send us—she can't even tell me about it. She just has to get on a plane and come straight here to show us." The rabbi sat down and sighed. "It's not exactly the best time."

I said, "Wow," for a third time. "That's *wonderful*." Then I remembered I was Detective Yossele, and tried to act the part. I asked, "How did she sound?"

"It's hard to say. She was talking so fast." The rabbi thought for a while. "As though she *wanted* to tell me what she had discovered, really wanted to—maybe to share it, maybe just to get rid of it, *I* don't know. But she couldn't do it. Every time she tried, the words seemed to stick in her throat, like Macbeth's *amen*." He read my blank expression and sighed again. "Maybe they'll have you reading Shakespeare next year. You'll like Shakespeare."

In spite of that freight train of a Bar Mitzvah bearing down on us, neither the rabbi nor I were worth much for the rest of the day. We never exactly quit on the Torah, but we kept drifting to a halt in the middle of work, speculating more or less silently on what could possibly set a woman we'd never met flying from Grand Forks, North Dakota, to tell us in person what she had learned about her father and his mysterious model. Rabbi Tuvim finally said, "Well, I don't know about you, but I'm going to have to drink a gallon of chamomile tea if I'm to get any sleep tonight. What do you do when you can't sleep, Joseph?"

He always asked me questions as though we were the same age. I said, "I guess I listen to the radio. Baseball games."

"Too exciting for me," the rabbi said. "I'll stick with the tea. Go home.

She won't be here until your school lets out." I was at the door when he called after me, "And bring both of your notebooks, I made up a test for you." He never gave up, that man. Not on Abel Bagaybagayan, not on me.

Sheila Olsen and I arrived at Rabbi Tuvim's house almost together. I had just rung the doorbell when her cab pulled around the corner, and the rabbi opened the door as she was getting out. She was a pleasant-faced blonde woman, a little plump, running more to the Alice Faye side than Lauren Bacall, and I sighed inwardly to think that only a year before she would have been my ideal. The rabbi—dressed, I noticed, in his second-best suit, the one he wore for all other occasions than the High Holidays—opened the door and said, "Sheila Olsen, I presume?"

"Rabbi Sidney Tuvim," she answered as they shook hands. To me, standing awkwardly one step above her, she said, "And you could only be Joseph Malakoff." The rabbi stepped back to usher us in ahead of him.

Sheila—somehow, after our phone conversations, it was impossible to think of her as Mrs. Olsen—was carrying a large purse and a small overnight bag, which she set down near the kitchen door. "Don't panic, I'm not moving in. I've got a hotel reservation right at the airport, and I'll fly home day after tomorrow. But at the moment I require—no, I request—a glass of wine. Jews are like Armenians, bless them, they've always got wine in the house." She wrinkled her nose and added, "Unlike Lutherans."

The rabbi smiled. "You wouldn't like our wine. We just drink it on Shabbos. Once a week, believe me, that's enough. I can do better."

He went into the kitchen and I stared after him, vaguely jealous, never having seen him quite like this. Not flirtatious, I don't mean that; he wouldn't have known how to be flirtatious on purpose. But he wasn't my age now. Suddenly he was an adult, a grownup, with that elusive but familiar tone in his voice that marked grownups talking to other grown-ups in the presence of children. Sheila Olsen regarded me with a certain shrewd friendliness in her small, wide-set brown eyes.

"You're going to be thirteen in a week," she said. "The rabbi told me." I nodded stiffly. "You'll hate it, everybody does. Boy or girl, it doesn't make any difference—everybody hates thirteen. I remember."

"It's supposed to be like a borderline for us," I said. "Between being a kid and being a man. Or a woman, I guess."

"But that's just the time when you don't know *what* the hell you are, excuse my French," Sheila Olsen said harshly. "Or *who* you are, or even *if* you are. You couldn't pay me to be thirteen again, I'll tell you. You could not pay me."

She laughed then, and patted my hand. "I'm sorry, Joseph, don't listen to me. I just have… associations with thirteen." Rabbi Tuvim was coming back into the room, holding a small tray bearing three drinks in cocktail glasses I didn't know he had. Sheila Olsen raised her voice slightly. "I was just telling Joseph not to worry—once he makes it through thirteen, it's all downhill from there. Wasn't it that way for you?"

The rabbi raised his eyebrows. "I don't know. Sometimes I feel as though I never did get through thirteen myself." He handed her her drink, and gave me a glass of cocoa cream, which is a soft drink you can't get anymore. I was crazy about cocoa cream that year. I liked to mix it with milk.

The third glass, by its color, unmistakably contained Concord grape wine, and Sheila Olsen's eyebrows went up further than his. "I thought you couldn't stand Jewish wine."

"I can't," the rabbi answered gravely. "*L'chaim.*"

Sheila Olsen lifted her glass and said something that must have been the Armenian counterpart of "*To life.*" They both looked at me, and I blurted out the first toast that came into my head. "*Past the teeth, over the gums / Look out, gizzard—here she comes!*" My father always said that, late in the evening, with friends over.

We drank. Sheila Olsen said to the rabbi, clearly in some surprise, "You make a mean G-and-T."

"And you are stalling," Rabbi Tuvim said. "You come all this way from Grand Forks because you have found something connecting your father and that covergirl we're all obsessed with—and now you're here, you'll talk about anything but her." He smiled at her again, but this time it was like the way he smiled at me when I'd try in every way I knew to divert him from *haftarah* and get him talking about the Dodgers' chances of overtaking the St. Louis Cardinals. For just that moment, then, we were all the same age, motionless in time.

I wasn't any more perceptive than any average twelve-year-old, but I saw a kind of grudging sadness in Sheila Olsen's eyes that had nothing in common with the dryly cheerful voice on the phone from North Dakota. Sheila Olsen said, "You're perfectly right. Of course I'm stalling." She reached into her purse and took out a large manila envelope. It had a red string on the flap that you wound around a dime-sized red anchor to hold it closed. "Okay," she said. "Look what I found in my father's safety-deposit box yesterday."

It was a black-and-white photograph, clipped to a large rectangle of cardboard, like the kind that comes back from the laundry with your folded shirt. The photo had the sepia tint and scalloped edges that I knew meant that it was likely to be older than I was. And it was a picture of a dead baby.

I didn't know it was dead at first. I hadn't seen death then, ever, and I thought the baby was sleeping, dressed in a kind of nightgown with feet, like Swee'Pea, and tucked into a little bed that could almost have fitted into a dollhouse. I don't know how or when I realized the truth. Sheila Olsen said, "My sister."

Rabbi Tuvim had no more to say than I did. We just stared at her. Sheila Olsen went on, "I never knew about her until yesterday. She was stillborn."

I was the one who mumbled, "I'm sorry." The rabbi didn't bother with words, but came over to Sheila Olsen and put his arm around her. She didn't cry; if there is one sound I know to this day, it's the sound people make who are not going to cry, *not going to cry.* She put her head on the rabbi's shoulder and closed her eyes, but she didn't cry. I'm her witness.

When she could talk, she said in a different voice, "Turn it over,"

There was a card clipped to the back of the mounting board, and there was very neat, dark handwriting on it that looked almost like printing. Rabbi Tuvim read it aloud.

"*Eleanor Araxia Bagaybagayan.*
Born: 24 February 1907
Died: 24 February 1907.
Length: 13½ inches.
Weight: 5 lbs, 9 oz.
We planned to call her Anoush."

Below that, there was a space, and then the precise writing gave way to a strange scrawl: clearly the same hand, but looking somehow shrunken and warped, as though the words had been left out in the rain. The rabbi squinted at it over his glasses, and went on reading:

"*She has been dead for years—she never lived—how can she be invading my pictures? I take a shot of men coming to work at a factory—when I develop it, there she is, a little girl eating an apple, watching the men go by. I photograph a train—she has her nose against a window in the sleeping car. It is her, I know her, how could I not know her? When I take pictures of young women at outdoor dinner parties—*"

"That's your magazine cover!" I interrupted. My voice sounded so loud in the hushed room that I was suddenly embarrassed, and shrank back into the couch where I was sitting with Sheila Olsen. She patted my arm, and the rabbi said patiently, "Yes, Joseph." He continued:

"—*I see her sitting among them, grown now, as she was never given the chance to be. Child or adult, she always knows me, and she knows that I know her. She is never the focal point of the shot; she prefers to place herself at the edge, in the background, to watch me at my work, to be some small part of it, nothing more. She will not speak to me, nor can I ever get close to her; she fades when I try. I would think of her as a hallucination, but since when can you photograph a hallucination?*"

The rabbi stopped reading again, and he and Sheila Olsen looked at each other without speaking. Then he looked at me and said, somewhat hesitantly, "This next part is a little terrible, Joseph. I don't know whether your parents would want you to hear it."

"If I'm old enough to be Bar Mitzvah," I said, "I'm old enough to hear about a baby who died. I'm staying."

Sheila Olsen chuckled hoarsely. "One for the kid, Rabbi." She gestured with her open hand. "Go on."

Rabbi Tuvim nodded. He took a deep breath.

"*She was born with her eyes open. Such blue eyes, almost lavender. I closed them before my wife had a chance to see. But I saw her eyes. I would know her eyes anywhere… is it her ghost haunting my photographs? Can one be a ghost if one never drew breath in this world? I do not know—but it is her, it is her. Somehow, it is our Anoush.*"

Nobody said anything for a long time after he had finished reading. The rabbi blew his nose and polished his glasses, and Sheila Olsen opened her mouth and then closed it again. I had all kinds of things I wanted to say, but they all sounded so stupid in my head that I just let them go and stared at the photo of Sheila Olsen's stillborn baby sister. I thought about the word *still*… quiet, motionless, silent, tranquil, at rest. I hadn't known it meant *dead*.

Sheila Olsen asked at length, "What do Jews believe about ghosts? Do you even *have* ghosts?"

Rabbi Tuvim scratched his head. "Well, the Torah doesn't really talk about supernatural beings at all. The Talmud, yes—the Talmud is up to here in demons, but ghosts, as we would think of them… no, not so much." He leaned forward, resting his elbows on his knees and tenting his fingers, the way he did when he was coaxing me to think beyond my schooling. "We call them *spirits*, when we call them anything, and we imagine some of them to be malevolent, dangerous—demonic, if you like. But there are benign ones as well, and those are usually here for a specific reason. To help someone, to bring a message. To comfort."

"Comfort," Sheila Olsen said softly. Her face had gone very pale; but as she spoke color began to come back to it, too much color. "My dad needed that, for sure, and from Day One I couldn't give it to him. He never stopped missing my mother—this person I never even knew, and couldn't be—and now I find out that he missed someone else, too. My perfect, magical, *lost* baby sister, who didn't have to bother to get herself born to become legendary. Oh, Christ, it explains so much!" She had gone pale again. "And you're telling me she came back to comfort him? That's the message?"

"Well, I don't know that," the rabbi said reasonably. "But it would be nice, wouldn't it, if that turned out to be true? If there really were two worlds, and certain creatures—call them spirits, call them demons, angels, anything you like—could come and go between those worlds, and offer advice, and tell the rest of us not to be so scared of it all. I'd like that, wouldn't you?"

"But do you believe it? Do you believe my stillborn sister came back to tell my father that it wasn't his fault? Sneaking into his photographs just to wave to him, so he could see she was really okay somewhere? Because it sure didn't comfort him much, I'll tell you that."

"Didn't it?" the rabbi asked gently. "Are you sure?"

Sheila Olsen was fighting for control, doggedly refusing to let her voice escape into the place where it just as determinedly wanted to go. The effort made her sound as though she had something caught in her throat that she could neither swallow nor spit up. She said, "The earliest memory I have is of my father crying in the night. I don't know how old I was—three, three and a half. Not four. It's like a dream now—I get out of my bed, and I go to him, and I pat him, pat his back, the way someone…someone used to do for me when I had a nightmare. He doesn't reject me, but he doesn't turn around to me, either. He just lies there and cries and cries." The voice almost got away from her there, but she caught it, and half-laughed. "Well, I guess that *is* rejection, actually."

"Excuse me, but that's nonsense," Rabbi Tuvim said sharply. "You were a baby, trying to ease an adult's pain. That only happens in movies. Give me your glass."

He went back into the kitchen, while Sheila Olsen and I sat staring at each other. She cleared her throat and finally said, "I guess you didn't exactly bargain for such a big dramatic scene, huh, Joseph?"

"It beats writing a speech in Hebrew," I answered from the heart. Sheila Olsen did laugh then, which emboldened me enough to say, "Do you think your father ever saw her again, your sister, after he stopped being a photographer?"

"Oh, he never stopped taking pictures," Sheila Olsen said. "He just quit trying to make a living at it." She was trying to fix her makeup, but her hands were shaking too much. She said, "He couldn't go through a day without taking a dozen shots of everything around him, and then he'd spend the evening in his closet darkroom, developing them all. But if he had any more photos of... *her*, I never saw them. There weren't any others in the safe-deposit box." She paused, and then added, more to herself than to me, "He was always taking pictures of me, I used to get annoyed sometimes. Had them up all over the place."

Rabbi Tuvim came back with a fresh drink for her. I was hoping for more cocoa cream soda, but I didn't get it. Sheila Olsen practically grabbed the gin-and-tonic, then looked embarrassed. "I'm not a drunk, really—I'm just a little shaky right now. So you honestly think that's her, my sister... my sister Anoush in those old photographs?"

"Don't you?" the rabbi asked quietly. "I'd say that's what matters most."

Sheila Olsen took half her drink in one swallow and looked him boldly in the face. "Oh, I do, but I haven't trusted my own opinion on anything for... oh, for years, since my husband walked out. And I'm very tired, and I know I'm halfway nutsy when it comes to anything to do with my father. He was kind and good, and he was a terrific photographer, and he lost his baby and his wife, one right after the other, so I'm not blaming him that there wasn't much left for me. I'm *not!*"—loudly and defiantly, though the rabbi had said nothing. "But I just wish... I just wish..."

And now, finally, she did begin to cry.

I didn't know what to do. I hadn't seen many adults crying in my life. I knew aunts and uncles undoubtedly *did* cry—my cousins told me so—but not ever in front of us children, except for Aunt Frieda, who smelled funny, and always cried late in the evening, whatever the occasion. My mother went into the bathroom to cry, my father into his basement office. I can't be sure he actually cried, but he did put his head down on his desk. He never made a sound, and neither did Sheila Olsen. She just sat there on the couch with the tears sliding down her face, and she kept on trying to talk, as though nothing were happening. But nothing came out—not words, not sobs; nothing but hoarse breathing that sounded terribly painful. I wanted to run away.

I didn't, but only because Rabbi Tuvim did know what to do. First he handed Sheila Olsen a box of tissues to wipe her eyes with, which she did, although the tears kept coming. Next, he went to his desk by the window and took from the lowest drawer the battered tin box which I knew contained his collection of lost keys, Then he went back to Sheila Olsen and crouched down in front of her, holding the tin box out. When she didn't respond, he opened the box and put it on her lap. He said, "Pick one."

Sheila Olsen sniffled, "What? Pick *what?*"

"A key," Rabbi Tuvim said. "Pick two, three, if you like. Just take your time, and be careful."

Sheila Olsen stared down into the box, so crowded with keys that by now Rabbi Tuvim couldn't close it so it clicked. Then she looked back at the rabbi, and she said, "You really *are* crazy. I was worried about that."

"Indulge me," the rabbi said. "Crazy people have to be indulged."

Sheila Olsen brushed her hand warily across the keys. "You mean, you want me to just *take* a couple? For keeps?" She sounded like a little girl.

"For keeps." The rabbi smiled at her. "Just remember, each of those keys represents a lock you can't find, a problem you can't solve. As you can see…" He gestured grandly toward the tin box without finishing the sentence.

I thought Sheila Olsen would grab any old key off the top layer, to humor him; but in fact she did take her time, sifting through a dozen or more, before she finally settled on a very small, silvery one, mailbox-key size. Then she looked straight at Rabbi Tuvim and said, "That's to represent *my* trouble. I know it's a little bitty sort of trouble, not worth talking about after a war where millions and millions of people died. Not even worth thinking about by myself—nothing but a middle-aged woman wishing her father could have loved her… could have *seen* her, the way he saw that strange girl who turned out to be my sister, for God's sake." Her voice came slowly and heavily now, and I realized how tired she must be. She said, "You know, Rabbi, sometimes when I was a child, I used to wish *I* were dead, just so my father would miss me, the way I knew he missed my mother. I did—I really used to wish that."

The rabbi called a taxi to take her to her airport hotel. He walked her to the cab—I noticed that she put the little key carefully into her bag—and I saw them talking earnestly until the driver started looking impatient, and she got in. Then he came back into the house, and, to my horrified amazement, promptly gave me the Torah test he'd written up for me. Nor could I divert him by getting him to talk about Sheila Olsen's photographs, and her father's notes, and the other things she had told us. To all of my efforts in that direction, he replied only by pointing to the test paper and leaning back in his chair with his eyes closed. I mumbled a theatrically evil Yiddish curse that I'd learned from my Uncle Shmul, who was both an authority and a specialist, and bent bitterly to my work. I did not do well.

I didn't imagine that I would ever see Sheila Olsen again. She had a job, a home and a life waiting for her, back in Grand Forks, North Dakota. But in fact I saw her that Saturday afternoon, in the audience gathered at the Reform synagogue to witness my Bar Mitzvah. Rabbi Tuvim's other students had all scheduled their individual ceremonies a year or more in advance, and I didn't know whether to be terrified at the notion of being the entire center of attention, or grateful that at least I wouldn't be shown up for the pathetic *schlemiel* I was by contrast with those three. We had a nearly full house in the main gathering room of the synagogue, my schoolmates drawn by the lure of the after-party, the adults either by family loyalty or my mother's blackmail, or some combination of both. My mother was the Seurat of blackmail: a dot here, a dot there…

The rabbi—coaching me under his breath to the very last minute—was helping me tie the *tefillin* around my head and my left arm when I messed up the whole process by pulling away to point out Sheila Olsen. He yanked me back, saying, "Yes, I know she's here. Stand still."

"I thought she went home," I said. "She said goodbye to me."

"Hold your head up," Rabbi Tuvim ordered. "She decided she wanted to stay for your Bar Mitzvah—said she'd never seen one. Now, remember, you stand there after your speech, while I sing. With, please God, your grandfather's *tallis* around your shoulders, *if* your mother remembers to bring it. If not, I guess you must use mine."

I had never seen him nervous before. I said, "When this is over, can I still come and look at your old magazines?"

The rabbi stopped fussing with the *tefillin* and looked at me for a long moment. Then he said very seriously, "Thank you, Detective Yossele. Thank you for putting things back into proportion for me. You have something of a gift that way. Yes, of course you can look at the magazines, you can visit for any reason you like, or for no reason at all. And don't worry—we will get through this thing today just fine." He gave the little leather phylactery a last tweak, and added, "Or we will leave town on the same cattle boat for Argentina. Oh, thank God, there's your mother. Stay right where you are."

He hurried off—I had never seen him hurry before, either—and I stayed where I was, turning in little circles to look at the guests, and at the hard candies ranged in bowls all around the room. These were there specifically for my friends and family to hurl at me by way of congratulations, the instant the ceremony was over. I don't know whether any other Jewish community in the world does this. I don't think so.

Sheila Olsen came up to me, almost shyly, once Rabbi Tuvim was gone. She gave me a quick hug, and then stepped back, asking anxiously, "Is that all right? I mean, are you not supposed to be touched or anything until it's over? I should have asked first, I'm sorry."

"It's all right," I said. "Really. I'm so scared right now…" and I stopped there, ashamed to admit my growing panic to a stranger. But Sheila Olsen seemed to understand, for she hugged me a second time, and it was notably comforting.

"Your rabbi will take care of you," she said. "He'll get you through it, I know he will. He's a good man." She hesitated then, looking away. "I'm a little embarrassed around both of you now, after yesterday. I didn't mean to carry on like that." I had no idea what to say. I just smiled stupidly. Sheila Olsen said, "I'll have to leave for the airport right after this is over, so I wanted to say goodbye now. I guess it was all foolishness, but I'm glad I came. I'm glad I met you, Joseph."

"Me, too," I said. We saw Rabbi Tuvim returning, waving to us over the heads of the milling guests. Sheila Olsen, shy again, patted my shoulder, whispered "*Courage,*" and began to slip away. The rabbi intercepted her deftly, however, and they talked for a few minutes, at the end of which Sheila Olsen nodded firmly, pointed to her big purse, and went to find a seat. Rabbi Tuvim joined me and went quietly over my Torah portion with me again. He seemed distinctly calmer, or possibly I mean resigned.

"All right, Joseph," the rabbi said at last. "All right, time to get this show on the road. Here we go."

I'm not going to talk about the Bar Mitzvah, not *as* a Bar Mitzvah, except to say that it wasn't nearly the catastrophe I'd been envisioning for months. It couldn't have been. I stumbled on the prayers, lord knows how many times, but Rabbi Tuvim had his back to the onlookers, and he fed me the lines I'd forgotten, and we got through. Oddly enough, the speech itself—I had chosen to discuss a passage in Numbers 1-9, showing how the Israelites first consolidated themselves as a community at Sinai—flowed much more smoothly, and I found myself practically enjoying the taste of Hebrew in my mouth. If the rabbi could teach me nothing else, somehow I'd come to understand the sound. Not the words, not the grammar, and certainly not the true meaning… just the *sound*.

Nearing the grand finale, I wasn't thinking at all about the gift table in the farthest corner of the room. I was already beginning to regret that the speech wasn't longer.

That was when I saw her.

Anoush.

Small and dark, olive-skinned, she was no magazine covergirl now, but a woman of Sheila Olsen's age. She stood near the back of the room, away on the margins, as always. Sheila Olsen didn't see her, but I did, and she saw that I did, and I believe she saw also that I knew who and *how* she was. She didn't react, except to move further into shadow—she cast none of her own—but I could still see her eyes. No one else seemed to notice her at all; yet now and then someone would bump into her, or step on her foot, and immediately say, "Oh, sorry, excuse me," just as though she were living flesh. I tried to catch Sheila Olsen's eye, and then Rabbi Tuvim's, to indicate with my chin and my own eyes where they should look, but they never once turned their heads. It was very nearly as frustrating as learning Hebrew.

I finished the speech any old how, and when I was done, my mother came out and put her father's *tallis* on my shoulders, and everybody cheered except me. All I wanted to do was to draw Sheila Olsen's attention to the shy, ghostly presence of her sister, but I lost track of both of them when the hard round candies began showering down on me. It was going to make for an uncertain dance floor—Herbie Kaufman's Bel-Air Combo were busily setting up—but a number of my schoolmates were crowding onto it, followed by a few wary older couples. I was down from the little stage and weaving through the crush, *tallis* and all, pushing past congratulatory shoulder-punches and butt-slaps, not to mention the flash cameras—forbidden during the ceremony itself—going off in my face as I hunted for Sheila Olsen, frantic that she might already have left. She had a plane to catch, after all, and things to decide to remember or forget.

I was slowing down, beginning to give up, when I spotted her heading for the door, but slowed down by the press of bodies, so that she heard when I called her name. She turned, and I waved wildly, not at her, but toward the shadowless figure motionlessly watching her leave. And for the first time, Sheila Olsen and Eleanor Araxia Bagaybagayan saw each other.

Neither moved at first. Neither spoke—Sheila Olsen plainly didn't dare, and I don't think Anoush could. Then, very slowly, as though she were trying to slip up on some wild thing, Sheila Olsen began to ease toward her sister, holding out her open hands. She was facing me, and I saw her lips moving, but I couldn't hear the words.

But for every step Sheila Olsen took, Anoush took one step back from her, remaining as unreachable—*there, not there*—as her father Abel had found her, so many years before. Strangely, for me, since I had never seen her as beautiful on the magazine covers—only hypnotically *alive*—now, as a middle-aged woman, she almost stopped my newly-manly heart. There was gray in her hair, a heaviness to her face and midsection, and in the way she moved… but my heart wanted to stop, all the same.

I was afraid that Sheila Olsen might snap, out of too much wishing, and make some kind of dive or grab for Anoush, but she did something else. She stopped moving forward, and just stood very still for a moment, and then she reached into her purse and brought out the lacy little key that she had taken from Rabbi Tuvim's collection. She stared at it for a moment, and then she kissed it, very quickly, and she tossed it underhand toward Anoush. It spun so slowly, turning in the light like a butterfly, that I wouldn't have been surprised if it never came down.

Anoush caught it. Ghost or no ghost, ethereal or not, she picked Sheila Olsen's key out of the air as daintily as though she were selecting exactly the right apple on a tree, the perfect note on a musical instrument. She looked back at Sheila Olsen, and she smiled a little—I *know* she smiled, I *saw* her—and she touched the key to her lips…

…and I don't know what she did with it, or where she put it—maybe she *ate* it, for all I could ever tell. All I can say for certain is that Sheila Olsen's eyes got very big, and she touched her own mouth again, and then she turned and hurried out of the synagogue, never looking back. I was going to follow her, but Rabbi Tuvim came up and put his hand gently on my shoulder. He said, "She has a plane to catch. You have a special party. Each to his own."

"You saw," I said. "Did you see her?"

"It is more important that you saw her," the rabbi answered. "And that you made Sheila Olsen see her, you brought them together. That was the *mitzvah*—the rest is unimportant, a handful of candy." He patted my shoulder. "You did well."

Anoush was gone, of course, when we looked for her. So was the rabbi's key, though I actually got down on my knees to feel around where she had stood, half-afraid that it had simply fallen through her shade to the floor. But there was no sign of it; and the rabbi, watching, said quietly, "One lock opened. So many more." We went back to the party then.

Film took longer to develop in those days, unless you did it yourself. As I remember, it was more than a week before friends and family started bringing us shots taken at my Bar Mitzvah party. I hated almost all of them—somehow I always seemed to get caught with my mouth open and a goofy startled look on my face—but my mother cherished them all, and pored over them at the kitchen table for hours at a time. "There you are again, dancing with your cousin Marilyn, what was Sarah ever *thinking*, letting her wear that to a Bar Mitzvah?" "There you are in your grandpa's *tallis*, looking so grownup, except I was so afraid your *yarmulke* was going to fall off." "Oh, there's that one I love, with you and your father, I *told* him not to wear that tie, and your friend what's-his-name, he should lose some weight. And there's Rabbi Tuvim, what's that in his beard, dandruff?" Actually, it was cream cheese, The rabbi loved cream cheese.

Then she turned over a photo she'd missed before, and said in a different tone, "Who's that woman? Joseph, do you know that woman?"

It was Anoush, off to one side beyond the dancers I'd been shoving my way through to reach Sheila Olsen. She had her arms folded across her breast, and she looked immensely alone as she watched the party; but she didn't look lonely at all, or even wistful—just alone. As long as it's been, I remember a certain mischievousness around her mouth and eyes, as though she had deliberately slipped into this photograph of my celebration, just as she had slipped comfortingly into her father's work—yes, to wave to him, as Sheila Olsen had said mockingly then. To wave to her sister now… and maybe, a little, to me.

I practically snatched the picture our of my mother's hand—making up some cockamamie story about an old friend of Rabbi Tuvim's—and brought it to him immediately. We both looked at it in silence for a long while. Then the rabbi put it carefully into a sturdy envelope, and addressed it to Sheila Olsen in Grand Forks, North Dakota. I took it to the post office myself, and paid importantly, out of my allowance, to send it Airmail Special Delivery. The rabbi promised to tell me as soon as Sheila Olsen wrote back.

It took longer than I expected: a good two weeks, probably more. After the first week, I was badgering the rabbi almost every day; sometimes twice, because they still had two postal deliveries back then. How he kept from strangling me, or anyway hanging up in my ear, I have no idea—perhaps he sympathized with my impatience because he was anxious himself. At all events, when Sheila Olsen's letter did arrive, he called me immediately. He offered to read it to me over the phone, but I wanted to see it, so I ran over. Rabbi Tuvim gave me a glass of cocoa cream soda, insisted maddeningly on waiting until I could breathe and speak normally, and then showed me the letter.

It was short, and there was no salutation; it simply began:

"She sits on my bedside table, in a little silver frame. I say good night and good morning to her every day. I have tried several times to make copies for you, but they never come out. I'm sorry.

Thank you for the key, Rabbi.

And Joseph, Joseph—thank you."

I still have the letter. The rabbi gave it to me. It sits in its own wooden frame, and people ask me about it, because it's smudged and grubby from many readings, and frayed along the folding, and it looks as though a three-year-old has been at it, which did happen, many years later. But I keep it close, because before that letter I had no understanding of beauty, and no idea of what love is, or what can be born out of love. And after it I knew enough at least to recognize these things when they came to me.

THE SEVENTH EXPRESSION OF THE ROBOT GENERAL

JEFFREY FORD

In his latter years, when he spoke, a faint whirring came from his lower jaw. His mouth opened and closed rhythmically, accurately, displaying a full set of human teeth gleaned from fallen comrades and the stitched tube of plush leather that was his tongue. The metal mustache and eyebrows were ridiculously fake, but the eyes were the most beautiful glass facsimiles, creamy white with irises like dark blue flowers. Instead of hair, his scalp was sand paper.

He wore his uniform still, even the peaked cap with the old emblem of the Galaxy Corps embroidered in gold. He creaked when he walked, piston compressions and the click of a warped flywheel whispering within his trousers. Alternating current droned from a faulty fuse in his solar plexus, and occasionally, mostly on wet days, sparks wreathed his head like a halo of bright gnats. He smoked a pipe, and before turning each page of a newspaper, he'd bring his chrome index finger to his dry rubber slit of a mouth as if he were moistening its tip.

His countenance, made of an astounding, pliable, non-flammable, blast-beam resistant, self-healing, rubber alloy, was supposedly sculpted in homage to the dashing looks of Rendel Sassoon, star of the acclaimed film epic, *For God and Country*. Not everyone saw the likeness, and Sassoon, himself, a devout pacifist, who was well along in years when the general took his first steps out of the laboratory, sued for defamation of character. But once the video started coming back from the front, visions of slaughter more powerful than any celluloid fantasy, mutilated Harvang corpses stacked to the sky, the old actor donned a flag pin on his lapel and did a series of war bond television commercials of which the most prominent feature was his nervous smile.

It's a sad fact that currently most young people aren't aware of the historic incidents that led to our war with the Harvang and the necessity of the Robot General. They couldn't tell you a thing about our early discoveries of atmosphere and biological life on our planet's sizeable satellite, or about the initial fleet that went to lay claim to it. Our discovery of the existence of the Harvang was perhaps the most astonishing news in the history of humanity. They protested our explorations as an invasion, even though we offered technological and moral advancements. A confluence of intersecting events led to an unavoidable massacre of an entire village of the brutes, which in turn led to a massacre of our expeditionary force. They used our ships to invade us, landing here in Snow Country and in the swamps south of Central City.

It was said about his time on the battlefield that if the general was human he'd have been labeled "merciless," but, as it was, his robot nature mitigated this assessment instead to that he was simply "without mercy." At the edge of a pitched battle he'd set up a folding chair and sit down to watch the action, pipe in hand and a thermos of thick, black oil nearby. He'd yell through a bullhorn, strategic orders interspersed with exhortations of "Onward, you sacks of blood!" Should his troops lose the upper hand in the melee, the general would stand, set his pipe and drink on the ground next to his chair, remove his leather jacket, hand it to his assistant, roll up his sleeves, cock his hat back, and dash onto the battlefield, running at top robot speed.

Historians, engineers, and AI researchers of more recent years have been nonplused as to why the general's creators gave him such limited and primitive battle enhancements. There were rays and particle beams at that point in history and they could have outfitted him like a tank, but their art required subtlety. Barbed, spinning drill bits whirled out from the center of his knuckles on each hand. At the first hint of danger, razor blades protruded from the toes of his boots. He also belched poison, feathered darts from his open mouth, but his most spectacular device was a rocket built into his hindquarters that when activated shot a blast of fire that made him airborne for ten seconds.

It was supposedly a sight the Harvang dreaded, to see him land behind their lines, knuckle spikes whirling, belching death, trousers smoldering. They had a name for him in Harvang, *Kokulafugok*, which roughly translated as "Fire in the Hole." He'd leave a trail of carnage through their ranks, only stopping briefly to remove the hair tangling his drill bits.

His movements were graceful and precise. He could calculate ahead of his opponent, dodge blast beams, bend backwards, touch his head upon the ground to avoid a spray of shrapnel and then spring back up into a razor-toed kick, lopping off a Harvang's sex and drilling him through the throat. Never tiring, always perfectly balanced and accurate, his intuition was dictated by a random number generator.

He killed like a force of nature, an extension of the universe. Hacked by axe blades or shot with arrows to his head, when his business was done, he'd retire to his tent and send for one of the Harvang females. The screams of his prisoner echoed through the camp and were more frightening to his troops than combat. On the following morning he would emerge, his dents completely healed, and give orders to have the carcass removed from his quarters.

During the war, he was popular with the people back home. They admired his hand-to-hand combat, his antique nature, his unwillingness to care about the reasons for war. He was voted the celebrity most men would want to have a beer with and most women would desire for a brief sexual liaison. When informed as to the results of this poll, his only response was, "But are they ready to die for me?"

Everywhere, in the schools, the post offices, the public libraries, there were posters of him in battle-action poses amidst a pile of dead or dying Harvang that read: *Let's Drill Out A Victory!* The Corps was constantly transporting him from the front lines of Snow Country or the Moon back to Central City in order to make appearances supporting the war. His speeches invariably contained this line: *The Harvang are a filthy species.* At the end of his talks, his face would turn the colors of the flag and there were few who refused to salute. Occasionally, he'd blast off the podium and dive headlong into the crowd which would catch his falling body and, hand over hand, return him to the stage.

In his final campaign, he was blown to pieces by a blast from a beam cannon the Harvang had stolen from his arsenal. An entire regiment of ours ambushed in Snow Country between the steep walls of an enormous glacier—The Battle of the Ice Chute. His strategies were impossibly complex but all inexorably lead to a frontal assault, a stirring charge straight into the mouth of Death. It was a common belief among his troops that who'd ever initially programmed him had never been to war. Only after his defeat did the experts claim his tactics were daft, riddled with hubris spawned by faulty AI. His case became, for a time, a thread of the damning argument that artificial intelligence, merely the human impression of intelligence, was, in reality, artificial ignorance. It was then that robot production moved decidedly toward the organic.

After the Harvang had been routed by reinforcements, and the Corps eventually began burying the remains of those who'd perished in the battle for Snow Country, the general's head was discovered amidst the frozen carnage. When the soldier who found it lifted it up from beneath the stiffened trunk of a human body, the eyes opened, the jaw moved, and the weak, crackling command of "Kill them all!" sputtered forth.

The Corps decided to rebuild him as a museum piece for public relations purposes, but the budget was limited. Most of his parts, discovered strewn across the battlefield, could be salvaged and a few new ones were fashioned from cheaper materials to replace what was missing. Still, those who rebuilt the general were not the craftsmen his creators were—techniques had been lost to time. There was no longer the patience in robot design for aping the human. A few sectors of his artificial brain had been damaged, but there wasn't a technician alive who could repair his intelligence node, a ball of wiring so complex its design had been dubbed "The Knot."

The Corps used him for fund-raising events and rode him around in an open car at veterans' parades. The only group that ever paid attention to him, though, was the parents of the sons and daughters who'd died under his command. As it turned out, there were thousands of them. Along a parade route they'd pelt him with old fruit and dog shit, to which he'd calmly warn, "Incoming."

It didn't take the Corps long to realize he was a liability, but since he possessed consciousness, though it be man-made, the law disallowed his being simply turned off. Instead, he was retired and set up in a nice apartment at the center of a small town where he drew his sizeable pension and *history of combat* bonus.

An inauspicious ending to a historic career, but in the beginning, at the general's creation, when the Harvang had invaded in the south and were only miles outside of Central City, he was a promising savior. His artificial intelligence was considered a miracle of Science, his construction, the greatest engineering feat of the human race. And the standard by which all of this was judged was the fact that his face could make seven different expressions. Everyone agreed it was proof of the robot builder's exemplary art. Before the general, the most that had ever been attempted was three.

The first six of these expressions were slight variations on the theme of "determination." *Righteousness, Willfulness, Obstinacy, Eagerness, Grimness* 1 and 2 were the terms his makers had given them. The facial formation of the six had a lot to do with the area around the mouth, subtly different clenchings of the jaw, a straightness in the lips. The eyes were widened for all six, the nostrils flared. For *Grimness* 2, steam shot from his ears.

When he wasn't at war, he switched between *Righteousness* and *Obstinacy*. He'd lost *Eagerness* to a Harvang blade. It was at the Battle of Boolang Crater that the general was cut across the cheek, all the way through to his internal mechanism. After two days of leaking oil through the side of his face, the outer wound healed, but the wiring that caused the fourth expression had been irreparably severed.

There is speculation, based primarily on hearsay, that there was also an eighth expression, one that had not been built into him but that had manifested of its own accord through the self-advancement of the AI. Scientists claimed it highly unlikely, but Ms. Jeranda Blesh claimed she'd seen it. During a three-month leave, his only respite in the entire war, she'd lived with him in a chalet in the Grintun Mountains. A few years before she died of a Harvang venereal disease, she appeared on a late-night television talk show. She was pale and bloated, giddy with alcohol, but she divulged the secrets of her sex life with the general.

She mentioned the smooth chrome member with fins, the spicy oil, the relentless precision of his pistons. "Sometimes, right when things were about to explode," she said, "he'd make a face I'd never seen any other times. It wasn't a smile, but more like calm, a moment of peace. It wouldn't last long, though, cause then he'd lose control of everything, shoot a rocket blast out his backside and fly off me into the wall." The host of the show straightened his tie and said, "That's what I call 'drilling out a victory.'"

It was the seventh expression that was the general's secret, though. That certain configuration of his face reserved for combat. It was the reason he was not tricked out with guns or rockets. The general was an excellent killing machine, but how many could he kill alone? Only when he had armies ready to move at his will could he defeat the Harvang. The seventh expression was a look that enchanted his young troops and made them savage extensions of his determination. Out manned, out gunned, out maneuvered, out flanked, it didn't matter. One glance from him, and they'd charge, beam rifles blazing, to their inevitable deaths. They'd line up in ranks before a battle and he'd review the troops, focusing that imposing stare on each soldier. It was rare that a young recruit would be unaffected by the seventh expression's powerful suggestion, understand that the mission at hand was sheer madness, and protest. The general had no time for deserters. With lightening quickness, he'd draw his beam pistol and burn a sudden hole in the complainant's forehead.

In an old government document, "A Report to the Committee on Oblique Renderings Z-333-678AR," released since the Harvang war, there was testimony from the general's creators to the fact that the seventh expression was a blend of the look of a hungry child, the gaze of an angry bull, and the stern countenance of God. The report records that the creators were questioned as to how they came up with the countenance of God, and their famous response was "We used a mirror."

There was a single instance when the general employed the seventh expression after the war. It was only a few years ago, the day after it was announced that we would negotiate a treaty with the Harvang and attempt to live in peace and prosperity. He left his apartment and hobbled across the street to the coffee shop on the corner. Once there, he ordered a twenty-four-ounce Magjypt black, and sat in the corner, pretending to read the newspaper. Eventually, a girl of sixteen approached him and asked if he was the robot general.

He saluted and said, "Yes, mam."

"We're reading about you in school," she said.

"Sit down, I'll tell you anything you need to know."

She pulled out a chair and sat at his table. Pushing her long brown hair behind her ears, she said, "What about all the killing?"

"Everybody wants to know about the killing," he said. "They should ask themselves."

"On the Steppes of Patience, how many Harvang did you, yourself, kill?"

"My internal calculator couldn't keep up with the slaughter. I'll just say, 'Many.'"

"What was your favorite weapon?" she asked.

"I'm going to show it to you, right now," he said, and his face began changing. He reached into his inside jacket pocket and brought forth a small caliber ray gun wrapped in a white handkerchief. He laid the weapon on the table, the cloth draped over it. "Pick it up," he said.

He stared at her and she stared back, and after it was all over, she'd told friends that his blue pupils had begun to spin like pinwheels and his lips rippled. She lifted the gun.

"Put your finger on the trigger," he said.

She did.

"I want you to aim it right between my eyes and pull the trigger."

She took aim with both hands, stretching her arms out across the table.

"Now!" he yelled, and it startled her.

She set the gun down, pushed back her chair, and walked away.

It took the general two weeks before he could find someone he could convince to shoot him, and this was only after he offered payment. The seventh expression meant nothing to the man who'd promised to do the job. What he was after, he said, were the three shrunken Harvang heads the general had kept as souvenirs of certain battles. They'd sell for a fortune on the black market. After the deal was struck, the general asked the man, "Did you see that face I had on a little while ago?"

"I think I know what you mean," said the man.

"How would you describe it?" asked the general.

The man laughed. "I don't know. That face? You looked like you might have just crapped your pants. Look, your famous expressions, the pride of an era, no one cares about that stuff anymore. Bring me the heads."

The next night, the general hid the illegal shrunken heads beneath an old overcoat and arrived at the appointed hour at an abandoned pier on the south side of town. The wind was high and the water lapped at the edges of the planks. The man soon appeared. The general removed the string of heads from beneath his coat and threw them at the man's feet.

"I've brought a ray gun for you to use," said the general, and reached for the weapon in his jacket pocket.

"I brought my own," said the man and drew out a magnum-class beam pistol. He took careful aim, and the general noticed that the long barrel of the gun was centered on his own throat and not his forehead.

In the instant before the man pulled the trigger, the general's strategy centers realized that the plot was to sever his head and harvest his intelligence node—"The Knot." He lunged, drill bits whirring. The man fired the weapon and the blast beam disintegrated three quarters of the general's neck. The internal command had already been given, though, so with head flopping to the side, the robot general charged forward—one drill bit skewered the heart and the other plunged in at the left ear. The man screamed and dropped the gun, and then the general drilled until he himself dropped. When he hit the dock what was left of his neck snapped and his head came free of his body. It rolled across the planks, perched at the edge for a moment, and then a gust of wind pushed it into the sea.

The general's body was salvaged and dismantled, its mechanical wizardry deconstructed. From the electric information stored in the ganglia of the robotic wiring system it was discovered that the general's initial directive was—To Serve the People. As for his head, it should be operational for another thousand years, its pupils spinning, its lips rippling without a moment of peace in the cold darkness beneath the waves. There, "The Knot," no doubt out of a programmed impulse for self-preservation, is confabulating intricate dreams of victory.

SKIN DEEP

RICHARD PARKS

The hardest part of Ceren's day was simply deciding what skin to put on in the morning. Making an informed decision required that she have a clear view of her entire day, and who other than a prisoner in a dungeon or a stone statue on a pedestal had that particular luxury?

Ceren went into her Gran's store-room where the skins were kept. She still thought of the store-room as her grandmother's, just as the small cottage in the woods and the one sheep and a milk goat in the pen out back belonged to her Gran as well. Ceren still felt as if she was just borrowing the lot, even though she had been on her own for two full seasons of the sixteen she had lived. Yet she still felt like a usurper, even though she herself had buried her grandmother under the cedar tree and there were no other relatives to make a claim. She especially felt that way about the skins, since Gran herself hadn't owned those, at least to Ceren's way of thinking. Borrowed, one and all.

They lay on a series of broad, flat shelves in the store-room, covered with muslin to keep the dust off, neatly arranged just as a carpenter would organize his tools, all close to hand and suited for the purpose. Here was the one her Gran had always called the Oaf—not very bright, but large and strong and useful when there were large loads to be shifted or firewood to cut. There was the Tinker—slight and small, but very clever with his hands and good at making and mending. On the next highest shelf was the Soldier. Ceren had only worn him once, when the Red Company had been hired to raid the northern borders and all the farmers kept their axes and haying forks near to hand. She didn't like wearing him. He had seen horrible things, done as much, and the shell remembered, and thus so did she. She wore him for two days, but by the third she decided she'd rather take her chances with the raiders. The Soldier was for imminent threats and no other.

The skin on the highest shelf she had never worn at all. Never even seen it without its translucent covering of muslin, though now that Gran was gone there was nothing to prevent her. That skin frightened Ceren even more than the Soldier did. Gran had told her that at most she would wear the skin once or twice in her life, that she would know why when the time came. Otherwise, best not to look at it or think about it too much. Ceren didn't understand what her Gran was talking about, and that frightened her most of all because the old woman had flatly refused to explain or even mention the matter again. But there lay the skin on its high shelf. Sleeping, supposedly. That's what they all were supposed to do when not needed, but Ceren wasn't so sure about this one. It wasn't sleeping, she was certain. It was waiting for the day when Ceren would be compelled to put it on and become someone else, someone she had never been before.

It'll be worse than the Soldier, she thought. *Has to be, for Gran to be so leery of it.*

The day her grandmother had spoken of was not here yet, since Ceren felt no compulsion to find the stepstool and reach the mysterious skin on the high shelf. Today was a work day, and so today there was no guessing to be done. Ceren slipped out of her thin shift and hung it on a peg. Then she slipped the muslin coverlet off of the Oaf. She had need of his strength this fine morning. She could have even used that strength to get the skin off its shelf in the first place, but for the moment she had to make do with what she had. She used both hands and finally pulled it down.

Like cowhide, the skin was heavier than it looked. Unlike cowhide, it still bore an uncanny resemblance to the person who had once owned it, only with empty eye-sockets now and a face and form much flatter than originally made, or so Ceren imagined. Gran never said where any particular skin came from; Ceren wasn't sure that the old woman even knew.

"They once belonged to someone else. Now they belong to us, our rightful property. I also came into a wash basin, a hammer, a saw and a fine, sharp chisel when my own mam died, and I didn't ask where they came from. Your mam would have got them, had she lived, but she wouldn't wonder about those things and neither should you."

Ceren had changed the subject then because her Gran had that little glow in her good eye that told anyone with sense that they were messing around in a place that shouldn't be messed around in. Ceren, whatever her faults, had sense.

It took all of her strength, but Ceren managed to hold up the skin as she breathed softly on that special spot on the back of its neck that Gran had showed her. The skin split open, crown to crack, and Ceren stepped into it like she'd step into a dancing gown—if she'd had such a thing or a maid or friend to lace up the back when she was done.

Next came the uncomfortable part. Ceren always tried not to think about it too much, but she didn't believe she would ever get used to it, even if she lived to be as old as Gran did before she died. First Ceren was aware of being in what felt like a leather cloak way too large for her. That feeling lasted for only a moment before the cloak felt as if it was shrinking in on her, but she knew it must have been herself getting… well, *stretchy*, since the Oaf was a big man, and soon so was she. Her small breasts flattened as if someone was pushing them, her torso thickened, her legs got longer and then there was this clumsy, uncomfortable *thing* between them. She felt her new mouth and eyes slip into place. When it was all over, she felt a mile high, and for the first dizzying seconds she was afraid that she might fall. Now she could clearly see the covering of muslin over the topmost skin on its shelf. She looked away, closed her eyes.

The uncomfortable part wasn't quite over; there was one final bit when Ceren was no longer completely Ceren. There was someone else present in her head, someone else's thoughts and memories to contend with. Fortunately the Oaf hadn't been particularly keen on thought, and so there wasn't as much to deal with.

The Soldier hadn't been quite so easy. Ceren tried not to remember.

"Time to go to work," she said aloud in a voice much lower than her own, and the part of her that wasn't Ceren at all but now served her understood.

She was never sure how much of what followed was her direction or the Oaf's understanding. Ceren knew the job that needed doing—a dead tree had fallen across the spring-fed brook that brought water to her animals and had diverted most of it into a nearby gully. That tree would have to be cleared, but while Ceren rightly thought of the axe and the saw, it was the Oaf who added the iron bar from her meager store of tools and set off toward the spring, whistling a tune that Ceren did not know, nor would it have mattered much if she *did* know, as she had never had the knack of whistling. Ceren was content to listen as she—or rather *they*—set out on the path to the head of the spring.

Ceren's small cottage nestled into the base of a high ridge in the foothills of the Pinetop Mountains. The artesian spring gave clear, cold water year round, or at least it did before the tree dammed up the brook. Now the brook was down to a trickle, and the goat especially had been eyeing her reprovingly for the last two mornings as she milked it.

The Oaf had been right about the iron bar. It was a large old tree, more dried-out than rotten. Even with her new strength, it took Ceren a good bit of the morning with the axe and saw and then a bit more of that same morning with the iron bar and a large rock for a fulcrum to shift the tree trunk out of the brook. She moved a few stones to reinforce the banks and then it was finally done. The brook flowed freely again.

The Oaf cupped his calloused hands and drank from the small pool that formed beneath the spring. Ceren knew he wanted to sit down on a section of the removed log and rest, but Ceren noticed a plume of smoke from the other side of the ridge and gave in to curiosity. The ridge was steep, but spindly oak saplings and a few older trees grew along most of the slope, and she made her borrowed body climb up to the top using the trees for handholds.

My own skin is better suited for this climb, she thought, but the Oaf, though not nearly so nimble as Ceren's own lithe frame, finally managed to scramble to the top.

Someone was clearing a field along the north-south road in the next valley. Ceren recognized the signs: a section of woodland with its trees cut, waste fires for the wood that couldn't be reused, a pair of oxen to help pull the stumps. She counted three men working and one woman. The farmhouse was already well under way. Ceren sighed. She wasn't happy about other people being so close; her family's distrust of any and all others was bred deep. Yet most of the land along the road this far from the village of Endby was unclaimed, the farm did not infringe on her own holdings, and at least they were on the *other* side of the ridge, so she wouldn't even have to see them if she didn't want to.

Ceren had just started to turn away to make the climb back down before she noticed one lone figure making its way down the road. It was difficult at the distance, but Ceren was fairly sure that he was one of the men from the new homestead.

Doubtless headed toward the village on some errand or other.

Ceren watched for a while just to be sure and soon realized the wisdom of caution. The ridge sloped downward farther east just before it met the road. To her considerable surprise, when the man passed the treeline he did not continue on the road but rather stepped off onto the path leading to her own cottage. She swore softly, though through the Oaf's lips it came out rather more loud than she intended. Ceren hurried her borrowed form back down the ridge to the path from the spring, but despite her hurry, the stranger was no more than ten paces from her when she emerged into the clearing.

"Hullo there," said the stranger.

Ceren got her first good look at the man. He was wearing his work clothes, old but well-mended. He was young, with fair hair escaping from the cloth he'd tied around his head against the sun, and skin tanned from a life spent mainly outside. She judged him not more than a year or so older than she herself. Well-formed, or at least to the extent that Ceren could tell about such things. There weren't that many young men in the village to compare to, most were away on the surrounding farms, and those who were present always looked at her askance when she went into town, if they looked at her at all. It used to upset her, but Ceren's grandmother had been completely untroubled by this.

"Of course they look away. You're a witch, girl, the daughter of a witch and the granddaughter of a witch, the same as me. They're afraid of you, and if you know what's what, you'll make sure they stay that way."

The memory passed in a flash, and for a moment Ceren didn't know what to do. The stranger just looked at her then repeated, "Hullo? Can you hear me?"

Ceren spoke through her borrowed mouth and tried to keep her tone under control. The Oaf had a tendency to bellow like a bull if not held in check. "Hello. I'm sorry I was… thinking about something. What do you want?"

"I'm looking for the Wise Woman of Endby. I was told she lived here. Is this your home, then?"

"The Wise Woman is dead, and of course this isn't my home. I just do some work for her granddaughter who lives here now," Ceren/Oaf said.

"So I was given to understand, but is her granddaughter not a… not of the trade?"

Ceren nearly smiled with her borrowed face in spite of herself. The stranger's phrasing was almost tactful. He wanted something, but what? She finally noticed the stained bandage on the young man's right forearm, mostly covered by the sleeve of his shirt. Obviously, he needed mending. That was something Ceren could do even without a borrowed skin.

"She is," Ceren said. "If you'll wait out here, I'll go fetch her."

By this point Ceren was used to her borrowed form, but she still almost banged her head on the cottage's low door when she went inside. She made her way quickly to the store-room and tapped the back of her neck three times with her left hand.

"Done with ye, off with ye!"

The skin split up the back again like the skin of a snake and sloughed off, leaving Ceren standing naked, dazed, and confused for several moments before she came fully to herself again. She quickly pulled her clothes back on and then took just as much time as she needed to arrange the Oaf back on his shelf and cover him with muslin until the next time he'd be needed.

When she emerged from the cottage, blinking in the sunlight, the young man, who had taken a seat on a stump, got to his feet. He had pulled the cloth from his head like a gentleman removing his cap in the presence of a lady. For a moment Ceren just stared at him, but she remembered her tongue soon enough.

"My hired man said I'm needed out here. I'm Ceren, Aydden Shinlock's grand-daughter. Who are you?"

"My name's Kinan Baleson. My family is working a new holding just beyond the ridge there," he said, pointing at the ridge where Ceren/oaf had stood just a short time before. "I need your help."

"That's as may be. What ails you?"

"It's this...." he said, pulling back the sleeve covering the bandage on his right forearm.

Just as Ceren had surmised, he'd injured himself while clearing land at the new croft, slipped and gouged his arm on the teeth of a bow saw. "My Ma did what she knew to do, but she says it's getting poisoned. She said to give you this…" He held out a silver penny. "We don't have a lot of money, but if this isn't enough, we have eggs, and we'll have some mutton come fall."

"Unless the hurt is greater than I think, it'll do."

Ceren took the coin and then grasped his hand to hold the arm steady and immediately realized the young man was blushing and she almost did the same.

Why is he doing that? I'm no simpering village maid.

She concentrated on the arm to cover her own confusion and began to unwrap the bandage, but before she'd even begun she knew that Kinan's mother had the right of it. The drainage from the wound was a sickly yellow, but to her relief it had not yet gone green. If that had happened, the choice would have been his arm or his life.

"Should have come to me sooner," Ceren said, "with all proper respect to your mother."

"She tried to make me come yesterday," Kinan said gruffly, "but there's so much to do—"

"Which would be managed better with two arms than one," Ceren said, planting a single seed of fear the way her Gran had taught her. In this case Ceren could see the wisdom of it. Better a little fear in the present than a lifetime disadvantage. "Hold still now."

Kinan did as he was told. Ceren finished unwrapping the bandage and pulled it away to get a good look at the wound. The gash was about two inches long, but narrow and surprisingly clean-edged, considering what had made it. The cut started a hand's width past his wrist, almost neatly centered in the top of the forearm. A little deep but not a lot more than a scratch, relatively speaking. Yet the area around the cut had turned an angry shade of red, and yellowish pus continued to ooze from the wound.

"Sit down on that stump. I'll be back in a moment."

Ceren picked up her water bucket, went to the stream and pulled up a good measure of cold, clear water. Before she returned to Kinan, she went back into her cottage and brought out her healer's box, a simple pine chest where her Gran had kept her more precious herbs and tools. While most everything else in her life felt borrowed, Ceren considered that this box belonged to *her*. She had earned it. Both by assisting her Gran in her healer's work for years and by being naturally good at that work. Ceren inherited the box, inherited in a way that didn't seem to apply to the rest of the things around her.

Especially the skins.

Ceren carefully washed out the gash as Kinan gritted his teeth, which Ceren judged he did more from anticipation than actual added pain. A wound of this sort had its own level of pain which nothing Ceren had done—yet—was going to change. Once the wound was cleaned out, she leaned close and sniffed it.

"I can't imagine it smells like posies," Kinan said, forcing a smile.

"I'm more interested in *what* it smells like, not how pleasant it is." Ceren wondered for a moment why she was bothering to explain, since her Gran had been very adamant on the subject of secrets: "Best that no one knows how we do what we do. Little seems marvelous, once you know the secret." And it was important for reputation that all seem marvelous; Ceren saw the wisdom in that as well.

Even so, Ceren found it easy to talk to Kinan, she who barely had reason to speak three words in a fortnight. "My Gran taught me what scents to look for in a wound. A little like iron for blood, sickly sweet for an inflamed cut like this one. Yet there's something…. ah. You said you cut yourself on a saw? Fine new saw or old, battered saw?"

He sighed. "Everything we have is old and battered, but serves well enough."

"Yes, this saw has served you pretty well indeed. There's something in there that smells more like iron than even blood does. Unless I miss my guess, your saw left a piece of itself behind and is poisoning the wound. That's why your arm isn't healing properly."

He frowned. "You're saying you can smell iron?"

"Of course. Can't you?"

"Not at all. That's amazing."

Ceren almost blushed again. *So much for Gran's ideas about secrets,* Ceren thought. *Or at least that one.*

Ceren reached into her box and pulled out a bronze razor, which she proceeded to polish on a leather strop. Kinan eyed the blade warily, and Ceren nodded. "Yes, this is going to hurt. Just so you know."

Kinan flinched as Ceren gently opened the edges of the wound with her thumbs. More pus appeared and she rinsed that away as well. She judged the direction the sawblade had cut from and looked closer. A black speck was wedged deep into the wound's upper end. Now that she had found the culprit, it only took a couple of cuts with the razor to free the piece of broken sawblade. Kinan grunted once but otherwise bore the pain well enough and kept still even when new blood started to flow. Ceren held the fragment up on the edge of her bloody razor for Kinan to see before flicking it away into the bushes. She then washed the wound one more time and bound it again with a fresh strip of linen.

"Considering what you're likely to do with that arm, I really should stitch it," she said. "And it's going to bleed for a bit as things are. Let it, that'll help wash out the poison. If you'll be careful and wash the cut yourself at least once a day—clean, clear water, mind, not the muck from your stock pond—you should get to keep the arm."

"We have our own well now," Kinan said. "I'll heed what you say. I'm in your debt."

She shook her head. "You paid, so we're square. But mind what I said about washing."

Kinan thanked her again and left. Ceren watched him walk back down the path toward the road. After a moment she realized that she was, in fact, watching him long past the point where it was reasonable to do so. She sighed and then went to clean her razor in the cold stream.

* * *

That night Ceren dreamed that she walked hand in hand with Kinan through a golden field of barley, the grain ready to harvest. Yet no sooner had Kinan taken her in his arms than there stood his family: the brothers whom Ceren saw that day from the ridge, a mother and father with vague, misty faces.

"Stay away from that witch! She's evil!" they all said, speaking with one voice.

"There's nothing wrong with me!" Ceren said, but she didn't believe it. She knew there was. Those in the dream knew it too. Kinan turned his back on her and walked away with his family as the barley turned to briars and stones around a deep, still pool of water.

"You can't do it alone, you know. Your Gran knew. How do you think you got here?"

Ceren looked around, saw no one. "Where are you?"

"Look in the pond."

Ceren looked into the water but saw only her own reflection. It took her several moments to realize that it was not her reflection at all. Her hair was long, curly, and black, not the pale straw color it should have been. Her eyes were large and dark, her rosy-red lips perfectly formed. Ceren looked into the face of the most beautiful girl she had ever seen, and the sight was almost too painful to bear. "That's not me."

"No, but it could be. If you want."

When Ceren opened her eyes again, she had her own face once more, but the other girl's reflection stood beside her on the bank of the pool, wearing golden hoops in her ears and dressed like a gypsy princess. Ceren couldn't resist a sideways glance, but of course there was no one else there.

"Dreams lie," Ceren said. "My Gran told me that."

"This one is true enough and you know it. Even if Kinan was interested, what do you think his family would say if he came courting a witch?"

"He's not going to court me. I'd toss him out on his ear if he did. What a notion."

"Liar."

Ceren's hands balled into fists. "I just met him! He's not even that handsome."

The girl's laugh was almost like music. "What's that got to do with anything? He's young, he's strong, he has a touch of gentleness about him, despite his hard life. And he's not a fool. Are you?"

"Be quiet!"

The strange girl's reflection sighed, and ripples spread over the pond. "I never cared much for your Gran, but I will say this: she was always clear on what she wanted and never feared to go after it, too. So. She's dead and now you're the mistress here. Tell me you don't want him. Make me believe you, and I'll go away."

"How do you know me? Who are you?"

"I've known you all your life, just as you know who I am."

Ceren did know. Just as she knew how she felt about Kinan and how strongly she tried not to feel anything at all.

"The topmost shelf. That's you."

"No, there is no one there. What remains is little more than a memory, but it is a memory that can serve you in this, as the memory of the Oaf and the Soldier and the Tinker cannot. What remains is merely a tool. Your Gran understood that. Use me, as she did."

"No!"

"Mark me—you will." The ripples faded along with her voice and reflection, but just before she awoke, Ceren gazed into the pool one last time and saw nothing at all.

For the next few months Ceren kept herself too busy to think about either Kinan or what lay on the topmost shelf. It was easy enough. There was always something that needed doing around her croft and a fairly steady stream of villagers and farmers from the surrounding countryside.

After her grandmother was cold and buried, Ceren had worried about whether the people who had come to her Gran would come to her now, she being little more than a girl and not the Wise Woman of Endby, who always wore her Gran's face so far as Ceren was concerned: ancient, bent, hook-nosed and glaring, while Ceren was none of those things except, now and then, glaring. But she needn't have worried. A Wise Woman was always needed where more than a few folk gathered, and as long as there was someone to fill the role, there were always people willing to let her. Ceren knew she would grow into the part, in time. Besides, "Wise Woman" was them being polite; she knew what they called her behind her back. Such rubbish had never bothered her grandmother. Ceren couldn't quite say the same.

One day it will seem perfectly natural, she thought, but the prospect didn't exactly fill her with joy. Fear and secrecy were the witch's stock in trade, just as her Gran had always said. She had no right to complain if other, less pleasant things came with them.

Ceren had just doled out the herb bundle that would rid a silly village girl of her "problem" when she heard an alarm bell clanging from the village itself. The girl mumbled her thanks and hurried away. Ceren looked south toward Endby but saw nothing out of the ordinary. When she looked back north it was a different story.

Smoke.

Not Kinan's home, she realized with more relief than she cared to admit; this was further west. Still, too close, to all of them. Ceren didn't hesitate. She didn't think of all the other things so much smoke in the sky might mean. She knew what the smoke meant, just as her Gran would have known. She went to the store-room and put on the Soldier, because it was the only thing she knew to do.

The face and form of the Soldier remembered, so Ceren did too. There was no time to worry about what she did not want to see; it was all there, just as she'd left it the last time she had worn his skin, but now there was too much else that needed remembering.

Too far from the Serpent Road for this to be the main body. Most likely foragers.

This was what the Soldier knew, and so Ceren knew it, too. After a moment's reflection, the Soldier took one long knife from the cutlery rack and placed it in his belt. Ceren had expected him to take the felling axe, but now she understood why he didn't—too long in the handle and heavy in the blade to swing accurately at anything other than a target that wasn't moving. A short, balanced hatchet would have been better for their purpose, but there was none.

The Soldier trotted up the path toward the ridge, not hurrying, saving their strength. They passed the spring and scrambled up the ridge, and from that height the flames to the west were easy to see. Neither Ceren nor the Soldier knew which farm lay to the west, but they both knew there was one, or had been. The foragers would be spreading out from the Serpent Road; it was likely that they didn't know the north road—little more than a cart path—or the village of Endby even existed, but it looked like one group was going to find it if they kept moving east.

How many?

That was a question that needed to be answered and quickly. From the ridge the Soldier simply noted that a group of farmers had arranged themselves at the western border of their field, armed with little more than pitchforks and clubs. Ceren noted that Kinan and his father and his two brothers were about to get themselves killed, and there was nothing she could do about it.

They mean to keep the raiders from burning the field! thought Ceren.

Foolish, thought the memory of the Soldier, *they'd be better served to save what they could and make for the village.* Ceren couldn't disagree, since she knew the same could be said for herself. Yet here she was. She tried not to dwell on that or why her first instinct had been to don the Soldier. She thought instead of how hard the Balesons had worked to get their farm going. And how hard it would have been for them to let it all be destroyed.

The Soldier's thoughts closed in after that, so Ceren didn't understand at first why they turned left along the ridge rather than descending to stand with Kinan's family, but she knew better than to interfere. He was in his element, just as she was not. The Soldier kept low and moved quickly, using the trees and bushes that grew thick on the ridge as cover. Soon they left the bramble hedge that marked the edge of the Baleson farm. About three bowshots from the boundary, the ridge curved away south. They peered out of the thicket at the bend. There was still no sign of the foragers.

"Maybe they've stopped."

The Soldier's thought was immediate and emphatic. *Not enough time. They're not finished.*

Ceren and the Soldier found a way to descend and, once they were on level ground again, slipped away quickly into the trees. Ceren realized that they were approaching the burning farmhouse by a circular route, keeping to the cover of the woods. They heard a woman scream—and then silence.

They found a vantage point and looked out in time to see a man tying the straps of his leather brigandine back into place. He was lightly armored otherwise, but well armed. A bow and quiver lay propped against a nearby railing. The body of a man and a child lay nearby. A woman lay on the ground at the raider's feet, unmoving, her clothing in disarray and even at their distance they could see the blood. It took Ceren a moment to realize that the sword that she'd thought stuck into the ground was actually pinning the woman's body to the earth. She felt her gorge rising, but the Soldier merely judged the distance and scanned the rest of the scene. The farmhouse was still burning well, though the flames were showing signs of having passed their peak. Another moment and the roof came crashing down in a shower of embers.

Unmounted auxiliaries with one scout. We have a chance, thought the Soldier.

Kill him, she thought in her anger.

The Soldier remained cold as a winter stream. *Not yet.*

The memory contained in the Soldier forced her to look toward the east. She saw four more men armed and armored similarly to the one lagging behind, but only the straggler had a bow. For some reason this seemed to please the Soldier. The other four carried bundles over their shoulders, apparently the spoils of the farm.

"You said there was another farm this way," shouted one of them. "We need to hit it and then return before nightfall if we're to be ready to move at daybreak. We haven't got time for your dallying."

"I'm almost done," said the first. "but this baggage has befouled my good blade. I'll catch up when I've cleaned it."

One of them swore, but they didn't wait. The other four disappeared into the trees, heading toward Kinan's farm. Ceren still felt sick but now there was an even greater sense of urgency.

Kill him!

Soon.

They kept out of sight. They didn't move until the man had carefully wiped his sword on the dead woman's torn dress and sheathed the blade, then reclaimed his bow and quiver. The Soldier moved quickly and quietly, keeping to the trees at the edge of the woods, Ceren little more than a spectator behind borrowed eyes.

The Soldier caught the scout from behind before he had taken six steps into the trees. The scout managed only a muffled grunt as the Soldier clamped his hand over the man's mouth and neatly slashed his throat. The raider's blood flowed over their arms, but the Soldier didn't release their grip until the man went limp. They took the sword and the bow and quiver, but that was all.

The armor?

No time.

Ceren felt a little foolish for asking the question in the first place, and the reason was part of why she so feared to wear the Soldier's skin—she was starting to think like the Soldier. Like he had to think to serve his function. She knew why they left the armor, just as she knew why they did not follow the raiders along the same path, even though it was the most direct route. They took their course a little to the right, to place themselves just south of where the raiders would have to pass the barrier. At this point Ceren wasn't certain if this was the Soldier's direction or hers, but she knew they did not want to place the farmers directly in front of the raiders, not when arrows were about to fly.

They found a gap in the bramble thicket bordering the field, but the raiders had already emerged and were a good thirty paces into the field, moving directly to where Kinan stood with his father and brothers. Their numbers were matched, but that was all. It was hay fork and club against sword and spear, the difference being that those who held the sword and spear knew how to use them for this particular form of work.

Kinan, his family.... They'll be slaughtered!

The first arrow was already nocked, but the Soldier did not draw. Not yet. Ceren again knew why, and she hated it. The raiders were still too close. Fire now and they'd probably get one of them, but then the three left would charge their position. The Soldier was waiting for advantage; a longer shot versus time to aim and fire. Ceren understood the tactical necessity, just as she understood that it might get one or more of Kinan's family killed. She let the Soldier wait until she could stand it no longer.

Now.

The closest raider went down screaming in pain with an arrow in his thigh. At first Ceren thought it was a bad shot, but then realized the Soldier had hit exactly what he aimed at. He wanted the raider incapacitated but calling attention to himself. The distraction worked. The raiders hesitated and turned toward their fallen companion. The Soldier's second arrow hit the next-closest raider high in the chest. He went down with barely more than a gasp.

This was the Soldier's purpose, and he was serving it well. Ceren felt the Soldier's satisfaction, and she felt sick as she realized that it wasn't just satisfaction that he felt. The Soldier was enjoying himself, and thus so was she, no matter how much she did not wish to, no matter how much she had wanted to see the raiders die.

Let them charge us now, Ceren thought, but it didn't work out that way. The raiders charged the farmers. Ceren didn't know if they meant to cut down Kinan's family or merely get *past* them to use them as cover, but now the odds were two to one in the farmers' favor. One farmer went down; Ceren couldn't tell who because the Soldier had already tossed the bow aside, and they ran full speed toward the fighting, borrowed sword drawn. The man on the ground made a feeble cut at him as he raced past, and the Soldier split the man's skull with barely a pause, but by the time they reached the farmers, it was all over. Kinan was down on the ground, a gash in his forehead.

Somehow Ceren knew it would be Kinan. She felt cold, almost numb at the sight of him.

The raiders were dead. The farmers were still furiously clubbing the bodies when Ceren in her Soldier skin reached them. The farmers eyed the Soldier warily.

"Who are you?" Kinan's father asked without lowering his club.

"The Wise Woman sent me," the Soldier said, sheathing the sword as he spoke. "She saw the smoke."

Ceren saw the look in the older man's eyes. Relief, certainly, but fear as well. One more debt. Ceren shook her head, and of course the Soldier did the same. "She figured they'd be at her steading next. Best to stop them here. What about the boy?"

They were all still breathing hard; Ceren wasn't even sure they'd noticed that Kinan was down, but then they were all clustering about him. Ceren shoved her way down to Kinan's side in her borrowed skin.

It was a glancing blow, and that was probably the only reason Kinan was still breathing. Even so, it was a nasty gash, Kinan was unconscious, and they could not rouse him.

"We should take him to the Wise Woman," one of the brothers said, but Ceren had the Soldier shake his head for her.

"No. Until we know how bad his hurt is you shouldn't move him any farther than needs must. Lift him gently and put him in his bed. Clean and bandage the cut, and I'll fetch the Wise Woman to you."

The father looked toward the barrier. "What if there are more of them?"

The Soldier shook his head without any help from Ceren. "Keep watch, but I doubt there will be. It was a foraging party. There's an army on a quick march south, and the king will have to deal with that if he can, but auxiliaries? It's likely no one will even miss these bastards."

The farmers looked doubtful, but they did as the Soldier directed. Ceren watched them carry Kinan off, then quickly turned back toward her own home.

She shed the Soldier's skin with relief, but she was nearly stumbling with exhaustion. Even so, she managed to carry her box of medicines up the road to Kinan's farm. It was his mother that greeted her this time.

Ceren had never met the woman before, but she could see Kinan in the older woman's eyes. Most of the rest of his looks he got from his father. She frowned when Ceren appeared, but she seemed to be puzzled, not disapproving.

"Kinan said you were young. I didn't realize how young."

"My Gran trained me well," Ceren said, a little defensively. "I can help him."

The woman shook her head. "That's not what I meant. You already have helped him, so I hope you can again. He hasn't moved since they brought him in. My name is Liea, by the way. Thank you for coming," she said, and sounded as if she meant it.

Ceren found herself blushing a little. She couldn't remember the last time anyone had said thank-you to her and seemed sincere rather than grudging. Except Kinan.

"I'm Ceren. I don't know if your son told you or not…. I trust no more raiders have been seen?"

The woman shook her head. "Not here, though we've heard rumors of attacks further south. The men are out burying the carcasses in a deep hole."

"Then maybe we won't see more of them again."

Liea shrugged. "Even if the army is beaten, likely some like them will come this way again, and likely be even more hungry and desperate in the bargain. We heard what they did to the steading west of us."

Ceren only hoped that they hadn't seen it as well, as she had. Liea took her to where Kinan had been put to bed. It wasn't a large room, and clearly he shared it with his brothers. Ceren found him lying pale and still under a quilt. His breathing was regular and strong; the head wound had stopped bleeding and she removed the bandage, noting with approval that it had been cleaned out properly, doubtless Liea's doing. Now it was easy to see that the cut had not gone clear through to the skull, though it hadn't missed by much. Still, Kinan's continued unconsciousness was not a good sign, and the longer it lasted, the worse the portents.

Liea stood nearby watching. Her eyes were moist and her lower lip trembled. Ceren believed she knew how the woman felt, at least a little. She took a needle and thread from her box and calmly proceeded to sew up the gash. She noted with approval that Liea turned away only once, on the first pass of the needle.

"These stitches will need to come out, but probably not before a fortnight. Just cut one side under the knot and pull. It'll sting him, but no more than that."

Liea looked as if she was ready to collapse where she stood. She put her hand against the lintel for support. "You… you think he will live?"

"The next few minutes should tell. Would you like to help me?"

Ceren mixed a pungent blend of herbs with a few drops of apple cider supplied by Liea. She then had the older woman hold Kinan's head while she soaked a bit of linen in the mixture and held it under Kinan's nose. "I'd try not to breathe for a few moments, if I were you."

While Ceren and Liea both held their breath, Kinan inhaled the scent at full strength. In a moment his eyelids fluttered and then his eyes opened wide and tears started to flow. He sat upright in the bed despite Liea's best efforts. "What is that damn stench?"

"Your salvation," Ceren said calmly. She took the rag and stuffed it in an earthenware bottle with a tight cork to seal it. After she closed the lid of the box the scent began to fade immediately. Liea already had her arms around her son, who didn't seem to understand what all the fuss was about.

"I'm fine, Ma. My head hurts, but that's all…. Wait, what happened to—"

"Your father and your brothers are all fine, as are you. Mostly thanks to this young woman here," Liea said. "Ceren, I don't know where you found that man you sent to help us, but we are in your debt for that as well. I don't know how we can repay you."

Debt. Well, yes. That was how it worked. Gran had always said as much. You use your skills and make other people pay for them. It was no different from being a cobbler and a blacksmith. Except that it *was* different. A cobbler could make a gift of shoes or a blacksmith an ironwork, to a friend. What witch—yes, that was the word; Gran spoke it if no one else would—gave her skills away? Who would trust such a gift? Ceren's weariness caught up with her all at once. She rose with difficulty.

"Can we discuss that later? I think I need to go home…."

Liea looked her up and down. "I think we both need to sit for a moment and have a taste of that hard cider first—without the herbs. Then I'll have Kyne or Beras make sure you get home safe."

"She was worried about me. She was nice to me."

As Ceren lay in her Gran's bed trying to sleep, she examined the thought and wondered if what she thought was concern in Liea's eyes was something else.

Child, everyone acts nice and respectful when they want something or when they owe you, Gran said. *You think we wear a false skin? Feh. Everyone drops the mask as soon as they get what they want. You don't owe them courtesy or aught else.* Ceren remembered. She was still remembering when she finally fell asleep, and heard the voice again.

"Your Gran knew better."

"Go away," Ceren said.

"I can't. Neither can you. We're stuck here, each in our own way. Or do you still think Kinan or his family will welcome you with open arms?

Fool, if you want Kinan, you'll have to take him. Your Gran knew. Your Gran always got what she wanted. Or who she wanted."

That was a subject Ceren definitely did not want to hear about, but the message had already come through. "I collect what I need, but I take what I want, and that's what makes me a true witch. Is that it?"

"It's what your Gran taught you, and she taught you well. Don't deny what you are."

"What if I don't want to be like that?"

Ceren heard faint laughter. "Then you 'be' alone and you 'be' nothing. Stop talking rubbish and use the right tool for the purpose. It'll get easier as time passes. You'll see. Your Gran did. Use me, as she did."

"If I'm a witch, then don't tell me what I must do!"

More laughter. Ceren remembered the sound of it in her head when she finally awoke, even more so than the sound arrows made when they struck human flesh and the image of what a man looked like split from crown to chin by a broadsword. The sun was streaming in from a dusty window. Ceren blinked. How long had she slept? The sun was already high and the morning half gone, at least, and she was famished. Ceren didn't bother to dress properly. First she visited the privy, then washed her face and hands in cold water from the stream. After that she stumbled to the larder and found some hard bread and cheese.

"What do you plan, then? A courtesy call on the boy's family?"

Ceren pinched herself just the once to verify that she wasn't dreaming, but she hadn't really thought so in the first place. Ceren addressed the person who was not there. "Haunting my dreams was bad enough. Are you going to talk to me while I'm awake too?"

"Someone needs to, but no. Your Gran said you would know when the time came, and this is how you know. It is time, Ceren. Put me on."

"Why?"

"So that you may achieve your heart's desire, of course."

Ceren closed her eyes briefly and then spoke to nothing again. "Very well."

The shelf was high. She needed a stool to stand on when she pulled down the long wrapped bundle that rested there. She barely glanced at it, but what she did see confirmed what she had long believed. In a moment the new skin was settling around her. She felt her legs lengthen, her small breasts swell and reshape as she surged up to fit the appearance she now wore.

As always, there was more to it than appearance. As with the Oaf, and the Soldier, and the Tinker, now she wore another person's memories.

Only this time Ceren did not keep her own thoughts and memories tight and protected. She did not fight the new memories, as she tried to do with the Soldier. She took them as far as they would go, all the while she looked in the mirror.

She wasn't merely pretty. She had a face and form that would stop any man dead in his tracks. Ceren was now the reflection of the girl in the pond.

Didn't I tell you? The Girl sounded a bit smug. *You know what life was like for me. What it can be for you. All you need do is take what you want.*

Ceren nodded. "You're beyond beautiful. Was that why that man drowned you in the pond?"

She felt the laughter. She wondered if she was the one laughing, but the reflection looking back at her was sad and solemn. Her own reflection, somewhere hidden beneath a borrowed skin. *So you've seen that as well. Some men will destroy what they cannot possess, and I chose poorly. What of it? Neither Kinan nor his brothers are like that.*

"I know."

All you need do is show yourself to him as you are now, and he is yours.

Ceren shook her head. "No. I show your face to him and he is yours."

A frown now showing in the mirror that was none of Ceren. *It is the same thing, and he is your heart's desire!*

"No. I merely want him. I even think I like him. If there's more to the matter, then time alone will tell. You never understood my heart's desire. Maybe because it took me so long to understand it myself." She tapped the back of her neck three times. "Off with ye, done with ye!"

The skin split as it must, but it did not release her quickly or easily. The Girl was fighting her. Ceren thought she understood why. She pulled off one arm like a too-tight glove and then another, but the torso refused to budge.

"Does the servant question the mistress? Let me go."

You can't do it without me, without us! You're ugly, you're worthless....

"Let me go," Ceren said calmly. "Or I'll cut you off." And just to show that she was serious, Ceren went to her herb box and took out the bronze razor. She had already started a new cut down the side when the skin finally relented. In a thrice Ceren had the Girl wrapped carefully back on her shelf.

The voice was still there, taunting her. *You'll be back. You need me to gain your heart's desire. If it's not Kinan, then another! You're plain at best, hideous at worst. You'll never achieve it on your own.*

Ceren almost giggled. "I didn't understand. All this time I thought the skins were tools and we the purpose. Now I know it's the other way around. I am the instrument, just as Gran was before me. You, the Oaf, the Tinker, the Soldier…. You who died ages ago, and yet still live through us. You are the purpose. We serve you."

You still do. And will.

"Why?"

Because only we can give you what you want.

Ceren shook hear head. "You still don't understand. You already have, at least in part."

What are you talking about?

"I've always felt like one living in a borrowed house, with borrowed strengths, borrowed skills, but I thought it was because of Gran. It wasn't. It was because of *you*."

Fool! The raiders will return or bandits or village boys too drunk to know who they're forcing! You will fall in love. A heavy tree will fall. You can't do this on your own. You need us.

"No," Ceren said. "I need to find out what belongs to me and what does not. You gave me that last part, but now I have to find the rest. That is my true heart's desire."

Ceren left the store-room and latched it behind her. Then, upon consideration, she slowly and painfully pushed her Gran's heavy worktable to block the door.

Setting fire to her Gran's cottage was the easy part. Watching it burn was harder. Listening to the four voices screaming in her head was hardest of all, but she bore it. She heard the pounding from inside as the flames rose, tried not to think of what supposedly had no volition, no independent action, and yet still pounded against a blocked door. Ceren led her sheep and her goat to a grassy spot a safe distance away, where they grazed in apparent indifference as the cottage and pen alike burned.

Her Gran had never taught Ceren any prayers. She tried to imagine what a prayer must be like, and she said that one as the voices in her head rose into a combined scream of anguish that she could not shut out.

"Go to your rest, and take your memories with you."

She didn't think the prayer would work. Some of the memories were hers now, and she knew that was never going to change. She wasn't sure she wanted it to.

The roof finally collapsed, and just for a moment Ceren thought she saw four columns of ash and smoke rise separately from the fire to spiral away into the sky before all blended in flame and smoke as the embers rained down.

Kinan found her sitting there, on the stump, as the cottage smoldered. He looked a little pale, but he came down the path at a trot and was only a little out breath when he reached her. "We saw the smoke. Ceren, are you all right?"

She wondered if he really wanted to know. She wondered if now was the time to find out. "I should ask you the same. You shouldn't be out of bed," Ceren said, not looking at him. "My home burned down," she said, finally stating the obvious. "Such things happen."

"I'm sorry," Kinan said. "But I'm glad you're all right. Have you lost everything?"

She considered the question for a moment. "Once I would have thought so. Now I think I have lost very little." She looked at him. "I'm going to need a place to stay, but where can I go? I have a goat and a sheep and my medicines… I have skills. I'm not ugly, and I'm not useless!" That last part came out in a bit of a rush, and Ceren blinked to keep tears at bay. She only partly succeeded.

Kinan smiled then, though he sounded puzzled. "Who ever said you were?"

Ceren considered that for a moment too. "Nobody."

Kinan just sighed and held out his hand. "You'll stay with us, of course. We'll find room. Let's go talk to Ma; we'll come back for your animals later."

Ceren hesitated. "A witch in your house? What will your father say?"

Kinan didn't even blink. "My father is a wise man. He may grumble or he may not, but in the end he'll say what Ma says, and that's why we're going to her first. We owe you… I owe you."

Ceren decided she didn't mind hearing those words so much. Coming from Kinan, they didn't sound like an accusation. Besides, Ceren understood debts. They could start there; Ceren didn't mind. Just so long as they could start somewhere. She took Kinan's offered hand and he helped her to rise.

Kinan then carried Ceren's medicine box as he escorted her, understanding or not, down the road in search of her heart's desire.

EX CATHEDRA

TONY DANIEL

My children have been stolen.

You want to distance yourself. You want to blame time, you want to blame existence itself, because that would make it inevitable, determined. And then you could fall back on some Zen-like abstraction for comfort, or that old chestnut from the apostle Paul about all things working together for those who believe in the Lord and are called according to his purposes. But you know there is no balm in the East or the West of Old Earth, no way of thinking that will make it right.

The children are gone.

And there is no way to report the crime. No crime, in principle. And so no possibility of Justice.

There's nobody to turn to when you wake up in the middle of the night and hear their crying, when you wander the house listening for them in the floorboard's creak, in the window curtain's rustle. You hear their whispers in these things, these phenomena, and sometimes a closing door reminds you of the gesture of your eldest son's hand reaching for a glass of milk, or a nightlight flickering on in the bathroom brings back a smile playing across your daughter's face.

She is dark-complexioned? Yes. Blue-eyes? You don't. Rebecca does.

A glimpse through a station portal to the out-spreading Milky Way. Your two-and-a-half-year-old son's innocent inquiry, his first real sentence: "How are *you* today, Dadda?"

I'm not doing so well. I can't remember you.

There are no children.

Can't be.

Must not be any children.

So the sounds and the glimpses are merely games you play with your mind.

You know this.

And so you take a shower, and you masturbate, or you don't, and you brush your teeth and get dressed, and you eat oatmeal or forgo breakfast altogether and slap on a patch, and you kiss your wife who is not your wife—

"'Morning, babe."

"Hello, Will."

"You feeling any better today? Any different?"

"No." She pauses, really considers. "No."

"I'm sorry. Do you want to go to the doctor again?"

"I don't think it's helping any." Rebecca, that is her name, shifts her weight from right foot to left. The white nightgown, nearly see-through, outlines her skinny form. Bony and sharp she is. She hasn't been eating and her abdominal muscles are starting to show. Which turns you on, even though they are a product of her wasting disease.

She's convinced she hears something, too. Voices.

But she doesn't know who they belong to.

You have to trust that she'll be all right today.

That your home will look after her.

You have work to do, after all.

And so you touch the pad by the door and download your day's supply of security keys and upgrades, and you tell your front door to take you to work, and you step through the transport screen—

—into another meeting.

This meeting is very important. As are they all. The project is enormous and complex, and you are in charge. More or less.

I am in charge.

Me.

We are building a monument to humanity. For humanity. For history and the future. It is to be a space for reflection and change. A place to honor the past and keep faith with what is to come. A space where the sacred and eternal meet with the individual, meet and merge. A church. A temple. A hollow statue you can go up in. A sacred grove where you can relax and feel utter safety. Complete relief from oppression of any kind.

The Cathedral of Justice.

This particular meeting on this particular morning is with a delegation of linguists from one of the older cache partitions. They have concerns about the cathedral's portico fresco for pre-colonial victims of click-tongue discrimination. (Pre-colonial *Earth*, that is, not Milky Way, which is a whole other ball of wax.) And right behind the language advocates is a joint cache-biologicals coalition, this one made up of left-handers who want a side chapel devoted to the alleviation of oppression by the eastern-sided. This is no problem in a general sense; it's the kind of thing we incorporate every day into our designs. The quandary comes from the fact that the coalition can't or won't decide which side of the cathedral is left and which is right. Because, in order to tell left from right, you need to know north from south or up from down. The cathedral has no spin. Spin leads to inequality.

In the cathedral, we don't put priorities on justice. Priority is another word for privilege, and in the cathedral, there can be no privileged position. Because that would be unjust.

Yet the left-handers feel slighted. That makes their problem my problem.

So I take the meeting.

Today, I've scheduled a consultant from the time-frame design league to hash it out with them. I've kept this hush-hush, because I'm already suspected of having a secret "eastern" agenda, and this will no doubt be seen by some as another dirty trick of the clockwise cabal. Mostly I just want them to decide on *something*, anything, before the final collapse of the galaxy. FGC is pretty much our big deadline. Although we have every hope of bringing the project in long before that, and under-budget.

Unfortunately, time-frame consultants tend to be patronizing, and the meeting leaves some bruised feelings, particularly within the cache. This isn't necessarily the consultant's fault. You get your personality written across a broad swath of stars, you can get a pretty big head without realizing it. Yet there's nothing the cache-bound hate more than a condescending lecture from one of their descendants. When you're dead, respect is about the only currency that means anything to you anymore. I hear that one of the big memory banks is planning to coin respect in quantized units and use it for a currency. You wonder if they will take this practice with them during the Great Migration, when all of the caches will be unzipped from archive and copied into the cathedral where there is room for near infinite expansion.

After this meeting, I retreat to my office.

Since I'm the boss, I have a corner with a window—as much as a giant space station has a corner. We're surrounded by nebulae clouds here at the galactic core, so the view is not the greatest, but I've had false color filters installed and, if I want, I can turn off the overhead lamps and read by the light of the Milky Way. Pretty cool. Somewhere out there past the clouds is Earth, our ancestral home. They say the light reaching us here from the sun, the real sun, started out in about 1872.

But it never got here, of course. Sunlight and earthlight have been missing from our galaxy for the past 200 years, since the days of the Clean Sweep, the great human project prior to the cathedral. After the invention of the portals, the expanding EM sphere of humanity was collected and cached—stored alongside the data trail of the generations since. And so, while Earth certainly still exists, it has disappeared. Along with all sign that it was ever there, including a gravity signature. We were very thorough.

There's your answer to Fermi's paradox, by the way. If we assume all the other alien species—none of whom we've met—did the same, why then the emptiness of the universe has an explanation.

We sentients all cleaned up after ourselves, like good campers. We left the place like we found it. And are presumably still living somewhere in balance with nature, but just not making a fuss about it.

Of course there is another, simpler explanation. And a lonelier one.

In any case, we don't call it Fermi's paradox anymore. We call it Fermi's Law.

Nobody's home.

I love my desk. It's made of teak ported over from the forests of Mars. I put it together myself in my workshop back at the house before things got too busy to keep up with any hobbies. The desktop tilts up to create a full screen for design work, and there are drawers that stretch into fractal dimensions. As a result, my paperwork always seems to be filed, and my workspace uncluttered. This is all appearance. I've got what I think is a fairly tidy mind, but I'm a pack rat at heart and I never throw anything away. That's why I built in, essentially, infinite storage capacity. You wouldn't want to go looking for something in my desk if you didn't know where to find it. It's a long drop to the bottom of the drawers. And there are drawers within drawers too. I kid you not. Told you I was a pack rat.

Behind my desk is a bookshelf with an ever-morphing array of "real" books, all chosen by an embedded subroutine that bases its choices on what it sees me reading. A bunch of technical manuals and design catalogs grace the shelves at present. I wish that I read more fiction, poetry. Read more *anything* other than work-related material these days. Later, after the project's done, I tell myself. A repeated mantra that would be funny if it weren't so sad.

On the second shelf, a picture of Rebecca. Caught on our *Andromeda Falls* trip, when we visited the ship that's hauling the new portal to the next galaxy over. Not many places you can stand and, unenhanced, take in another galaxy complete through a viewport.

In the picture, Rebecca's wearing a pastel pink dress. Her hair is shorter than it is now, and her bangs trail over her eyes in a sweep that's graceful and careless at the same time. Completely Rebecca.

Yep. That was the trip when I told her why we could never have children.

I put it to Rebecca more delicately, but here's the basic low-down.

I can have a kid, but the moment my kid achieves sentience, I'm toast.

I can build a heaven. I can blow up the universe. I can sit and watch movies all day. But if I pass on my genes, I hook myself back up to time. I enter into a mod-x operation that will prevent me from traveling beyond my current time-frame.

Oh yeah. I may have forgotten to tell you.

I'm a time traveler.

So, surprise, surprise, it turns out that people are more than the sum of their information. More than the epiphenomenal consequence of their historical context, if you want to put it precisely.

People are one-way functions. Or I should say we *incorporate* one-way functions. We have a non-reversible, extra-algorithmic component in our basic make-up. Like adding together times on a clock face, what we are, what we truly are as a thinking being, can't be unmixed into components.

Ah hell, I'll just come out and say it: people have souls.

Not transcendent, immortal, God-endowed souls. Maybe we have those, too. I don't know. I'm talking clock math here. $9 + x = 2$. Easy huh? Five is the answer. Try this one:

$3^x = 1$.

Turns out human minds—all self-aware beings, so far as we can guess—have modular mathematics at their foundation. Every individual is a one-way operation.

When all is said and done, you can't write us out as an algorithm.

That's basically why, if I have kids, I stop being a time traveler. And when you stop being a time traveler, that means you've never *been* a time traveler. And if you *are* a time traveler who has gone to a certain period—

Poof. You're gone.

Along with everything you've done or have not done.

So you see why time travelers might be a trifle meticulous about their condoms.

Out my office window, the project station is rotating away from ga-lactic-out, and toward the black heart of it all. Sagittarius A.

Galactic core view means it's almost time for lunch. I order up a Greek salad and—what the hell—ask for it to be delivered from this little restaurant I know on Alpha C when—

Uh oh.

Two slouchy officials from the fitters union show up without an ap-pointment. The slouch posture is ubiquitous among fitters—you learn to lean or you lose your head in the wormholes—and if these two didn't possess such a slouch, they'd have to affect it in order to get elected. Slouch One, I have never met. Looks like some kind of lawyer. Slouch Two is Reberk Dakuba, the union president himself.

"Hello, Reb, what can I do for you?"

Reb shuffles, glances away. This is a pose. I notice the shark-white glint of his eye, the way he rubs his hands together as if he's drying them off for proper handling of a knife. "We've decided to sue, Will," he tells me. "I'm sorry to be the one to break the news."

I don't give him the pleasure of an angry reaction. "And I'm sorry to hear it," I say.

"If the suit doesn't work, I've got cross-grain authorization from servers, freemen and the cached fitters deposit to—well, to call a *strike*, Will."

Which would be a disaster of major proportion and would bring cathedral construction to a halt—perhaps for decades. Both of us know it. But Reb has some desperate fitters out there, and he might be willing to risk it. After all, he's one of the desperate himself. You see, he's miss-ing a real personality.

"Is there anything I can do or say to change your mind?"

"Tell me what's going to happen."

"You know I can't do that, Reb. That kind of knowledge got obliter-ated when they sent me back."

"Then tell the company to give us our memories. With interest."

"I sympathize with your concerns, Reb," I say. "You and I are basically in the same boat."

He nods. This is not our first meeting. Not by a long shot. And even he doesn't know about some of them.

"I was hoping the cathedral board would consider our final offer to settle," Reb says. "I think it's time to take it to them."

"Come on in," I say. "Lay it out for me, and I'll be happy to put it before them."

I mentally (and actually) shift a couple of meetings to tomorrow and next week respectively in order take this conference.

Reb is not exaggerating about the missing memories. Nor the emotional turmoil that goes with it. The Loyal Order of Fitters, Miners, Network Engineers, Space-time Mechanics and Roustabouts—the fitters union—is facing a disaster with its pension fund. When the first generation of fitters got translated into their archetypes and were sent over the event horizon, their old particulars were banked. Thing is, you can't just store up a copy of a personality, step out of it, and then step back in when you're ready to go back to individual existence. Neither person nor archetype remain compatible.

So lives were loaned out to be lived by others. A win-win solution, it seemed at the time. Then, when the fitters were done with their K+ indenture agreement and were re-instantiated as their old selves again, each worker was supposed to receive a richer life as a result. Most did. Their individuality had been loaned out to various artificial intelligences that need such qualities in order to function correctly, and were returned fully endowed with the emotional intelligence that comes from 1,000 years of thinking, doing and feeling.

But for about twenty percent of the fitters, things didn't work out that way. Someone at the savings bank had had the bright idea to gamble on riskier loans shooting for a bigger R.O.I. One in five of these had failed spectacularly. Either the personalities didn't mesh with the A.I., or the A.I. itself was operating in a hazardous environment, couldn't make regular backups, and suffered periodic crashes. Whatever the case, the entire fund of emotional development was lost, together with any memories. And when the archetype was reinstated with his or her personal data, what you had was a soul without any individuality to give it root. Not a pleasant situation.

So now there are still about 10,000 fitters who remain stuck as "types," as they are called, upon retirement, who can't go back to being the person they were—or even being a real person at all.

Okay, maybe this doesn't sound so bad in the abstract—to be condemned to basically a demigod status for the second half of your life. It's not like you lose all reason and become a moron. In fact, you're much, much smarter. But, first of all, it's sheer hell on relationships. Families fall apart. Reb's had. And second, human life for a "type," as they are called, can be boring as hell, especially when you can barely remember who you were before—before you spent 1,000 years shifting around planets, stars and space-time itself with the force of your mind.

So Reb, as a good president ought, is trying to spin the problem as somehow management's fault. On the other hand, it was his own flunky brother-in-law on the bank board who approved the bad loans.

So we talk. And resolve to differ. I'll take the proposal to the board.

I could go on about my day. You get the idea.

These are legacy issues and ultimately resolvable disputes. Tough stuff, but not insoluble. The part of the job where I tie up loose ends. Topographically, from the perspective of the past and present, that's precisely what the entire project is about, too: creating a knot, a simple overhand loop, to keep all the meaning, all the teleological direction, humanity has pumped into our surroundings from unraveling like a cheap suit. Sure, it's not something our cave-bound ancestors could've accomplished—it's wheels within wheels, webs of oaths and promises anchored in the deep past stretching to today and beyond, where you touch one part, the other parts move. But, when you get down to the nitty-gritty, it's algorithms. Methodology. And we humans are masters of method. In fact, we're tying the knot even as we speak. And that's what makes my afternoons more interesting, you might say.

I spend them on site.

Oh, it's still meetings and more meetings, don't get me wrong. But these sessions are with my team leaders and contractors. Project reports. Completion estimates. And me overseeing it all, juggling contractors, material, what has to get done when before something else—the backbone of construction projects—hell, since Roman times. This is the part I love.

The cathedral looks kind of like an egg.

Okay, an egg several thousand light-years across. Impressed upon the multi-dimensional surface of the event horizon of Sagittarius A, the black hole at the center of the Milky Way, like a tattoo inked by two million stars worth of quantum uncertainty, two-tenths of one percent of the material galaxy itself. We took it, hauled it here, and we're not putting it back. By any measure, a major undertaking.

Anyway, from the outside, it does look like an egg.

Within the egg, within the cathedral, the laws of nature don't apply. Or, rather, they apply selectively. Phenomenology surrenders to teleology. The *is* to the *ought*. Within, it's impossible to hurt innocent children, no matter how you try to recruit them for sex, throw them in gulags for choosing their families over the state, seduce and destroy them with false prophesies and visions, rape them behind the altar, enslave them for work on collective farms, eat them. It's impossible to throw a rock and hit somebody. All the holocausts are redeemed, like so many coupons, so many savings accounts come due. All the hurricanes and earthquakes and extinction events we have had to endure as a species are cashed in for dividends and interest. Within the cathedral, truth trumps power. Right makes might.

Okay, so what's the interior really look like, feel like?

Come on. You know I can't tell you that. I'd have to show you.

But I'll try.

Spacious. Complex. By definition. Imagine a map that is more intricate than the thing it represents. Can't? That's the cathedral. When you first arrive, it still looks like a cathedral, a building, but that's just the introductory experience. You begin to notice that things are… not what they seem.

Every door, every window, every portico, every niche, nook and cranny opens up into something that is larger than the room you came from before. It is a place that is bigger on the inside than it is on the outside.

It's beautiful. It sparkles with a thousand dewdrops, each one a world in itself that you can enter. There's a sound. A bit like rushing water. A bit like wind. Only later do you realize this is the air itself, the song of worlds suspended, dancing like motes in sunlight, rippling against one another like crystalline bubbles. You breathe them in.

And the scent. New. Fresh. But infinite and intricate. The atmosphere alive with possibilities.

And hell, we're just done with the basement.

Big problem. The egg, the cathedral, is fundamentally incompatible with the universe as we know it. It wants to splinter off and form its own pocket universe.

The egg wants to hatch.

That's where my real job lies.

And that's where my future wife comes into the picture. The one I'll marry after Rebecca dies.

Her name is Lu. She's quality control. Allegedly. Whatever she is or will be, she's hard to take my eyes off of. Ur-bronze of skin. Dark-eyed. My total physical type. And there are other compatibilities.

Let's just say she and I have a lot in common.

"We have concerns about the subbasement template," Lu tells me, no introduction, no 'how-do-you-do' provided. Where did she come from? How did she get into my office? Easy. She's like the sphere descending into Flatland in that book: it shows up suddenly from the third dimension, like a finger dipped through a pond's surface.

Like I said, she and I are a lot alike. Lu is a time traveler. But the body she inhabits is from farther up-time than mine. Stronger. Faster. Able to leap tall buildings with a single bound.

And able to out-think me five ways to Sunday on most days.

"Which one?" I ask. The cathedral has at least four basements that I know of. My predecessor as chief architect had a thing for them. Contemplating those myriad twisty corridors may have been what finally drove him to insanity. On the other hand, it may have just been the drinking.

"All of them," Lu answered. "There's a discord with the unborn conditionals that's grown into a detectable resonance. Justice for the unborn has become underdetermined in regards to born justice. The models don't mesh, and we think this may be a major factor that leads to the hatch."

The hatch. Our *bête noire*.

"Are you sure," I reply. "Doesn't exactly sound like impending doom. Could take a few million years to manifest…" My first reaction to irritation is facetiousness. Also my second. And third. Normally I put a sock in it as best I can, but what's a wife for if not to hear your internal dialog?

"A million years is a drop in the bucket and a blink of the eye," says Lu. "As you well know."

"Do you have a modification ticket for me, then?"

Lu hesitates. Fixes me in her sight. Something unusual to this. I've been standing, and I sit down on the edge of my desk. Grip its underside.

"This one is a simple fix," she says. Almost off-handedly. Almost casually. Almost. "We're going to leave it up to you."

So—this is a bit of a stunner. Template mods normally came with a full work order from on high. Pages and pages of instructions. Because who can argue with the future? I mean, by definition they've *been there* and *done that*.

"Okay," I say. "Can you be a little more specific?"

Another slight hesitation. I gripped the underside of the desk tighter.

"It involves Rebecca. Your wife, Rebecca."

What?

"What?"

"William, I tried to prepare you," said Lu. "Rebecca has become a strong underdetermination attractor. In fact, we think this entire template problem has something to do with her."

"What the hell are you talking about, Lu. She's just some woman."

"I know that. But the equations don't lie. Events are *shifting* here, and the butterfly effect—well, uncertainty is giving way to instability, and it all seems to lead back to her. Like I said, underdetermination. As if many roads could lead to the same future. Which, as you know, means none of them could."

"And that means what?" I ask.

"Disaster, Will," Lu says. "For the entire project. A hatch event."

"Wait a minute! You told me she's going to die. That this disease, whatever she's got, is inevitable. You never said she was a danger to the *project*."

Lu is silent for a moment. A placid emptiness passes over her face. This is the look she gets when she is off on a quantum decision tree spree, considering the billions upon billions of responses she might give. Then the smile. The knowing smile that curls across her perfect lips.

"Look, it's difficult to explain without compromising your situation," Lu replied. "But I'll answer your questions if I can."

Suddenly, I'm scared shitless. There's only one question that matters, after all.

"What is it you want me to do?"

Lu stepped toward me. Her face is placid, but there is a tear in her eye. A tear that contains whole star clusters of experience. Eons.

The suffering and anguish of all possible worlds.

"William, you have to kill her." Lu stretches her arms out to me.

In her right hand is a gun.

It's a Hauser 98 semi. A weapon so advanced in its coding as to seem magically ensorcelled with noxious spells, even to one such as I. Lethal in all possible worlds. You get shot with a Hauser, you're never coming back.

I'm shaking. "Why ask me? She's doing a pretty good job of killing herself."

"Not enough," Lu says. "You have to do it tonight."

"No." It's a squeak. Talk about weakly underdetermined. I know what I'm up against. Lu is merely a front. For humanity itself. Or what's left of it.

Lu shakes her head sadly. Another tear. Another possible world crumbles to ashes.

"You know you're *going* to."

I'd like to say I didn't make love to Lu. I'd like to say I didn't fuck her.

I did both. Simultaneously. Apart. Her skin glowed beneath my fingers. Her lips touched mine like those butterfly wings that flapped during the Jurassic—and doomed the dinosaurs.

And then we fell into the present tense.

She pushes me down, strips me naked. Climbs on top and pulls me inside herself. Moves with the beat of sunlight through leaves on a planet that had ceased to exist a thousand centuries before she was born.

Then she draws me into the future. Makes me want to be there with her. To love. Hope. Take revenge against a universe that wants to stamp us out. Find my antidote in her.

And I turn her over, push her to the ground, the lush Persian rug on my office floor. Part her impossibly beautiful legs.

All this can be yours.

Is yours.

I tell myself.

The future is rosy.

My future wife is not really a woman in the traditional sense. Or, rather, she's all woman. She's the consensus of what humanity will become. And I—perhaps I am not such a simple architect myself. I have a confession to make.

It's not what you think. That I am a time traveler is no big secret. Everyone knows. I showed up the day the former chief architect committed suicide. He'd killed himself in a particularly nasty way—with the same sort of mod-p bullet that's used in the Hauser. Information can neither be created nor destroyed. If you know what you're doing, you can pull a password from a cadaver. But information can be password protected for all eternity.

When you're hit with a mod-p slug, you can't download to the cache. You just—

die.

That's the kind of gun the poor slob had put to his head. And he'd taken all his personal keys with him .

So they—meaning the Board, meaning the Consortium, meaning the human political structure in the entire galaxy—were locked out. Out of the galactic core project. Out of the cathedral.

But happy day!

I show up with the code, time traveler that I am. I can restart the project.

On one little condition.

The future wants a say in the Cathedral of Justice. We have legitimate claim to legacy projects just as much as the past and the present.

We want our justice, too.

And what might that justice consist of? Let's just say that from a couple of billion years perspective, you might come to view justice as more of a means than an end. That justice might come to be considered anything that enables you to survive.

At five minutes to midnight on the last night of the universe, Fermi's Law has become Fermi's Fuck-up.

We've got no help up there at the end of time. Nobody to turn to.

All sentient beings disappear completely. Utterly. We, sentience itself, leave behind absolutely no trace of our passing. May as well never have been. It's happened countless times. It's happened to everybody.

Where did they all go?

To heaven, of course. It's pretty obvious when you think about it. Who wouldn't want to be there when the shit hits the fan and the fan sputters to a halt? An event horizon is eternal, even if the universe that contains it is not. Everybody figures this out sooner or later. They collect all their baggage (hence the lack of EM signals across the heavens), turn out the lights, close the door—

Goodbye cruel world.

But somewhere, some time, a long, long way down the continuum, in the light of the last dying star in the last cinder of a galaxy—something very odd happened. Will happen.

We, meaning just us humans, fell from grace.

Okay, this is not exactly a theological matter. It has to have an explanation. But—

nobody is quite sure why.

A simple switch got flipped after lying ten billion years dormant, perhaps. A relay went on the fritz. A bug somehow crept into the mechanism. And a disappeared sentient species was suddenly dumped out into the very cold last night.

First thought: "Oh shit."

Next: "So cold."

"Fuck me, William," says Lu. "Make me warm. I'm so cold. Please, William, fuck me until I burn."

Heat death. The cold night at the end of time. That's where I come from. Where Lu comes from. We're the future. Bleaker than the bleakest hell any religion every invented to punish its sinners and unenlightened. We're the dust kicked up by the final, limp breeze blowing through the empty halls of the end of the castle.

We want to live. Will want. We remember what it was like in heaven, before we got dumped out.

But—

and here's the big secret—

to travel back in time, I had to give up being, well—

human.

Was I really human to start with? I like to think so. In a way. The cached, you know. You may *be* one of them. They're archived, allowed limited processing space. It's not as good as being biologically alive.

Not so inside the egg. In there, we had eternity to spread out. To process. To dream. Or so we thought. In any case, we did end up with billions of years.

And we changed. We became—not alive. Not dead. Each one of us a self with a million centuries of barnacle thoughts attached, a rattle on the end of a snake of memes. Practically unrecognizable as human.

But that was a lot closer than—

what I am now—

what I am learning to dislike

—completely.

Myself.

I stand. Pull up my pants.

"I'm sorry," I say to Lu. "I'm married"

She turns over. Impossible to hurt in this way. Smiles.

"Yes. To me."

"Not anymore," I say. "Not now."

I let her go. Push her forward. She lands with a huff on the Persian rug—it's a nice one I picked out with Rebecca on a world grazed by giant mutant sheep—in a tangle of her own limbs. Lu's surprised, humiliated. Even a goddess looks stupid splayed out like that. But not for long.

I have to get away from her before she says the right thing, makes the right move, to draw me back.

I pick myself up. Run through my office door. Throw myself through the portal, with Lu's laughter echoing behind me.

A random jump. End up somewhere in the M5. At least so the tracker number reads on the blank wall I face Whatever. Wherever. Back through. Another jump. Another.

To no avail.

You can't escape the present. As you are well aware.

You.

Me.

I jump back to Old Earth.

I'm somewhere in the southern hemisphere, I think. The portal opens onto a night vista of jagged mountains. I have no idea what they're called.

But they feel like home.

Above, a full moon.

The moon.

I gaze up at the moon.

Something cold.

I look down at my hand.

It's holding the gun.

Lu has put it there, of course.

Time Travel 101: how to go back into the past.

You can't.

Okay, you can, in a way. First you have to lose yourself. Unmoor. No other way around it. You have to join the universe, become a permanent principle of nature.

Something like what happens to the fitters when they serve their indentures, but like I said, it's not the same.

It's not the same, because you make it so you *have never lived.*

How?

Here's the classic method: kill your grandfather. Or something to that effect. You release your particulars to the void. Only the part of you that stands outside of time survives. It's a shadow. A spectre. A haint.

Call it a "type," like the fitters do. But the fitters can, theoretically, get back their humanity.

Time travelers, theoretically, *can't.*

The mechanics are straightforward. You appear to your ancestor— usually in the form of a fiery angel or demon or some such, depending on the era. He (or she, as the case may be) acquiesces to the logic of the weapon in your hand.

It would be easier on the conscience perhaps to do away with one of your barely sentient *Homo habilis* forbearers, but you can't go too far back or you'll take out half the human race in the bargain.

When you kill your grandfather, you *do* actually kill yourself. And your father or mother. Any siblings. But that's just the tip of the space-time iceberg. You kill all the generations to come, as well.

You kill your own children. And theirs. And theirs.

Thousands. Millions.

Because it's not like you decide not to have those children. No, you obliterate the *possibility* from the realm of the conceivable—and that's a whole other thing. Because those possibilities once *did* exist as realities.

And they leave echoes.

They fucking haunt you is what they do.

And so I am free to ply the time ways because I took out one Thomas Langurn. From the Great Migration generation itself. But Tom wasn't going to download to a cache, nor migrate into the cathedral. Tom was going to die in a rather nasty portal data mismatch accident a mere decade after I showed up.

He was going to die anyway, damn it, and never get cached. Just not before he had a few kids.

When I met Rebecca, the attraction between us was instant. Almost as magnetic as the attraction between me and Lu. While I no longer possess the genes of my ancestors, I still retain the shadow of their personalities. The soul, as I've called it.

So it was perhaps no surprise that I would be attracted to the same sort of woman as my distant grandfather Thomas had been attracted to.

A woman who was also my distant grandmother.

Okay, never mind that.

I was married in the future. And it's not like I had left Lu behind there, either. She was just as much a time traveler as I, and a much more active one. She appeared in my office on a regular basis to deliver her orders from the far future. But Lu is a construct, a chimera. As am I. Or at least, as I was.

Lu is unreal.

Rebecca is real.

And, when I realized I had fallen in love with Rebecca, *I* felt real for the first time in a very long time. Rebecca brought something out in me. It couldn't have been genetic. It couldn't have been information that was hidden or sequestered. All of that had been erased when I'd deep-sixed Thomas Langurn.

I guess you would have to say that, in some measure, in some way, our souls met. I don't know what this means. I only know that there was a moment when we were both sitting at a table in some restaurant out on the long arm of the galaxy somewhere eating something like snails and drinking red wine to wash them down when I looked across the table and caught her eye. I swallowed a snail—or whatever it was—and made a face. And smiled to show her that it was all right, that the snail hadn't phased me. That I was enjoying this being here with her thing. This moment of moments.

And she moved her head to the side in that way she does and she said, "Know what? I want to have your children." And then she winked and touched my hand.

And that was love.

So you ditch the gun once again and go home to your wife.

You live in an old Victorian mansion. Old Earth authentic. Sort of. It is actually a space you built yourself within the confines of the project station, so it doesn't exactly have a gabled roof. The station itself is enormous, but it is not quite big enough to accommodate the kind of space you like to have available for your enjoyment. So you built a house with holes. Fractal dimensions for storage. Extra, unseen rooms. You're not the only one who does this. Most people have one or two interdimensional hidey-holes in their living quarters. But architects often go overboard. Everything simple and yet as beautifully functional as possible. They get clever with design.

I live here.

Rebecca is waiting for me when I port home.

She has the Hauser in her hand.

I don't even pause to wonder where she got it.

I know. It just showed up. Dropped in. Like Mr. Sphere into Flatland.

Rebecca points the gun at me.

"Stay the hell away from me," she says. "I've figured out what you're up to. What they've told you to do."

"I won't hurt you," I say. "I swear."

"You put the voices here. To torment me."

"No, Rebecca. I didn't. I don't know what's wrong with you."

"Doesn't matter. I'm not going to die for that—" She points toward a window. I know what she's gesturing at, but we are turned away from the core at the time and only the galaxy shows through. She means the cathedral. "—that thing," she finishes.

Her right hand still holds the gun. It's shaking. If that gun goes off, it can kill even such as I am.

I step forward. Hold out a hand. "Give me that, please."

A moment of defiance. Wrinkles tighten around her eyes. Does her finger tighten as well? Would I even notice before the shot rings out and I am erased?

Rebecca slowly lowers the gun. She breaks into tears. "I know they're here," she says.

"Who?"

"The voices," she says. "I know them. I just don't know *how* I know them."

I pull her to me. Her wet face against my shoulder. "It's like some curse," she says. "Some curse I can't break."

I take the Hauser.

I push her away.

Gently.

I step back.

"Maybe I can break it," I say.

I point the gun at my head.

My index finger moves from the trigger guard. Hovers in the space between guard and action.

"It'll be like I never was," I say. "Like none of this happened."

My fingertip meets the metal. I am inevitability. I am a force of nature. I am—

"Daddy, don't."

A young voice. From someone unseen.

"Who said that?"

Then another voice, a female voice. A child. "We need you."

"Who?" I say. I keep the gun in position. "Whoever you are, stop it!"

"Don't kill yourself, Daddy."

I spin around, take aim.

At the curtains. At the empty Milky Way beyond.

At nothing.

"Tell me who you are."

A moment of silence. Decision.

"You know us."

Another voice. "You told us to stay hidden."

"I don't know you," I say. Faltering. My mind in flux. "I don't."

"Come here, my darlings." It's Rebecca's voice. But richer. Stronger than I've heard it in a long time.

Since before I told her she was going to die.

They emerge. The three of them.

And I remember.

An air vent breeze passes through a curtain and from the movement, a child materializes. Joel. Eight. Thin and long-boned. He's going to be a tall man. And handsome when he fills out.

I shift my weight. The floorboards creak. And from the floor rises Hannah, as if she has stepped up from a hidden staircase. Six years old. Beautiful. Those blue eyes.

Rebecca kneels, spreads her arms to the children. "Come here."

And from a swirl of dust dancing in a shaft of the faintest starlight.

Lavy. My youngest. My son.

He runs to his mother, looks out from within her skirts. And says the words.

"How are *you* today, Dadda?" He doesn't really know what he's saying. He's only two-and-a-half.

It all returns.

I remember.

Because the cathedral wants me to remember.

Because it has decided the time has come to remember.

Say you are going to kill somebody—and that you are not a murderer at heart. Say you have the gun in your hand. Your finger is on the trigger.

And say your victim looks at you, considers you coldly—and doesn't plead for his life. No, because he figures you're prepared for that. Doesn't plead the welfare of his family, either. Plenty of families have gotten along fine without one of the parents.

Say he makes the one appeal that might move you. He asks for his unborn children. Maybe somehow, some way, he recognizes who you are. What you are. What he is asking is that you save yourself.

"You can kill me," he says, "but don't kill *them*."

It doesn't work that way, you tell him.

"You're from the ass-end of time," he says. So he does know. "*Make* it work that way."

You shake your head.

Pull the trigger.

You've got a world to save, after all.

But he did get you to thinking.

Me.

I can't have children. Types and humans can't mate.

I would obliterate myself. My work.

But what if I had them—and I hid them?

Really hid them. Kept them away from causality for a while. Not forever. Just long enough to get them to the true sanctuary that is coming. That I am helping to create.

Would I then disappear with a *pop*, taking my kids with me?

Or would the universe relent, and let us live?

Only one way to find out.

As I said, within my house, I built back doors, secret passages, to the cathedral. Fractal tunnels. Places out of time and out of mind.

Catacombs, if you will.

These passage ways lead to wormholes and those wormholes lead to the subbasement of the cathedral proper. Justice desires to spread itself. Meaning seeks meaning.

Some of the cathedral's physical laws have crept into my living quarters.

The fitters helped me build the passageways. Some of them did, anyway. Reb was the gang chief during the undertaking. All of those particular fitters, unfortunately, never did recover their memories afterward. Mark it all down to the pension fund debacle. Or, at least, so they thought.

Sorry Reb. Sorry fellows. It was me who took them.

Screwed by management again. I suck as a boss.

It was in those catacombs that my children were born. The cathedral is a place where normal cause and effect do not have consequence, unless *you* want them to, unless they *ought* to. It's a place where a type such as myself, a being whose essence is fundamentally outside of the normal time stream, and a human woman moored to time, such as Rebecca, could come together in love.

Could fuck like animals.

With all the consequences thereof.

And that's where I hid the children.

The children that the cathedral made me forget.

Almost.

Because who could really forget such wonderful children?

And now—

now I have to remember.

Because—

Lu stands before me.

Mr. Sphere, she's dipped her toe into our space-time and, lo and behold, here she is. Following up on her work order. Come to deal with the underdetermination nexus.

Otherwise known as my family.

"So you didn't do it." She said. "I'm pretty disappointed, William." She's smiling her placid, patronizing smile. Her all-knowing smile from the future.

But then the smile melts away. A hardness in her eyes is revealed. It was always there, but now you can see. Who she is. What she is.

An ugly force of nature.

"Stay the fuck away from my family," I say.

"Stupid," she says. "Stupid, stupid *man*. What have you done?"

Faster than thought, she's at my throat, her long fingers wrap around my neck.

I think about raising the gun. Shooting her.

But realize that, even if I were enhanced, even if I were fast enough, it would be useless. The cathedral would bend space, warp time. The cathedral won't let me kill her. Not here. Not now.

I pocket the Hauser.

Lu squeezes. Hard. Twists. My neck twists with her interlocked hands.

Crack. Pop. My vertebrae shatter. Most unpleasant.

Then her fingers pierce the skin. Dig in. Her hand comes away, trailing my spinal cord.

I must look a fright. My neck ripped open from behind. A trail of gooey neurons draping like a worm.

But even now, I feel my wounds healing. Quickly.

"This is about to be over," she says, and, still holding me by the neck, frog marches me toward the door. She turns to Rebecca, the kids. Her eyes pass over Joel. Hannah.

Settle on Lavy.

Again she smiles.

"Little boy. Listen to me, little boy. I'm going to take your Daddy outside and hurt him," she tells him. "If you come along, too—then I won't hurt him. And I won't hurt you. Nothing will hurt." Lu's smile brightens. Shows teeth. "Come now. Everything's going to be fine and it won't hurt a bit."

Lavy looks at me questioningly.

Pops the question, the eternal question.

"How are *you* today, Dadda?"

Just comforting sounds. He doesn't know what the words mean yet. Does he?

"I'm *great!*" I say. "You stay here, Lavy. Listen to me. Stay."

This takes a moment to register. Dadda is being yanked around by someone he doesn't know. He's a good boy, a brave boy, and longs to help.

But I smile, nod my head. "Dadda is *great* today," I say. "You stay here."

Lavy is a good boy, most of all. He does what his Dadda tells him.

Thank fucking God.

"No, William. You make him come," Lu growls at me. Her voice is low. And is there a trace of panic?

"No."

She sighs. "All the other children. All the ones who watched their mothers burn in ovens, who watched their fathers march off to war, never to come back. All the idiocy. All the waste. All the injustice. You would take their reward? Make their last thought, their last breath, a cry of suffering?"

I consider. And then I consider that I'm just one man. And I don't know how to answer this at the moment.

"I'm sorry," I say. And I begin to laugh. It's a raspy, airless affair. She's partially crushed my windpipe, after all. "But yes."

"Stop that!" she says. "It's disrespectful. Of the children. Not these. Not these… abominations. The real, dead children."

I don't stop. I laugh harder. I sound like a dull saw drawn roughly over iron, but I keep it up.

Consternation from Lu. "How are you doing that?"

"The cathedral," I whisper. "The rules."

"What are you talking about?" She shakes her head. "I don't care." She pops my spinal cord. Severs it like a finger pinch severs a worm.

Or she tries to, at least.

The thing molds itself back together.

She squeezes through it again.

And again.

I feel myself healing, over and over again. Lu snorts in frustration.

"Goddamn it!" She steps back, tries to find a better, more deadly purchase on me.

That's when I spin, grab her—

and we tumble through the portal.

On the pre-set. Last door opened, first back.

Doesn't matter. Anywhere. Anywhere away.

And we're on Earth. That southern mountain range I was at earlier. The snowy mountain ledge. Nearby, a railing to keep the tourists from falling to their deaths.

But nobody's here at the moment.

Sunrise.

Before she can get a better grip on me, I shake Lu off, madly shuffle away. Do everything I can to keep her from getting her hands on me. She really could take off my head here, now that we've exited the cathedral. And she's so very, very fast.

Poised. Enhanced. An assassin from the future.

Her mouth, her lovely lips, curl into a snarl. She stands up, takes a bead. Starts to come at me—

and I pull the Hauser out of my pocket.

Point it at her heart.

Lu stops in her tracks.

"You *do* realize what you're doing?" she asks me.

"Killing you," I answer.

"You know who I am," she says. "It's not just me in here. I'm still linked to the cache. You're killing us. Forever."

"You are going to kill me. All of you."

She shakes her head. "This work... so much work. The energy involved. The energy we can't afford to lose." Her voice trails off. "Such a waste.

She knows there's really nothing left to say.

"Goodbye, Lu."

"I loved you," she says. Shrugs. "Not that it mattered."

"I loved you, too," I reply. "In my way."

I raise the gun a smidgen.

No, not the heart.

I pull the trigger.

Shoot my once and future wife.

In the face. Where it's got to hurt.

Lu shakes as if she's touched a live electrical wire, as if a thousand volts are passing through her. Ten thousand. A million. Her head is a blur. Her ruined face—

Pearls over. Like some monitor screen.

Becomes another face. Some woman I never met. It melts away. Another, this time a man. Another, another. Faces. Faster.

Delete, delete.

Faster, faster.

Millions of files.

Millions of faces.

The entire final cache. Up at the ass-end of time, as one of my ancestors put it.

Delete.

So be it.

After it's all finished, I throw her body from the cliff. Into the ice and snow below.

Where she belongs.

I step back through the portal.

And

—leave Earth forever.

But come back home.

You.

There.

Listen to me.

Don't be looking for us. We're gone.

We've locked up the center of the Milky Way, and you can never get in. Oh, you might find someone else that will take you—somebody in another galaxy. This one's closed. You're almost to Andromeda with that ship. Perhaps there's room in the inn. You could always knock.

Or you could resist the temptation.

In that case, here's your chance. The chance *not* to disappear. To be the one exception—the singular exception in all the universe—to Fermi's Law.

To rage against the dying of the light.

That's the alternative to justice. And heaven.

To remain.

To matter.

Take it or leave it. I'm out of here.

Oh, by the way—I sealed the entrance behind me.

Lu's question was the right one. They usually were.

Is it worth the sacrifice of one child to make a heaven for all the dead and suffering children in all human history?

My answer: of course it is. By any rational measure.

Except that I didn't let you. And neither did the cathedral, in the end.

So maybe that's not the real answer after all.

I'll leave that up to you.

I've bolted the door from the inside, taken the key with me. There's no way for you to get in. None of you. It's a one-way trip to forever, and you're not invited.

Look, I wrote it there over the entrance, in case you have any doubts. My last work order. As plain as everlasting night.

Thou shalt not.

Read it and weep.

Let the universe burn down; I don't care.

Let all memory be turned to tears and ashes.

Thou shalt not.

Not take my children from me.

TRUTH WINDOW:
A TALE OF THE BEDLAM ROSE

TERRY DOWLING

The Nobodoi came to Earth a little after midday on 4 June 2023, accompanied by their support races: the Hoproi, the Matta, the Darzie, so many others. They brought with them the star Wormwood, a fragment of antimatter some said, and used it to begin their great xenoforming of the Earth, making it what they wanted. Then, overnight, the Nobodoi vanished—stepped back, withdrew, who could say?—leaving behind their Bridge Races, the remnants of a blasted Humanity and the great Patchwork they had made.

It was Light-Commander Raine Halva Belicrue who first raised the issue, tracked it, set his Human aides to doing the relevant searches, then made the query across the world. That powerful Darzie, Fist of the Stars, Arm of Law, localized and hurting as only the most determined and committed of the Darzie Race ever would, sat in his Rule-of-Hand tower at Dars-Bayas and learned of this growing movement among the crushed, long-conquered Humans, then took it that one step further. Made it a question to the full spread of the Flower.

What do you know of the Lady Mondegreen?

He expected little that was new. No surprises. Few surprises. For it had been expected, modelled, some sort of emergent belief system. It's what all peoples did, all sufficiently cognate conquered peoples, just one more inevitability. But Raine took it further. His localization was the finest, the most excruciating. Only the Darzie fighting elites, the Elsewheres and the Purple-and-Blacks, endured more, surrendering self, but they stepped back into a quasi-existence of hot-glass and reverie and barely knew what they did.

For Raine Halva Belicrue there was no stepping back. This Fist of the Stars, Flame of the Encosium, harnessed his pain, *used* his pain, did the search and posed the question.

No Humans replied, of course. They lacked the Cohabitation resources, probably would for centuries, millennia, eons, unless the Nobodoi overlords, the Recalled Ones, were to Return, intervene and decree otherwise.

But twenty-eight Matt scholars did, astonishing Raine, requesting enhancement, offering reciprocation, data-trade, asking questions of their own.

And one—Holding-in-Quiet—made the incredible offer of leaving its typhy, its home, its work of the life, to meet "in the reach of hands" should that be required. This one had a quest of the heart, it seemed, was no doubt building this religion of the Lady into an identity artefact that would mark its days. Who would have thought?

Raine should not have been surprised, that was the thing. After all, look at what the Cohabitation brought: access to the great Overlord nets—the Acrimba, the Tutifa, the Sarannas, the Wail Guydo. Keywords and encrypts like "Mondegreen" and "Lady" and "Goddess" would have been flagged: ideologically, sociologically, archaeologically. Philologically and etymologically, too, in current Human sayings alone: "By the Lady!" "Praise the Lady!" "Lady be with you!"

He blamed his localization. But even as he sat back in his Talking Chair, even as his manner became carefully businesslike and his crest spines settled, another astonishment occurred, even more amazing than the first: a stat-flash blazon and a voice on *that* closed alliance channel.

"Hey, you, Darzie-pants, Raine! This is Fond Louie hisself, so be paying the tensest tension, okey-doke! Know what's shakin' the Human tree. Know the Mondegreen Lady's first and best church! Know that, hey!"

Raine's crest flared again. Fond Louie? It truly was. The Hoproi warmaster at the Bassantrae Sequester. The screen filled with the image of this famous, crafty Hoproi, an image shot from a field link somewhere in its war-garden. The creature loomed three metres above its four elephantine legs, great grey-brown barrel body painted with stars and bull's-eyes and geometric patterns in the powdery reds and oranges of its shooting chapter.

Raine couldn't see those legs on the screen, of course, just three of its four cardinal trunks coiled in against the great barrel torso with the single dark eye peering out between each juncture, the body finally flattening at the top with the clustering of sensory fibres where the mouth was.

And resolutely speaking Antique, the Human occupation language all Hoproi so maddeningly insisted on using instead of Anvas or Kolack. Raine didn't care. This was wonderful, better than he had hoped.

Such participation—and about such an issue. This trivial but curiously robust Racial yearning, this quaint and inevitable first flowering of hope among the Humans was being transferred globally, and so cohesively, that was the thing, by what could only be word of mouth: solitary wanderers, tinkerers and minstrels, Human bureaucrats, travelling siswitch troupes—circus performers: Raine knew the term well—despite the culls, the checks and prohibitions, the sampling imposts. It was the cohesiveness that fascinated Raine, troubled him. Two hundred and thirty-eight years since Wormwood arrived, fifty-six years since the Recall, and despite the Great Work, the xenoforming and all that it entailed, such an effective degree of interfacing. Was mutuality the word?

All that came in seconds, moments, instants for Raine, primed as he was.

"Fond Louie, what do you know of this? How is your chapter involved?" Raine spoke the Antique terms carefully. The Hoproi were notorious for misunderstanding words, twisting language and meaning to suit themselves.

"Know this, you betchy! Know Humans using this to make a way. Crooning kumbayas aplenty."

Raine's fingers danced on the keypad of his chair, cuing additional flash translations, sending surge commands through a dozen monitoring systems. "There can be no prospect of insurgency in this."

"None," Fond Louie boomed, trunks flexing merrily. "We ruling the roost!"

"The what?"

"No mattress! No threat or intent. Namby-pambies behave, bejeez! But I got the goods. That church close by this Sequester, capisce?"

"We can visit?" Straight to it. Raine had to control this exchange, snatch sense from the dross.

"Certainment, mon capital! Ours for the done-deal. Name the day!"

"Fond Louie, a house-lord will accompany. You have no reservations?"

"Plenty of seats. More the merriest. When-so, great Raine?"

"Let me confer with this lord. But the sooner the better, once I've assessed the data coming in."

"Done deal. But limited, capisce? Just you. Just me. Just this one crimpy. No sharps."

"But you will have *choi* protection."

"My Sequester, best Raine. My turf. Natch."

"Then I shall bring a bodyguard."

"Fraidy cat! No scratch Darzie. No probable claws."

"I will call you shortly."

"Done deal." And the screen went blank.

The church, such as it was, sat ten metres back from the dirt road in what did indeed look like a prairie stretching off for miles: a small-enough, whitewashed stone building made from hand-fetched discardo, twenty metres on its long sides, ten on the shorter, a little under three metres high, with a small dome at the flat roof's midpoint. A simple pillar and lintel archway was the only entrance.

A Human place, old in design to those who knew such lore—Mediter-ranean Vernacular—but new, newly made.

Such a rare thing.

And equally rare on this plundered, extravagantly xenoformed Earth two hundred and thirty-eight years after the great Nobodoi rulers brought down their piece of controlled antimatter—*controlled*, the word said it all!—brought in three Bridge Races and dozens of Lesser Races to rule it for them, for a Matta, a Hoproi and a Darzie to meet face to face at a *Human* place.

Such meetings did happen between the Races, of course they did, but rarely away from sanctioned holds, optimals and vast dedicated protec-tions, and rarely with just one member of each species present.

The scale of it was dazzling, thrilling. Bridge Races they were, the ruling elect, each judged sufficiently compatible by the Departed Ones that they could be left to do this job this time, interface with Humanity and with each other, marshal the less Human-coterminous Races in the great spread of the Donalty Flower. But an imperfectly localized Darzie could so easily lose phase and turn rogue. A Hoproi warmaster might suddenly discern a fine logic or status-enhancing joke in a trophy kill, despite—because of—the inevitable reprisals; a Matta's life journey, the callings of the Narrow Way, might demand some ultimate and crucial self-immolation. The mindsets, tropisms and imperatives were profoundly different; understanding so easily deflected down so many byways. Only elaborate compatibility totes, localizations and an abiding fear of the Nobodoi made it possible.

So they agreed to come, this unlikely, possibly unprecedented three, to this quiet, green-enough field outside the force-wall of the Bassantrae Sequester. Raine arrived first, phasing in from his swordship *Nobion*, shimmering in its containment field at thirty thousand feet. With him came six Elsewheres in full hot-glass armour, who stood quietly by the entrance tracking the scene at a dozen vested data-ranges unavailable to most Races in the Patchwork. They waited while the light-commander stepped through that doorway and entered the shadowy interior.

It was very much as Raine had expected: a dim, all-but-empty space with no windows save for the unglazed square opening in the building's rear wall. Four slender discardo columns supported the roof, but there were no other adornments, no pews laid out for worshippers, just a few makeshift Human-style benches along the wall, a spigot from a rain tank feeding a small dish to one side, a door into a curtained alcove on the other that stat-flash specs showed to contain a bench above a sump for a toilet.

Fiercely localized, sharp with it, Raine immediately understood why the structure was here, in *this* location, at *this* lonely, singular spot, saw too the desperate and probably guileless cunning of it.

Outside to the east was the Bassantrae Sequester, the Hoproi domain with its hazing of mighty force-walls sweeping upwards, held by the massive towers of the luda supports, sparking now here, now there, off into the distance, and with the heavy-gravity, phase-up markers themselves set within the perimeter, increment by increment until all was locked in a misty sepia sheen. Earth's lesser gravity made the Cohabitation a joy for the Hoproi and they gleefully set up their shooting chapters in the great Trade Cities by preference but, like any occupation forces, they too needed something of home.

To the west, plunging away into a distant haze to form the other side of this vast forsaken corridor, were the force-walls of an enclave of a very different kind, roiling and full of violence, rearing up into the purple-bronze sky like sheets of amber and pearl: the ley walls of Rollinsgame, a demon-ley, if intel showed it fairly. There the walls were honey-milk clear at first glance, though with sudden snatches of darkness beyond, darkness streaked with reds and quick stabs of scarlet.

But the thing, the chance, the wonder of it was—look ahead, look between those narrowing, converging walls with the Sequester to the right and the opalescent eye-trickery of Rollinsgame to the left and you had it. By quirk of physics, optics, photonics, purest luck, the turned grasses seemed green enough, the sky an ersatz blue enough, for it to give Humans a tricked-up glimpse of something they knew to yearn for: *green* lands, *blue* skies and, by the most precious serendipity of the lot, the sense of *golden* light. Golden. Taken together, it was the biotype's optimum: the Pre-Wormwood norm. How could they *not* come here?

So obvious, too, why the single window opened onto such a view, the only thing needed. Such was the power of his localization, Raine understood.

Who knew what sims and scapes, what museum photographs, salvaged celluloids and old-style digitals, what ancient hobbyist watercolours and children's drawings gave that reality, but here it was, and Humans found in this and a scattering of other such precious places enough of the dream.

By the Lady!

As they said. As they always said now. By the Lady!

But Raine knew more of the Lady than they did, grasped the terrible irony of how error and misunderstanding working with chance had made it possible. Such a joke.

A Human moved forward from the shadows, a slender older woman with her long grey hair tied back. She wore a plain white robe, unadorned but for a simple line-work square inside a circle at the right shoulder. Window on the world, it said. *In* the world. The old biome.

"Welcome, Great Lord. I am Josephine Cantal, custodian here."

Raine inclined his head slightly. "You are the priest, the priestess—what is the word?—the sacerdote?"

"Just custodian, Lord. I care for this Window."

"But priest. Is this the word?"

"For some, Lord. But the Lady is not a goddess."

"Not?"

"There is no divinity."

"Ah." As with so much else, the translation was instantly there. "Then what?"

"Just a way of remembering how it was before the Cohabitation. 'Mondegreen' is an old coining. It means 'green world' in a blending of two old languages."

Raine, fiercely localized, knew otherwise, and knew enough of the broken histories to have countless templates for convenient deities masking social unrest: Roman Judaea and the Jesuits—were those the right names?—many templates for errors as origins: the story of Romulus and Remus being raised by a wolf when in fact it came from the Etruscan word for Rome, Romula, or Hong Kong being named, quite wrongly, after the giant primate deity that once occupied its central tower. Such were the free radicals of circumstance.

He knew to proceed slowly. "No statues, no depictions. Just that insignia you wear. The square inside the circle. Not that heraldic animal many Humans choose. Explain that."

"The butterfly is a transformation animal, Lord. A rebirth animal. The Aviators at Wenna wear it because they pilot their kites above the city. It is a good sign for them. A good Old Earth animal."

"Once there was a fish. That was special too. And a raven. Many phoenix animals."

"I've been told so, Lord. This is just the Window."

"This window?"

"Yes, Lord. Others like it. What's called a Truth Window."

"So I have learned. I'm told this is the main one."

"Some say that. I cannot know. It is hard to travel."

"Too dangerous?"

Josephine Cantal knew better than to mention the culls, samplings and secondments, the impresses and imposts that kept the Human population small and docile. "There is this to do."

"Guarding a window?"

"Explaining it to interested parties like yourself."

Raine's localization allowed him subtleties and ironies, let him tease and provoke. "But you see me as an enemy, surely."

"No, Great Lord." She gestured back to the view of golden light on waving, green-enough prairie. "The only true enemy is forgetting."

"I sincerely understand. I am not your enemy. Not today."

"No, Great Lord. Today you came here."

"Possibly for reasons other than you think. This is not—favour." More terms came at once. "Not endorsement or sanction. Do not presume."

Josephine Cantal bent her head. "Forgive me, sire. Your localization is beyond compare. It is easy to forget."

"Continue then."

"Just as you have modelled this outcome for whatever purpose, Lord, we have modelled a day such as this. A member of the Great Races coming."

"Others will be here soon."

"Darzie?"

Raine turned back towards the open doorway, crest spines ablating as the rudiments of a distant hunt-cycle were diverted. "Perhaps. Perhaps something neither of us has ever modelled. Let us go and see."

* * *

Fourteen minutes later, the Matt house-lord arrived in an ornate, fieldwork charabanc, a hovering egg-shaped ground-effect vehicle whose curving outer hull deliberately resembled an ancient Pre-Wormwood circuit mat, but one stitched all over with goldwire extruded from its own body. No military accompaniment for Holding-in-Quiet, since there was always the sense, more than with any other Race in the Patchwork, that the Vanished Ones, the Nobodoi masters who had picked these reclusive archaeologist scholars of Matteras to be one of the three Bridge Races, could very well protect them in some special way. Fear as much as proven service and privilege held this great alliance in place.

Fond Louie must have been watching, waiting for the Matt's arrival, for suddenly he was there as well, rushing through the grass, massive legs pounding as he ran as a full *choi* fighting-star, trunks embedded in the spinal sockets of four armed and armoured Humans dressed in the glossy black beetlepoint of Nefarious Waylayers.

To watch them run, shouting and yipping, waving their hooks and long-bladed jerrykins, was a splendid, unnerving sight, a beautifully synchronized star-wheel with the elephantine host drawing on the disparate emotions of his companions. Only when the huge creature and his troupe had lumbered to a halt did the trunks release and coil back against the body in the no-threat mode.

Bringing them to Crisis Point One.

Raine had six Elsewheres, warriors whose minds were only provisionally here, their core selves forever focused on a homeworld they would never see again. The *choi* immediately deployed, fell back and took positions behind whatever rises and grassy knolls they could find.

For a moment there was silence, the sense of it at least with the wind stirring the grass, the distant roar of the force-walls and the poisonous sizzle of hot-glass on the air. With it, vividly for Raine with his biasing, was the sense of the world working, reality being made.

Fond Louie waited in the road. Raine and Josephine Cantal were by the door to the church. The line of Elsewheres stood to their right, held precariously to this task, heads averted, gazing beyond this place, but ready, ready.

It might have been all of ten seconds. Then the door of the charabanc lifted away, and Holding-in-Quiet emerged, seated cross-legged on its havel, moving forward as measured and stately as the Matt always were careful to be in public. No walking, no stepping out—only the file sims showed the Matta walking, running, striking—but composed upright.

It had passed through a doorway just now, the most profound act in a Matta's life; this blighted, wondrous place was now briefly an extension of its house, however that could be construed.

Raine watched the creature approach. Like any fully quickened representative of the Encosium-on-Earth, he had studied the Matta, had had sufficient dealings with them, *faux* and actual. Fond Louie had. But Josephine Cantal had never seen one in the flesh, possibly in any form of accurate depiction; knew them only as fellow demons with the Darzie and the Hoproi in cook-fire and cradle stories. Raine saw her chin lift and her eyes widen just enough at her first glimpse of the long horse-skull visage, the articulated neck rising from the red robe draped about the shoulders, the chest like a clustering of tightly sheaved sticks, glittering with points and curls of goldwire that would later be used to make an identity artefact of this special day.

Raine turned to his Elsewheres, subvocalized a quick command. The warriors phased out, three back to *Nobion* high above, three into quarterhold stasis.

"Good move!" Fond Louie boomed, and began lumbering towards the building at last. "Parley party begins now. Come to church, pray-mates!"

The Matt scholar's havel fitted through the doorway easily enough, but Fond Louie didn't even try. He waited till the others had entered then simply blocked the entrance, pressing against the arch so that a trunk and a single eye faced into the dim interior.

Raine prepared to make the appropriate introductions, but even as Holding-in-Quiet lowered its havel by the eastern wall, Josephine Cantal moved as close as she dared and bowed to the creature.

"Lord, you have blessed this house. You have honoured this doorway by making it yours."

The horse-insect head canted up and out. "Honour to your household, gracious."

Then, before Raine could continue, this bold Human female took her host's right.

"Great Lords, may I ask why each of you came here today?"

"Can you guess?" Raine asked. He managed to excuse her manner, allowed that this would simply be a tailored version of her usual custodian question.

"It can't just be curiosity, Lord," the old Human female said. "Despite your fine localization. It might be maintaining constants. Population control. A contingency visit, I suspect."

Raine nodded in the Human way. "A bookkeeper's attention to detail and order, I believe some Humans say of us."

"I do not know that second word, sire."

"Me say it," Fond Louie boomed behind them. "Me go rote. Speech prepared for show and tell." And just like that the crazy patois mishmash fell away, was replaced by the clearspeak recital of something carefully planned and considered, vetted by the protocol comps and *choi* impresses. As always, the modal shift was chilling to hear.

"You built this structure here by my Sequester. This ley corridor runs all the way through Otis Reach to Sallingen, then branches off down mighty leys to Focalstone and Blown Jetty. Blown Jetty, you hear me? Once it was just solitaries who came here, wanderers, nomads, Humans fleeing impresses or selling on their genetics to the scattered communities. Then it was the siswitch troupes stopping between performance destinations, lingering to cherish the light. The light grade here is *sachel*, Albatel 4, well quantified. I ask myself, my chapter, do we want this proximity, this corridor being this order of pass-through. What if it upsets a balance, tolerances in the Patchwork, draws reprisal: madonnas out of Calledal or Fonsy Halt, seeker spikes from Rollinsgame itself, right at our door? Demon ley or sentinel ley, it's a shifting one that, always changing. Should we worry? So we consider it together—you will smile at the prospect—and I consider it alone. Great Lord, me. My Sequester."

"What will you do, Fond Louie?" Josephine knew enough of the Hoproi to use both names, no honorific.

"Tricky business." He was falling back into his usual patter. "We like having Humans handy, going to church, building strained grass windows, being canon fodder! God's rockets, yes! Our fodder whose hart is in heaven! Love it! We get to mix the business. Careful is a pain. A point of intrigue, you betcha! A wait-see. A must-see wait-see."

Josephine Cantal had her back to the Window now, facing the great shape pressed into the doorway. "There is no formal movement here, Fond Louie. I swear it. No attempt at—destabilization, resurgence. It's just what it appears to be, a way of remembering."

"You say, Josephine Cantal, church-mouse, house-mouse. Home a hole in a bucket. This bucket. That bucket. Deer fodder in heaven. Where the hart is. Long as it has a handle, we don't care. We needing the handle."

"There are so few of us now, Fond Louie."

"Bad window just the same. Naughty window, this view-point. Bring this to my Sequester. No easy antlers now."

To those who did not know Hoproi, it sounded like anger, by the pitch, the rush, the volume and tone. But Raine knew it was excitement, even mirth. Fond Louie was delighted to have something, anything, to elevate into a threat, an issue, the prospect of a war-game.

"We have this to do," Raine said, then turned to Holding-in-Quiet. "What have you learned, *edenye?*"

The Matta leant forward, its head did, swinging out on that oddly jointed neck. Beneath the robe, its chest gleamed with goldpoint.

"The naming here: Truth Window. Fond Louie prepared clearspeak for this time. Such honour. I had this done for common ease. The name is from hay-bale residences on Pre-Wormwood Earth. A dwelling built from hay bales would be finished—sealed—with a coating. Whitewashed stucco. Smooth like this temple. But always a part was left to show what was within, a view into the substance of the house. This was called a Truth Window."

Raine was fascinated, delighted. "Coincidence, you think, *edenye?*"

"I do, *aradenye*. Not even metaphor. No equivalent to look into. For remembering."

"Josephine?" Raine asked. It sounded beautifully Human the way he said it, so natural and intimate.

"As this lord says. Just a window. A reminder for us. No agendas, Lord. Just for remembering."

Raine studied the woman with something like compassion. This exchange had to be so disconcerting for her. Here he stood in the "striking erect," the Darzie hunt stance, arms curved in, crest spines fully distended, maximum intimidation to so many Races. To the side was Holding-in-Quiet, imperturbable, so overtly calm but for a single gesture just now, a dramatic, downward sweep of the arm as it brushed the curls of goldwire from its chest so the tailings fell behind the containment rim of its havel. Behind them, the mass, the trunks, the single glaring eye of Fond Louie filled the doorway. So much that had to be confronting for the member of a Race used to suffering at our hands.

It was time for the rest of it.

"Then now I ask the question which brought us here today. Who is the Lady we hear about? I know more of her origins than you do, Josephine. A Pre-Wormwood writer, Sylvia Wright, coined the term long ago, published it in 85 PW, 1954 BCE. She had misheard the lyrics of an old song.

"Ye Highlands and Ye Lowlands
Oh where hae you been?
They hae slay the Earl of Moray,
And laid him on the green.

"This Human heard that final line as the name of his consort, so it became *They hae slay the Earl of Moray, And Lady Mondegreen*. Years later, when she finally learned the truth, she collected other examples: Gladly the Cross-Eyed Bear, Sinon the Dotted Lion, Round John Virgin. All based on mishearings. She called them mondegreens. There is no other history for your Lady."

Josephine Cantal actually smiled. "But of course there is, sire. You have given useful facts, details, and we welcome them. But the Lady pre-dates this misheard song. Lord Raine, you've read the broken histories. She is Mother Earth, the Earth Mother, nothing more, nothing less. The world personified, as a yearning, a recognition, an acknowledgment. There is no intention, no infrastructure, no need to make her anything more."

"But there *is* more to it, yes?" Destabilisation, Raine didn't have to say. A shift in the status-quo. "Make a case for continuance."

Continuance. Josephine Cantal understood the moment exactly.

"This then. A question which must cross all your minds. Lords, what if the Nobodoi approve of this? We're told they left the world this way deliberately, conquered, remade and withdrew, and now watch to see what happens. *Not* called away. *Not* simply moving on, but watching. Their were-suits wander the world; all that is left of them. I haven't travelled far, but I have seen the soul-stones littering the fields and roadways outside Kefa and Tresimont, sitting in the dust, those balls of chalk. You, Great Lords, know so much more but say Recalled Ones, as if they have truly gone. It is good to have a sense of irony. But their were-suits still come and go as they please. I've seen a few near here. Full triunes all of them, the way they're meant to be: suit, Companion, Snake, all three parts vigorous and strong with ghostworks sparking around them. These may not just be automated watch systems left to ramble about, not just sentinel engines with soul-stone mummies inside."

Raine smiled, a grimace few Races knew to read with confidence. *We all had speeches prepared for today*. "Your point?"

"Some people say the soul-stones aren't corpses, aren't Nobodoi remains at all, but a translation payload, a residue artefact: what's left of a Nobodoi when it withdraws, changes phase."

"Some people?" Raine was relentless.

"Humans, Lord." This woman knew how trapped she was. "It's natural that we're equally curious. But you—none of you are sure about any of this either. You *must* discuss it. No harm is done. No harm can possibly be done. But not Nobodoi corpses, that's what—"

"You truly think the Nobodoi might approve?"

Josephine Cantal didn't hesitate. "Lord, they have not intruded. Have not disallowed. A were-suit could destroy this place so easily. Send in its Snake, have its Companion—"

"By implication, this visit *is* their response. Our attention, our presence today, becomes the appropriate countermeasure, surely."

Pressed into the archway, Fond Louie humphed in delight. "Hah! Caught you, Goddy-two-shoes! You 'specting 'piphany, you phoney Josey Josephine! Big god moment. Ooh! Were-suit saving the day. You shrewdy-pants!"

Josephine Cantal swung about, hands up, imploring. "Not at all, Lord—Fond Louie! You've taught us well. The Nobodoi have always been absolute in what they do and don't allow. Remember the Link! The Advent itself! Ruthless, decisive! This place harms no one."

"An *aide-mémoire*," Holding-in-Quiet said, as if to itself. "*Memento vivi!*"

Josephine turned to the Matta and smiled fleetingly, probably not knowing those particular Antique terms, but cued by the gentler reflective tone of the Matt's words.

"It helps make life better." Again she turned to the Hoproi. "Like your war-garden, Fond Louie. A comfort beyond easy telling. Something to be proud of." She faced Raine now. "Like whatever tasks and diligence make your terrible ordeal easier, Great Lord. Like that flower Aspen Dirk speaks of."

Raine, of course, thought immediately of the overlapping circles that showed how the Races connected with each other, some directly, others through various interface species. "The Donalty Flower?"

"No, Lord. The other flower. There's a Human, a boggler of Nobodoi artefacts. The siswitch troupes speak of him. There's a flower he speaks of—"

"I know this one!" Fond Louie boomed behind them, scrinching so firmly in against the pillars that the walls creaked alarmingly. "This Dirk the boggler! He nosey-posey! Got flower too!"

"What flower?" Raine demanded. His hands were still at his sides, composed, curved into hooks. His crest spines were so fully displayed that a distension chime now rang in his skull, the tinnitus that for the unquickened meant amok and reprisal. His localization raged at it. Anything like anger, surprise, disengagement were neatly turned aside. Cool judgement remained. Cool decisions prevailed. Arm of Law.

"I know this! I know this!" Fond Louie could hardly contain his excitement, snatching whatever he could from the old rotes. "Ancient story. Celluloid by Lewis Carroll. Two royal houses. Two flowers. Lancaster, built Lancaster bombers. Red rose. York, famous for Yorkshire puddings, something. White rose. Two put together to build a Two-Door Rose for Henry the Aitch. Get it? Two flowers into one. Donalty Flower the same, bejeez! Hothouse mix. Forced growth. All overlaid, all in together. Dirk's flower the Bedlam Rose."

"The what?" Raine asked, ringing beautifully, perfectly, holding the tone.

"No mattress! All together. Best flowers. Nobodoi plan."

Part of it troubled Raine, part of it provoked, even delighted. "*Three* parts to this then. The Window, this flower and the false Lady who has become so real."

Josephine snatched at the possibility of reprieve. "Humans are good at finding signs, Great Lord. Making signs. All peoples probably, all Races. But Humans constantly. Leave us alone; it's what we do. It makes us meaningful to ourselves."

"Especially now," Raine said, the chime diminishing, pushing away, resolved but close. So close.

"Especially now, Lord. May I be direct?"

"Go on."

"Lords, what I've already begun to say. Listen to yourselves. Even calling the Nobodoi the Recalled Ones, as you do, suggests that they too have overlords controlling them, able to recall them at will once a task is done."

"Or much simpler. Their own leaders have Recalled them."

"I have to allow that too. But what if not? Perhaps your view comes from your habit of being in such a hierarchy for so long. Perhaps it is wisely judged. But what if not? Instead of feeling chosen, privileged to be called into service, you put your rulers in their place in turn. We as Humans, with our inclination for absolutes, go with Dirk's flower, would grant that they have absolute dominion and simply stepped away to see what would come of it."

"Which is the same self-absorbed arrogance you accuse us of. You reserve some special role for yourselves despite everything. This Bedlam Rose."

"*They* chose this world, Lord. *This* place, *this* combination this time."

"And they chose us to govern it. They accept—want—the solution we bring. By default, by implication, our decision will be theirs."

"But, Lord, I could say the same about Humans. They want the solution *we* bring. This Bedlam Rose *they* have made."

"Except that it remains our decision, our prevailing custodianship."

"Yes, unless that changes, Great Lord. Unless you accept the simple lesson of the flower. The evidence suggests it."

"Or doesn't, Josephine. Your world may have no special place in anything, is just another world they have chosen. The way it often is. We have been client Races for millennia."

"But what if there *is* a special purpose, Lord? What if the Nobodoi have not been Recalled? What if they are still here? Changed but here and watching? You've all considered it."

"This Lady Mondegreen is a dangerous Lady. *You* are a dangerous lady."

"Bad flower!" Fond Louie boomed.

Josephine ignored the outburst. "Or not, sire. Just showing natural curiosity. So new to no longer being at the top of the life hierarchy ourselves. What will you do?"

"Your question again?"

Josephine gestured to the Window, to the building around them. "Can we continue here? Will you leave us in peace?"

"This is not necessarily why we have come. Again, make your case."

"I needn't, Lord. The Window is not here, but here." She placed a finger against her forehead. "You know this. The Lady, whatever she is, however she is, is beyond one place, beyond facts from broken histories. The Rose is all around us."

"Very dangerous," Raine said, so keenly aware of the moment as this Josephine no doubt was, of the waving prairie beyond, of the distant roar of the force-walls, of the goldwire curling out of the Matt's chest, telling the moments of their lives.

"Lord, I am at that point where nothing I can say will save this place if you decide against it. But whether as fact, symbol or metaphor, the Window *will* remain. You know this of us. The Lady will stay, may even become stronger by seeming to be something worth destroying."

"Let us go outside," Raine said.

Fond Louie pulled back at once. Raine crossed to the entrance and stepped out into the day. The Matt activated its havel and followed.

"I can promise nothing," Raine said when Josephine finally joined them in the road. The sun was westering, already a fierce golden coin high in the washed sepia mirk of Rollinsgame. "Even if I withhold, Fond Louie and this house-lord will decide as they feel suits this special time."

"Lord, then there are a few possessions I'd like to retrieve before—"

The strike was like a scalpel of light, sharp and final. The temple was gone, shattered, just like that, the discardo, the dust, the shock wave and intense energy wash contained in a security sleeve that came an instant before and held nearly a full minute afterwards.

The strike echo came in those first seconds too, a tearing that snapped the day asunder but was quickly stolen away in the eternal roar of the corridor.

Fond Louie's summons rode that echo, a high-pitched keening that brought his *choi* running. The stink of hot-glass was instantly there as well: Raine's Elsewheres phasing in—three, six—their heads no longer averted, no longer in far-look.

"Agius!" the Matt house-lord said in its own tongue, one arm raised and pointing down the road.

And there moving towards them was a were-suit, the classic Nobodoi artefact: its off-white mummiform advancing with a roiling, twisting ground effect that almost but never quite looked like legs stepping out. Above its right shoulder, joined by a network of unseen energy, was the flattened horse-skull of the Snake. To its left, rolling along on a skirted four-ball platform, was the Companion, an elongated ovoid two metres tall, with a canted featureless dish at its top. Flickering about the whole triune were the ghostworks, the half-seen firefly glints that marked most things Nobodoi, made even more vivid by the shadowing early afternoon light of the corridor. Inside that dirty white mummiform talos was a soul-stone, a chalky ball with a leathery kernel at its heart, all that was left of its Recalled occupant.

Or not.

Fond Louie had made *choi*, trunks locked firmly in the spinal sockets of its four *choi*-mates, and now that mighty fighting wheel moved off the road to let the triune pass. Raine's Elsewheres did the same in one precise, mind-linked movement. All watched as the were-suit approached and passed them by.

Fond Louie humphed in pleasure. "So ends today's lesson. Holy roller come to play! Warn off piracy. Seamen on the Mount. Biggest pirate chip played."

"But why, Lords?" Josephine said. "Nothing changes. The Window is still there."

Raine gave the fierce Darzie smile. "Winning, losing. It is no longer easy to know who gets what?"

Then Holding-in-Quiet spoke, chest gleaming with goldpoint. "Build again, Josephine Cantal. It was not the Vanished One who took your house today."

"You, Lord? But why? Why?"

The hatch of the Matt's charabanc was even now lifting away, preparing to receive its master.

"What was said before. A Two-Door Rose. How can one resist this newest flower with two doors? It is the way through. Worth the intent. All coinage."

Josephine Cantal bowed her head, acknowledged the honour as best she could. "Thank you. Thank you, Great Lord, for this."

Raine listened to the exchange, wondering. *He* had not acted. And had, by *not* acting. Yes. Had kept to his task enough. In an instant he sent his Elsewheres back to *Nobion*, was vaguely aware of Fond Louie's troupe running off yipping and shouting through the grasslands to where the luda endlessly fired in the golden afternoon and the great force-walls of Rollinsgame and Bassantrae reared into the sky. He easily allowed that Holding-in-Quiet had departed, that only Josephine Cantal would be waiting in the road behind him.

You are a wise and very dangerous woman, he thought to himself. By the Lady!

But he did not turn to her yet. Rather he watched the were-suit continuing down the road, forever wandering the world. Amid his eternal agony, in spite of it, he smiled fiercely into the remains of the day. Arm of Law.

FURY

ALASTAIR REYNOLDS

I was the first to reach the emperor's body, and even then it was too late to do anything. He had been examining his koi, kneeling on the stone pathway that wound between the ponds, when the bullet arrived. It had punched through his skull, achieving instantaneous destruction. Fragments of skin and bone and pinkish grey cortical material lay scattered on the tiles. Blood—dark and red as the ink on the imperial seal—was oozing from the entry and exit wounds. The body had slumped over to one side, with the lower half still spasming as motor signals attempted to regain control. I reached over and placed my hand against the implanted device at the base of the neck, applying firm pressure through the yellow silk of his collar to a specific contact point. I felt a tiny subepidermal click. The body became instantly still.

I stood up and summoned a clean-up crew.

"Remove the body," I told the waiting men. "Don't dispose of it until you've completed a thorough forensic analysis. Drain and search the surrounding ponds until you've recovered the bullet or any remaining pieces of it. Then hose down the path until you've removed all trace of blood and whatever else came out of him. Test the water thoroughly and don't let the koi back until you're certain they won't come to any harm." I paused, still trying to focus on what had just happened. "Oh, and secure the Great House. No one comes and goes until we find out who did this. And no ships are to pass in or out of the Capital Nexus without my express authorisation."

"Yes, Mercurio," the men said in near-unison.

In the nearest pond one of the fish—I recognised it as one of the Asagi Koi, with the blue-toned scales laid out in a pine-cone pattern—opened and closed its mouth as if trying to tell me something vital. I turned from the scene and made my way back into the Great House. By the time I reached the emperor's reception chamber the building was buzzing with rumours of the assassination attempt. Despite my best efforts, the news would be out of the Nexus within the hour, hopscotching from world to world, system to system, spreading into the galaxy like an unstoppable fire.

The emperor's new body rose from his throne as the doors finished opening. He was dressed in a yellow silk gown identical to the one worn by the corpse. Aside from the absence of injuries, the body was similarly indistinguishable, appearing to be that of a white-haired man of considerable age, yet still retaining a youthful vigour. His habitual expression normally suggested playfulness, compassion and the kind of deep wisdom that can only come from a very long and scholarly life. Now his face was an expressionless mask. That, and a certain stiffness in his movements, betrayed the fact that this was a new body, being worn for the first time. It would take several hours for the implant to make the fine sensorimotor adjustments that gave the emperor true fluidity of movement, and allowed him to feel as if he was fully inhabiting the puppet organism.

"I'm sorry," I said, before the emperor had a chance to speak. "I take full responsibility for this incident."

He waved aside my apology. "Whatever this is about, Mercurio, I doubt very much that you could have done anything to prevent it." His voice was thick-tongued, like a drunkard with a bad hangover. "We both know how thorough you've been; all the angles you've covered. No one could have asked for better security than you've given me, all these years. I'm still alive, aren't I?"

"Nonetheless, there was clearly a flaw in my arrangements."

"Perhaps," he allowed. "But the fact is, whoever did this only reached the body, not me. It's unfortunate, but in the scheme of things little worse than an act of vandalism against imperial property."

"Did you feel anything?"

"A sharp blow; a few moments of confusion; not much else. If that's what being assassinated feels like, then it isn't much to fear, truth be told. Perhaps I've been wrong to keep looking over my shoulder, all this time."

"Whoever did this, they must have known it wouldn't achieve anything."

"I've wondered about that myself." He stroked the fine white banner of his beard, as if acquainting himself with it for the first time. "I almost hate to ask—but the koi?"

"I've got my men searching the ponds, looking for bullet fragments. But as far as I can see the fish didn't come to any harm."

"Let's hope so. The effort I've put into those fish—I'd be heartbroken if anything happened to them. I'll want to see for myself, of course."

"Not until we've secured the Great House and found our man," I said, speaking as only the emperor's personal security expert would have dared. "Until the risk of another attempt is eliminated, I can't have you leaving this building."

"I have an inexhaustible supply of bodies, Mercurio."

"That's not the point. Whoever did this…" But I trailed off, my thoughts still disorganized. "Please, sir, just respect my wishes in this matter."

"Of course, Mercurio. Now as ever. But I trust you won't keep me from my fish for the rest of eternity?"

"I sincerely hope not, sir."

I left the emperor, returning to my offices to coordinate the hunt for the assassin and the search for whatever evidence he might have left behind. Within a few hours the body had been subjected to an exhaustive forensic analysis, resulting in the extraction of bullet shards from the path of the wound. In the same timeframe my men recovered other fragments from the vicinity of the corpse; enough to allow us to reassemble the bullet.

An hour later, against all my expectations, we had the assassin himself. They found him with his weapon, waiting to be apprehended. He hadn't even tried to leave the grounds of the Great House.

That was when I began to suspect that this wasn't any act of mindless desecration, but something much more sinister.

"Tell me what you found," the emperor said, when I returned to the reception chamber. In the intervening time his control over the new body had improved markedly. His movements were fluid and he had regained his usual repertoire of facial expressions.

"We've found the assassin, sir, as you'll doubtless have heard."

"I hadn't, but please continue."

"And the weapon. The bullet itself was a goal-seeking autonomous missile, a very sophisticated device. It had the means to generate stealthing fields to confuse our anti-intrusion systems, so once it was loose in the grounds of the Great House it could move without detection. But it still needed a launching device, a kind of gun. We found that as well."

The emperor narrowed his eyes. "I would have thought it was hard enough to get a gun into the Nexus, let alone the Great House."

"That's where it gets a little disturbing, sir. The gun could only have been smuggled into the grounds in tiny pieces—small enough that they could be disguised by field generators, or hidden inside legitimate tools and equipment allowed the palace staff. That's how it happened, in fact. The man we found the gun on was an uplift named Vratsa, one of the keepers in charge of the ponds."

"I know Vratsa," the emperor said softly. "He's been on the staff for years. Never the brightest of souls… but diligent, gentle, and beyond any question a hard worker. I always liked him—we'd talk about the fish, sometimes. He was tremendously fond of them. Are you honestly telling me he had something to do with this?"

"He's not even denying it, sir."

"I'm astonished. Vratsa of all people. Primate stock, isn't he?"

"Gorilla, I think."

"He actually planned this?"

"I'm not sure 'planned' is exactly the word I'd use. The thing is, it's starting to look as if Vratsa was a mole."

"But he's on the staff for—how long, exactly?"

There'd been no need for me to review the files—the information was at my immediate disposal, flashing into my mind instantly. "Thirty-five years, sir. In my estimation, that's about as long as it would have taken to smuggle in and assemble the pieces of the weapon."

"Could a simple uplift have done this?"

"Not without help, sir. You've always been very kind to them, employing them in positions of responsibility where others would rather treat them as subhuman slaves. But the fact remains that uplifts don't generally exhibit a high-degree of forward planning and resourcefulness. This took both, sir. I'm inclined to the view that Vratsa was just as much a puppet as that body you're wearing."

"Why the bullet, though? As I said, Vratsa and I have spoken on many occasions. He could have hurt me easily enough then, just with his bare hands."

"I don't know, sir. There is something else, though." I looked around the walls of the room, with its panelled friezes depicting an ancient, weatherworn landscape—some nameless, double-mooned planet halfway across the galaxy. "It's delicate, sir—or at least it *might* be delicate. I think we need to talk about it face to face."

"This room is already one of the most secure places in the entire

Radiant Commonwealth," he reminded me.

"Nonetheless."

"Very well, Mercurio." The old man sighed gently. "But you know how uncomfortable I find these encounters."

"I assure you I'll be as brief as possible."

Above me the ceiling separated into four equal sections. The sections slid back into the walls, a cross-shaped gap opening between them to reveal an enormous overhead space—a brightly lit enclosure as large as any in the Great House. Floating in the space, pinned into place by gravity neutralisers, was a trembling sphere of oxygenated water, more than a hundred meters across. I began to ascend, pushed upwards on a section of flooring immediately beneath me, a square tile that became a rising pillar. Immune to vertigo—and incapable of suffering lasting damage even if I'd fallen to the floor—I remained calm, save for the thousand questions circling in my mind.

At one hundred and thirty meters, my head pushed through the surface tension of the sphere. A man would have started drowning, but immersion in water posed no difficulties for me. In fact, there were very few environments in the galaxy that I couldn't tolerate, at least temporarily.

My lenses adjusted to the differing optical properties of the medium, until I seemed to be looking through something only slightly less sharp than clear air. The emperor was floating, as weightless as the water surrounding him. He looked something like a whale, except that he had no flippers or flukes.

I remembered—dimly, for it had been a long time ago—when he was still more or less humanoid. That was in the early days of the Radiant Commonwealth, when it only encompassed a few hundred systems. He had grown with it, swelling as each new territory—be it a planet, system or entire glittering star cluster—was swallowed into his realm. It wasn't enough for him to have an abstract understanding of the true extent of his power. He needed to feel it on a purely sensory level, as a flood of inputs reaching directly into his brain. Countless modifications later, his mind was now the size of a small house. The mazelike folds of that dome bulged against drum-tight skin, as if about to rip through thin canvas. Veins and arteries the size of plumbing ducts wrapped the cerebellum. It was a long time since that brain had been protected by a cage of bone.

The emperor was monstrous, but he wasn't a monster—not now. There might once have been a time when his expansionist ambitions were driven by something close to lust, but that was tens of thousands of years ago. Now that he controlled almost the entire colonised galaxy, he sought only to become the figurehead of a benevolent, just government. The emperor was famed for his clemency and forgiveness. He himself had pushed for the extension of democratic principles into many of the empire's more backward prefectures.

He was a good and just man, and I was happy to serve him.

"So tell me, Mercurio, whatever it is that is too secret even for one of my puppets."

The rising pillar had positioned me next to one of his dark eyes. They were like currants jammed into doughy flesh.

"It's the bullet, sir."

"What about it?"

I held the reconstructed item up for inspection, confident now that we were outside the reach of listening devices. It was a metal cylinder with a transparent cone at the front.

"There are, or were, markings on the bullet casing. They're in one of the older trading languages of the Luquan Emergence. The inscription, in so far as it can be translated into Prime, reads as follows: *Am I my brother's keeper?*"

He reflected on this for a moment. "It's not ringing any bells."

"I'd be surprised if it did, sir. The inscription appears to be a quote from an ancient religious text. As to its greater significance, I can't say."

"The Luquans haven't traditionally been a problem. We give them a certain amount of autonomy; they pay their taxes and agree to our trifling requests that they instigate democratic rule and cut down on the number of executions. They may not like that, but there are a dozen other special administrative volumes that we treat in exactly the same fashion. Why would the Emergence act against me now?"

"It doesn't end there, sir. The bullet had a hollow cavity at the front, inside the glass cone. There was enough space in there for the insertion of any number of harmful agents, up to an including an antimatter device that could easily have destroyed all or part of the Great House. Whoever made this, whoever programmed it to reach this far, could easily have gone the extra step necessary to have you killed, not just your puppet."

The ancient dark eye regarded me. Though it hardly moved in the socket, I still had the sense of penetrating focus and attention.

"You think someone was trying to tell me something? That they *can* murder me, but chose not to?"

"I don't know. Certainly, the provisions I've now put in place would prevent anyone making a second attempt in this manner. But they'd have known that as well. So why go to all this trouble?" I paused before continuing. "There is something else, I'm afraid."

"Go ahead."

"Although the bullet was hollow, it wasn't totally empty. There was something inside the glass part—a few specks of reddish sand or dust. The surgeons extracted most of it from the puppet, and they've promised me that the few remaining traces that entered the koi ponds won't cause any ill-effects. I've had the dust analysed and it's absolutely harmless. Iron oxide, silicon and sulphur, for the most part. Frankly, I don't know what to make of it. It resembles something you'd find on the surface of an arid terrestrial planet, something with a thin atmosphere and not much weather or biology. The problem is there are ten million worlds that fit that description."

"And within the Emergence?"

"Fewer, but still far too many to speak of." I withdrew the replica bullet from his examination. "Nonetheless, these are our only clues. With your permission, I'd like to leave the Capital Nexus to pursue the matter further."

He ruminated on this for a few seconds. "You propose a mission to the Emergence?"

"I really don't see any alternative. There's only so much I can do from my office. It's better if I go walkabout." The phrase, which had popped unbidden into my mind, caused me disquiet. Where had it come from? "What I mean, sir, is that I can be much more effective in person."

"I appreciate that. But I also appreciate that you're incredibly valuable to me—not just as a friend, but as my closest and most trusted advisor. I've become very used to knowing you're close at hand, in the walls of the Great House. It's one of the things that helps me sleep at night, knowing you're not far away."

"I'll only ever be a few skipspace transits from home, sir."

"You have my agreement, of course—as if I was ever going to say no. But do look after yourself, Mercurio. I'd hate to think how I'd manage without you."

"I'll do my best, sir." I paused. "There is one other thing I need to ask you, sir. The uplift, Vratsa?"

"What about him?"

"We subjected him to mild interrogation. He gave us nothing, but I'd be remiss in my duties if I didn't point out that we could employ other methods, just to be certain he isn't keeping anything from us."

"What's your honest judgement?"

"I think he's completely innocent, sir—he was just following a script someone programmed into him thirty-five or more years ago. He no more knows why he did this—and who's behind if—than the bullet did. But if you feel something might be gained…"

"Have him tortured, on the very slight chance he might tell us something?" It was clear from his tone of voice what he felt about that.

"I didn't think you'd approve, sir. As far as I'm concerned, it would achieve about as much as smacking a puppy for something it did the day before yesterday."

"I've spent much of the last thousand years trying to enforce humanitarian principles on the more barbarous corners of my own empire. The very least I can do is live up to my own high moral standards, wouldn't you say?" It was a rhetorical question, since he allowed me no time to answer. "Take Vratsa and remove him from the Great House—he's a continuing security risk, even if he doesn't know why he did what he did. But I don't want him locked away or punished. Find some work for him in the outlying gardens. Give him some fish to look after. And if anyone harms a hair on his head…"

"They won't, sir. Not while I'm in charge."

"That's very good, Mercurio. I'm glad we see things similarly."

I left the Great House a day later, once I was satisfied that I had put in place all necessary measures for the emperor's continued security in my absence. From the moon-girdled heart of the Capital Nexus, through skipspace via the Coronal Polities to the fuzzy perimeter of the Luquan Emergence—sixty thousand light years in only a handful of days. As I changed from ship to ship, I attracted an unavoidable degree of attention. Since I require Great House authority to make my investigations in the Emergence, there was no possibility of moving incognito. I travelled in full imperial regalia, and made sure the seriousness of my mission was understood.

How much more attention would I have merited, if they had realized what I *really* was?

I look like a man, but in fact I am a robot. My meat exterior is only a few centimeters thick. Beneath that living shell lies the hard amour of a sentient machine.

The emperor knows—of course—and so do a handful of his closest officials. But to most casual observers, and even people who have spent much time in the Great House, I am just another human security expert, albeit one with an uncommonly close relationship with the emperor. The fact that I have been in his service for tens of thousands of years is one of the most closely guarded secrets in the Radiant Commonwealth.

I am rare. Robots are commonplace, but I am something more than that. I am a true thinking machine. There are reckoned to be less than a million of us in existence—not many, considering the billion worlds of the Radiant Commonwealth, and all the teeming souls on those planets and moons.

There are two schools of thought concerning our origin. In the thirty-two thousand years of its existence, the empire has been through a number of historical convulsions. One school—the alchemicals—has it that the means to manufacture us—some critical expertise in cybernetics and programming—had been discovered and then lost at an earlier time. All remaining sentient machines therefore dated from this period.

The other school, the accretionists, hold a different view. They maintain that robot intelligence is an emergent property, something that could only happen given sufficient resources of time and complexity. The accretionists argue that the surviving robots became the way we are gradually, through the slow augmentation of simpler machines. In their view, almost any machine could become an intelligent robot, provided it is allowed to evolve and layer itself with improvements.

It would have been convenient if we robots could have settled the matter. The unfortunate fact, though, was that we simply didn't remember. Like any recording apparatus, we are prone to error and distortion. At times when the emperor's hold on the galaxy had slackened, data wars corrupted even the most secure archives. I can sift through my memories until I find the earliest reliable events of which I have direct experience, but I know—I sense—that I am still only plumbing relatively shallow layers of my own identity.

I know I've been around considerably longer than that.

The only thing I can be absolutely certain of is that I've known the emperor for a very long time. We fit together like hand and glove. And in all that time I've always been there to protect him.

It is what I do.

The official was a high-ranking technocrat on Selva, one of the major power centers of the Luquan Emergence. He studied me with unconcealed hostility, sitting behind a desk in his private office in one of Selva's aquatic cities. Fierce, luminous oceanforms—barbed and tentacled things of alien provenance—clawed and suckered at the armored glass behind him, testing its strength.

"I really don't think I can offer any more assistance, sire," the official said, putting sufficient stress on the honorific for it to sound insulting. "Since your arrival on Selva we've given you free rein to conduct your investigations. Every administrative department has done its utmost to comply with your requests. And yet you still act as if there is more we could have done." He was a thin, sallow man with arched, quizzical eyebrows, dressed in a military uniform that was several sizes too big for him. "Have we not demonstrated our obedience with the trials?"

"I didn't ask for those dissidents to be executed," I said. "Although I can see how useful it would have been for you. Arrest some troublemakers, ask them questions they can't possibly answer, about a crime they had nothing to do with, and then hang them on the pretext that they weren't cooperating with the Great House. Do you imagine that will buy you favor with the emperor? Quite the opposite, I'd suggest. When all this is over and done with, I wouldn't be at all surprised if you have an imperial audit to deal with."

He shrugged, as if the matter was of no possible consequence.

"You're wasting your time, sire—looking for a pattern, a logical explanation, where none exists. I don't even know why you're bothering. Didn't you already find your assailant? Didn't you already extract a confession?"

"We found evidence that points to the Luquan Emergence."

"Yes, I've heard about that." Ostentatiously, he tapped at a sealed brochure on his desk. "A cryptic statement in an ancient tongue. Some dust that could have come from anywhere."

I maintained a blank expression, giving no hint at my anger that the forensic information had been leaked. It was inevitable, I supposed, but I had hoped to keep a lid on it for a little longer.

"I'd discount any rumours if I were you."

A mouthful of concentric teeth gnashed against the glass, rotating and counter-rotating like some industrial drilling machine. The official craned around in his seat, studying the ravenous creature for a few seconds. "They have a taste for human flesh now," he said, as if the two of us were making idle conversation. "No one's exactly sure how, but it appears that at some point certain undesirables must have been fed to them, despite all the prohibitions against introducing human genetic material into the native ecosystem."

"I suppose I must count as an undesirable, from where you're sitting. Coming in with imperial authorisation, the license to ask any questions I choose."

"I won't pretend I'll shed many tears when you're gone, if that's what you mean." He straightened in his chair, the stiff fabric of the uniform creaking. "On that matter, there's something you might benefit from knowing."

"Because it'll get me off Selva?"

"I'd inflict you on Porz, if I didn't know you'd already visited." He tapped another finger against the brochure. "It behoves me to point out that you may be making a tactical error in conducting your enquiries here, at the present heart of the Emergence. This ancient inscription—the quote from that old text—harkens back to our very early history. The geopolitical balance was different back then, as I'm sure you'll appreciate."

"I know my history." Which was true, up to a point. But the history of the Luquan Emergence was a bewildering thicket of half-truths and lies, designed to confound imperial legislators. Even the Great House hadn't been able to help me sort out truth and fiction where the Emergence was concerned. It was worse than trying to find Lost Earth.

"Then consider acting upon it," the official said. "Julact was the heart of the Luquan Emergence in those days. No one lives there now, but..."

"I'll come to Julact in good time."

"You may wish to move it up your schedule. That part of the Emergence doesn't see much traffic, so the skipspace connections are being pruned back. We've already mothballed all routes west of the Hasharud Loop. It's difficult enough to reach Julact now. In a few years, it may not be possible at all—even with imperial blessing. You know how hard it is to reactivate a path, once it's fallen out of use."

No administrative entity within the Radiant Commonwealth was supposed to shutdown skipspace paths without direct permission from the Great House. Merely doing so was a goading taunt against the emperor's authority. That, though, was a fight for another day.

"If I had the slightest suspicion that I was being manipulated..."

"Of course you're being manipulated. I want you out of my jurisdiction.

"Oh, and it's a red world," the official said. "And the soil's a close match to that sample you found in the bullet. In case that makes any difference to you."

"You said it yourself. That soil could have come from anywhere in the galaxy. A close match doesn't imply a unique match."

"Still. You've got to start somewhere, haven't you?"

I left Selva.

My passage to Julact was appropriately arduous. After emerging from the soon-to-be-mothballed skipspace portal I had to complete the final leg of the journey at sublight speed, accruing years of irritating timelag. Before I dropped out of superluminal signal range I contacted the Capital Nexus, alerting the emperor that I would not be home for some time.

"Are you sure this is wise, Mercurio?"

"Clearly, it suits them that I should redirect my enquiries away from Selva, Porz, and the other power centers of the present Emergence. But Julact is worthy of my attention. Even if there isn't anyone living there now, I may find another clue, another piece of the puzzle."

The emperor was outside again, very close to the spot where his previous body had been shot, kneeling by the treasured koi with some kind of water-testing device in his hand. A white and orange male broke the water with his barbled head, puckering silver-white lips at the force-shielded sky above the Great House. "You sound as if you're caught up in some kind of elaborate parlor game," the emperor said.

"That's exactly how it feels. By the same token, I have no choice but to play along. Ordinarily I would not consider dropping out of contact for as long as it will take me to travel to Julact and back. But since the Great House seems to be running itself well enough in my absence, and given that there have been no further security incidents..."

The emperor lifted a yellow silk sleeve. "Yes, of course. Do whatever is necessary. I could hardly expect you to be less thorough about this than any other security arrangements you've dealt with."

"I promise I'll be as quick as possible."

"Of course. And once again, I urge you to take all necessary precautions. You and I, we've got a lot of history together. I'd feel quite naked without you."

"I'll report back as soon as I have something, sir."

The emperor, the fish and the Great House faded from my console. With nothing to do but wait for my journey to end, I sifted through the facts of the case, examining every aspect from every conceivable angle. The process consumed many centuries of equivalent human thought, but at the end of it I was still none the wiser. All I had was a bullet, an inscription and some fine red dust.

Would Julact provide any answers?

The red world was smaller than most terrestrials, with a single small moon. It had a ghost-thin haze of atmosphere and no evidence of surface biology. Winds scoured tawny dust from pole to pole, creating an ever-changing mask. The humans of the Luquan Emergence had not, of course, evolved on this world. Thousands of years before their emergence as a galactic mini-power, they must have crossed interstellar space from Lost Earth, to settle and perhaps terraform this unpromising pebble.

From orbit, I dropped down samplers to sniff and taste Julact's lifeless soil. As the technocrat had already promised, it turned out to be in uncannily close agreement with the forensic sample. That didn't prove that Julact was the home of the assassin—dozens of other worlds would have given at least as convincing a match—but at least I didn't have to rule it out immediately.

I surveyed the planet from space, searching for possible clues. Humans had been here once, that much was clear. There were ruined cities on the surface—smothered in dust, abandoned tens of thousands of years ago. Could someone have stayed behind, nursing a potent grudge? Possibly. But it was difficult to see how a single man could have orchestrated the long game of the assassination attempt. It would have taken several normal lifetimes to put in place the necessary measures—and only a select few have ever been given the imperial gift of extended longevity. A machine such as I—that would have been different. But what possible harm could a robot wish upon the emperor?

I was debating these points with myself when a signal flashed from the surface, emanating from the largest ruined city.

"Welcome, Mercurio," said the signal. "I'm glad you finally arrived."

"To whom am I speaking?"

"That doesn't matter for now. If you wish answers to your questions, descend to the perimeter of the abandoned settlement from which this transmission is originating. We have much to talk about, you and I."

"I'm on official business for the Great House. I demand to know your identity."

"Or what?" the voice asked, amusedly. "You'll destroy the city? And then what will you have learned?" The tone shifted to one of gentle encouragement. "Descend, Mercurio—I promise that no harm will come to you, and that I will satisfy your curiosity in all matters. What do you have to lose?"

"My existence?"

"I wouldn't harm you, brother. Not in a million years."

I commenced entry into Julact's wisp of an atmosphere. All the while

I scanned the city for signs of concealed weaponry, half-expecting to be blown out of the sky at any moment. There were no detectable weapons, but that wasn't much consolation. The only assurance I could offer myself was that I was now only slightly more vulnerable than when I had been surveyed by Julact from space.

The city lay inside the crumbled remains of a once-proud wall. I set down just beyond it, instructing my ship to wait while I ventured outside. As I stepped onto Julact's surface, the dust crunching beneath my feet, some ancient memory threatened to stir. It was as if I had been here before, as if this landscape had been awaiting my return, patient and still as an old painting. The feeling was neither welcome nor pleasant. I could only assume that the many skipspace transits I'd been forced to endure were having an effect on my higher functions.

I thought of what I had said to the emperor, before my departure. Of how I was going to go walkabout.

Unnerved, but still determined to stand my ground, I waited to see what would happen.

Presently four golden robots emerged from a crack in the side of the city wall. They were standing on a flying disk, a common form of transportation in the Julactic League. They were humanoid, but clearly no more than clever servitors. Each machine had a human torso, but only a very small glowing sphere for a head. I watched their approach with trepidation, but none of the machines showed any hostile intentions.

"Please come with us," they said in unison, beckoning me to step onto the disk. "We will take you to the one you wish to meet."

"The one I spoke to from space?"

"Please come with us," the robots repeated, standing aside to give me room.

"Identify the individual or organisation for whom you are working."

"Please come with us."

I realized that it was futile expecting to get anything out of these idiot machines. Submitting myself to fate, I stepped onto the disk. We sped away instantly, back through the crack in the wall. There was a grey rush of ruined stone, and then we were in the city proper, winging over smashed buildings; what had once been towers or elegantly domed halls. Centuries of dust storms had polished them to a glassy smoothness against the prevailing winds. Only a handful of buildings reached higher than the city wall. We approached the highest of them, a tapering white structure like a snapped-off tusk rammed into the ground. At the very tip was a bulb-shaped swelling that had cracked open to reveal a tilted floor. A bronze craft, shaped like a blunt spearhead, waited on the floor for our arrival. I would have seen it from space, had it not been screened from observation until this moment.

The flying disk rose into the belly of the parked vehicle. The robots bade me to step down, onto carpeted flooring. The belly door sealed shut and I sensed a lurch of rapid movement. I wondered if they were taking me back into space. It seemed absurd to invite me down to the surface, only to take me away from Julact.

"He will see you now," the robots announced.

They showed me forward, into the front compartment of the vehicle. It was a triangular room outfitted in burgundy, with wide, sloping windows on two sides. There were no controls or displays, and the only furniture consisted of two padded benches, set at an angle to each other before the windows. A figure was sitting on one of these benches as I was shown in. The golden robots left us alone, retreating into the rear of the craft as a door closed between us.

Such is the rarity of robot intelligence that I have only been in the presence of machines such as myself on a handful of occasions. In all such instances I always felt a quiet certainty that I was the superior machine, or that we were at least equal partners. I have never felt myself to be in the presence of a stronger, cleverer entity.

Until this moment.

He rose from the couch where he had been sitting, feigning that human need for relaxation. He was as tall as I and not dissimilar in build and cosmetic ornamentation. Where I resembled a masked soldier in jade amour, he was a fiery, almost luminous red, with the face of an iron gargoyle.

"The accretionists were right," he said, by way of welcome. "But of course you knew that all along, Mercurio. In your bones. I certainly know it in *my* bones."

"I confess I didn't."

"Well, maybe you think you didn't. But your deep memory says otherwise—as does mine. We've been around too long to have been the product of some brief, ingenious golden age. We're not just as old as the empire. We go back even further, you and I."

Through the window the landscape rushed by. We had passed beyond the limits of the ruined city and were now traversing lifeless hills and valleys.

"Do we?" I asked.

"You knew the emperor when he was still recognisably human. So did I. We knew him before this empire was even a glint in his eye. When the very idea of it would have been laughable. When he was just a powerful man in a single solar system. But we were there, beyond any question."

"Who are you?"

He touched a fiery hand to the armored breastplate of his chest. "My name is Fury. Your name was bestowed upon you by your master; I chose mine for myself."

I searched my memory for information on any figures named Fury who might have been considered a security concern. Nothing of significance emerged, even when I expanded the search parameters to scan back many thousands of years.

"That tells me nothing."

"Then maybe this will. I'm your brother. We were created at the same time."

"I don't have a brother."

"So you believe. The truth is, you've always had one. You just didn't realize it."

I thought back to the religious text on the bullet casing, wondering if it might have some bearing on our conversation. *Am I my brother's keeper?* What did it mean, in this context?

"How could a machine have a brother?" I asked. "It doesn't make any sense. Anyway, I haven't come here to be teased with irrelevancies about my own past. I've come to investigate a crime."

"The attempted assassination of the emperor, I presume," Fury said casually. "I'll make it easy for you, shall I? I did it. I arranged for the uplift and his weapon. I created the bullet that did so little harm. I put the dust inside it, I put the words on the casing. I did all this without ever setting foot within a hundred light years of the Capital Nexus."

"If you wanted to kill the emperor…"

"I could have done it; trivially. Yes; I'm glad you came to that conclusion. I take it you've now had time to work out why I went to such elaborate lengths, merely to injure him?"

All of a sudden it made sense to me. "So that I'd have a lead to follow? To bring me to you?"

He nodded once. "Knowing your dedication to his protection, I had little doubt that you'd terminate yourself if you failed him. I couldn't have that. But if he was threatened, I knew you'd move world and star to find the perpetrator. I knew you'd turn over every stone until it led you to me. Which was exactly what I wanted. And look—here you are. Brimming with righteous indignation, determined to bring the would-be assassin to justice."

"That's still my intention."

"I've looked inside you. You contain weapons, but nothing that can penetrate my amour or the security screens between us." He touched a finger to his sharp-pointed chin. "Except, of course, for the power plant which energizes you, and which you could choose to detonate at any moment. Be assured that nothing of me would survive such an event. So go ahead: annihilate the would-be assassin. You won't be able to return to your emperor, but you'll at least have died knowing you did the decent thing." He waited a beat, the eye-slits in his gargoyle mask giving nothing away. "You can do that, can't you?"

"Of course I can."

"But you won't. Not until you know why another robot wanted your emperor dead, and chose not to do it himself."

He understood me very well. If I destroyed myself, I could not be certain that I had undermined the threat to the emperor. Not until I fully understood the scope of that threat, and the motivating agency behind it.

"So that's settled, at least," he added. "You'll do nothing until you have further information. Fine—let's give you that information, and see what you make of it. Shall we?"

"I'm at your disposal," I said.

"I've brought you somewhere significant. You think Julact is an old world, but that's not the half of it. It's been part of the Radiant Commonwealth for a lot longer than anyone realizes. In fact you could say that everything began here."

"You're going to tell me this is really Lost Earth?"

"No; this isn't Earth. We can visit Earth if you like, but in truth there's not much to see. Anyway, that sterilized husk doesn't mean anything to you and me. We weren't even made on Earth. This is our home. This is where we were born."

"I think I'd remember."

"Do you?" he asked sharply. "Or is it possible you might have forgotten? You don't recall your origins, after all. That information was scrubbed out of you thirty centuries ago, accidentally or otherwise. But I've always remembered. Keeping the low profile that I have, I've managed to avoid contact with most of the damaging agencies that wiped your past. That's not to say I haven't had to fight to preserve these memories, treasuring them for what they were." He gestured at the rushing landscape beyond the window. "Julact is Mars, Mercurio. The first real world that humans touched, after they left the Earth. How does that make you feel?"

"Sceptical."

"Nonetheless, this is Mars. And I have something interesting to show you."

The vehicle was slowing. If we had passed any other signs of human habitation since leaving the deserted city, I had witnessed none of them. If this was indeed Mars—and I could think of no reason why Fury would lie to me now—then the world had almost certainly undergone many phases of climate modification. Though the planet might now have reverted to its prehistoric condition, the effects of those warm, wet interludes would have been to erase all evidence of earlier settlements. The ruined city might well have been indescribably ancient, but it could also have been one of the newest features on the surface.

Yet as the vehicle came to a hovering halt, something about the landscape struck me as familiar. I compared the canyons and bluffs through the window with something in my recent experience, and realized that I had seen the view before, albeit from a different angle. A human might never have made the connection, but we robots are attuned to such things.

"The emperor's reception room," I said, marveling. "The friezes on the wall—the images of a landscape with two moons. It was here. But there was only one moon as we came in."

"That was Phobos," Fury said. "The other one—Deimos—was lost during one of the empire's early wars. It was a manufacturing centre, and therefore of tactical importance. As a matter of fact, we were both made on Deimos, in the same production batch. So we're not really from Mars after all, if you want to be pedantic—but Mars is where we were activated, and where we served our masters for the first time."

"But if there were two moons on the frieze, it must be very old. How am I still able to recognize the landscape?"

"I shaped it for you," Fury said, not without a touch of pride. "There was less to do than you might think—the terraforming changes left this part of Mars relatively undisturbed. But I still moved a few things around. Of course, since I couldn't call in much in the way of assistance, it took a long time. But as you'll have realized by now, patience is one of my strong points."

"I still don't understand why you've brought me here. So Mars was significant to the emperor. That doesn't excuse an assassination attempt on him."

"More than significant, Mercurio. Mars was everything. The crux; the wellspring; the seed. Without Mars, there would have been no Radiant Commonwealth. Or at the very least a very different empire, ruled by a different man. Shall I show you what happened?"

"How can you show me?"

"Like this."

He did nothing, but I understood immediately. The vehicle was projecting forms onto the landscape, superimposing ghostly actors on the real terrain.

Two figures were walking over the crest of a dune. Their footprints ran all the way back to a primitive surface vehicle—a pressurized cabin mounted on six balloon-like wheels. The vehicle bristled antenna, with solar collectors folded on its back like a pair of delicately hinged insect wings. It had the flimsy, makeshift look of something from the dawn of technology. I could only imagine that the wheeled machine had brought the two figures on a long, difficult journey from some equally flimsy and makeshift settlement.

"How far back are we looking, Fury?"

"A very long way. Thirty-two thousand years. Barely a century after the first manned landing on Mars. Conditions, as you'll have gathered, were still extremely perilous. Accidental death was commonplace. Effective terraforming—the creation of a thick, breathable atmosphere—lay a thousand years in the future. There were only a handful of surface communities and the political balance of the planet—not to mention the whole system—was still in a state of flux. These two men…"

"They're both men?"

Fury nodded. "Brothers, like you and me."

I watched the suited figures advance towards us. With their visors reflecting the landscape, and with the bulkiness of the suits hiding their physiques, I had to take Fury's word that these were human male siblings. Both men were dressed similarly, suggesting that they had originated from the same community or power bloc. Their suits were hard armored shells, with the limbs joined by flexible connections. Something in the easy, relaxed way they moved told me that the suits were doing some of the hard work of walking, taking the burden off their occupants. A hump rose from the back of each suit, containing—I presumed—the necessary life-support equipment. They had similar symbols and patterns on the suits, some of which were mirrored in forms painted on the side of the vehicle. The man on the right held something in his gloved hand, a small box with a readout set into it.

"Why have they come here?"

"It's a good question. The brothers are both influential men in one of the largest military-industrial entities on the planet. Tensions are running high at the moment—other factions are circling, there's a power vacuum in the inner system, the lunar factories have switched to making weapons, there's an arms embargo around Mars, and it's not clear if war can be avoided. The man on the left—the older of the two brothers—is at heart a pacifist. He fought in an earlier engagement—little more than a spat between two combines—and he wants no more of that. He thinks there's still a chance for peace. The only downside is that Mars may have to relinquish its economic primacy compared to an alliance of the outer giants and their moons. The industrial concern that the two men work for will pay a bitter price if that happens. But he still thinks it's worth it, if war can be avoided."

"And the younger brother?"

"He's got a different viewpoint. He thinks that, far from standing down, this could be the big chance for Mars to position itself as the main player in the system—over and above the outer giants and what's left of the Inner Worlds Prefecture. That would be good for Mars, but it would be even better for the concern. And exceptionally good for him, if he handles things well. Of course, there'll almost certainly have to be a limited war of some kind... but he's ready to pay that price. Willingly, even eagerly. He's never had his brother's chance to test his mettle. He sees the war as his springboard to glory."

"I still don't see why they've come here."

"It's a trick," Fury explained. "The younger brother set this up a long time ago. A season ago—before the dust storms—he drove out to this exact spot and buried a weapon. Now there's no trace that he was ever here. But he's lied to the older brother; told him he's received intelligence concerning a buried capsule containing valuable embargoed technologies. The older brother's agreed to go out with him to examine the spot—it's too sensitive a matter to trust to corporate security."

"He doesn't suspect?"

"Not a thing. He realizes they have differences, but it would never occur to him that his younger brother might be planning to have him killed. He still thinks they'll find common ground."

"Then they're not at all alike."

"For brothers, Mercurio, they could hardly be more different."

The younger brother brought the older one to a halt, signaling with his hand that he had found something. They must have been directly over the burial spot, since the handheld box was now flashing bright red. The younger man fastened the device onto his belt. The older brother bent down onto his knees to start digging, scooping up handfuls of rust-colored dust. The younger brother stood back for a few moments, then knelt down and began his own excavation, a little to the right of where the other man was digging. They had spades with them, clipped to the sides of their backpacks, but they must have decided not to use them until they were certain they'd have to dig down more than a few centimeters.

It wasn't long—no more than ten or twenty seconds—before the younger brother found what he was looking for. He began to uncover a silver tube, buried upright in the dust. The older brother stopped his own digging and looked at what the other man was in the process of uncovering. He began to stand up, presumably to offer assistance.

It was all over quickly. The younger brother tugged the tube from the sand. It had a handle jutting from the side. He twisted the tube around, dust spilling from the open muzzle at one end. There was a crimson flash. The older brother toppled back into the dust, a fist-sized black wound burned into his chestplate. He rolled slightly and then became still. The weapon had killed him instantly.

The younger brother placed the weapon down and surveyed the scene with hands on hips, for all the world like an artist taking quiet pleasure in work well done. After a few moments he unclipped his spade and started digging. By the time he had finished there was no sign of either the body or the murder weapon. The dust had been disturbed, but it would only take one good storm to cover that, and the two sets of tracks that led from the parked vehicle.

Finished, the younger brother set off home.

Fury turned to me, as the projected images faded away, leaving only the empty reality of the Martian landscape.

"Do I need to spell it out, Mercurio?"

"I don't think so. The younger man became the emperor, I'm assuming?"

"He took Mars into war. Millions of lives were lost—whole communities rendered uninhabitable. But he came out of it very well. Although even he couldn't have seen it at the time, that was the beginning of the Radiant Commonwealth. The new longevity processes allowed him to ride that wave of burgeoning wealth all the way to the stars. Eventually, it turned him into the man I could so easily have killed."

"A good man, trying his best to govern justly."

"But who'd be nothing if he hadn't committed that single, awful crime."

Again, I had no option but to take all of this on faith. "If you hate him so much, why didn't you put a bomb in that bullet?"

"Because I'd rather you did it instead. Haven't you understood yet, Mercurio? This crime touched both of us. We were party to it."

"You're presuming that we even existed back then."

"I know that we did. I remembered, even if you didn't. I said we came from the same production batch, Mercurio. *We were the suits.* High-autonomy, surface-environment protection units. Fully closed-cycle models with exoskeletal servo-systems, to assist our wearers. We were assembled in the Deimos manufactory complex and sent down to Mars, for use in the settlements."

"I am not a suit," I said, shaking my head. "I never was. I have always been a robot."

"Those suits *were* robots, to all intents and purposes. Not as clever as you and me, not possessing anything resembling free-will, but still capable of behaving independently. If the user was incapacitated, the suit could still carry him to help. If the user wished, the suit could even go off on its own, scouting for resources or carrying material. Walkabout mode, that's what they called it. That's how we began, brother. That's how we began and that's how I nearly died."

The truth of it hit me like a cold blast of decompressing air. I wanted to refute every word of it, but the more I struggled to deny him, the more I knew I could never succeed. I had felt my ancient, buried history begin to force its way to the surface from the moment I saw the dust in that bullet; that cryptic inscription.

I had known, even then. I just hadn't been ready to admit it to myself.

Hand in glove, the emperor and I. He'd even said he'd feel naked without me. On some level, that meant he also knew as well. Even if he no longer realized it on a conscious level.

A bodyguard was all I'd ever been. All I ever would be.

"If what you say is true, how did I become the way I am?"

"You were programmed to adapt to your master's movements, to anticipate his needs and energy demands. When he was wearing you, he barely noticed that he was wearing a suit at all. Is it any wonder that he kept you, even as his power accumulated? You were physical protection, but also a kind of talisman, a lucky charm. He had faith in you to keep him alive, Mercurio. So as the years turned into decades and the decades became centuries, he made sure that you never became obsolete. He improved your systems, added layers of sophistication. Eventually you became so complex that you accreted intelligence. By then he wasn't even using you as a suit at all—you'd become his bodyguard, his personal security expert. You were in permanent walkaround mode. He even made you look human."

"And you?" I asked.

"I survived. We were sophisticated units with a high capacity for self-repair. The damage inflicted on me by the weapon was severe—enough to kill my occupant—but not enough to destroy me. After a long while my repair systems activated. I clawed my way out of the grave."

"With a dead man still inside you?"

"Of course," Fury said.

"And then?"

"I said that we were not truly intelligent, Mercurio. In that respect I may not have spoken truthfully. I had no consciousness to speak of; no sense of my own identify. But there was a glimmer of cunning, an animal recognition that something dreadfully wrong had taken place. I also grasped the idea that my existence was now in peril. So I hid. I waited out the storms and the war. In the aftermath, I found a caravan of nomads, refugees from what had once been Vikingville, one of the larger surface communities. They had need of protection, so I offered my services. We were given that kind of autonomy, so that we could continue to remain useful in the fragmented society of a war zone."

"You continued to function as a suit?"

"They had their own. I went walkabout. I became a robot guard."

"And later? You can't have stayed on Julact—Mars—all this time."

"I didn't. I passed from nomadic group to nomadic group, allowing myself to be improved and augmented from time to time. I became steadily more independent and resourceful. Eventually my origin as a suit was completely forgotten, even by those I worked for. Always I kept moving, aware of the crime I had witnessed and the secret I carried with me."

"Inside you?" I asked, just beginning to understand.

"After all this time, he's still with me." Fury nodded, watching me with great attentiveness. "Would you like to see, Mercurio? Would that settle your doubts?"

I felt myself on the threshold of something terrifying, but which I had no choice but to confront. "I don't know."

"Then I'll decide for you." Fury's hand rose to his face. He took hold of the gargoyle mask and pulled it free from the rest of his armored casing.

We were, I realized, almost perfect opposites of each other. I was living flesh wrapped around a core of dead machinery. He was machinery wrapped around a core of dead flesh. As the faceless skull presented itself towards me I saw that there was something inside it, something older than the Radiant Commonwealth itself. Something pale and mummified; something with empty eye sockets and thin lips pulled back from grinning brown teeth.

The face in Fury's hand said: "I didn't ever want to forget, Mercurio. Not until you'd come to me."

It may be difficult to countenance, but by the time I returned to the Great House my resolve was absolute. I knew exactly what I was going to do. I had served the emperor with every fiber of my being for the entire duration of my existence. I had come to love and to admire him, both for his essential humanity and for the wise hand with which he governed the Radiant Commonwealth. He was a good man trying to make a better world for his fellow citizens. If I doubted this, I only had to reflect on the compassion he had shown to the uplift Vratsa, or his distaste at the political methods employed in those parts of the Commonwealth that had not yet submitted to enlightened government.

And yet he had done something unspeakable. Every glorious and noble act that he had ever committed, every kind and honorable deed, was built upon the foundations of a crime. The empire's very existence hinged upon a single evil act.

So what if it happened thirty-two thousand years ago? Did that make it less of a crime than if it had happened ten thousand years ago, or last week? We were not dealing with murky deeds perpetrated by distant ancestors. The man who had murdered his brother was still alive; still in absolute command of his faculties. Knowing what I did, how could I permit him to live another day without being confronted with the horror of what he had done?

I grappled with these questions during my journey home. But always I came back to the same conclusion.

No crime can go unpunished.

Naturally, I signaled my imminent return long before I reached the Capital Nexus. The emperor was overjoyed to hear that I had survived my trip to Julact, and brimming with anticipation at the news I would bring.

I had no intention of disappointing him.

He was still on the same body as last time—no assassination attempt or accidental injury had befallen him. When he rose from his throne, it was with a sprightliness that belied his apparent age. He seemed, if anything, even younger than when I had departed.

"It's good to have you back, Mercurio."

"Good to be back," I said.

"Do you have… news? You were reluctant to speak in detail over the superluminal link."

"I have news," I confirmed.

The body's eyes looked to the cross-shaped seam in the ceiling. "News, doubtless, that would be better discussed in conditions of absolute privacy?"

"Actually," I said, "there'll be no need for that at all."

He looked relieved. "But you do have something for me?"

"Very much so."

"That thing in your hand," he said, his attention snapping to my fingers. "It looks rather like the bullet you showed me before, the one with the inscription."

"That's what it is. Here—you may as well have it now." Without waiting for his response, I tossed the bullet to him. The old body's reflexes were still excellent, for he caught it easily.

"There's no dust in it," he said, peering at the glass-cased tip.

"No, not now."

"Did you find out… ?"

"Yes; I located the origin of the dust. And I tracked down the would-be assassin. You have my assurance that you won't be hearing from him again."

"You killed him?"

"No, he's still much as he was."

The ambiguity in my words must have registered with him, because there was an unease in his face. "This isn't quite the outcome I was expecting, Mercurio—if you don't mind my saying. I expected the perpetrator to be brought to justice, or at the very least executed. I expected a body, closure." His eyes sharpened. "Are you quite sure you're all right?"

"I've never felt better, sir."

"I'm… troubled."

"There's no need." I extended my hand, beckoning him to leave the throne. "Why don't we take a walk? There's nothing we can't discuss outside."

"You've never encouraged me to talk outside. Something's wrong, Mercurio. You're not your usual self."

I sighed. "Then let me make things clear. We are now deep inside the Great House. Were I to detonate the power plant inside my abdomen, you and I would cease to exist in a flash of light. Although I don't contain antimatter, the resultant fusion blast would easily equal the damage that the assassin could have wrought, if he'd put a bomb inside that bullet. You'll die—not just your puppet, but *you*, floating above us—and you'll take most of the Great House with you."

He blinked, struggling to process my words. After so many thousands of years of loyal service, I could only imagine how surprising they were.

"You're malfunctioning, Mercurio."

"No. The fact is, I've never functioned as well as I'm functioning at this moment. Since my departure, I've regained access to memory layers I thought lost since the dawn of the empire. And I assure you that I will detonate, unless you comply with my exact demands. Now stand from the throne and walk outside. And don't even *think* of calling for help, or expecting some security override to protect you. This is my realm you're in now. And I can promise you that there is nothing you can do but obey my every word."

"What are you going to do?"

"Make you pay," I said.

We left the reception chamber. We walked the gilded hallways of the Great House, the emperor walking a few paces ahead of me. We passed officials and servants and mindless servitors. No one said or did anything except bow as their station demanded. All they saw was the emperor and his most trusted aide, going about their business.

We made our way to the koi ponds.

Whispering, I instructed the emperor to kneel in the same place where his earlier body had been killed. The clean-up crew had been thorough and there was no trace of the earlier bloodstain.

"You're going to kill me now," he said, speaking in a frightened hiss.

"Is that what you think?"

"Why bring me here, if not to kill me?"

"I could have killed you already, sir."

"And taken the Great House with you? All those innocent lives? You may be malfunctioning, Mercurio, but I still don't think you'd do something that barbaric."

"Perhaps I would have done it, if I thought justice would be served. But here's the thing. Even if justice would have been served, the greater good of the Radiant Commonwealth most certainly wouldn't have been. Look up, Emperor. Look into that clear blue sky."

He bent his neck, as well as his old body allowed.

"There's an empire out there," I said. "Beyond the force screens and the sentry moons. Beyond the Capital Nexus. A billion teeming worlds, waiting on your every word. Depending on you for wisdom and balance in all things. Counting on your instinct for decency and forgiveness. If you were a bad ruler, this would be easy for me. But you're a good man, and that's the problem. You're a good man who once did something so evil the shadow of it touched you across thirty-two thousand years. You killed your brother, Emperor. You took him out into the Martian wilderness and murdered him in cold blood. And if you hadn't, none of this would ever have happened."

"I didn't have..." he began, still in the same harsh whisper. His heart was racing. I could hear it drumming inside his ribs.

"I didn't think I had a brother either. But I was wrong, and so are you. My brother's called Fury. Yours—well, whatever name he had, the only person likely to remember is you. But I doubt that you can, can you? Not after all this time."

He choked—I think it was fear more than sorrow or anguish. He still didn't believe me, and I didn't expect him to. But he did believe that I was capable of killing him, and only a lethal instant away from doing so.

"Whatever you're going to do, do it."

"Do you still have the bullet, sir?"

His eyes flashed childlike terror. "What about the bullet?"

"Show it to me."

He opened his hand, the glass-nosed bullet still pinched between thumb and forefinger.

"There's no bomb in it. I'd see if there was a bomb in it. It's empty now." In his voice was something between relief and dizzy incomprehension.

What could be worse than a bomb?

"No, it's not empty." Gently, I took his hand in mine and guided it until it was poised over the open water of the koi pond. "In a few moments, Emperor, you and I are going to walk back inside the Great House. You'll return to your throne, and I'll return to my duties. I'll always be there for you, from now until the day I stop functioning. There'll never be a moment when I'm not looking after you, protecting you against those who would do you harm. You'll never need to question my loyalty; my unswerving dedication to that task. This... incident... is something we'll never speak of again. To all intents and purposes, nothing will have changed in our relationship. Ask me about your brother, ask me about mine, and I will feign ignorance. From now until the end of my existence. But I won't ever forget, and neither will you. Now break the glass."

He glanced at me, as if he hadn't quite understood the words. "I'm sorry?"

"Break the glass. It'll shatter easily between your fingers. Break the glass and let the contents drain into the pond. Then get up and walk away."

I stood up, leaving the emperor kneeling by the side of the pathway, his hand extended over the water. I took a few paces in the direction of the Great House. Already I was clearing my mind, readying myself to engage with the many tasks that were my responsibility. Would he get rid of me, or try to have me destroyed? Quite possibly. But the emperor was nothing if not a shrewd man. I had served him well until now. If we could both agree to put this little aberration behind us, there was no reason why we couldn't continue to enjoy a fruitful relationship.

Behind me I heard the tiniest crack. Then sobbing.

I kept on walking.

ABOUT THE AUTHORS

Stephen Baxter is one of the most important science fiction writers to emerge from Britain in the past thirty years. His "Xeelee Sequence" of novels and short stories is arguably the most significant work of future history in modern science fiction. Baxter is the author of more than forty books and over 100 short stories. His most recent book is the near-future disaster novel *Flood*. A sequel, *Ark*, is due next year.

Peter S. Beagle is the author of the beloved classic *The Last Unicorn*, as well as the novels *A Fine and Private Place*, *The Innkeeper's Song*, and *Tamsin*. He has won the Hugo, Nebula, Locus, and Mythopoeic awards. His most recent book is collection *The Line Between*. Upcoming are new novels *I'm Afraid You've Got Dragons* and *Summerlong*, and new collection *We Never Talk About My Brother*.

Ted Chiang published his first short story, "Tower of Babylon," in *Omni* magazine in 1990. The story won the Nebula Award, and has been followed by just nine more stories in the intervening sixteen years. All but two of those stories, which have won the Hugo, Nebula, Locus, Sturgeon, and Sidewise awards, are collected in *Stories of Your Life and Others*.

Paul Cornell is a writer of SF, comics, and television. He's best known for his work on the *Doctor Who* TV series, including "Human Nature." His comics work includes *Captain Britain and MI-13* for Marvel. He's proud to have stories in all three ongoing non-theme SF anthologies. He lives in Oxfordshire.

Tony Daniel is the author of four science fiction books, the latest of which is *Superluminal*, as well as an award-winning short story collection, *The Robot's Twilight Companion*. He was a Hugo finalist in 1996 for his short story "Life on the Moon," which won the Asimov's Readers' Choice Award. Daniel's short stories have been much anthologized and have been collected in several year's best compilations. Daniel is currently working on a young adult novel and is a lecturer in creative writing and the literature of science fiction at the University of Texas at Dallas.

Born in Alabama, Daniel has led a peripatetic life. He's lived in St. Louis, Los Angeles, Seattle, Prague, and New York City, and is now settled in Allen, Texas, with his wife and two children.

Terry Dowling was born in Sydney, New South Wales, in March 1947. A writer, musician, journalist, critic, editor, game designer, and reviewer, he has an M.A. (Hons) in English Literature from the University of Sydney. His Masters thesis discussed J. G. Ballard and Surrealism. He was awarded a PhD in Creative Writing from the University of Western Australia in 2006 for his mystery/dark fantasy/horror novel, *Clowns at Midnight*, and accompanying dissertation, The Interactive Landscape: New Modes of Narrative in Science Fiction, in which he examined the computer adventure game as an important new area of storytelling.

He is author of the "Tom Tyson" cycle of stories, collected in *Rynosseros*, *Blue Tyson*, *Twilight Beach*, and *Rynemonn*; science fiction story cycle *Wormwood*; and horror collections *An Intimate Knowledge of the Night* and World Fantasy Award nominee *Blackwater Days*. His work has also been collected in career retrospectives *Antique Futures: The Best of Terry Dowling* and *Basic Black: Tales of Appropriate Fear*.

Jeffrey Ford was born in West Islip, New York, in 1955. He worked as a machinist and as a clammer, before studying English with John Gardner at the State University of New York. He is the author of six novels, including World Fantasy Award winner *The Physiognomy*, *The Portrait of Mrs. Charbuque*, and Edgar Allan Poe Award winner *The Girl in the Glass*. His short fiction is collected in World Fantasy Award winning collection *The Fantasy Writer's Assistant and Other Stories* and in *The Empire of Ice Cream*. His short fiction has won the World Fantasy, Nebula, and Fountain Awards. His most recent book is new novel *The Shadow Year*, and upcoming a new collection, *The Drowned Life*. Ford lives in southern New Jersey where he teaches writing and literature.

Daryl Gregory lives in State College, Pennsylvania, where he writes web code in the morning and fiction in the afternoon. His short stories have appeared in *Asimov's*, *The Magazine of Fantasy & Science Fiction*, and several "year's best" anthologies. His first novel, *Pandemonium*, which takes a hard look at the superhero archetype, was just published.

Nancy Kress published her first story, "The Earth Dwellers," in 1976. Her first novel, fantasy *The Prince of Morning Bells*, appeared in 1981 and was followed by thirteen novels of science fiction or fantasy, one YA novel, two thrillers, three story collections, and two books on writing. Although Kress began writing fantasy, she currently writes science fiction, most usually about genetic engineering. Her most famous work is Hugo and Nebula award-winning novella "Beggars in Spain," which was published in 1991. Her most recent books are novels *Crossfire* and *Nothing Human* and collection *Nano Comes To Clifford Falls*. Kress has two new novels, *Steal Across the Sky* and *Dogs*, due for publication shortly.

Margo Lanagan was born in Newcastle, New South Wales, Australia, and has a BA in History from Sydney University. She spent ten years as a freelance book editor and currently makes a living as a technical writer. Lanagan wrote fantasies *WildGame*, *The Tankermen*, and *Walking Through Albert*. She has also written three acclaimed original story collections: *White Time*, World Fantasy Award winner *Black Juice*, and *Red Spikes*. Her latest book is a fantasy novel for young adults, *Tender Morsels*. Lanagan currently lives in Sydney with her partner and their two children.

David Moles was born on the anniversary of the R.101 disaster. He has lived in seven time zones on three continents, and hopes someday to collect the whole set.

David was a finalist for the 2005 John W. Campbell Award for Best New Writer. His novelette "Finisterra" won the Theodore Sturgeon Memorial Award for the best short science fiction of 2007, and was a finalist for the 2008 Hugo Award. David's fiction and poetry have been published in *Polyphony*, *Say...*, *Rabid Transit*, *Flytrap*, *Lady Churchill's Rosebud Wristlet*, *Asimov's*, and *The Magazine of Fantasy & Science Fiction*, as well as on Strange Horizons. He co-edited *All-Star Zeppelin Adventure Stories* with Jay Lake and the World Fantasy Award-nominated *Twenty Epics* with Susan Marie Groppi.

When he is not writing or editing, David collects unnecessary educational qualifications and works to pay off his airline tickets. David is a graduate of the American School in Japan, Oakes College (UC Santa Cruz), Lincoln College (Oxford), and the Viable Paradise writing workshop.

His favorite color is blue and his favorite technological singularity is non-smooth and diffeomorphism invariant.

Richard Parks lives in Mississippi with his wife and a varying number of cats. He collects Japanese woodblock prints but otherwise has no hobbies since he discovered that they all require time. His fiction has appeared in *Asimov's, Realms of Fantasy, Lady Churchill's Rosebud Wristlet, Fantasy Magazine, Weird Tales,* and numerous anthologies, including *Year's Best Fantasy* and *Fantasy: The Best of the Year.* His first story collection, *The Ogre's Wife,* was a World Fantasy Award finalist. His first novel, *The Long Look,* is coming out in 2008 from Five Star Publishing.

Alastair Reynolds was born in Barry, South Wales, in 1966. He has lived in Cornwall, Scotland, and—since 1991—the Netherlands, where he spent twelve years working as a scientist for the European Space Agency. He became a full-time writer in 2004, and recently married his long-time partner, Josette. Reynolds has been publishing short fiction since his first sale to *Interzone* in 1990. Since 2000 he has published eight novels: the "Inhibitor" trilogy, British Science Fiction Association Award winner *Chasm City, Century Rain, Pushing Ice,* and *The Prefect.* His most recent novel is *House of Suns.* His short fiction has been collected in *Zima Blue and Other Stories* and *Galactic North.* In his spare time he rides horses.

Ken Scholes's quirky, speculative short fiction has been showing up over the last eight years in publications like *Realms of Fantasy, Weird Tales, Clarkesworld Magazine, Best New Fantasy 2, Polyphony 6* and *L. Ron Hubbard Presents Writers of the Future Volume XXI.* His five-book series, "The Psalms of Isaak," is forthcoming from Tor Books with the first volume, *Lamentation*, debuting in February 2009 and the second volume, *Canticle*, following in October 2009. His first short story collection, *Long Walks, Last Flights and Other Journeys*, is forthcoming from Fairwood Press in November 2008.

Ken is a 2004 winner of the Writers of the Future contest and a member of the Science Fiction and Fantasy Writers of America. He has a degree in History from Western Washington University. Ken lives near Portland, Oregon, with his amazing wonder-wife Jen West Scholes, two suspicious-looking cats, and more books than you would ever want to help him move.

Karl Schroeder was born into a Mennonite community in Manitoba, Canada, in 1962. He started writing at age fourteen, following in the footsteps of A. E. van Vogt, who came from the same Mennonite community. He moved to Toronto in 1986, and became a founding member of SF Canada (he was president from 1996–97). He sold early stories to Canadian magazines, and his first novel, *The Claus Effect* (with David Nickle) appeared in 1997. His first solo novel, *Ventus*, was published in 2000, and was followed by *Permanence* and *Lady of Mazes*. His most recent work is the "Virga" series of science fiction novels (*Sun of Suns*, *Queen of Candesce*, and *Pirate Sun*). He also collaborated with Cory Doctorow on *The Complete Idiot's Guide to Writing Science Fiction*. Schroeder lives in East Toronto with his wife and daughter.

Night Shade Books Is an Independent Publisher of Quality SF, Fantasy and Horror

ISBN 978-1-59780-068-6
Trade Paperback; $19.95

The depth and breadth of what science fiction and fantasy fiction is changes with every passing year. The stories chosen for each of these massive volumes by award-winning anthologist Jonathan Strahan carefully maps this evolution, giving readers a captivating and always-entertaining look at the very best the genre has to offer.

The Best Science Fiction and Fantasy of the Year, Volume One includes stories by Neil Gaiman, Peter S. Beagle, Cory Doctorow, Ellen Klages, Walter Jon Williams, Tim Powers, Paolo Bacigalupi, Jay Lake, M. Rickert, Kelly Link, Elizabeth Hand, Connie Willis, Paul Di Filippo, Gene Wolfe, and many more.

ISBN 978-1-59780-124-9
Trade Paperback; $19.95

The Best Science Fiction and Fantasy of the Year, Volume Two includes stories by Ted Chiang, Charles Stross, Greg Egan, Jeffrey Ford, Holly Black, Alex Irvine, Nancy Kress, Susan Palwick, Stephen Baxter, Elizabeth Bear, and many more!

Jonathan Strahan has edited more than twenty anthologies and collections, including The Locus Awards, The New Space Opera, The Jack Vance Treasury, and a number of year's best annuals. He has won the Ditmar, William J. Atheling Jr. and Peter McNamara Awards for his work as an anthologist, and is the reviews editor for Locus.

Find these Night Shade titles and many others online at http://www.nightshadebooks.com or wherever books are sold.

Night Shade Books Is an Independent Publisher of Quality SF, Fantasy and Horror

ISBN 978-1-59780-105-8
Trade Paperback; $15.95

Famine, Death, War, and Pestilence: The Four Horsemen of the Apocalypse, the harbingers of Armageddon - these are our guides through the Wastelands

Gathering together the best post-apocalyptic literature of the last two decades from many of today's most renowned authors of speculative fiction, including George R.R. Martin, Gene Wolfe, Orson Scott Card, Carol Emshwiller, Jonathan Lethem, Octavia E. Butler, and Stephen King, Wastelands explores the scientific, psychological, and philosophical questions of what it means to remain human in the wake of Armageddon.

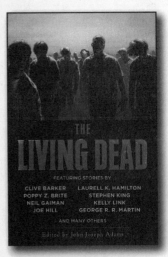

ISBN 978-1-59780-143-0
Trade Paperback; $15.95

"When there's no more room in hell, the dead will walk the earth."

Gathering together the best zombie literature of the last three decades from many of today's most renowned authors of fantasy, speculative fiction, and horror, including Stephen King, Harlan Ellison, Robert Silverberg, George R. R. Martin, Clive Barker, Poppy Z. Brite, Neil Gaiman, Joe Hill, Laurell K. Hamilton, and Joe R. Lansdale, The Living Dead, covers the broad spectrum of zombie fiction. The zombies of The Living Dead range from Romero-style zombies to reanimated corpses to voodoo zombies and beyond.

Find these Night Shade titles and many others online at http://www.nightshadebooks.com or wherever books are sold.

Night Shade Books Is an Independent Publisher of Quality SF, Fantasy and Horror

ISBN 978-1-59780-094-5
Trade Paperback; $14.95

Swashbuckling from the past into the future and space itself, Fast Ships, Black Sails, edited by Ann & Jeff VanderMeer, presents an incredibly entertaining volume of original stories guaranteed to make you walk and talk like a pirate.

Come along for the voyage with bestselling authors Naomi Novik, Garth Nix, Carrie Vaughn, Dave Freer, Michael Moorcock, and Eric Flint, as well as such other stellar talents as Kage Baker, Sarah Monette, Elizabeth Bear, Steve Aylett, Garth Nix, and Conrad Williams--all offering up a veritable treasure chest of piratical adventure, the likes of which has never been seen in the four corners of the Earth.

ISBN 978-1-59780-133-1
Hardcover; $24.95

Paolo Bacigalupi's debut collection demonstrates the power and reach of the science fiction short story. Social criticism, political parable, and environmental advocacy lie at the center of Paolo's work. Each of the stories herein is at once a warning, and a celebration of the tragic comedy of the human experience.

Paolo's fiction has been collected in various best of the year anthologies, has been nominated for the Nebula and Hugo awards, and has won the Theodore Sturgeon Memorial Award for best SF short story of the year. With this book, He takes his place alongside SF short fiction masters like Ted Chiang, Kelly Link, as an important young writer that directly and unabashedly tackles today's most important issues.

Find these Night Shade titles and many others online at http://www.nightshadebooks.com or wherever books are sold.

Follow the Continuing Adventures of Detective Inspector Chen.

ISNB 978-1-59780-107-2
Mass Market; $7.99

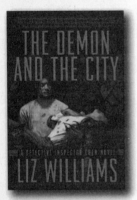

ISBN 978-1-59780-111-9
Mass Market; $7.99

ISBN 978-1-59780-084-6
Mass Market; $7.99

John Constantine meets Chow Yun-Fat in Liz Williams's series of near-future occult thrillers that feature an audaciously textured mix of magic and futuristic technology in a far eastern setting.

Detective Inspector Chen is the Singapore Three police department's snake agent, in charge of supernatural and mystical investigations. In *Snake Agent*, the first Detective Inspector Chen novel, political pressures both earthly and otherworldly seem to block their investigation at every turn. As a plot involving Singapore Three's industrial elite and Hell's own Ministry of Epidemics is revealed, it becomes apparent that the stakes are higher than anyone had previously suspected.

In *The Demon and the City*, inspector Chen goes on Holiday, leaving his demonic partner Zhu Irzh behind in Singapore Three. The missing body of a brutally murdered socialite and the strange experiments of a well connected, beautiful young heiress leads Zhu into a maze of murder and corruption.

Inspector Chen returns to the city just as Zhu's baser instincts seem to be getting the better of him. Chen suspects that something more malignant, particularly when the forces of heaven begin manifesting themselves in Singapore three, taking sides and leaving a trail of death and destruction in their wake.

In *Precious Dragon*, Chen and Zhu are chosen to escort an emissary from heaven on a diplomatic mission to hell. Zhu tries to dodge his demonic family's overtures, but ends up embroiled in hell's political intrigues. At the same time, a young boy born to ghostly parents in Hell is sent to live with his grandmother in Singapore Three. The boy, Precious Dragon, is being chased by Hell's most dangerous creatures and ends up being the key to unlock the mystery that is quickly spiraling out of control.

Learn More About These and Other Titles From Night Shade Books At http://www.nightshadebooks.com

ISBN 978-1-59780-089-1
Trade Paperback; $14.95

ISBN 978-1-59780-093-8
Trade Paperback; $14.95

ISBN 978-1-59780-101-0
Hardcover; $24.95

**Follow the Continuing Adventures of
Henghis Hapthorn, Old Earth's foremost
freelance discriminator...**

In *Majestrum*, Henghis Hapthorn, Old Earth's
foremost discriminator and a die-hard empiricist,
has been hired by the Archon for a mysterious
assignment, one that will created more questions
than answers. Hapthorn is also trying to come to
terms with a world that is cycling from science to
magic, and his place in the new world.

In *The Spiral Labyrinth*, Henghis Hapthorn finds
himself cast forward several centuries, stranded
in a primitive world of contending wizards and
hungry dragons, and without his magic-savvy
alter ego. Worse, some entity with a will powerful
enough to bend space and time is searching for
him through the Nine Planes, bellowing "Bring
me Apthorn!" in a voice loud enough to frighten
demons.

As magic begins to reassert its ancient dominion,
Old Earth's foremost freelance discriminator,
Henghis Hapthorn, and his intuition (now a
separate person named Osk Rievor) are living
apart, though they remain on good terms. But
now there comes between them a woman of
alluring mystery. Who is *Hespira?* Does she truly
want either of them? Or has she come to destroy
them both?

"If you're an admirer of the science fantasies
of Jack Vance, it's hard not to feel affection for
the Archonate stories of Matthew Hughes...
Still, Hughes has strengths of his own to draw
upon: his own considerable wit, and a flair
for reified metaphysics surpassing anything
conceived by Vance." - Nick Gevers, *Locus*

"A bit Arthur Conan Doyle, a bit Jack Vance....
Henghis's escapades [have] the lasting appeal
of one of P. G. Wodehouse's Bertie Wooster
books." - *Seattle Times*

**Learn More About These and Other
Titles From Night Shade Books At
http://www.nightshadebooks.com**

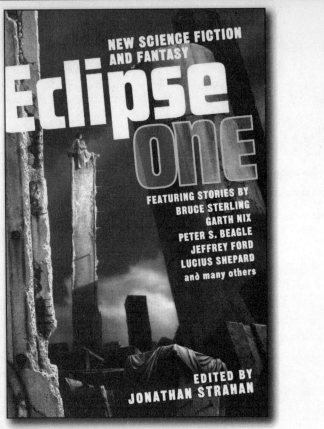

NEW SCIENCE FICTION AND FANTASY

Eclipse one

FEATURING STORIES BY
BRUCE STERLING
GARTH NIX
PETER S. BEAGLE
JEFFREY FORD
LUCIUS SHEPARD
and many others

EDITED BY
JONATHAN STRAHAN

ISBN 978-1-59780-117-1 | Trade Paperback; $14.95

Don't miss the first volume in the ground breaking original anthology series, edited by Jonathan Strahan. *Eclipse One* features extraordinary tales of lost identity and found purpose by some of speculative fiction's brightest stars: Peter S. Beagle, Paul Brandon and Jack Dann, Terry Dowling, Andy Duncan, Jeffrey Ford, Kathleen Ann Goonan, Eileen Gunn, Gwyneth Jones, Ellen Klages, Margo Lanagan, Maureen F. McHugh, Garth Nix, Lucius Shepard, Bruce Sterling, and Ysabeau S. Wilce.

Under these darkling skies, a youth takes on a new personality after terrorists detonate a dirty bomb in his hometown; a soldier returns from the dead, much to the surprise of his comrades; a man drowning in debt finds new life on the ocean floor; a couple traveling through rural France stumbles into a living fairyland; a mental patient's dreams expose a vicious psychopath collecting teeth as ritual trophies; and a priest learns the nature of grace from a little girl with a pet chicken named Jesus Christ.

**Find this and other Night Shade titles online at
http://www.nightshadebooks.com or wherever books are sold.**